Capri: Island of Pleasure

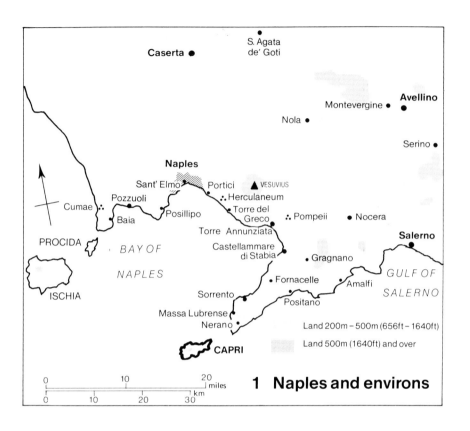

Caserta ●

S. Agata
de' Goti

Montevergine ● **Avellino** ●

Nola ●

Serino ●

Naples

Sant' Elmo ● Portici ▲ VESUVIUS
Pozzuoli ∴ Herculaneum
Cumae ∴ Posillipo ● Torre del
Baia Greco ∴ Pompeii ● Nocera
Torre Annunziata
PROCIDA Castellammare **Salerno** ●
BAY OF di Stabia
● Gragnano
NAPLES *GULF OF*
● Fornacelle *SALERNO*
ISCHIA ● Amalfi
Sorrento Positano
Massa Lubrense
Nerano Land 200m – 500m (656ft – 1640ft)

CAPRI Land 500m (1640ft) and over

| 0 | 10 | 20 miles |
| 0 | 10 | 20 | 30 | km |

1 Naples and environs

CAPRI
Island of Pleasure

by

JAMES MONEY

HAMISH HAMILTON

LONDON

First published in Great Britain 1986
by Hamish Hamilton Ltd
Garden House, 57–59 Long Acre, London WC2E 9JZ

British Library Cataloguing in Publication Data

Money, James
  Capri: island of pleasure.
  1. Capri Island (Italy) – Social life and customs
  I. Title
  945'.73   DG975.C2
  ISBN 0-241-11747-X

Typeset by Rowland Phototypesetting Ltd
Bury St Edmunds, Suffolk
Printed and bound in Great Britain by
Butler & Tanner Ltd, Frome, Somerset

In gratitude
to
Dr George William Weber, MD
for
his unfailing help

Contents

Maps (drawn by Patrick Leeson)

Acknowledgements

My opening acknowledgement must be to the late Sir Compton Mackenzie, whose entertaining novel *Vestal Fire* first aroused my interest in Capri.
The book had been introduced to my family, soon after its publication in
1927, by the late V. S. H. Russell, a Charterhouse master, who considered
it one of the funniest books he had ever read and persuaded my eldest
brother David, who had been one of his pupils, to buy it. My own interest
(I was only ten at the time) did not develop until later. By the end of the
'thirties, however, having read and re-read it several times, and his novel
Extraordinary Women too, I felt myself well acquainted with members of
Capri's foreign colony at the beginning of the century, although I did not
know their real names. After World War II, I acquired a few second-hand
books about Capri and in the late 'sixties bought *Octaves Four, Five* and *Six*
of Mackenzie's *My Life and Times*, which describe his years on Capri and
provide identification of several of the characters in *Vestal Fire* and
Extraordinary Women.

In 1973 I decided to visit the island, with the idea of writing a short
illustrated article about these characters and their homes. I already had
introductions to Carlo della Posta, Duca di Civitella and Barone Mario
Cottrau, and hoped that these would launch me successfully on Capri
society. Visiting the Italian Tourist Bureau in Regent Street for advice on
hotels, I found a Caprese behind the counter, who recommended the
Hotel Gatto Bianco, where I was hospitably received by the Esposito
brothers and their staff, who helped by providing information and
introductions. During my three weeks in Capri I ranged round the island,
photographing what seemed relevant, and in one way or another met:
Maria Aprea, Doreen and Adrian Berrill, Prof. Luigi Bladier, Laetitia
Cerio, the late Carlo Civitella, the late Barone Cottrau, Peter and Valerie
Davies, the late Duca Marino Dusmet and his wife Polly, the late General
Carlo Gardini, his wife Milly Gardini, Anne and Vittorio Gargiulo,
Graham Greene, Flora Massa, the late Giuseppina Messanelli, Mario
Morgano, the late Principe Gaetano Parente, the late David Rawnsley,
Giovanni Ruggiero, and Francis and Shirley Steegmuller, all of whom
showed interest and gave information and advice. Criticism and help from

the Steegmullers, who are professional writers, has always been specially valuable.

I spent long periods in the non-Catholic cemetery, which like all cemeteries contains a wealth of valuable material and is itself an extremely moving place. I was horrified at its neglected state, which I am sorry to say continues to this day. I have always aired my views on the subject with some force but unfortunately little result.

On my return to England I gave a few illustrated lectures on Capri to relations and friends, and, encouraged by their reactions, turned my thoughts to writing a book rather than an article, though still concentrating on the foreign colony described by Mackenzie. A few months later a letter arrived from Maurice Yates, then living in the nearby island of Procida, who, hearing from Laetitia Cerio of my quest for information about Mackenzie's characters, told me that he and Kenneth Macpherson, in whose house on Capri Norman Douglas had spent his last years, had intended to publish new editions of *Vestal Fire* and *Extraordinary Women*, with photographs of the characters and their villas. This project, however, had foundered with Macpherson's death in 1971. Yates obligingly sent me useful notes, suggestions for research and answers to a number of queries. I later established contact with Mark Holloway, whose detailed biography of Norman Douglas published in 1976 contained valuable material.

By this time I had decided to extend the book to embrace the whole of Capri's history, but the work proceeded slowly and painfully. Having returned to Capri in 1979 with an incomplete and unsatisfactory draft, I renewed my old contacts, established new ones and, what was crucially important, met Dr George W. Weber, who was visiting Capri from his home in Florida, and to whom my book is gratefully dedicated. We had many fruitful talks in the Gatto Bianco and later valuable correspondence. Born in Capri in 1894, the son of a German father and *caprese* mother, he lived there almost constantly until he emigrated to the United States at the end of 1929. After World War II he was frequently in Capri to see his relations and friends and always kept *au fait* with the affairs of the island which he loved so dearly. His effective knowledge of Capri, therefore, spans more than eighty years. By profession a doctor and possessed of a clear mind and retentive memory, he has been a gold-mine of information. He combines the thoroughness of a German with the lively spirit and ingenuity of an Italian, his training and work as a doctor have made him clinical and dispassionate in his treatment of evidence, and above all I have his confidence and his constant determination to help in the writing of what he sees as the first reasonably accurate account of the essential Capri. Weber has a poor opinion of Edwin Cerio's books, which he considers tiresomely repetitive, at times deliberately inaccurate and misleading, and agonising in their constant attempts to be humorous. He deplores the fact that Cerio, who had endless written and oral sources at his disposal, unlimited leisure, intellectual ability and a fluency in both Italian and English, never applied himself to writing a proper account of the island and its people. From 1979 until the present day George Weber has been indefatigable in providing information from his rich store of knowledge and answering my many questions about Capri. Without his help much of this book would have remained unwritten. In gratitude I asked a London bookseller to send him a second-hand copy of *Vestal Fire*. Weber read it and then returned it to me because at the back of the book there was a manuscript list identifying *all* the characters mentioned. The list is so detailed and so accurate that Mackenzie himself must have been the source. This indeed was a find.

My visit of 1979 was valuable for other reasons. I met and enlisted the help of Teodoro Pagano, friend of George Weber from their earliest years and himself an ardent collector of material about Capri's past. Always ready to meet me for discussion, he has a depth and length of knowledge which in several respects exceeds Weber's, having lived almost continually in the island since his birth in 1893, and, by his involvement in the family hotel which bears his name and in Capri politics, possesses extensive and deep knowledge over many fields. In 1979 too I met Aldo Aprea, whose study of Capri past and present and willingness to answer my many questions has been enormously helpful; and Antigone Pesce (Stavros), who, although a foreigner, has, after residence of many years and with an Italian husband, become immersed in the island.

During my later visits of 1979 and from 1981 to 1984, thanks to an introduction by Maurice Yates, I stayed at the Albergo Sanfelice, where I have always received a warm welcome and been helped in innumerable ways by Pietro Cerrotta, the late Gloria Magnus and Vincenzo (Enzo) Simeoli – both in the provision of information and in introductions to other helpful people. If the Gatto Bianco is disappointed at my defection after their kindness of 1973 – which was due solely to the fact that after a gap of six years I left my hotel arrangements in the hands of Maurice Yates – they have not shown it. Indeed Giuseppe, Giovanni and Tonino Esposito have been helpful in providing information about the history of their family, as well as other topics.

A good part of my research in Capri has been done in the Library of the Centro Caprense Ignazio Cerio, where Prof. Luigi Bladier has been obliging in locating and providing material.

I acknowledge gratefully the help often given by Mario Ferraro, *vice-segretario* of the *comune* of Capri, and Francesco Gargiulo, head of that section of the Servizi Demografisci which deals with births, marriages and deaths.

I could go on for much longer about individuals and institutions in Capri, the United Kingdom and elsewhere, who have contributed to the making of this book. It is at this point that I telescope the long years of research, during which my knowledge of the island has been broadened and deepened, and simply list those sources and helpers whom I have not already mentioned. If any name which ought to be here has been omitted, I hope I shall be forgiven. These kind people and organisations are: Gennarino Alberino, Roberto Alberino, the late Boris Alperovici, Etienne Amyot, Alan Anderson, Biagino Aprea, Michele Ascione, Mario Binyon, Rachel (Nini) Binyon, Robin Binyon, Ingolf Boisen, Gelvio Bottiglieri, Goffredo Buccini, J. D. Campbell (formerly HM Consul-General in Naples), Vittorio Canale, Giuseppe Catuogno, Carmela Celentano, Don Costanzo Cerrotta, Luigi Chierchia, Prof. Achille Ciccaglione, Prof. Sol Cohen, FRCS, Condé Nast Publications (Vogue), Prof. Attilio Coppola, Marchesa Tina De Forcade, Luigi De Gregorio, Barone Eric De Kolb, Ornella De Martino, Dr Costanzo Di Stefano, Raffaele Di Stefano, Lino Donnarumma, Uno Energren, Levente Erdeos, Paolo Falco, Michele Farace, Carlo and Venere Federico, Gianna Federico, Costantino Ferraro, Mario Ferraro (employee of the SIPPIC), Matteo Ferraro, Roberto Ferraro, Cicillo Foresta, Manfred Gräter, Ian Greenlees, Rev. Edward Holland, Brian Hubbard, Giorgio Iacono, International Rose O'Neill Club (Jean Cantwell), Daniel W. Jones Jnr, Humphrey Jones, Attilio Lembo, Costanzo and Maria Lembo, Mrs Lenon, The London Library, Islay Lyons, Maria MacGregor, Mario Maresca, Flora Massa, the late Clelia Matania, University of Michigan (Kelsey Museum of Ancient and Medieval Archaeology), Diana Money, Mark Morgan, Mario Morgano, Kathleen Nathan, Liberato Orlandi, Corrado Pagano, Marchese Ettore Patrizi, Baronessa Graziella Pennacchio, Contessa Maddalena Pozzo di Borgo, Hazel Provost, Conrad Rawnsley, Damon Rawnsley, Mary Rawnsley, Avv. Ugo Reiter, Crescenzo Ricci, Italia Rocchi, Don Gaetano Ruocco, Avv. Carmine Ruotolo, Francis Russell, Gigino Russo, Maria Russo, Vincenzo Russo, Arturo Salvia, Maria Salvia, Pino Salvia, the late Mrs Sandilands, Giovanni Schettino, Laura Scoppa, Meryle Secrest, Adriana Settanni, Silvana Settanni, Elio Sica, Giovanni Sinibaldi, Library of the Society for the Propagation of the Gospel in Foreign Parts (SPG), David Smurthwaite, Tonino Spadaro, Guido Staiano, Paolo Staiano, Maria Strina, Lidia Talamona, Prof. Richard Tedeschi, the late Gemma Terrasino (Lembo), Giovanni Tessitore, Norah Tew, Rev. Henry Thorold, Matteo Tommaiolo, Francesco Tortora, Baroness Dana Uexküll, Raffaele Vacca, The Hon. Elizabeth Varley, Prof. Gino Verbena, Costanzo Vuotto, Raffaele Vuotto, the late Patrick Wilkinson, Rev. Trevor Willmott, Andrew Wilton, Alessandra Zomack.

Nor can I forget the many pleasant meals taken in restaurants whose owners and staff often helped with information – Al Grottino, Da Gemma, La Capannina, La Cisterna, La Pigna, 'O Saraceno, Settanni, and Tip Top; the friendly Bar Biele, where one can drink without paying the preposterous prices of the Piazza bars and meet an interesting variety of Capresi and tourists; and the Embassy Bar, where Raffaele Vuotto often waylaid me on my evening promenade down Via Camerelle for a glass of brandy and conversation.

I am grateful to Aldo Aprea, Doreen Berrill, Ann Douglas, Derek Jennings, Alexandra Lima, George Money, Antigone Pesce, Pino Salvia, Prof. Richard Shannon, Enzo Simeoli, Francis and Shirley Steegmuller, and Myrtle Streeten, for reading some or all of my drafts, correcting mistakes and making valuable suggestions for improving the book.

I must thank Professor Sir John Hale, for helping with the translation of some Italian passages.

I acknowledge gratefully a grant from the Phoenix Trust towards my research expenses.

I have to thank the following for typing various parts of my manuscript: Angela Campbell, Doreen Gibson, my sister Rosemary Harley, and Felicity Tarrant.

As regards illustrations, ownership of copyright has been acknowledged at appropriate points. I am grateful to all who have let me reproduce their photographs. In the printing of photographs, good work has been done by my niece Lucilla Phelps.

I have been much helped by my sister Rosemary, who first put into my head the idea of writing a book, rather than an ephemeral article, who has advised me throughout and whose long experience of publishing has been invaluable.

Finally, I owe a great debt to my publisher Christopher Sinclair-Stevenson for his enthusiastic support and wise counsel, and to his editor Jonathan Hill.

The author and publishers acknowledge the following sources of quotations used in the text: Macdonald and Co. Ltd., for *Extraordinary Women* by Sir Compton Mackenzie; the Society of Authors, as the literary representative of the Estate of Sir Compton Mackenzie, for *Vestal Fire* and *Octaves 4 & 5*; Chatto & Windus Ltd., for *Looking Back* by Norman Douglas; Eland Books, for *Naples '44* by Norman Lewis; William Collins Sons & Co. Ltd., for *As Much as I Dare*, *More than I Should* and *Always Afternoon* by Faith Compton Mackenzie; Martin Secker and Warburg Ltd., for *The Exile of Capri* by Roger Peyrefitte, translated from the French by Edward Hyams; Aktiebolaget Allhem, Sweden, for *The Story of Axel*

Munthe, Capri and San Michele. All possible care has been taken to trace the owners of copyright material used in this book, to seek permission to reproduce it and make correct acknowledgement of its use. If any material has not been properly acknowledged, the author and publishers offer their apologies.

Introduction

The island of Capri, pronounced CAH-pri not Ca-PREE, lies 17 nautical miles due south of Naples, and 3 miles out from the Sorrentine peninsula. It is 3¾ miles long, varies in breadth from ¾ to 1¾ miles and covers an area of 2,560 acres, of which Capri occupies 988 and Anacapri 1,572. The high land in the west, which rises 1,932 feet to the peak of Monte Solaro, and the less elevated area in the east, rising to 1,099 feet at Monte Tiberio and there plunging precipitously into the sea, are formed of whitish-grey limestones. The intervening depression is filled by sandstones and marls. Capri abounds in natural grottoes; most are at sea-level, but a number are found at a considerable altitude. Capri was not always an island. It probably shook itself free from the mainland during eruptions which convulsed the whole Neapolitan region and left the deposits of volcanic tuff which occur above the limestone and immediately below the present land surface.

As to climate, Capri is small enough to feel the full effects of the sea, large and uneven enough to provide local variations. In winter and spring the prevailing winds are north (*tramontana*), east (*levante*) and north-east (*grecale*), alternating with south (*ostro*) and the humid south-west (*libeccio*) and south-east (*scirocco*). In summer westerly (*ponente*) winds prevail, particularly the north-west (*maestrale*), which ushers in the finest weather and blows constantly through most of the day until towards evening it gives place to the land breeze from the north. The winds from the south sometimes carry dust from Africa; and in late spring and early summer there is occasionally *bafuogno*, a condition with hardly any wind at all, when the air is hot and humid, the sea dead calm, clouds hang over Monte Solaro, and everyone is limp and in a bad humour. The annual rainfall is relatively light, and there is little or no rain at all between June and August. Owing to the precipitous character of the island, rain is caught only on the roofs and terraces of houses and stored in cisterns; the water supply thus provided is totally inadequate and has to be supplemented massively from the mainland. The mean annual temperature is about 60° Fahr. The diurnal range is exceptionally low and there is no sudden fall of temperature at sunset. Capri, which is generally mild in winter and cool in summer, is blessed not only with equability of temperature but also bright sunshine, which is almost constant in summer and comparatively frequent in winter. Climatic shocks, however, occur with little or no warning. There are sudden thunderstorms and destructive thunderbolts. September can be marred by short outbursts of high wind, sometimes of tornado force, and torrential rain. Most devastating are the fierce storms which not infrequently occur in the last few days of December and the beginning of January and can cause great havoc on the coast. For residence, a southern aspect is more suitable in winter and a northern in summer, but there is virtually no spot in the island which enjoys the advantage of both. On the whole it is best to avoid the northerly aspect, since houses facing north on Capri, however charming their prospect over the Bay of Naples, are not agreeable in the winter months when icy winds sweep over the island; north-facing houses can also be formidably damp.

The land surface is notably green, with large areas covered by trees, shrubs and vines. This description applies to much of Anacapri, the land between Anacapri and Marina Grande, Aiano, Torina, Matermania, and the slopes of Monte Tuoro and Monte San Michele.

The high land of Anacapri is isolated from the lower part of the island by a sheer cliff, which until 1874, when the carriage road between Capri and Anacapri was completed, could be scaled only by the Scala Fenicia, the ancient rock-cut staircase which led from Marina Grande to the gateway of Anacapri village, or by the Passetiello, a narrow and difficult mountain path linking the Torina zone of Capri with the upland plain of Cetrella. From earliest times remoteness from each other, persistent enmity, separate religious festivals and different characteristics have distinguished the two communities, which, if both were on the same level, would be only ten minutes walking-distance apart.

The island has always been noted for its clear air, the celebrated *aria di Capri*, to which the relaxed *mores* of the inhabitants and visitors are often attributed. In 1919 an English resident found it necessary to swathe her two female dogs in chastity belts: 'Must do it. Must do it. Dogs in Sirene most immoral dogs in the world. Everybody immoral in Sirene. It's the air. Dogs. People. Can't help it, poor dears.'[1] Capresi and Anacapresi attribute each other's failings to the difference between the upper and lower air. In 1890 a native of Capri told an English resident: 'These people of Anacapri are born thieves and liars . . . they cannot help it – the very air of Anacapri makes them thieves, whether they wish to be or not. You never see one of them without a sack on his shoulder to hide in it what he has stolen.' On the other hand, the people of Anacapri 'consider the air of Capri as deleterious to all moral principle; . . . they wonder how an honest stranger can remain any length of time among such corrupted and evil specimens of humanity.'[2]

What of the islanders today? They remain, as they have always been, totally involved with the island and its prosperity. There is a local saying: '*I Capresi sono attaccati all' Isola come le patelle agli scogli*' (the Capresi are attached to the island like limpets to the rocks). Since their prosperity depends entirely on the exploitation of foreigners – and this includes mainland Italians – everything is geared to this end and the characters of most of the islanders are moulded accordingly.

Long famous as the island of pleasure, it is this aspect in particular which they have been so successful in fostering. They start with a decided advantage in occupying an island which has an exceptionally benign climate, is free from the tectonic disasters which beset the mainland, and is a most impressive work of nature. Capri is endowed with spectacular beauty and extraordinary variations of form in a small space, ranging from remote and delectable corners in the countryside and on the coast, to the hum and excitement of the town – and everywhere eye-catching views of cliff and mountain, sea and ships. The pleasures provided are various, and no matter how eccentric or outrageous you may be in your pursuit of them, no one questions how you or other people live. In 1632 the pleasure-loving Parisian, Bouchard, found both the women and the boys beautiful and willing, and in the nineteenth century, amidst the stuffy morals of the rest of Europe, Capri enjoyed a sexual permissiveness, which was openly acknowledged, where rich women came happily to be bedded by the handsome and virile *marinai*, while homosexuals could enjoy the island's boys and young men – all, of course, at a price. There were quieter pleasures in the enjoyment of the climate, which was particularly suitable for invalids; in wonderment at the natural scenery and, if you were a painter, in the joy of depicting it; restaurants with delicious food and wine; *caffè* and bars where you could gossip; the aura of a welcoming, happy and good-looking people; and, most special to Capri, its quality as lotusland, where the outside world could be forgotten. All these things are still more or less true. Capri still maintains a bewitching air of exclusivity and charm in spite of widespread vulgarisation and, in the season, an apparently endless procession of conducted parties (*comitive*) spending a day there in their package tour of the Naples area; and hordes of day-trippers (*pendolari*), mostly from Naples, who cover the island like a swarm of untidy ants.

The islanders have never advertised their wares and have had no need to do so. Capri has acquired the reputation of being an earthly paradise, and the inhabitants take good care that this reputation persists. For the visitor, everything must appear to be *couleur de rose*. Thus, outwardly, there are no murders, and no muggings in alleyways; boats never collide in the harbour; and no one is ever injured by *cacciatori* shooting song-birds in the Anacapri woods. If by some unlucky chance any of these things happen, news of the event soon vanishes. It is perhaps not an accident that, apart from occasional pamphlets on social, political and environmental matters, issued by the local Communist Party, there is no local news-sheet, and current information about the island has to be sought in the Naples *Il Mattino*, which, of course, covers only major items.

The Capresi themselves are an enclosed and secretive people and usually put up every sort of defence – in the form of straightforward lies, half-truths, evasions, referring you to someone else (*scarica barile*) – against the over-inquisitive foreigner. On the other hand, they are tremendous gossips and, while usually prepared to talk in favourable terms about themselves, like nothing better than tearing apart another person's reputation. Thus diligent enquiry with A can produce basic information about himself and more colourful details of B and C, and *vice versa*. A resident foreigner advised me not to dig too deep and said that usually I would be told just as much as would be thought good for me; when once I sought information from her on a sensitive topic she declined to answer, saying 'I have to live with these people'. Nevertheless, although increasingly regarded as being *troppo insistente* and sometimes finding productive sources liable to dry up, I have obtained a great deal of useful material from the many helpers and sources noted in the Acknowledgements.

In disputes involving foreigners, the Capresi band closely together, and it will be a lucky foreigner who in a law case, for example, finds any islander ready to give evidence on his behalf against another islander – as the following cautionary tale shows. Many years ago a foreigner owned a large villa, which as a rule was let to suitable foreign tenants. At one point the villa was let to an Italian resident, who appeared to have good credentials, but in the event proved very unsatisfactory. Not only did he default on his rent and refuse to go, but also misappropriated some of the contents of the villa. Unfortunately no inventory had been made and when he was finally evicted and the owner complained about the missing objects, not a single Caprese could be found to give evidence that he or she had once seen such and such an item in the villa. Nor was this all. When he was on the point of death the major-domo of the villa asked the foreigner to visit him at home and with engaging frankness begged forgiveness for the theft of various objects which were clear to see scattered about his house.

What, for want of a better phrase, may be called 'cultural activities' are rare. Making money out of the visitors is the dominant activity, and this is done by the islanders with characteristic Italian ingenuity and skill. Because this makes them happy, most of them look happy. A glum face is rarely seen. By October, however, many Capresi look tired, because they have worked extremely hard since May keeping the system going – happy all the same for a successful season and because six months' rest, with the prospect of lazy days and perhaps a winter-cruise, lies ahead.

How the islanders dispose of all the money they make exercises the tax authorities, and there is a strong permanent team of the Guardia di Finanza – a marshal (*maresciallo*), a sergeant (*brigadiere*) and eight corporals (*appuntati*) – to enforce tax payments, both local and national, and prevent the illegal export of currency, by a population of only 12,500. Many islanders invest their profits in Buoni Ordinari Tesoro (BOT), which until recently paid an astonishing 18% tax free, but by 1984 was down to 15%.

Like all Italians, the Capresi are disillusioned and cynical about local politics. Even if they actually know which politicians belong to what party, they tend to regard them generally as *mascalzoni* (scoundrels) or *burattini* (puppets), but do not worry greatly, because the politicians seldom impinge on the tourist trade, from which the greater part of the population earn their bread and butter. While Anacapri could look back on continuity between 1947 and 1970, when the efficient Tommaso De Tommaso was *sindaco*, the instability of the Capri *comune* is illustrated by the fact that, on four occasions since 1944, Naples had to appoint a provincial administrator (*commissario prefettizio*) to the island, because the local politicians were unable to form a government.

Ultimately everything depends on the contributions made by foreigners. In the old days when the islanders were poor, they were grateful to British residents like Henry Wreford and George Clark, who helped them to develop. In the latter part of the nineteenth century there was a steady stream of well-heeled German tourists, and especially the munificent Fritz Krupp. There were the eccentrics and failures and well-to-do residents of the early 1900s, who spent their lives in Capri because they loved it. Between the wars, under the approving gaze of Mussolini, tourism made steady progress. After World War II the islanders began to revel in boom-time and Capri became fashionable world-wide. While individual foreigners have always been liked, either because they are *simpatici*, or talk Italian or take an intelligent interest in the island, the ever-increasing numbers of foreigners are in effect despised, as being no more than people to be provided with the varied pleasures they require, relieved of their cash and, as ephemeral creatures, sent on their way rejoicing.

As the 'eighties begin, Capri has ceased to be fashionable, has lost almost all the elegance which it had in the 'sixties and 'seventies, attracts fewer people who are prepared to contend with the ever-rising prices, and is beset by increasing hordes of *pendolari*, who contribute nothing to the economy and leave behind piles of rubbish. Whatever may be the future of this amazing island – and, as one who has greatly enjoyed his visits, I wish it and the islanders well – its past at least can be studied.

A word of warning to the reader. This does not set out to be a well-proportioned chronicle of Capri from start to finish. The book is biased towards a recital of the 'pleasure' theme and skips quickly over some periods and concentrates more on others, portraying at some length the individuals, both native and foreign, who enjoyed the island and enhanced its pleasures. Thus I move rapidly up to about 1880; expatiate on the next forty-five years; examine the effects of Fascism; look selectively at World War II and the post-war boom up to 1952; and end with reflections on various aspects of the island between 1952 and 1985. Unless otherwise stated, detailed information is correct only up to May 1984.

CHAPTER ONE

2,000 Years of Foreign Rule

The remains of various extinct animals, elephant, rhinoceros, hippopota-
mus, cave-bear, tiger, stag and tortoise, found in the Tragara valley under
volcanic deposits and modern soil, are evidence that in Quaternary times
Capri had a tropical climate and was connected to the mainland, the site of
these bones being possibly a watering place, which subsequently emptied
itself into the sea during a landslide.[1]

Prehistoric man is represented by stone implements and pottery, which
have been found in the Grotta delle Felci (Grotto of the Ferns) on the
eastern slope of Monte Solaro and at several open sites dotted around the
island. These remains suggest sparse occupation of an island which, apart
from its caves, was devoid of natural cover.[2]

Tradition represents Capri as being occupied by the Teleboae, members of a piratical race from north-west Greece. Their ruler Telon, then
an old man, embraced a nymph of the river Sebethos, near Naples, who in
due course gave birth to a son Oebalus – the first of many Capri scandals.

The Sirens, half women, half birds, were mythical beings who had the
power of enchanting by their song anyone who heard them. Ancient
writers were in doubt as to their location.[3] Although none placed the
Sirens in Capri, they are commemorated there by the Scoglio delle
Sirene, the rock which juts into the sea at Marina Piccola. What better
place could have been chosen by the Teleboan brigands, keeping watch
from their cave on the side of Monte Solaro, to lure passing boats ashore,
using their most attractive women as bait?

In the Odyssey[4] Homer describes how Odysseus escaped the lure of
the Sirens by inserting wax in the ears of his crew and having himself
bound to the mast of his ship; the event is recorded by the romantic
German painter Friedrich Preller, who places it in a Capri-type landscape.

*

The first mention of Capri in history is by Strabo, the Greek historian and
geographer, writing at the end of the first century B.C.: 'Capreai had two
small towns in ancient times, though later only one. The Neapolitans took

possession of this island too'.[5] Naples, founded around 600 B.C. by the
Greek colony of Cumae, soon became the centre of Greek culture in
Campania. In Capri two stretches of defensive wall, one known as *muro
greco*, still survive on the northern side of the town, but no early Greek
remains have ever been found in the island. The masonry of the town-wall
is like that of early Pompeii and other towns of Campania fortified from
the fourth century B.C. by the Etruscans. It is, therefore, in an Italic rather
than Greek context that the walled town should be placed.[6] The later,
single town, to which Strabo refers, was probably around Marina Grande,
which remained the principal centre throughout the secure years of the
Roman Empire and until Muslim pirates drove the inhabitants back to
their highland. Although Capri lacked early Greek artefacts, the islanders, as dependants of Naples, adopted and retained for many years the
Greek customs of that city.

Capri was 'discovered' by Octavian (later the Emperor Augustus) in
29 B.C., when he was returning to Italy from Egypt, with all his rivals
conquered and he himself commander of the legions and thus master of
the Roman world. While sailing towards Naples he landed on Capri, to be
greeted by a favourable omen – 'The branches of an old oak, which had
drooped right to the ground and were withering, suddenly regained their
vigour'[7] – which so delighted him that he arranged to buy the island from
Naples and gave them Ischia in exchange. Augustus paid many visits to
Capri and looked on it as an admirable place for a holiday. He had a
passion for building, and there can be no doubt that many of the Roman
structures belong to his reign. For the movement of building materials,
contact between Capri and Anacapri would have been essential, and it is
likely that the Scala Fenicia, the rock-cut stairway which joined Anacapri
to the lower region, if not already existing, was cut at this time.[8]

In the summer of A.D. 14, suffering from the stomach ailment which
ended in his death, Augustus visited Capri, 'where he gave himself up
wholly to rest and geniality. . . . He distributed Roman gowns (*togae*) and
Greek cloaks (*pallia*), stipulating that the Romans should use the Greek
dress and language, and the Greeks, the Roman. He continually watched
the exercises of the cadets (*ephebi*).[9] Afterwards he gave these young men a
banquet and not merely allowed but insisted on the playing of games and
scrambling for tokens which entitled the holders to fruit, sweetmeats and
the like. In fact he indulged in every sort of fun.'[10] He was unfavourably
impressed by the laziness of some of his staff who, now settled on the
island, were being affected by the Capri air, and as a parting shot dubbed
the island Apragopolis ('City of do-nothings').

Augustus crossed over to Naples, but feeling worse on the homeward
journey took to his bed at Nola, where he died in his seventy-sixth year.
He was succeeded as Emperor by his stepson Tiberius, who for the first

Capri from the air, looking west. Anacapri in background, with summit of Monte Solaro; part of Capri town and Marina Grande in middle ground; Faraglioni rocks and Monte Tiberio, with Villa Iovis, in foreground. *Courtesy of Italian Tourist Bureau, Capri*

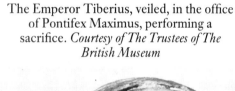

The Emperor Augustus, about 15 B.C. From a statue in the Vatican Museum

The Emperor Tiberius, veiled, in the office of Pontifex Maximus, performing a sacrifice. *Courtesy of The Trustees of The British Museum*

twelve years of his reign continued Augustus's policy of keeping the Empire within its existing boundaries and ruling it by a judicious mixture of force and diplomacy.

But he disliked Rome and the Romans disliked him. In A.D. 26, in his sixty-eighth year, Tiberius decided to leave Rome for ever and make his home in Capri. The island was his private property and by its seclusion offered the old man, who was still in excellent health, peace and enjoyment. According to Suetonius he was 'particularly attracted to the island because it was accessible only by one small beach, being everywhere else surrounded with sheer cliffs of great height and by deep water'.[11] Tacitus adds that there were 'no more than a few facilities for small ships, and no ship could put in unobserved by a coastguard. In winter the climate is mild; its summers catch the western breeze and are made extremely pleasant by the circling expanse of the open sea; it also overlooks . . . the most beautiful of bays.'[12]

Tiberius established himself in twelve villas, which must have included some already built by Augustus. He was thus able to take advantage of all the vagaries of the Capri climate.[13] Having settled himself on Capri, he continued in his care for the Empire, maintained links with Rome and took decisions on matters referred to him. In short, he continued to be an effective, if distant, ruler.

I do not wish to add to the already enormous volume of literature about the sensual and vicious behaviour to which, after a long life of self-control, Tiberius abandoned himself in the amiable surroundings of his private island, beyond quoting some of the relevant passages from Tacitus and Suetonius.[14] Here it must be said that both were writing in the early part of the second century A.D., many years after the death of their subject, both perhaps drawing on the same *chronique scandaleuse*.

Tacitus writes: 'Tiberius, once so much absorbed in the cares of State, now relaxed with equal application into secret indulgences and immoral pastimes.' Suetonius begins: 'Having gained the freedom of privacy and being no longer in the public eye, he at last gave vent to all the vices which he had for a long time tried unsuccessfully to conceal . . .' and then launches into his notorious account of the Emperor's pleasures.

'In his retreat on Capri, he devised special parlours of secret vices (*sellaria*) where bevies of girls and dissipated young men, collected from all quarters, and devisers of unnatural practices (*spintriae*), in groups of three, would perform sexual acts with each other in his presence, so as to stimulate his failing lust. He decorated apartments with pictures and statuettes of the most indecent paintings and figures, and equipped them with the works of Elephantis,[15] so that in each act that was to be performed the model for the required position would be available. In woods and glades he devised places for sex, and in caves and grottos young people of

Villa Iovis from the air, the ruins of Tiberius's villa surmounted by the church and statue of Santa Maria del Maria del Soccorso. *Photo: Herman Hammer, reproduced from illustration published by AB Allhem, Sweden*

both sexes, dressed as little Pans and Nymphs, offered their services.'

Tacitus mentions that these new words, *sellarii* and *spintriae*, were coined on Capri, 'one drawn from the obscenity of the place and the other from the versatility of the pathic. In kingly style he polluted with his lecheries the children of free-born parents. Nor were beauty and physical charm his only incitements to lasciviousness, but sometimes a boyish modesty and sometimes a noble lineage.' Boys were procured by threats, force and bribery. Amongst the *spintriae* was the future Emperor Vitellius, who was thus 'the cause of his father's first advancement, at the expense of his own chastity'.[16]

Suetonius continues: 'he trained small boys whom he called his "tiddlers" (*pisciculi*) to get between his thighs and play while he was swimming; exciting him with their tongue and nibbling . . . and he even put sturdier, though still unweaned, infants to suck his member like a nipple; it was to this type of pleasure that he was particularly prone both by inclination and age. And on this account, in respect of a picture by Parrhasius[17] depicting Atalanta sucking off Meleager, bequeathed to him on condition that, if he was offended by the subject, he could have 10,000 gold pieces instead, Tiberius not only preferred to keep the picture but assigned it to his own bedroom. It is related that once, while sacrificing, Tiberius was so struck by the appearance of the attendant who proffered the incense-casket that he could not control himself, but with the ceremony scarcely over hurried him aside and ravished him, and did the same to his brother, a flute-player. Soon afterwards, because the brothers complained of this outrage, he had their legs broken'.

No doubt, much of the Emperor's time was spent in the Villa Iovis, perched magnificently on the precipitous north-east tip of the island, and, according to Suetonius, it was here that unwanted persons were cast to their death from what is now called 'Il Salto' (the Leap).

Tiberius occasionally crossed to the mainland and in A.D. 32 advanced as far as his own gardens on the Vatican, but he did not enter the City and, sensitive about his decrepit appearance, placed soldiers to prevent anyone from coming near him.

Back in Capri the consciousness of his own wretchedness was expressed in a letter to the Senate which began: 'If I knew what to write to you, Conscript Fathers, or how to write it, or what not to write at this time, may the gods and goddesses destroy me more wretchedly than I feel myself to be perishing every day.'[18] In his seventy-eighth year, the lonely old man's robust health at last gave way. In the spring of A.D. 37 he became seriously ill and on 16 March had a fainting fit which was thought to be fatal. Gaius, his great-nephew and heir designate, was present and emerged to be saluted as Emperor. Tiberius, however, recovered and called for something to eat. The Prefect of the Pretorian Guard gave orders that a quantity of clothes should be thrown on Tiberius and that he should be left alone. He was thus smothered to death – only a few days after the lighthouse (Torre del Faro) below the Villa Iovis had been brought down by an earthquake.

So ended Capri's first 'crowded hour'. It was followed by many years of obscurity. No Caesar resided there, but Commodus banished his wife Crispina and sister Lucilla to Capri in 182. Dio Cassius, writing in about 200, says: 'It [Capri] lies not far from the mainland in the region of Surrentum and is good for nothing, but is renowned even to the present day because Tiberius had a residence there.[19] Capri probably remained the personal property of successive Emperors until 476, when Romulus August (Augustulus), the last ruler of the Western Empire, died. Thereafter it was joined to the territory of Sorrento, which was subject to the Dukes of Naples.

*

Around 530 the island was acquired by the monastery of Monte Cassino, which had just been founded by Saint Benedict, and sometime before the end of the sixth century a Benedictine monastery, dedicated to Saint Stephen, was established in Capri.

In the seventh century Capri was visited by Bishop San Costanzo, who there fell ill and died. He was buried near the Marina and was chosen as patron of Capri, with 14 May as the day of his *festa*. Later, at a date unknown, a small church was built over his tomb and in one form or another has continued to this day as the basilica of San Costanzo.[20] It was not until 1231, however, that Anacapri acquired its own patron saint and protector, Sant' Antonio da Padova, who, whatever he may have lacked as a late arrival, surpassed San Costanzo in achievement. After working many miracles in Ferrara, Padua and Lisbon, which were later recorded in paintings by Titian and other masters, he died near Padua on 13 June 1231 – the day of his annual *festa*, one month later than his Capri rival.

From the ninth to the eleventh century Capri was constantly under threat of North African marauders, variously called Moslems, Saracens, Corsairs and Tripoli pirates, and there was very little pleasure except for the marauders themselves, who plundered what was portable and carried off the men, women and children to be sold as slaves on the North African coast. In Capri, which in 868 had been transferred from the Duke of Naples to the Doge of Amalfi, fishing and viticulture were constantly interrupted by the need to take refuge inland – usually in the Grotta del Castiglione, which was shielded by a castle on top of the Castiglione hill. In quieter times the town on the Marina continued to be inhabited and was still standing in the eleventh century, when the contemporary writer

Edrisius says: 'There is in Capri a town of medium size in the very middle of which rises a spring of water' – referring evidently to the Marina and the Truglio fountain. In 994, under the papacy of John XVI, Capri achieved ecclesiastical autonomy, when its first Bishop, also named John, was consecrated by the Archbishop of Amalfi; the Cathedral was probably on the same site as the present church of Santo Stefano.

*

The arrival of the Normans, who quickly conquered Sicily and Southern Italy, brought no comfort to Capri, which they invaded in 1138. A group of Capresi, not wishing to submit, retreated to a fort, which since Byzantine times had guarded access to Anacapri; here they were blockaded and forced to surrender.

The twelfth century saw the emergence of one of Capri's oldest families, the Arcucci, who came to the island from the Amalfitan coast. One, Sergio Arcucci, married Gemma Strina, member of another ancient Capri family, a union which enabled both families to enlarge their domains within the island. Brief glory came to the family in 1230 when Eliseo Arcucci served as a sea-captain[21] in the fleet of Frederick II ('Stupor Mundi'), son of a German father and Norman mother, who became Emperor of Germany in 1198 and King of Sicily in 1220.

Frederick's death in 1250 was followed by a long struggle between Anjou and Aragon for the Kingdom of Sicily, which, it must be remembered, included Naples. Eventually a treaty between them acknowledged the separation and independence of the crowns of Naples and Sicily, the former being assigned to Anjou and the latter to Aragon.

Capri thus fell under the rule of Anjou. There were at this period in the island some 120 dwellings, representing a population of about 600. The islanders were extremely poor and, while fishing provided a modicum of food, there was never enough arable land, and in a bad year they would be on the brink of famine. It says much for the skill of Capri's nameless spokesmen, who never failed to extract from successive rulers special privileges, without which the island could not have survived – the most important being exemption from Royal dues and the right to import grain from the mainland.

In 1343 Queen Joanna I succeeded to the throne of Anjou. She renewed the islanders' privileges and appointed as her secretary and chamberlain Giacomo Arcucci, great-grandson of Eliseo, the sea-captain. In 1363, in fulfilment of a vow made to his protector, St James, Giacomo celebrated the birth of his first-born son by building a monastery, the Certosa di San Giacomo, in the valley between the Castiglione and Tuoro hills. The Queen helped to finance the project and granted

Arcucci considerable tracts of the best land of Capri for the use of the Carthusians. The building, whose architect is unknown, was completed in 1374. The Queen and later various Popes granted the monks special privileges, which gave them control of much of the agricultural and economic life of the island, as well as the right to levy taxes on the produce of land and sea. Amongst the Papal gifts was the right to acquire the possessions of any Caprese family which became extinct. Thus the Certosa steadily increased in wealth, property and power, housing monks who, though few in number, lived luxuriously, attended by numerous servants, and were far richer than the Bishop and his Clergy.

The last twenty years of the fourteenth century were rendered hideous by hostilities between rival Anjou factions. A notable casualty was Giacomo Arcucci, who was disgraced and stripped of all his wealth, property and honours. Old and destitute he sought shelter in the Certosa, and there he died in 1397; the monks, in gratitude to their founder and benefactor, gave him a sumptuous funeral.[22]

In 1435 war again broke out between Anjou and Aragon. The Capresi, learning that the Aragonese had a measure of support amongst influential Neapolitans, decided to change sides, handed over the island to Alfonso of Aragon and witnessed his capture of Naples in 1442.

During the next fifty years successive Aragonese Kings of Naples confirmed the privileges and exemptions which Capri had been granted by Anjou, and added a curious new benefit – the right to control the catching of garfish (*aguglie*) – a small eel-like fish with a long sharp nose, which is still caught and considered a delicacy.

*

In the sixteenth century control of Naples passed first to Ferdinand and Isabella, rulers of a United Spain, and then to Frederick's grandson Charles, the Austrian Hapsburg, who, already master of the Low Countries, became, on Frederick's death in 1516, ruler of an empire larger than any since the time of Charlemagne. He moved his court from Flanders to Spain and, having little concern for his South Italian possessions, except as a source of revenue from taxes, henceforth appointed Viceroys to rule them.

To Moorish piracy, organised from the Barbary coast, was now added the Ottoman assault against Europe by land and sea. In 1535 Kheir-eddin ('Barbarossa'), Admiral of the Turkish Fleet, after passing through the Straits of Messina, entered the Bay of Naples and ravaged its coasts and islands. Capri suffered the worst assault of its history. The fortress barring the Anacapri pass, which still bears Barbarossa's name, was partly destroyed, the ancient walls of Capri town were demolished and many of the inhabitants fled to the mainland. Another attack in 1553 by the Turkish admiral Dragut led to the sack and burning of the Certosa. In face of these attacks, which went unpunished, the Spanish Viceroy allowed the islanders to keep and carry arms, some kind of civilian militia was formed, and defensive works were established in various parts of the island.

By 1561 the population had risen to about 1500, living in 349 dwellings. Fabio Giordano, a contemporary historian of Naples, wrote of the catching and bottling of quails, of the water-springs of the island, of the Certosa monastery and the Faraglioni rocks, of the Grotta del Castiglione, in which the inhabitants took refuge during the hostile raids, and of the stairway to Anacapri, whose population he describes as 'deficient in virtue'. Capaccio summed up the islanders with Tacitean brevity: 'nevertheless they live in extreme poverty, vying with each other in pride, always liable to be preyed upon by the Turks, who daily carry them away into slavery as they fish or sail'.

In the first half of the seventeenth century Capri was one of the poorest dioceses of the Roman Church. The bishop of the time considered that the Pope had sent him to Capri as a penance for his sins. His successor wrote to the Pope in 1632 that his episcopal income, derived mainly from a tithe on quails, was only 160 ducats[23] a year, but even this he found difficult to extract from the poverty-stricken inhabitants. With this income the 'Bishop of Quails', as he became known, had to maintain the churches of Santo Stefano and San Costanzo, and pay numerous clerics, who, contrary to custom, retained three or four livings for their own use. The letter continued with more about the poverty and unruliness of the inhabitants, the rebelliousness of his clergy, and the high-handedness of the Carthusians, who claimed to be outside the jurisdiction of the Bishop and forbade the islanders to sell their produce, so that the market for the monks' own crops should not be spoiled.[24]

In the same year as this woeful tale, Jean-Jacques Bouchard, a pleasure-loving Parisian, who was also a scholar and antiquarian, after spending Easter in Naples, crossed over to Capri and has a strong claim to being the first tourist. He was unfavourably impressed by the narrow streets and the small, one-storey, vaulted houses. He noted that many houses, churches and chapels were in ruins. He lodged at the Certosa, where he was well entertained and was particularly struck by *certaines petites ricottes* – the renowned soft white cheeses (*ricottelle*) made from goats' milk, which were in great demand among *tous les grands de Naples*. At this time the monastery's income was more than fifty times greater than that of the Bishop. Bouchard formed a poor opinion of the islanders, whom he found 'very vicious, quarrelsome, rebellious, thievish, proud and all dying of hunger'. He had a good word, nevertheless, for the looks and willingness of the women and boys of Anacapri: '*Les femmes y sont fort belles, comme aussi les garçons, et les uns et les autres font volontiers la courtoisie.*' The women raised large numbers of silkworms, the silk from Capri being the most highly prized of all the silk coming from Italy. The island had an abundance of olive groves, vineyards, wheat, flax and vegetables on the lower ground towards the harbour. The mountains were covered with oaks, holly, laurel, arbutus, myrtle and rosemary. The greatest share of the produce went to the Carthusian monks. . . . Bouchard paid particular attention to the 'curiosities' (*anticaglie*) of the island and was impressed by the Villa Iovis and the Roman remains on Monte San Michele, at Tragara and at Palazzo a Mare.[25]

Religious affairs continued to agitate the island. In 1641 Monsignor Paolo Pellegrino[26] of Naples began a turbulent episcopate, which lasted some forty-two years, with a general visitation of the diocese. This revealed a state of such disorder that, to the dismay of all, he convened the first synod ever held in the island, and quickly put its recommendations for reform into practice. He antagonised his own clergy by enforcing that part of the synod which dealt *De vita et honestate clericorum*. They must wear their cassocks 'fastened at the neck, so that in no wise should the chest appear uncovered'. They were forbidden to wear coloured shoes and fancy laces; to bathe in the sea except in private and then suitably clad; to frequent shops, which the synod likened to taverns; or to be seen in the company of women. He quarrelled with the Certosa over the collection of tithes, their control of the wine-trade, which discriminated against the importation of wine from his own vineyards in Naples, and their privileges in the pasturing of livestock. He made plentiful use of excommunication and formed gangs of armed thugs (*percussori*) to enforce his will on the islanders.

Growing up in this troubled scene was a very determined young lady, Prudentia,[27] who was born in 1621, daughter of a Neapolitan merchant named Pisa and a *caprese* mother, Giustina Strina. At an early age she read 'Lives of the Martyrs', which had a profound effect on her mind. Inspired by the sufferings of the Saints she began to impose penances and tasks on herself which became ever more ingenious and severe. She had frequent converse with Jesus; 'numerous letters and poems to her Divine Lover . . . couched in language that might be addressed with equal propriety by some terrestrial Juliet to her Romeo'.[28] In 1641 she retired to a convent in Naples and four years later made her full profession as a Dominican. Having assumed the name Suor Serafina di Dio, she returned to Capri and there founded a small house of retreat for young women.

Early in 1656 Naples was attacked by the Plague, which in a short time devastated much of Southern Italy. The pestilence reached Capri in June and spread rapidly. Many of the clergy working amongst the victims were struck down, and it was no longer possible to administer sacraments to the dying. Bishop Pellegrino, who was among the survivors, begged the Prior of the Certosa, to send his monks to help care for the dying. But the Prior, claiming that the monks were 'vowed to the strict observance of the cloister', refused to help and barred the gates of the monastery against all comers.[29] The deaths became so numerous that burial was impossible, and corpses were left where they lay. Some were thrown by the infuriated survivors over the walls of the Certosa, but the monks remained unscathed. The Plague, which lasted for five months, claimed half of Capri's 1,700 inhabitants and completely wiped out many families. Invoking the ancient privilege by which they were allowed to inherit the possessions of families which had become extinct, the Carthusians added substantially to their already considerable estates.

The Plague did not quell either the intransigence of Bishop Pellegrino or the zeal of Suor Serafina. The former, after new quarrels with the Certosa, his own clergy and the civil authorities, was compelled to leave Capri and did not return until 1672. Serafina set about recruiting patrons and donors to support her work, to such good effect that in 1666 she was able to lay the foundation stone of a convent, named after Santa Teresa, whose life and circumstances so closely resembled her own;[30] and a year later that of its Church. This astonishing woman then turned her attention to the mainland, where three convents were built, and in 1683 a fifth was founded in Anacapri. One of the peculiarities of the organisation of these new convents was that their inmates were nearly always recruited from the first convent in Capri. This in its turn was replenished by girls from the mainland, since its life had little appeal to the islanders.

In the 1680s the tide turned against her. Growing old, fixed in her ways and no longer Superior of the convent in Capri, Serafina was unable to control its policies. She was distressed that the rigours of the old régime were relaxed, while she herself lacked authority and was neglected and even ill-treated by the other nuns. Worse, she came to the adverse notice of the Inquisition.

In her younger days she had been accused of immoral relations with her uncle, Don Marcello Strina. At various times she had been called a 'hypocrite, witch, drunkard, liar, lunatic, thief. . . . She was accused of necromancy and, strangest of all, of adorning herself with lace undergarments.'[31] Subjected to periodic investigation by the Holy Office, in 1689 the verdict went against her and, as punishment, she was imprisoned in her cell, without the consolation of the Eucharist. Eventually deemed to be innocent of the various charges laid against her she was released in 1691. Her last years were plagued with ill-health and continuing spite within the Convent of Santa Teresa. She died there on 17 March 1699 in her seventy-eighth year and, in a spirit of reconciliation and attended by a great concourse of people, was buried in the Convent Church of San Salvatore.[32]

In 1682, to general relief, Bishop Pellegrino resigned his see and died within a few months. His successor set in motion the complete rebuilding of the Cathedral Church of Santo Stefano. The work was given to Marziale Desiderio, a master-builder of Amalfi, where he had already achieved fame in the construction of vaultings and domes. These features he combined with traditional Caprese methods for surfacing roofs, to produce a complex arrangement of curved surfaces which united beauty with the practical function of collecting rain-water. The body and façade of the church were built in the Baroque style, but free of superfluous adornments. Desiderio left Amalfi and became a citizen of Capri, where he headed a long line of skilled builders who carried on his traditions and were nicknamed 'Marzianielli'; the Desiderio clan is still flourishing today.

In 1715 a magnificent silver statue of San Costanzo, patron saint of Capri, was commissioned, to replace the old wooden effigy housed in his church at the Marina, which had succumbed to the humidity and disintegrated. The new life-sized effigy was made of laminated silver, the layers held together by small nails. Fashioned by craftsmen in Naples and financed from public and private donations, it was lodged in the Cathedral of Santo Stefano. The Saint, represented as far as the waist, is in pontifical dress; he holds in his left hand a staff and book, and with his right hand bestows a benediction; amongst the adornments of his mitre are sapphires, garnets and beryls found at the Villa Iovis.[33] It is this same effigy which is still carried in procession by fishermen every year at his *festa* on 14 May.

*

In 1713 Spanish rule was brought temporarily to an end by a Hapsburg invasion from Austria. They in turn were driven out of Naples in 1734 by Don Carlos, son of the Bourbon King of Spain, who was crowned King Charles III of the Two Sicilies (Naples and Sicily). So began 136 years of Bourbon rule.

The Bourbons interested themselves in the excavation of antiquities. The Villa Iovis was explored, and a fine polychrome marble floor from it was presented to the Cathedral, where, in spite of the poor reputation enjoyed by the Emperor Tiberius, it was re-laid in front of the High Altar. But the Bourbons also wanted Capri's treasures for themselves. In 1750 four yellow and *cipolino* Roman columns were removed from the nave of the Church of San Costanzo and transplanted to the Royal Palace at Caserta, where they were converted into slabs and frames; their place in the church was taken by plain, granite columns, also of Roman origin.

In 1745 or 1746 occurred a notable event in the history of Capri, the arrival of the first foreign resident – Sir Nathaniel Thorold, last baronet of Harmston in Lincolnshire. Nothing is known of his birth or early life. At some stage he went on the Grand Tour and *c.*1740 had his portrait painted by an Italian artist. Later, and certainly before 1745, suffering from asthma and heavily in debt, he decided to leave England for ever. While in Holland, he met a wandering Jew from Leghorn (Livorno), who suggested that a fortune could be made in Italy, with its large Catholic population restricted to fish on Fridays, by anyone able to cure codfish so that it would last long enough to be eaten in the South. Thorold discovered that the technique used for salting herrings could also be applied to cod, and soon was in Leghorn supervising the arrival and disposal of the first cargo of salted codfish (*baccalà*). Thorold took lodgings in the house of Antonino Canale, an elderly apothecary and soon started an affair with his wife, Anna della Noce. The resulting scandal drove all three from Leghorn to Naples. Salted cod proved as popular in Naples as in Leghorn, and Thorold decided to make Capri his home and from it direct his growing business. He bought a property just outside the town-gate and commissioned Marziale Desiderio to construct a sumptuous dwelling overlooking the Bay of Naples. In the *palazzo* which Desiderio built for him Thorold installed English furniture, Greek and Roman antiquities, and every available comfort; the structure was liberally decorated with the Thorold coat of arms. Here he lived with his lover Anna, her official husband, Antonino Canale, and assorted children, who for the sake of propriety were all called Canale. Anna, born in 1743, may have been the daughter of Canale, but Nataniele (1745) must have been Thorold's child. At the end of 1749 Samuele, who became Thorold's favourite son, was born; others, including Carlo (1752), followed. These goings-on greatly displeased the Bishop, who in 1754 informed His Holiness that 'a scandal had been caused by the co-habitation . . . of a certain married woman . . . with an heretical English nobleman'. The Pope seems to have taken the matter calmly. The Bishop then tried hard to convert Thorold to the Catholic faith, but could never extract any reaction from him except the Italian word *pazienza*. After Canale's death the Bishop urged Thorold to marry Anna, but achieved nothing beyond the assurance that Thorold would consider the matter 'bye and bye'. In his will of 1763 the Baronet gave instructions that after his death Samuel should be sent to England and educated as a Protestant; on reaching the age of twenty-one he was to apply for naturalisation and the right to change his name from Canale to Thorold, whereupon he would inherit Nathaniel's English estates.

Nathaniel died peacefully on 28 August 1764. Anna, who, because she

Silver effigy of San Costanzo,
1715

Sir Nathaniel Thorald, c. 1740.
Photo: Alan Nesbit

was not married to him, could not inherit his wealth and property, persuaded a notary, Michele Pagano, to concoct a bogus will, whereby Nathaniel left all his worldly possessions, specified in full detail, to Anna. Unfortunately for her the authentic will soon came to light, and all that Nathaniel had planned for Samuel was carried out. The rest of his illegitimate children remained in Capri and were progenitors of later members of the Canale family. The Palazzo Inglese, as it was known, also passed into the possession of the Canale family, and its name changed accordingly. Thorold is commemorated in the language of the island, for when a Caprese wants to postpone something indefinitely, he says in dialect '*Baibai dicette 'u 'Nglese*'.[34]

During the second half of the eighteenth century, in spite of occasional raids by the Corsairs, the economic condition of the islanders improved, as business in the products of land and sea increased. The island had long been known for its wine, the white mostly from Anacapri, the red from Capri. Norbert Hadrawa,[35] secretary of the Austrian Legation in Naples and a frequent visitor at the end of the eighteenth century, both in the company of King Ferdinand IV and on his own to excavate Roman sites, considered Capri wine to be equal, if not superior, to the wine of Piedmont and the 'Lacrima Cristi' of the Vesuvian vineyards. Plentiful supplies of olive oil were produced. Oranges, lemons and melons were amongst the fruits grown for local consumption and for export. The only manufactures were fishing-nets, made by men and old women, and ribands and scarves, prepared by girls and young women from silk furnished by the merchants of Naples. Catches of fish, especially tuna, were abundant. In the summer young men went coral-fishing off Sardinia, but stood the risk of being captured by pirates and sold as slaves in North Africa.

There were some advances in education, thanks mainly to Monsignor Nicola Saverio Gamboni, who in 1777 became (the last) Bishop of Capri. Liberal, intelligent and energetic, he founded a seminary for training young priests, as well as four other schools, one of which was devoted to agriculture and naval affairs, and another to arts and crafts for girls.

The Certosa, which contained only fourteen monks, owned all the land in and around the Tragara Valley, and had many vineyards and olive-groves in other parts of the island, as well as possessions on the mainland. To judge from the steady and substantial income which the monks derived from their lands, they must have managed them efficiently. The monastery baked the best bread in the island and manufactured a liqueur, 'Certosino' (Capri version of Chartreuse), both of which were sold on behalf of the monks. With plenty of servants, they did themselves well in matters of food and drink. They continued to oppress the islanders with the exactions which had been their right since the earliest years of the monastery, but the most unpopular, the *pecunia maris*, levied on catches of fish, was abolished by Bishop Gamboni in 1786.

Fortunately for many islanders the trapping of quail in May and September, which was too widespread to be made a monopoly by either the religious or secular authorities, provided food for themselves during the two short seasons and a temporary income from the sale of the birds in Naples. Capri was a favourite landfall and resting-place for quail during their spring and autumn migrations. During the spring flight from North Africa both the *scirocco*, which otherwise had no friends, and San Costanzo, whose month is May, were blessed by the islanders. The autumn migration, when the birds flew south from Europe, was usually on a larger scale, and the birds, having fattened on the grain-fields along their route, were in prime condition. Thousands of quail were caught in nets hung on a long line of posts about 30 feet apart and 30 to 40 feet high, especially at what is now Due Golfi – the saddle of land between Torina and Capri town, from which the Bay of Naples and Gulf of Salerno are both visible – then called Le Parate ('things prepared' or traps for the quail). Birds blinded for the purpose were put as decoys in cages near the poles, so that their lamentations should attract new arrivals into the nets. When the nets were full enough they were hauled down, and the birds stuffed, still alive, into long cages for transport to the Naples market; many died during the journey. Other quail were caught individually by men with hand-nets, accompanied by boys to mark the quail and half-starved little dogs to flush them from their cover. Others, who had stunned themselves against the cliffs, were picked up by fishermen. As many as 12,000 quail could be taken in a single day and up to 150,000 in the fifteen days of a seasonal migration.

The King often visited Capri to hunt quail and partridge, and offered rewards for the killing of snakes which destroyed the eggs of the latter. To retrieve the birds from the undergrowth he employed a recent immigrant named Lembo,[36] who moved so swiftly and was so good at his job that he was nicknamed ''A Sorechella' (field-mouse). During his trips the King stayed in the Palazzo Canale, with its comfortable interior and splendid view of the Marina and the Bay of Naples, while two ships continually circled the island as protection against corsairs.

At the turn of the century Capri became embroiled in the Napoleonic wars. The French army swept down the peninsula, occupied Rome and moved on Naples. King Ferdinand and his court took refuge with the English fleet under Lord Nelson, which, after its victory at the Battle of the Nile in 1798, was anchored in the Bay of Naples, and were able to escape to Palermo. On 23 January 1799 the French entered Naples and proclaimed the Parthenopean Republic, to which many liberal and other anti-Bourbon elements rallied. In Capri an active supporter of the

Republic was Gennaro Felice Arcucci, doctor, savant and wine-producer, while, much to everyone's surprise, Bishop Gamboni praised the new régime in his sermons.

The Parthenopean Republic was short-lived. The reverses suffered by the French armies in northern Italy compelled the withdrawal from Naples of the bulk of their forces. The small garrison which remained was soon overwhelmed by English, Russian and Sardinian troops, and in June 1799 Ferdinand, protected by Nelson's fleet, returned to his capital. The restitution of the Bourbon monarchy was followed by a massacre of republicans and the execution of their leaders – a process enthusiastically supported by Nelson.[37] Arcucci was hanged in Naples on 18 March 1800. Gamboni was luckier. After being imprisoned and exiled from Capri, he retired to Rome. Finally in 1807 he was elevated to the Patriarchate of Venice, where he died in 1811.

After the Bourbon reoccupation of Naples Napoleon came to terms with the King, by undertaking to withdraw his forces from South Italy, if Ferdinand would prevent the Allies from using the ports of his Kingdom. The pact lasted until November 1805 when, with the consent of the King, a joint English and Russian force descended on Naples. Napoleon, infuriated, sent a strong French force against the city. The Allies withdrew, and on 12 February 1806 the Bourbon court fled once more to Palermo, while their troops retired to Calabria. The French were joined by the Emperor's brother Joseph, who entered the city, captured all the neighbouring islands except Ponza, and on 30 March was declared King of Naples.

The French garrisoned and fortified Capri against a likely assault by the English fleet, which since its victory at Trafalgar was set to dominate the Mediterranean. On 12 May 1806 a naval force under Sir Sidney Smith arrived unexpectedly off Marina Grande and landed without difficulty. The French commander was killed; his force lost courage and retired to the town, where on the next day they surrendered. They were given permission to retain their arms and baggage, and were sent over to the mainland in their own ships.

It was decided to make Capri a stronghold against the French in Naples, and Lieutenant-Colonel Hudson Lowe, whose service had included the fortress of Gibraltar, was appointed to command a re-inforced garrison of mainly English and Corsican troops. He made his headquarters in the Palazzo Canale and with a Caprese, Don Nicola Morgano, as director of fortifications, established defensive works on high points and in positions covering the two Marinas. Anacapri was garrisoned by a party of Corsican rangers commanded by the young and recently-promoted Captain Richard Church. Proud of his command and responsibilities, he was energetic in fortifying Anacapri, by erecting defences on the heights and above various coves on the west coast, where landings were possible.

The French, however, made no attack, and by the summer of 1808 the garrison had become bored and apathetic. In September, Church was replaced in Anacapri by Major John Hamill, in command of the Royal Regiment of Malta. Church and his Corsicans joined Lowe's forces in Capri. The garrison now totalled about 1,800.

On 1 August the dashing General Joachim Murat, Napoleon's brother-in-law, succeeded Joseph Bonaparte as King of Naples, with the title 'Gioacchino Napoleone', and was charged with the reoccupation of Capri, for which he made skilful plans.

On 27 September Lowe sent a letter from Capri ordering 'four dozen champagne; three dozen burgundy of three years old; three dozen burgundy of four years old; six dozen of the best wines, such as Frontignan, and any others which may be held in good estimation'.[38] Although agents in Naples had already warned him of an impending attack, Lowe appears to have relied on the strength of Capri's garrison and fortifications, and on the English fleet as his first line of defence. When, however, on 3 October he received firm intelligence that the attack had been fixed for the following day, the fleet was nowhere to be seen. It had gone to Ponza, to acquaint the Neapolitan squadron there and any other English ships which it encountered that an assault was imminent.

While Murat watched from Massa, at the end of the Sorrentine peninsula, naval forces and cargo ships, with 3,000 French and Neapolitan troops on board, under the command of General Lamarque, sailed from Naples. Feint attacks were made at the two Marinas to keep Colonel Lowe's forces occupied in Capri, while the main assault was launched on the inaccessible north-west coast of Anacapri. Equipped with ladders borrowed from the lamp-lighters of Naples, 80 men touched land before the Maltese were aware of the fact, and, having scaled the rocks, grouped themselves round a flag. 500 more were landed before there was any reaction at all from the defenders, and then, instead of charging and driving the invaders into the sea, the Maltese retreated slowly uphill. Most of them were taken prisoner, the Scala Fenicia was occupied, so that communications with Capri were cut off, and Major Hamill was killed. Completely demoralised, the remaining Maltese retreated to Monte Solaro, where they were forced to surrender, were marched with their arms and baggage into the French camp in the village of Anacapri, and sent over to Naples as prisoners of war.

Three companies of Corsican Rangers, of which one was under Captain Church, had already been despatched to reinforce Anacapri, but could achieve nothing in the face of this débâcle and, unable to use the Scala Fenicia, were guided by a peasant down the hazardous mountain-path called Passetiello and reached Capri safely with the loss of only one man.

Despite repeated requests by General Lamarque to surrender and attacks from all sides, including the bombardment of Capri town by a battery which the French in Anacapri had hauled up the mountain-side to the cliff edge at Cetrella, from where they could overlook the town, Colonel Lowe – hoping to be relieved by the Anglo-Sicilian fleet – held out in an increasingly desperate situation, in which many soldiers were killed and much damage caused to the buildings and walls of Capri. On the 16th, having lost hope of either success or relief, he hoisted the white flag, and on the 18th the island, with all its fortifications, magazines and war material, was surrendered to General Lamarque – just as the fleet from Sicily, bringing amongst other supplies Lowe's wine-order, hove into sight. The terms for Lowe and the depleted English and Corsican forces were not severe. After being mustered in the spacious confines of the Certosa, they were conveyed with arms and baggage in their own ships to Sicily, upon their parole not to fight against the Neapolitans or French or the allies of France for a year and a day. Lowe eventually had his revenge over the French by becoming Napoleon's gaoler on St Helena. Many years later Church became a much revered general in the Greek army.

The French left behind a garrison and strengthened the island's fortifications against further attack. Their rule was viewed with mixed feelings in Capri. The islanders had been content with the English, not least because they had been allowed to conduct extensive contraband trade with the mainland. The French stopped this tax-losing traffic and thus deprived Capri of a substantial source of income. On the other hand, many citizens approved French action against the religious foundations of the island. On 12 Novmeber 1808 the Certosa was suppressed, its wealth and property were confiscated, and the monks were dispersed.[39] Before the end of the year the same fate overtook the two convents of Santa Teresa in Anacapri and Capri. The established church, however, was not molested.

The defeat of the British in Capri was listed among the Napoleonic victories on the Arc de Triomphe and in 1811 a medallion, engraved by Louis Jaley, was struck to commemorate the victory in Capri, showing on the obverse Murat in one of his splendid uniforms and on the reverse the French fleet off Capri. The medal was not a moment too soon. The catastrophic campaign of 1812 in Russia was the prelude to a long series of French military disasters. In Italy Murat was defeated by the Austrians and in May 1815 fled from Naples to France, where the Emperor refused to meet or employ him. After his defeat at Waterloo on 15 June Napoleon abdicated and a month later surrendered to the British. But Murat did not abandon the struggle. Sailing from Corsica with a small band of supporters, in order to rouse the Italians against the Bourbon King, he landed in Calabria, but was soon rounded up. He was court-martialled, found guilty of inciting to civil war and of appearing in arms against the legitimate King, and shot on 13 October. So ended the period known in Italian history as the *decennio francese*, the ten years of French rule in the Kingdom of Naples.

*

In 1815 Ferdinand IV re-established his court in Naples and in December 1816 proclaimed himself Ferdinand I of the Two Sicilies (Naples and Sicily). In Capri the old order, joint rule by civil and military governors, returned. The Certosa was turned into a prison, and the Convent of Santa Teresa into a hospital for invalid soldiers. The various schools which had flourished under the liberal Bishop Gamboni were closed. The Bishopric of Capri was abolished, the Church of Santo Stefano lost the dignity of a cathedral, and the island was absorbed into the archdiocese of Sorrento, to which the episcopal records of Capri were transferred. Before the transfer many papers were destroyed as being of no value, and others were lost on the journey. The suppression of the Certosa and the sale at auction of its confiscated lands and property had mixed effects in Capri. Although some of the monks' possessions passed into the hands of Capresi, much was bought by persons who did not live in the island and did not give personal attention to estate-management, as the monks had always done. King Ferdinand, who was a friend of the Bishop of Ischia and wanted to do him a favour, gave instructions that part of the income derived from the Certosa's former possessions should be paid annually to the Bishop, and this galling payment is still made.

The Bourbons discouraged commerce, and their institution of a passport requirement for all visitors to what was now half-way to becoming a penal settlement inhibited travel to and from the island. In any case there was not a single inn in Capri. The island was at a very low ebb indeed.

In this gloomy year of 1818, however, a ray of hope emerged. Giuseppe Pagano, a local notary (*notaio*), opened in the middle of Capri town a *casa ospitale*, surrounded by a garden in which the most notable object was an imposing date-palm, perhaps a relic of the North African pirates. The Pagano family, which had originated in Calabria, had moved to Nocera around 1350 and one branch made its way to Capri; we have already encountered Michele, notary in the latter half of the eighteenth century, who concocted a bogus will for Anna Canale. At first, visitors to the house were guests (*ospiti*) of the Pagano family and lived with them free. In 1825

Giuseppe started a visitors' book, and in the next year transformed the house into an inn (*locanda*) and charged for board and lodging.

Amongst his visitors of August 1826 were two Germans, August Kopisch, a painter and poet, and his friend Ernst Fries, also a painter. They were intrigued by Pagano's account of a cave which could be reached only from the sea and was said to be haunted by evil spirits. Many years earlier two priests had swum into it, but had retreated hastily, scared by the strange colour of the water and the presence of what seemed to be an altar and statues. The cave was known to fishermen and one in particular, Angelo Ferraro, who had entered it in 1822. The visitors decided to explore it and accompanied by Pagano, his young son, and suitable equipment, including two large tubs and a cauldron of pitch to light the interior of the cave, they packed into a small boat, which was towed to the scene by Ferraro in a larger craft. They swam in through the low, narrow entrance, and Ferraro followed with the lighted pitch in one of the tubs. The swimmers were astonished by the vibrating silvery-blue water and the reflections from the white sandy bottom of the cave to its roof and sides. They returned to the hotel, and Kopisch wrote enthusiastically of it in the visitors' book of the hotel.

And so the Blue Grotto was discovered, or rather rediscovered. That it was known to the Romans is clear from their masonry work at the back of the cave, and from the recent uncovering on its bottom of four Roman marble statues, which are at present housed in the Certosa. It was no doubt remains of this sort that had terrified the aquatic priests. Immediately above the cave are the ruins of a small Roman villa (Villa di Gradola) and on old maps the cave is marked 'Grotta Gradola'.

A host of romantic writers, poets and painters, mostly German, visited Capri, stayed at Pagano's and contributed to the saga of the Blue Grotto.[40] All this was very good for the island. Edward Lear, however, who paid a brief call in 1838, later advised a friend to stay at Pagano's and 'see Tiberius's villa – and blue grotto, if you please, but I think it a bore.'[41]

Capri was also being discovered by artists. Corot included it in his Italian tour of spring 1828 and painted an attractive view of the town and Monte Solaro seen from the olive-groves of Tragara.[42] More important for our knowledge of Capri's vanished topography are the works of Neapolitan artists – notably Giacinto Gigante, who between 1823 and 1843 did a series of careful and pleasing topographical drawings.[43] Capri had a remarkable effect on Ivan Constantinovich Aivasovsky, a talented painter of seascapes, from the Crimea. Arriving in 1840, at the age of twenty-three, he was astonished by the effects of the southern sun sparkling over land and sea. Faced with an intensity of light he had never seen before, he abandoned his studio and took to painting in the open air. His exhibition of these paintings in St Petersburg got a frosty reception.

The critics said that Capri had spoilt him, so that, abandoning naturalism, he had employed imaginary colours of impossible brilliance. Poor Aivasovsky destroyed the Capri canvases and, to restore his reputation, repainted the scenes from memory with an acceptable Russian palette.

In May 1832 William Ewart Gladstone, then aged twenty-three, and two young companions, Count Orlovsky, a Russian Pole, and Arthur, fourteenth child of Sir Thomas Pakenham, made a quick tour of the island, but bad weather denied them entry to the Blue Grotto:

Thursday May 10 1832
Sailed for Capri [from Sorrento] about six – we all had a tedious and I a sick passage, of near four hours. Mounted to the town and lodged ourselves at Giuseppe Pagano's.
Friday May 11
After breakfast a donkey cruise to the villa of Tiberius – pharos – mosaics – and a smirking friar, who begged of us and was refused. In this small isle are forty priests. Want of timber. Coasts magnificently precipitous. Salto of Tiberius awful. Found the boatman most rascally – the innkeeper civil and respectable. After dinner set out for Ischia. I was very sick or should have enjoyed it much. Orlowsky and Pakenham also sick. There being some sea, we were unable to enter the newly discovered cavern. Wind got round – after some tossing and several hours sailing, it was found impossible to get to 'Isch', as the boatmen call it (all the inhabitants here abscide the termination and mangle moreover; for Capri they say Crapi); and we sailed with a fair wind for Naples.[44]

In 1837 Francesco Alvino, a Neapolitan engineer, who spent two days on the island, described the inhabitants as 'sober, hard working and quick in their movements, but extremely avaricious. Whenever a stranger is seen, rich and poor, large and small surround him and clamorously beg for money. The women wear gaily coloured gowns, with red or green silk aprons, and bodices adorned with gold braid; the arms of their chemises are tied up with red ribbons. They dress their hair with ribbons, dividing it into two tresses, which are plaited, then rolled up behind the head, and supported by large silver or gilt silver pins. The men wear long trousers, red Neapolitan fishing caps, and go barefoot. The people of Anacapri do not come in contact with the convicts, who remain at Capri, and therefore the manners of the Anacapriotes are more simple and natural; the women are more affable and pleasing, and there are some, who have perfect Greek faces. Not only do they dance the Tarantella, but also another dance which they call Trescone or Tarascone. It is a Greek dance and is danced by four or eight couples, who turn round and round, then all form into a grand circle, snapping their fingers and clapping their hands.'[45] Mary Shelley, second wife of the poet, who was there in 1841, commented on the widespread poverty and prevalence of begging.[46] At this time the population of 3,237 – 1,833 in Capri and 1,404 in Anacapri – was some 260 fewer than in 1792.

In 1842 Henry Wreford was posted abroad by *The Times* on account of lung disease. After trying the Riviera, he moved to Italy and there established himself as the paper's special correspondent. One day in Naples he took a trip to Capri, fell in love with it, decided to make it his home and kept house there until his death fifty years later. Wreford was a scholarly and cultured man, energetic, courageous and firmly devoted to the English love of liberty. It did not take him long to become a bitter opponent of Bourbon misrule and injustice, and to identify himself with the revolutionary movement. On account of his critical despatches to *The Times* he became a marked man in Naples and was also much disliked by the Vatican. Although much of Wreford's work kept him on the mainland, he was able to relax in his Capri home in the Villa Croce, at the north-east corner of Capri town. He would not have found much local wine and fruit there, for in 1839 a fierce attack of phylloxera plant-lice had made great havoc amongst the vines and fruit-trees. San Costanzo's intervention was sought and must have been temporarily successful, because he was presented with a silver bunch of grapes and a lemon, which thereafter hung from his wrist. But the disease struck again in 1846–7 and by 1850 not a single barrel of wine was produced on the island. This total failure of the vintage reduced many of the inhabitants to a condition below their usual state of poverty, and Ferdinand Gregorovius, the young German historian who stayed in Capri for a month in the summer of 1853, records that, to avoid becoming penniless, peasant women 'sold all their neck-laces, earrings and rings, and this is a sign of the direst disasters, for only extreme desperation can separate a woman from her ornaments.'

In his book, *The Island of Capri – a Mediterranean Idyll*, Gregorovius provides a wide-ranging, if somewhat flowery, survey of the island at this period. He came ashore dry-shod at Marina Grande by way of a wooden bench pushed into the sea by a fisher-girl. On the beach he found relics of 1806–8 – deserted trenches and rusty cannons overgrown with genista. Having climbed the steep path to Capri town, he established himself at Pagano's, just as a religious procession of men in white cowls, crowned with twisted blackberry-branches, and women in long white veils, peni-tents on account of the phylloxera plague, followed a crucifix on its way past the hotel.

Most of the farm-houses belonged to Neapolitans, the tenants relying on profits from wine, oil, fruit, cheese-making and cattle-breeding to pay their rent; in autumn and spring also the catching of quails usually

Capri Fisherman, c. 1850, by
T. Valério. *Photo: Allhem*

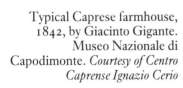

Typical Caprese farmhouse,
1842, by Giacinto Gigante.
Museo Nazionale di
Capodimonte. *Courtesy of Centro
Caprense Ignazio Cerio*

provided some profit. The average farm-house was on two floors. The ground floor was used as a stable for one or more cows (who were often kept in total darkness and whose droppings were the only fertiliser available) for chickens and even for pigs, while the upper floor was the living-quarters and was reached by an exterior staircase; the roof was vaulted in the traditional *caprese* manner. The main industry was fishing, which continued the whole year round, and as a rule only the fishermen owned any property – namely their boats. Every year also about two hundred young men, mostly from Anacapri, worked for the coral-merchants of Torre del Greco, leaving for the Straits of Bonifacio and the North African coast in March, and hoping to return in October with enough money to marry their sweethearts. At home, meanwhile, the women and girls wove silk and cotton for the Neapolitan merchants, who gave them 'scant pay for their unceasing labour'. Gregorovius was astonished by the ability of the women and even young girls to carry heavy loads on their heads and watched as lumps of tufa brought over from Naples were borne in this way from the marina up the steep path, for the repair of buildings in the town. Begging by children was universal – 'being so poor it appears to them natural that those who are richer should assist them'. The Certosa, no longer a jail, housed retired soldiers who had suffered in the Napoleonic Wars and the Sicilian revolution of 1848–9. They came from every part of the Kingdom of Naples, and many were blind. Since there were no carts or carriages in the island, they could safely wander the streets without guides, groping their way with sticks – a favourite walk being along the level path of Tragara. At Marina Piccola there was 'a tiny beach on the southern side' and 'two fishermen's dwellings . . . built like hermits' cells into the rocks, which afford a scanty shelter for a couple of barques'. There was a semaphore station, which was mainly used to give Naples 'early warning' of ships approaching from the south. The key position was on Monte Tuoro (still called 'Semaforo' or 'Telegrafo'), where an official manned two telescopes – one trained on the top of Monte Solaro, from where an approaching ship would be first seen, and the other on Massa Lubrense, which was Capri's link with the mainland. Massa communicated with the Royal Palace in Naples by intermediate stations at Castellammare and Castel St Elmo. This solitary official, accompanied only by his dog, sat day after day on Tuoro passing traffic to and from Naples. He lived not near his work, but in Anacapri, journeying out in the early morning and back in the evening by the Scala Fenicia.[47]

In 1855, for the first time, Capri was given a place in Murray's *Handbook for Travellers in Southern Italy*, which advised that the island was best visited from Sorrento, where a six-oared boat could be hired for 4 to 6 francs[48] (3 to 5 shillings); the crossing took about two hours. For travellers who intended to spend only a day on Capri a very early start was recommended, as it required 'several hours to examine even superficially the principal objects of interest in the island; a calm day should be chosen to prevent disappointment in seeing the Grotta Azzurra and the Grotta Verde'.[49] A cheaper but longer voyage could be made from Naples by the market- or fish-boats, which left at 1 p.m., took 3 to 4 hours and therefore required the traveller to remain in Capri overnight. For visitors who wished to stay, there was a hotel at the Marina; and three in Capri town – all offering 'clean and tolerably comfortable accommodation'. For visitors prepared to take the time Murray recommended the Villa Iovis, The Metromania (sic) grotto,[50] Roman remains on the top of Monte San Michele, the long row of arches called Le Camerelle,[51] the Castiglione hill with its crowning *castello*, and the Roman remains at Palazzo a Mare near the port. Donkeys and guides were desirable in view of the fatigue caused by continual ascents. To visit Anacapri the traveller could climb the Scala Fenicia or 'if unable to incur the fatigue of doing so on foot . . . be carried in a chair (*portantina*)'. Having reached the top of the steps and being prepared to mount still higher he could climb to the Castle of Barbarossa, the Chapel of Santa Maria a Cetrella and finally the summit of Monte Solaro. There was then a steep descent to Anacapri village, where he could find 'refreshments and decent accommodation for the night . . . at a house kept by a woman called Brigida', and, if he wished, do more sight seeing.

In the 'fifties a Scot and two Englishmen, all of different character and pursuits, made Capri their home and married local girls. George Sidney Clark, born in Scotland in 1819, qualified as a doctor and practised medicine for some years, until the spirit moved him to settle in Capri, where he devoted himself and his wealth to the good of the island, giving free medical service to the poor and helping in other ways. His wife Anna bore him two sons and four daughters. Before his death in 1868 he was made an honorary citizen of Capri.[52]

Of the two Englishmen, Thomas Brinsley Norton, 4th Baron Grantley, born in 1831, had a fall out hunting with the York and Ainsty hounds and received 'a head injury which affected his conduct for the rest of his life'. He went to live in Capri and in 1854 married the daughter of a local lawyer, and sired a son and heir, John, and daughter Carlotta.[53] The other, James Talmage White, born in London in 1837, the son of James White, a Liberal MP, was destined by his father for commerce, but instead decided to become an artist. After studying first in Switzerland, he joined Jean François Millet's circle in Paris. Having espoused the cause of the Italian patriots and become an admirer of Garibaldi, he went south to Capri, bought property there and in Amalfi, established a studio in the island, and married a local girl; their son Alberto Garibaldi was born in Amalfi in 1861.

While Capri was gradually being discovered by foreigners, in Naples
and Sicily the Bourbons were becoming increasingly unpopular and
ineffective, and the revolutionary movement correspondingly stronger.
On 5 May 1860 Garibaldi, with just over a thousand volunteers, left
Genoa in two small paddle-steamers, which they had stolen, and arrived
six days later at Marsala. Although confronted by superior forces he
defiantly proclaimed himself Dictator, ruling on behalf of Vittorio
Emanuele, King of Piedmont, and, quickly winning popular support,
swept away the last relics of Bourbon rule. Francis II and his demoralised
forces retreated first to Messina and then over to the mainland and to
Naples. Similar movements started in southern Italy, and the nationalists
appealed to Garibaldi for help. Vittorio Emanuele forbade him to cross
the Straits of Messina, but he did so and then advanced on Naples.
Deserted by most of his soldiers, Francis abandoned Naples, and next day
Garibaldi entered the capital. Meanwhile, in support of popular movements in Umbria and the Marches, the Italian army invaded the Papal
States and defeated the Papal army at Castelfidardo. The King's forces
pushed on into Neapolitan territory and took over the authority which
Garibaldi had assumed. Garibaldi was warmly thanked by the King for
what he had done, but he refused all rewards and retired to his home in
Sardinia.

In the plebiscite of 21 October 1860 Capri joined Naples in voting
overwhelmingly (1,303,064 to 10,312) for annexation to the new Kingdom of Italy. The Capresi 'gave themselves up to such riotous demon-
strations (*baccani e dimostrazioni*) that one would have thought they had
taken leave of their senses'.[54] The town-councillors, however, some of
whom had Bourbon sympathies, took a cooler look at the situation, and
instead of removing the shield with the Bourbon coat of arms, which stood
above the town-gate, ordered that it should be plastered over to hide the
fleur de lys, but in such a manner that, if Bourbon rule was ever restored,
the plaster could quickly be removed.[55] Before this exciting year came to
an end, disaster nearly overtook the effigy of San Costanzo. The new
Government gave orders for the weighing of the Saint, with a view, it was
suspected, of his being boiled down and turned into five-franc pieces.
The islanders were panic-stricken. Calamity was only averted by the
'munificent action of one of the Canons, who handed over to the
authorities a sum in hard cash equivalent to the value of the precious
metal'.[56]

CHAPTER TWO

The First Foreign Residents

Soon after self-government, a town-council (*consiglio*) was established in Capri, under a mayor (*sindaco*), who, although unpaid, held a position which, as well as being prestigious, was a useful power-base and could be lucrative. Capri's days of military involvement being at last ended, its forts were abandoned, and military stores transported to the mainland. In other respects the events of 1860 made very little difference to the inhabitants, who remained backward, very poor and much dependent on foreign residents for initiating and guiding such advances as were made. We are indebted to Wreford, the *Times* correspondent, who in 1861 was appointed honorary inspector of schools, for a wide range of information not only about education but also other aspects of the island in the early years of Italian independence.[1] Valuable also are the researches of John Cly Mackowen,[2] an American who lived in Capri from 1876 to 1900; and essays by John Richard Green,[3] the English historian who visited Capri in the early 'seventies.

Plaster was removed from the Bourbon shield, now only an historical curiosity, which was still over the town gate in Mackowen's day, 'to prove that the spirit of Machiavelli hovers over Capri and inspires its inhabitants'.[4] Wreford found Capri 'governed by a ruling clique who in municipal elections tell people how to vote, while nothing is done for the people'. In municipal affairs *lucro* was the 'sole motive power'. The roads and footpaths were in a terrible state of dilapidation. The streets were full of filth, 'the most disgusting refuse of the houses being suffered to run off or thrown on the public paths'. There was a great shortage of water, and the poor had sometimes to 'toil a mile for the precious liquid, which is doled out in quantities just sufficient to keep body and soul together, but not a drop to spare for bodily cleanliness . . . yet an abundant supply might be provided with one tenth part of the money expended on *festas* and other mysterious matters'.[5]

The new Government of Italy under the House of Savoy had achieved unification of most of the peninsula, but it had also inherited the debts of the old States. To resolve these debts, they confiscated Church properties and sold them at auction, where the Church appointed members of the laity to bid for them, making it clear that the Church stooges were not to be run up by private bidders. Property thus obtained very cheaply was later resold at its market value, and the Church pocketed the difference.[6]

In the Capri sales, however, not everyone was prepared to accommodate the Church. In particular, the Ferraro family, headed by Don Giacinto, bid for and obtained for themselves several Church properties. Giacinto's father, who had been a butcher, had done well and used the profits of his business for the dexterous granting of life-annuities (*vitalizi*) against the eventual acquisition of the grantees' property. He specialized in old people without sons and thus obtained, to the detriment of the nephews, a variety of properties.[7] A small group led by Costanzo Serena, a tax-collector (*esattore*), and including Giacinto Ferraro, assembled enough money to bid for the Convent of Santa Teresa, which was the second largest building in Capri after the Certosa. The money was entrusted to Ferraro, who was sent to Naples to bid on behalf of the group. When he returned to Capri he was at first evasive about the results of the sale, but, when pressed, admitted that he had used the money to buy the convent in his name only. Later he repaid the money, but the convent remained his property.[8] The convent of Santa Teresa in Anacapri was sold to a Society of Evangelists, who must have had an uphill task amongst a people which had 'an eye for colour and the beautiful, who rejoiced in processions, flowers, wax-candles, altars, pictures and incense'.[9]

Fishing still provided the wherewithal for many of the islanders, but it was a hand-to-mouth existence. Wreford described the routine of the sardine-fishers, who in the morning spread out, mended and cleaned their nets on the marina; set forth in the evening in twenty to thirty boats, with sails spread to catch the *maestrale*; spent the night toiling round the coast of Massa or in the strait which separated Capri from the mainland. The excitement of pulling in a good catch was tempered by the thought that profits would have to be divided into seven parts – one each for the captain and his crew of four, and two for the *padrone*. Were it not for this good luck, any of these fishermen might have been visited by the bailiff's man (*piantone*) or been compelled to put off his daughter's marriage for another year. It was a precarious way of life, and there was no economy or prudence amongst the people; a good haul was soon dissipated in paying up arrears, or in extra food and drink; and, as the season came around again, the same tale was told.[10]

The wine-trade had not yet recovered from the ravages of phylloxera, and the islanders derived no benefit from the spurious Capri wine now being fabricated in the vineyards north and east of Naples. Olive- and fruit-trees provided a small income for a lucky few. Apart from fishing, much store was still set on the earnings of young men and boys who every spring joined the coral-fleets at Torre del Greco.[11]

Begging, which earlier visitors had noted as unusually prevalent, continued unabated. Baedeker (1867) observed that, if more than the smallest coin was bestowed on the woman who placed the wooden bench in the sea to facilitate the visitor's landing, it would 'act as an incentive to the keen-eyed beggars who infest the spot. Mendicancy prevails here to a greater extent than in other parts of Italy; nor is it begging pure and simple; dancing and singing are attendant tortures, whilst the cry resounds: "*un bajocc, Signoria! Eccellenza! un bajocc!*" '[12]

There were four municipal schools – one for boys and one for girls in Capri town; and the same in Anacapri. The boys' schools were run by priests and, in Wreford's opinion, well-conducted, especially that in Capri. He was less impressed by the girls' schools. There was an infant-school (*asilo infantile*), 'established by an English gentleman who passes his summer in the island' (perhaps Wreford himself), and maintained by him and some friends. This Englishman also set up 'an evening-school, which existed for some time and bore good fruit', but by 1868 had 'been closed from want of funds to pay an efficient master'. Wreford considered this a sad loss, because it would have benefitted the coral-fishers and other young men with time on their hands during the winter. 'But there is no one amongst the natives', he complained, 'to give the impulse, and the governing body display the greatest indifference to such subjects . . . the teachers complain that they are not supported, for, with the exception of the foreigners, no one goes near them to give a word of encouragement. . . .'

As for medical care, Wreford prayed 'most devoutly' that he would never be ill in Capri. There was a municipal *medico*, who, according to public accounts, was paid 36 ducats (about £6 sterling) a month, but in fact received only 24 ducats. What became of the balance? he asked. 'It is to such a miserable practitioner as can be provided from this sum that are confided the lives of many hundreds of persons; lives too of much greater value to their families than those of the wealthy'. Wreford summed up: 'Mind and body are alike neglected by what is called the governing body of lower Capri.'[13]

For burial, Anacapri had its *camposanto* outside the village, but in Capri the situation was far from satisfactory. Up to about 1600 you would have been dumped in a common burial-ground (*fossa carnaia*) in the middle of what is now the Piazza. In the seventeenth century the *fossa carnaia* was moved to a vault or cavity under the Church of Santo Stefano. Into this hole bodies were shot head-first and uncoffined, until in the early 1870s it was discovered that the floor of the church was unsafe and that the living were in danger of joining the putrefying remains of the dead; the vault was then closed. Corpses were also stuffed into old drains under the Camerelle. A scathing commentary on these insanitary arrangements was included in an official report of 1876–7 by the Naples health authority.[14]

Writing in 1868 Wreford said that nominally a new cemetery had just been established, but he had not been able to trace it. He had been told that a *custode* 'had been appointed with a small salary to watch over what cannot be said to exist'.[15]

What of foreign visitors? Travel to Italy had been improved by the spread of railways, which by 1866 linked Rome and Naples with north Italy and the Middle European network. Journeys could be planned and made in comparative comfort, without hired coaches, bad hotels and possible attacks by bandits. Shortly after 1860 Naples started a spasmodic steamboat service 'on Sundays and holidays in summer, sometimes on other days', which did a round trip to Sorrento, Capri and back. Baedeker, however, did not recommend it, as the boat would not start until enough passengers had been secured, and the whole journey was extremely hurried.

The spectacular beauty and admirable climate of Capri attracted many northern artists in these years. Of these one of the most faithful was the Alsatian, Jean Benner, who arrived in 1866 at the age of thirty and, apart from portraits, painted little else but Capri scenes until his death in Paris in 1909. He became a permanent fixture at Pagano's, married Margherita, daughter of Michele Pagano, who had succeeded his father Giuseppe as proprietor, and produced an artistic son, Emmanuel. Michele encouraged foreign artists to decorate the hotel. Benner did murals, and another Frenchman, Tristan Corbière, painted and enlivened the visitors' book with caricatures of himself and other inmates.[16]

Edward Binyon, sea and landscape painter, member of the Society of Friends and cousin of the poet Laurence Binyon, came to Capri in 1867 after a spell in Algeria and Morocco. One day he saw a pretty little girl and asked if he could paint her. Emilia Settanni, very properly, referred the painter to her father, Michele. At the Settannis' house Binyon met Emilia's elder sister Maria and fell in love with her. Since Maria was barely eighteen and Edward was a Quaker, Michele refused to let them marry, so they ran away together to Naples, where the British Consul helped to arrange their marriage in 1869. They had three children – Algernon, Bianca, and Bertram. After their marriage Edward gave Maria a dress allowance, which she saved up and, when she had enough money, bought some land on Via Pastena, which she presented to Edward – and he bequeathed it to his three children. Edward's life came to a sudden and untimely end in 1876, when in his fiftieth year he died from the effects of bathing while overheated.

In Algeria, many years earlier, Edward had made friends with another artist, Principe Giovanni Giudice Caracciolo di Leporano, a member of the numerous Neapolitan clan. Caracciolo too came to Capri and fell for the beautiful and now nubile Emilia, whom he married, and between 1879

Hotel Pagano at the end of the 19th century

Hotel Quisisana, c. 1900

and 1901 sired a steady succession of children, of whom ten survived. He took as his Capri home the Villa Monte San Michele, which included ownership of the whole of the mountain of that name north-east of Capri town.[17]

Around 1860 the benevolent Dr Clark had built the Quisisana ('Here one gets better') as a sanatorium (*casa di cura*) 'in the most sheltered and sunny position he could find on the island, suitable for invalids, especially those suffering from rheumatism and chest infections'. The establishment, which had extensive grounds, lay in what was still open country, just outside the south-east corner of the town, protected from the north-east winds by Monte San Michele and by the saddle of land which lay between San Michele and Castiglione; it commanded fine views to the south. Before his death Clark transformed the Quisisana into a hotel with a *pension* of about 7 to 8 *lire* a day, and after his death in 1868 it was managed by his widow Anna and younger son, Alfredo. Among the staff there was an ambitious young waiter, Federico Serena, who gave Anna to understand that, in exchange for a thirty-year lease of the hotel, he would marry her. As she and Alfredo were not doing particularly well, she accepted his proposition. As soon as the formalities of the lease had been concluded, Serena got rid of the Clarks and instead married the maid of a foreign lady staying in the hotel. Later the Clarks sold the hotel outright to Serena in exchange for an annuity and a villa near the hotel.[18] Under Serena's management the Quisisana became the best hotel in the island and the favourite resort of English visitors. Facilities included 'excellent filtered water for table use'; milk and eggs from the hotel's own cows and poultry-yard; good drainage; and 'Moule's earth-closets carefully tended and kept in perfect condition'. The *pension* was 8 francs a day, with extra for wine, fires and candles; and 25 centimes for meals served in bedrooms.[19]

Another doctor, a young Italian named Ignazio Cerio, was also beginning to make his mark on Capri. Born in 1840 at Giulia Nova di Abruzzo, he studied medicine and, after graduating in 1860, joined Garibaldi in Sicily. Later in that year he took a commission in the new Italian Army and saw varied service on the mainland. In 1868 he was posted to Capri as medical officer of the Fifth Provost Company, a disciplinary unit which since 1860 had occupied the Certosa. The inmates, who were from the mainland, were a mixture of offenders against military discipline and individuals with revolutionary or anarchistic ideas. They enjoyed a few hours of liberty each day, when they could visit the Piazza. As it was customary to march them in and out six-abreast, the gate of the Certosa was widened to admit a column of this breadth. Dr Cerio lived in what became known as the Palazzo Cerio, the old Palazzo Arcucci, which overlooked the Piazza. He married Elizabeth Grimmer, an Englishwoman from East Anglia, who bore him six children, of whom three – Arturo (1860), Giorgio (1865) and the youngest, Edwin (1875), later played significant parts on the Capri stage. Soon after the birth of her children Elizabeth went mad.

In 1870 Dr Cerio became official doctor of the Capri municipality, a post which he held for fifty years. For some time, holding the honorary rank of Captain, he continued as medical officer of the Certosa, and Edwin recalls how every morning his father would don military uniform to take sick-parade, and return at eleven to change into civilian clothes for the morning surgery.[20] Ignazio had many interests besides medicine – geology, sea-shells, botany, zoology and antiquarian matters – in all of which he was an enthusiastic and successful investigator. He cared little for money, and, when he treated the peasants, did not charge them if they were poor, but, if they had, say, a geological specimen in which he was interested, would take that instead. In religious matters he was a freethinker with a tendency towards Protestantism. Throughout his long life he was much respected as doctor, savant and man.

One of the direct results of the end of the American Civil War in 1865 was to precipitate John Cly Mackowen, member of a rich slave-owning family in Louisiana, into Europe and finally Capri. After the war, Mackowen, who had enrolled with the Confederate army, was compelled to free all his slaves and, disgusted with the Yankees, went to Europe, settled down in Bavaria to study medicine and qualified as a doctor with a thesis on 'Atrophy of the Kidneys'. On a visit to Capri in 1876 he liked the island and decided to stay there. Having bought an estate in Anacapri at Damecuta and a plot of land at Marina Grande, where he built a house, he took as his partner an Anacapri girl, Mariuccia Cimino, but never married her, and proceeded to enlarge her house into what later became the Casa Rossa in Via Giuseppe Orlandi. He usually wore topee, boots and spurs, and carried a whip which he was ready to use on any peasant who displeased him, but later would send money and food to the man's home – which earned him the nickname '*ciacca e mereca*' (he strikes and heals). He often went further in kindness and treated the poor when they were ill and kept them supplied with medicines. Mackowen was more than slave-owner *manqué*. During his first six years on Capri he collected material for a book about the island, working with the objective precision of a doctor, and in 1883 published *Capri* – the first critical and modern account of the island, its geology, topography and climate, history, habits and customs, antiquities, churches and grottos. His book was from the first and still is a prime source of information about the island.

In 1858, at the age of eighteen, another American, Charles Coleman, arrived in Italy from Buffalo, New York, to study painting. Attracted by Garibaldi he nearly joined the patriotic movement, but instead went back to America to fight for the Union. He returned to Rome in 1866, and in 1870, after an unsuccessful marriage, came to Capri, where he bought what had once been the guest-house of Madre Serafina's convent, notable for a magnificent oleander which was growing in the cloister. Here he made some 'baroque' alterations which he imagined to be in keeping with the second half of the seventeenth century, and started to fill 'The House of the Oleander' with classical antiquities and medieval bric-à-brac. Vesuvius was visible from the north window of his studio and he was always ready to depict the changing moods of the volcano, and the effects it created on the clouds above and the sea below. While Vesuvius was his stock-in-trade, he also painted imaginary scenes of Capri under the Roman Emperors; studies of handsome islanders, particularly women; religious canvases to decorate altars; and graceful views of Capri gardens.

The most notable event of the 'seventies was the building of a carriage-road linking Capri and Anacapri by way of the precipitous cliff which for so long had isolated the two communities. The road was conceived by Giuseppe Orlandi, a politician, whose family, although mainly resident in Naples, had a house in Anacapri, and was built by Emilio Mayer, civil engineer of the *prefettura* in Naples. The Scala Fenicia, however, continued to be used by the strapping women who for centuries past had carried their burdens up and down it. Two years after the opening of this vital road, and probably on account of the increased flow of goods between highland and lowland zones which the road engendered, Capri was made a *comune chiuso* and became liable to taxes from which it had previously been immune. Anacapri, however, remained exempt. Consumption in Capri of every commodity except bread, macaroni and vegetables, was taxed. Wine carried a tax to the grower of 2.30 lire a barrel. Salt was so jealously guarded by the authorities that the bringing up of a bottle of sea-water for cooking or any other purpose could land the offender in jail. Anyone who wished to slaughter a pig had to make a formal declaration to the authorities, who, if at all suspicious of the owner, would superintend the weighing of the carcass. While passage of produce from Capri to Anacapri was free, that coming in the reverse direction was subject to toll at the commune-boundary. Smuggling was dangerous, and it was not unknown for the coachman, certain of payment for his treachery as he passed the toll-house (*uffizio daziario*), to indicate to the official with a particular jerk of his whip that contraband was on board.[21] All this did nothing to dissolve the perennial hostility between the two communes, which Orlandi had hoped would follow the new road.

In 1873 cholera broke out in Naples and spread to Capri. It continued into 1874, with many deaths, and a special cemetery for Capresi smitten

Women on the Scala Fenicia, c. 1874

Antonio Scoppa, 1891, by C. W. Allers

Francesco Spadaro

by the plague was opened on the hillside in the Torina zone, while the Anacapri victims were buried in the mountain valley of Cetrella.

Whether or not a cemetery for ordinary burials existed in the late 'sixties and early 'seventies – Wreford was doubtful, but another source speaks of a graveyard on the top of the Castiglione – it is certain that the present Catholic cemetery was inaugurated on 23 March 1875 on the hillside between Aiano and Corigliano. Among the earliest burials was that of Lord Grantley, in spite of the fact that he was a Protestant and, therefore, a heretic. A huge and powerful man, with an immense beard, he had become more and more violent and unbalanced. His wife Maria, in spite of being fat and lazy and unable to cope with the English language, was the only person capable of managing him. In a fit of temper he killed his 'valet' (euphemism for male nurse) and was only saved from prison by the influence of his friend Garibaldi. His erratic life came to an end in 1877.[22]

The Church in Capri, which had now at last got a proper burial-ground for the faithful departed, showed no concern whatsoever about the general fate of non-Catholic corpses. Edwin Cerio, in a biography of his father, says that they were treated as *bestie* and just abandoned in the Piazza and buried like carrion (*carogne*) in the open country.[23] In view of the debt which nineteenth-century Capresi owed to non-Catholic foreigners, this was ungenerous of the Church.

By the 'seventies there was a sizeable foreign colony of non-Catholics, and in 1876, if not earlier, at the request of the Bishop of Gibraltar, the Society for the Propagation of the Gospel in Foreign Parts (SPG) established a chaplaincy in Capri during the season (December to May) for British residents and visitors who wanted to attend services on Sundays. During the winter of 1879–80 a harmonium was bought and services were held in a room provided by Dr Cerio. Shortly before 1878 a group of foreigners presided over by George Hayward, an Englishman from near Bury St Edmunds, and actively encouraged by Ignazio Cerio, decided to found a non-Catholic cemetery (*cimitero acattolico*) for 'all non-Catholics, irrespective of race or religion'. They bought about 1,000 square metres of land adjoining the new Catholic cemetery and 'laid it out into an attractive resting-place for all non-Catholic residents of Capri who wished to be buried there'. In spite of hostile public opinion and bitter opposition by the Catholic Church, the cemetery was authorised by the Prefect of Naples and opened in 1878. The decision to allow its establishment may have been helped by the fact that Dr Cerio had now added politics to his many interests and had been elected a member (*consigliere*) of the communal council. The two earliest graves were those of Alfred Stanford (d. 1874); and of Lorenzo Mackens who died in 1875, aged twenty, and whose tomb was *eretto da alcuni amici dolentissimi in segno della loro stima* (erected by some grief-stricken friends as a mark of their respect). Where, one may ask, had these two rested in the intervening years? The next burial was of Hayward himself in April 1878.[24]

In 1881 the population was 4848 – 2,827 in Capri and 2,021 in Anacapri – an increase of just under fifty percent in forty years with a slight preponderance in favour of Capri. There was an established and growing tourist industry, which required hotels, restaurants, *caffè* and shops, while foreign residents needed houses, gardens, cooks and servants. At this stage few islanders had the foresight and energy to exploit this favourable situation for the creation of real wealth. An increasing number, however, profited directly and indirectly, by providing services of various kinds and devising ingenious ways of relieving foreigners of their money. Begging by children was still widespread, to which was now added their facility for guiding tourists to the Blue Grotto, the Villa Iovis, or the top of Monte Solaro.

We are lucky in finding at the beginning of the 'eighties two foreigners, one American and the other English, with a discerning and critical eye, sympathy for this welcoming and attractive people, and a love of the island, who wrote in detail about them. Mackowen we already know; the other, Alan Walters, after living in Ceylon, moved to the Mediterranean and became 'a lotus-eater in Capri'.

Mackowen noted physical differences between Capresi and Anacapresi. The former were a mixture of every strain that had impinged on the island – Greek, Latin, Saracen, Turkish and Spanish in their day; Jewish immigrants at the beginning of the sixteenth century and during the eighteenth. The Anacapresi, isolated until the building of the road in 1874, maintained what Mackowen considered to be Greek characteristics, as well as instances of fair or reddish hair and blue eyes (possibly English/Irish traces from 1806–8), and not without the occasional dark, frizzy hair of the Saracen – 'Ciammurri' to their fellow-islanders.

Mackowen devotes a long passage to the avariciousness of the islanders and their skill in exploiting the foreigner. He evens the score, however, by observing that 'the good qualities of the Capriote far outnumber his bad qualities; he is temperate in all things, is neither impertinent, nor impudent, is industrious, is very much attached to his family, is of a peaceful disposition, and when aroused never uses a knife or revolver like his countrymen across on the mainland, but resorts to the weapons provided by nature.'

Most of the men were absent from the island for much of the year 'at sea, either coral-fishing, or employed in the coasting trade or on long voyages'; others were doing national service with the armed forces. Mackowen, therefore, saw more of the women, on whom fell a large variety of tasks, the most remarkable being the carriage of heavy loads on their heads – 'straightbacked handsome women with their burdens and graceful poses, their dark, laughing, eyes, their clear, brown, healthy complexions and gay chatter among the narrow and rocky paths of Capri . . . ; it is no exaggeration to say that all the houses in Capri have been carried to their present sites on the heads of women.'[25] Their journeys along the country paths were made barefoot. In the Piazza and other level ground they wore clattering wooden clogs (*zoccoli*); in *caprese* slang *zoccola* means 'willing' (of a woman).

Since the creation of the Kingdom of Italy in 1860, there had been an increase in the spread of education and liberal ideas amongst the peasants, particularly the young men, many of whom did service with the army and navy, travelled, and saw places and customs in other parts of Italy. These young men also encountered new ideas; learned to look after themselves; if illiterate, were taught to read and write; and had the opportunity of acquiring the virtues of obedience, patriotism and hygiene. Their experiences put them at a distinct advantage when they returned to their peasant communities, not least in their dealings with the priests, who for so long had enjoyed 'the power placed in their hands by the confiding ignorance of the peasant population'.[26]

The peasants ate frugally, consuming large quantities of bread, to which they added boiled beans with oil and raw onions, or a salad of boiled potatoes and wild herbs; now and then they would take fish. On Sundays and holy-days they ate macaroni. Except at wedding-feasts, meat was usually restricted to the *feste* of Christmas, Epiphany, Easter and San Costanzo, and was accompanied by *pizza* or snails in garlic and oil. In summer, when vegetables were plentiful, many boiled or fried dishes of these were consumed; Mackowen found them 'very good even to the palate of a foreigner.'[27]

In 1875 'La Pigna' restaurant was opened in Strada Nuova (now Via Roma) as a place where the *contadini* could eat fish and drink wine and coffee; later the restaurant raised its standard, so as to appeal to foreigners. On the east side of the Piazza, Antonio Scoppa provided beer, wine, spirits and coffee in his 'Caffè al Vermouth di Torino'. A hundred yards down Via Hohenzollern (now Via Vittorio Emanuele), which ran from the south-east corner of the Piazza to the Quisisana, was the *caffè* 'Zum Kater Hiddigeigei', run by a Sorrentine immigrant named Staiano, who rented the premises from the Ferraro family.[28]

Coleman had given up Rome entirely and now lived permanently in Capri, where he was often visited from the capital by his old friend and fellow-artist, Elihu Vedder. A few doors away, in the Villa Castello, were an English couple, both artists, Sophie and Walter Anderson, who had been in Capri since 1871. The Villa Castello had a large garden and no less than seven doors giving access from the house and garden to the Via

Castello on which it fronted and the narrow alleys which enclosed the other three sides of the property. Sophie, an imposing woman and known locally as the 'cauliflower lady' on account of her mass of white hair, held a leading place in society. She enjoyed entertaining 'the right sort of people' and is remembered for the famous incident of an uninvited guest, an English nobleman, said to have been Lord Grantley,[29] who on the occasion of one of her afternoon parties rang the bell and on being admitted was found to be naked. Striding past the swooning maid, he emerged on the *terrazza*, where the guests were eating their strawberries and cream. After pausing long enough to take a good look at him, the ladies also swooned in their chairs, and the intruder was man-handled into the street by Mr Anderson and the male guests. To prevent any repetition of such an unseemly incident, four holes were bored in the front door, so that any future visitor could be scrutinized as to his apparel before being admitted. Mrs Anderson had exhibited regularly at the Royal Academy since 1855. Amongst her pupils was Ignazio Cerio, whose son Edwin observed that in her depiction of the nude Sophie Anderson had the remarkable gift of depriving it of all sensuality and 'in making classical art presentable even in the most proper of Victorian drawing-rooms'.[30]

Jean Benner and his artist son, Emmanuel, were still painting at Pagano's, and there was a French painter named Daras and his wife at the Villa Discopoli on Via Tragara. A photograph of *c.* 1877–8 shows the Cerios, Benners, Andersons, Daras and others relaxing at a game of *bocce* – an Italian version of bowls – on the *terrazza* of Pagano's.

John Singer Sargent, after studying in Paris and falling under the influence of the Impressionists, spent the summer of 1878 in Capri, where he met and depicted the model Rosina 'an Anacapri girl, a magnificent type, about seventeen years of age, her complexion a rich nut-brown, with a mass of blue-black hair, very beautiful and of an Arab type'.[31] Augustus Hare, competent artist, as well as inveterate traveller, visiting Capri a year or two later, found the inhabitants 'quite unlike the Neapolitans, pleasant, civil in their manners and full of courtesies to strangers. The women are frequently beautiful, and good models may be obtained here by artists more cheaply than anywhere else. One franc a day is the usual price of a model, and yet the artist may feel he is doing no injustice, as 60 centimes a day would be the wages of a day's hard work in the fields.'[32]

In far-away Bavaria, after a conventional secondary education, August Weber, member of a well-to-do Munich family, enrolled at the Polytechnic of that city, with the idea of studying architecture, but soon moved to the Academy of Arts and took up painting. One day he noticed in an art shop several photographs of Italy, and one which particularly impressed him, of a beach with some houses and mountains in the background. There was no name on the picture, and he was too shy to go in and ask what it represented. Having graduated, his father already dead and his sisters married, he set up a studio at home with his mother and younger brother. Although he sold a few paintings, he found little enthusiasm for his classical figures amongst a people used to Bavarian or Tyrolean styles. In the winter of 1879, despondent at his failure, he set off for Italy with a small allowance from his mother, going first to Rome and in the summer of 1880 to Naples, where he camped in a straw hut in the vineyards of Posillipo. One day he decided to explore other parts of the Bay and bought a rowing-boat. Having rowed hither and thither for some days, he headed for Capri and landed at the Bagni di Tiberio. With his long beard and looking very dishevelled, he was arrested on suspicion of being an escaped convict and taken to Marina Grande. Watching all this from his house on the Marina was Mackowen, who intervened and, judging that Weber was not a criminal, persuaded the guards to release him, and invited him to lunch. It now dawned on Weber that Capri was the subject of the photograph in Munich which had attracted him and he knew he had reached journey's end. After enjoying Mackowen's hospitality, he put out again in his boat and started rowing westwards round the island. After visiting the Grotta Azzurra and the Grotta Verde, he came to the tiny beach of Marina Piccola, where he found two houses – one intact but uninhabited, and the Spadaro family living in the ruins of the other. The Spadaro family, Corsican in origin, had come to Capri for the coral-fishing and settled there. Later one of the sons, Francesco, with his bushy white beard and long clay pipe, was to feature on countless postcards and in cheap oil-paintings as the archetypal boatman/fisherman of Capri.

Weber became a paying guest of the family, but, when in October 1880 they asked him to go up with them to Capri, he declined and instead found a small grotto at the foot of the Castiglione, which, with the help of a bricklayer, he turned into a little house. In 1882, for 5 lire a month, he rented a room in the *fortino* – relic of the British/French occupation – which had just been bought by John Shortridge, a British merchant-seaman and his Sorrentine wife, Carmela Esposito. Weber was determined to put down his roots at the Marina and for 600 lire bought a piece of land on which he built a rudimentary studio and resumed his painting. Later he hired a master-mason, Ciro Spadaro, another son of his first landlord, to build three rooms as the start of a real house. Sometime in the early 'eighties he met Raffaella Desiderio, daughter of the family which owned the other house on the Marina. Raffaella's father Michele was a direct descendant of Marziale, who near the end of the seventeenth century had moved from Amalfi to Capri to build the cathedral. Michele was the only 'Marzianiello' who had not followed the traditional family occupation of building. Instead, until the early 'eighties, when the new steamboats between Naples and Capri deprived him of his job, he had carried the official mail to and from the mainland, and three days a week, with two sons and some hired labour, had plied between Marina Grande and Sorrento, ferrying not only the mail but passengers and merchandise. He also had a butcher's shop at the Piazza end of the Via Hohenzollern.[33] Having lost his contract to carry mail, he retired to his house at Marina Piccola and became a fisherman.

Raffaella and Augusto fell in love, but there were formidable obstacles to their plans of marriage ('*Il mio desiderio era di sposare Raffaella Desiderio*,' said Weber). At that time it was considered almost a duty for any self-respecting family to have a son in the priesthood and, if there was also a daughter, she would be expected to remain unmarried, in order to be able to keep house for her brother. Michele placed his youngest boy, Vincenzo, in a seminary at Sorrento and decreed that Raffaella, his only daughter, should not marry, so that she could take care of her brother after his ordination. The fact that Weber was a foreigner and a Protestant, and that Michele disliked all foreigners, made the prospects even bleaker. During the long years of waiting Weber went back to Munich four times, travelling both ways entirely on foot, sleeping under hedges and haystacks, and buying bread, cheese, fruit and milk from the peasants. He converted to Catholicism, but for their marriage they had to wait for Vincenzo's ordination in 1893, because no other priest in Capri dared to defy Michele's wrath. Eventually they were married by Vincenzo at ten o'clock on a September evening in a small chapel in Capri, while the bride's parents were asleep at the Marina. Giuseppe and Lucia Morgano, who had bought from Schiano the lease of 'Zum Kater Hiddigeigei', were witnesses at the wedding. Michele was furious and refused to speak to his daughter, until he was softened by the birth of her first child, Giorgio, in the following July.[34]

Around 1880 a mysterious Frenchman arrived, bought a *casetta* on the east side of Via Tragara, enlarged it and called it 'La Certosella' (The Little Charterhouse). No one knew who he was or anything of his past. He was a recluse and rather bad-tempered; the islanders called him ''U Francesiello', and the English, 'The Acid Drop'. Usually to be seen in an impeccable French *complet*, which was eccentric enough, one day he attracted attention by appearing in a suit and cape of rough, uncoloured wool from Amalfi, such as fishermen wore. Soon this rustic garb became fashionable amongst foreigners in Capri and for a time there was a profitable new industry of handwoven woollen fabrics. It was not until he died in 1903 that his identity became known. He was Camille Du Locle, who for many years had played an important part in the musical and theatrical life of France. He had been librettist of several operas, including Verdi's *Aïda*, had married a niece of Emile Perrin, Director of the Grand Opéra of Paris, and Du Locle himself had become director of the Opéra Comique. In March 1876, for reasons unknown, he had suddenly abandoned his post, moved first to Rome and then Castellammare, before slinking off to Capri. A single personal recollection of Du Locle is provided by Norman Douglas, who knew him in his last years – 'that witty old reprobate . . . of whom I could tell some unprintable stories'.[35]

At the beginning of 1881 a severe epidemic of typhus had struck the island. Staying there at the time was Axel Munthe, a twenty-four-year-old Swede, who had just qualified as a doctor. After an undistinguished career at school and as a medical student at Uppsala University, ill-health drove him south to Italy and it is possible that he spent a day in Capri in the spring of 1876.[36] He resumed his studies at Montpellier University, specialising in gynaecology, and later moved to the Medical Faculty of Paris, where in August 1880 he qualified with a thesis on *Prophylaxie et traitement des hémorrhagies post-partum*. Nine months later he married Ultima Hornberg, a chemist's daughter, and took her for a long stay on Capri.

There were only three doctors in the island – Dr Ignazio Cerio; Dr Gustavo Rispo; and Dr Henry Thompson Green, an Englishman living in what is now the Villa Rosa in Anacapri, who, although not practising officially, was always ready to give medical aid. Munthe's help, therefore, in the typhus epidemic was welcome. He worked unsparingly amongst the peasants. 'In every cottage, hovel and mountain shepherd's cave he sought out the sick and dying and stopped with them throughout their misery until the scourge passed.' In March 1881 Ischia was struck by an earthquake. With the same restless energy Munthe moved there to do what he could to alleviate suffering. In the autumn he returned to Paris to start his medical career.[37]

As long as the weather was favourable and there were enough passengers, the Società Procida-Ischia ran daily steamboats ('rickety and roll horribly in the slightest swell' according to Augustus Hare) from Naples to Capri; and the Società Manzi, four a week. The trip was via Sorrento and then direct to the Blue Grotto, on to the Marina at midday for a three-hour stay ashore and then back to Naples in the early evening. Hare adds that 'the steamers are always accompanied by a number of singers, guitar players, and *mercanti ambulanti* (of coral, inlaid wood, walking sticks and music), who will usually ask literally six times the sum with which they are satisfied in the end.'[38] In bad weather, however, the boats did not sail at all, and when the wind was in the east or the north the Blue Grotto was inaccessible, a fact which the captain of the steamer was careful not to mention, and 'on such days,' warns Baedeker, 'the roughness of the water is apt to occasion seasickness.' The market-boats still plied, somewhat irregularly, between Naples and Capri, and there were four-oared boats from Sorrento for the travellers who wanted to spend the night in Capri and return on the next day. Baedeker advises against the day-trip, which, 'unless the traveller is much pressed for time, is a most unsatisfactory mode of visiting beautiful Capri as, in addition to the Blue Grotto, he will barely have time to visit the Villa of Tiberius. The view from the latter, moreover, is far less attractive in the middle of the day than by evening light. One whole day at least should be devoted to the island, as there are many other beautiful points beside the two just mentioned. . . .' The advice in the visitors' book at Pagano's hotel should in any case be taken to heart: '*Ne quittex pas la Grotte d'Azur sans voir Capri.*' Visitors making the day-trip from Sorrento 'had better first visit the Blue Grotto, then order dinner at one of the inns on the Marina, ascend to Capri and go direct to the Punta Tragara, for a view of the Faraglioni rocks, or the Villa di Tiberio, if time and energy permit, and finally return to the beach.' A longer stay could include a descent to the Marina Piccola, a boat to the Green Grotto 'or better still the *giro* of the whole island by boat (3–4 hours)'. Anacapri and Monte Solaro could also be visited. As regards transport, a donkey from the Marina to the village of Capri was 1¼ fr. (one shilling) a horse 1½ fr.; in the reverse direction 1 or 1¼ fr.; to the Villa di Tiberio and back 2½ or 3 fr., and a small fee; per day, 5 or 6 fr., and the same for the ascent of Monte Solaro – 'guides are quite unnecessary unless time is very limited. A boy to show the way may be engaged for several hours for ½–1 fr.' Baedeker of 1883 is the first guide-book to make a special point of recommending to 'tolerable walkers' the ascent of Monte Solaro. He describes a 'route easily found' by paved path, bridle path, past the Hermitage of Cetrella ('good wine for which Pater Anselmo, the hermit, expects a trifling fee'), finally after a fatiguing ascent of about twenty minutes more over debris the traveller reaches the summit, from which 'the view is superb, embracing Naples with the whole of its bay, as well as that of Salerno as far as the ruins of Paestum. Towards the north the bay of Gaeta is visible, and towards the west the group of the Ponza Islands. The spectator also obtains a survey of the chain of the Appenines, bounding the Campanian plain in a wide curve, and culminating in Monte Vergine near Avellino. Capri itself and the peninsula of Sorrento lie in prominent relief at the spectator's feet'.[39] Such views would have been hardly possible earlier in the nineteenth century, when Monte Solaro supported an abundance of timber. By the 'eighties, however, it was being progressively deforested by the depredations of the peasants and the nibbling of sheep and goats, to become the 'barren desolation' from which it never recovered.[40]

In January 1883 the 'Società Operaia di Mutuo Soccorso', organised on the lines of a 'friendly society', was founded for the benefit of professional and working people (*operai*); its office was and still is on the Piazza in the second floor of the building which adjoins the bell-tower. Members, who paid one lira per month, were given financial help during illness, and the Society's physician gave them free advice and treatment. When a member died all fellow-members foregathered at the Cemetery to see him on his way, and a fixed sum was paid to the bereaved family. The officers of the Society included a wide variety of the Capresi who mattered at this period. The first President was Dr Gustavo Rispo, but he soon gave place to Vincenzo Serena, a clerk at the *municipio*, and became the Society's first doctor; the Presidency was a life-long appointment which Serena held for forty years. Arcangelo Trama, carpenter and picture-frame maker, with a shop in Via Hohenzollern, and Manfredi Pagano, eldest son of Michele the hotelier, were Vice-Presidents. The Secretary was Antonino Russo, who operated the Capri branch of the Italian State Lottery (Banco Lotto) and ran a grocery, called 'Coloniali' in Via Hohenzollern. Russo was one of the few even slightly educated Capresi of his day and was much in advance of most other islanders in seeking to do good and help people who were out of work or otherwise in trouble, rather than exploiting them. The Treasurer was Giuseppe Federico, nicknamed ' 'O Truglio', because he owned a bit of land in the Truglio district between the town and the Marina. He owned one or two of the barks which plied between Capri and Torre del Greco and Torre Annunziata on the mainland, in order to keep Capri supplied. They displaced 50 to 80 tons, had lateen sails and were manned by a crew of five or six men. Each had a stove on which the crew cooked beans and other simple food. They used the sails when there was a wind and four long oars when it was calm. The ships carried every sort of staple requirement from flour to tufa stone and lime, but no perishable goods, because their schedule depended on the weather. As *relatore*, Ignazio Cerio was responsible for delivering the Society's annual report and in due course succeeded Rispo as its doctor.[41]

In November 1883 there was a serious outbreak of cholera in Naples, which raged throughout the following year. The only places in the immediate neighbourhood which escaped were Amalfi, and the island of Capri, where rigid quarantine was imposed. While on a holiday in Lapland Munthe read about the plague in a discarded copy of *The Times* and hurried south to work in the cholera hospital of Naples and amongst victims in the houses and streets.[42] In 1885 he repaired to Capri, in order to recover from the strain and exhaustion of Naples, but was given little peace by the islanders, who remembered his good work in 1881 and besieged his door, either to pay their respects or seek cures for their ailments. Later in the year he returned to Paris, where, under the influence of Jean-Martin Charcot, he turned from gynaecology and surgery, in which he had qualified, to the dark and largely uncharted areas of nervous disorders and madness. He haunted Charcot's Salpêtrière hospital for women suffering from chronic diseases, and would sit by the beds of the dying, not to comfort them, but to study them just before and in death itself.[43] Munthe's medical career in Paris, now set along new paths, was prosperous but exacting; as his fame increased, so also did his restlessness, inconsistency and loneliness. Björnstjerne Björnson, the Norwegian playwright, who encountered him there, described him thus:

> You write that I am too hard on Dr Axel Munthe. Yes, perhaps so. There is no kinder, more generous disposition, and he has a gift, so fine and great and so prepared for comprehensive thought that it ought to be able to accomplish rare things. But he is so unsettled by his meditations, so taken up with self-admiration and the admiration of others, that he no longer gets peace with himself. And so afraid of becoming common-place, that he seldom tells the same thing to two persons. He can make great efforts to reach a goal and, when he has reached it, he is as a rule utterly tired of the thing it has as its object. He also allows himself to be dominated by his fancies. So restless a nature is never happy longer than a moment at a time, and he involves those who surround him in his mood. There are few people I have been able to care for like this insinuating genius, but, whilst I derive pleasure from him, I know that he is already tired of me.[44]

In 1887, thoroughly exhausted, Munthe left Paris. In 1888 he divorced his wife, with whom he appeared to have no common interests, and returned to Anacapri, where he lived in a small house, with Giovannina, a fourteen-year old Capri girl, as his servant, and his dog Tim (short for Timberio). In July 1889 he wrote: 'I have killed myself with overwork, and here I sit in my solitary Anacapri, like a hermit, with destroyed health and a future of incurable hypochondria before me, a future which may be long and weary, for I am only 32 years old.'[45] In 1890 he felt strong enough to resume work and set up a practice in Rome, but not before he had bought a property at the north-east end of Anacapri, which included the remains of a Roman villa, the ruined chapel of San Michele and a vineyard, with the intention of building a house on it and spending his summers in the island. In Rome he occupied the house beside the Spanish Steps, where Keats and Shelley had lived, and quickly became a fashionable doctor.

*

It is time to consider the political pattern of Capri, some twenty-five years after the emancipation of Italy and the institution of self-government.

Michele Pagano, *sindaco* for five years until his death in 1877, had been succeeded by Filippo Trama, who owned property between the Quisisana Hotel and the Piazza. In 1885 Trama was followed as *sindaco* by Michele's son, Manfredi. For the next twenty-five years Capri politics were dominated by Federico Serena, proprietor of the Quisisana, and Manfredi Pagano – the two principal hoteliers of the island. Serena and his supporters were termed '*clericali*', and the Pagano faction '*anticlericali*'. Although politically speaking Serena did have some bias towards the priests (*appogiava i preti*), the distinction was largely meaningless. There were about twenty priests in Capri at this time; some were in the Pagano camp and others supported Serena. Women had no vote, and eligible male voters amounted to only a few hundred. At election times the few leading families who supported either Pagano or Serena would round up their retainers and as many uncommitted voters as they could muster, to vote for their candidate. Serena usually had the edge on Pagano.

The Ferraro family, led by Don Giacinto, who after 1860 had done well by buying confiscated Church property, were in the Pagano camp, but, in spite of their affluence, played little part in politics. Their interest lay in real estate, of which they acquired an extraordinary amount. Success may have partly been due to the fact that the family were tax-collectors (*esattori*) and were thus in a position to acquire property from the illiterate poor, who, when they could not pay their taxes, were compelled to sign a paper, which they probably did not understand, pledging their property for the debt. Giacinto had two brothers who were priests – Enrico, archpriest of the chapter (*archiprete del capitolo*), a fat, jovial character, who was an excellent cook, and Don Dionisio, who was a canon. Being priests they did not marry – so all their property remained in the family. They lived in the Palazzo Ferraro at the north-east end of Via Hohenzollern. The house had three floors, each with a large entry hall, a spacious drawing-room, dining-room and enough bedrooms to accommodate the entire family on the first and second floors, while the third was usually let; the ground floor (where Ferragamo now is) was occupied by Filippo Ferraro, who belonged to another family.[46] Among their properties and adjoining the Palazzo Ferraro was the *caffè* 'Zum Kater Hiddigeigei', the lease of which now belonged to Giuseppe and Lucia Morgano.

Giuseppe was born in 1850, the son of Mariano, and was grandson of Don Nicola Morgano, Colonel Lowe's director of fortifications during the Franco-British war. As a young man Giuseppe had become prosperous by lending money and foreclosing on mortgages. His first wife, Maria Mazzola, died in 1876, soon after bearing him a daughter Anna (Nannina). His second wife, Lucia Iuliano, from Torre del Greco, was barely fifteen when they married. Their eldest son Mariano was born in 1880, their second, Enrico, in 1885 and the youngest, Nicola, in 1893. 'Morgano's', as the *caffè* soon became known, developed a special character and power of its own and during its career of some thirty-five years achieved a unique position in the social life of the island. Although used mainly by Germans, for whom imported beer was always available, it also sold English and American stores – coffee, wines and spirits, groceries, books, papers and souvenirs of Capri; and 'afternoon tea' soon made its appearance for the growing number of English residents and tourists. Don Giuseppe and Donna Lucia, as they became in later years,[47] took special care of the interests of foreign residents. Giuseppe cashed their cheques or lent them money, and Lucia found them cooks and servants. Both were usually ready to help foreigners in distress. Those who were put in jail for drunkenness or involvement in an affray were sent fresh linen, good meals and, if necessary, provided with a lawyer. Although the Morgano family seldom left the *caffè*, they kept abreast of all that was going on in the island, and in particular made it their business to know in advance of any foreigner who was likely to be arrested for serious infringements of the law.

Physically, both Giuseppe and Lucia were fat and so were their children, which was due mainly to their greediness about food. But in character they were different. Lucia was 'one of those classical figures of humanity' – very intelligent, sane and compassionate, always ready to help anyone who needed her care – be it aid to foreigners in trouble with the authorities, or consolation and sweets to her own children when Giuseppe was being stern with them. Sitting and often dozing behind her counter at the back of the *caffè*, she presided, as a tutelary goddess, over its life and customers. If she had a fault, it was in being *politicante* – perhaps remarking happily to some very ordinary-looking man, woman or child, '*Com' è bello/bella*', and paying other compliments to the point of insincerity.

Giuseppe had a dark beard and a hooked nose, and invariably 'wore a skull-cap that gave his personality a most definite suggestion of the ghetto. He had none of the joviality one expects from fat men, and even in the tone of his welcome to entering customers there was a kind of cynical contempt as if a huge spider whose web had long been overcrowded by flies was expressing his indifference to new customers'.[48]

Giuseppe had a brother Enrico – a colourful character, who had a picture gallery on the Piazza and was also equipped to extract teeth. He often ran for a seat on the municipal council and during the election campaign would address the people from the terrace of the Società Operaia. Their sister Giacomina was married to Manfredi Pagano's brother, Nicola – and politically the whole Morgano family were in the Pagano camp.

South-east of Capri town lay the district of Tragara, reached along Via

Camerelle and itself served by Via Tragara, which had the merit of being almost flat and, therefore, possible for the most delicate promenaders. On account of its favourable position, facing south and west and protected by high ground on the north and east, it had been extensively built on by the Romans. In the period of which we are speaking, however, it was largely open country, with only a handful of houses, mostly belonging to the peasant families who owned the surrounding land. The two principal land-owners were the families Esposito[49] and Federico, who were still unconscious of the enormous potential value of their holdings.

The Esposito family owned most of the upper part of Tragara, from Via Camerelle to Punta Tragara and up the slopes of Monte Tuoro. At this time it was shared by three brothers – Giovanni, whose house lay about halfway along and just below Via Tragara; Luigi, married to Maria Cerrotta and with a son Antonio; and Filippo, married to Maria's sister Carmela. A handsome and capable woman, Carmela started a *caffè* at the end of Via Tragara. The spot was well chosen. After a level walk from the town you came to Punta Tragara, where on a terrace in front of a large room and kitchen you could sit drinking wine, vermouth, coffee or tea and enjoy stupendous views of the blue sea rippling far below, the Faraglioni rocks, Monte Solaro and Marina Piccola.

Much of the lower part of Tragara, stretching down towards Unghia Marina, belonged to the brothers Luigi and Raffaele Federico. The latter was known as 'Il Verginiello' (little virgin), because as a young man and unmarried he had been so-called by the municipal authorities, in order to distinguish him from another Raffaele Federico, who was older and married.

In 1890 the character of Tragara was transformed irrevocably by the arrival in Capri of the German artist Christian Wilhelm Allers.

CHAPTER THREE

The Gay 'Nineties

Shortly after his arrival in Capri, Allers bought a piece of land from the Esposito family halfway along the upper part of Tragara and built a villa in what was still open country. Born in 1857 at Hamburg, he had studied art at the Karlsruhe Gymnasium and become a very skilful draughtsman, particularly of figures, with an extraordinary facility for fluent and expressive line. After a short career as a sailor in the German Navy, he based himself in Germany, travelled widely through the rest of Europe and issued a steady stream of drawings and lithographs. He attracted the attention of Bismarck and was invited to stay at Friedrichsruhe, where he made many drawings of the Chancellor, including a head that was reproduced all over Germany.

He filled Villa Allers with quantities of uncomfortable Renaissance-style furniture, rugs, tapestries and hangings, medieval arms and armour, relics of Bismarck, and his own works. It became a nodal point for the entertainment of German visitors. With Teutonic energy and thoroughness Allers explored every corner of the island, recording in meticulous detail all that he encountered – it is altogether a vivid and invaluable record of Capri in the early 'nineties. There are drawings of leading citizens, priests, old women, young women, fishermen and fisherboys, a coachman, the Caffè Morgano, German women at the Villa Allers, German women drawing a model, foreigners watching the procession of San Costanzo, and a middle-aged German professor bargaining with a boy to accompany him to the Grotta Azzurra.

These and many other brilliant drawings were published by Allers in two books of engravings in 1892 and 1893, and by his friend Dr Alexander Olinda, in *Freund Allers* in 1894. Olinda was a German philologer 'with grey hair and a smooth-shaven, comical face. It was an unusually round and ruddy face, and, to make it still funnier, he wore enormous old fashioned goggles'.[1] To be near Allers, he started to build a house high up on the slope of Tuoro overlooking the Faraglioni rocks.

Allers's first boy-friend was a young sailor named Alberino from Marina Grande, who became general factotum in the villa. Later, Allers found other boys he liked better and replaced Alberino, who acquired the nicknames *'Miezo Culillo'* (Half Arse) and *'Meza Recchia'*. In explanation of the latter it should be noted that *recchia* is a corruption of *recchione*, shortened form of *orecchione* (big ear), which is slang for 'homosexual'; if you want to indicate this of a person, you flip the lobe of your ear. Allers's relations with local boys, who often posed as models in his studio, or perhaps with one in particular, eventually brought him to the adverse notice of the *questura* in Naples, who made an expulsion order against him and sent over two policemen in civilian clothes to enforce it. Wind of these events reached Donna Lucia Morgano, who warned Allers of his impending arrest and helped to procure him a boat, in which he was conveyed in the nick of time to a point on the Italian mainland outside the jurisdiction of Naples. The police arrived to find that the bird had flown. 'No one had any knowledge of him. No one knew when and how he had departed. *Sacra omertà isolana.*'[2] For many years Allers hid himself in another island – Samoa – and was soon forgotten. Poor Olinda departed too and the beginnings of his house soon crumbled to a ruin. Allers returned to die in Karlsruhe in 1915. Fame came to him in 1969, when in a set of German stamps issued to commemorate national artists no less than three were devoted to his works.

Henry Wreford, *doyen* of the English colony, died on 26 March 1892 at the age of 86 and received the honour of a public funeral. On his gravestone in the *cimitero acattolico* was inscribed what he had most valued: FOR FIFTY YEARS A RESIDENT OF CAPRI. During his long stay he had acquired many friends and substantial amounts of property. He deeded one of his houses to Arcangelo Trama, in gratitude for the friendship of Arcangelo's young son, Giovanni. Wreford died in his home, at the Villa Croce and bequeathed this and his other house, Villa Cesina, which lay on the north-east slope of Monte San Michele, to Brigida Scoppa, a cousin of the *caffè*-owner, Antonio. Wreford's many services to the island were commemorated in 1908 in a tablet which adorns the courtyard of the *municipio*.

Another Englishman who loved the island and acquired much property in it was the artist Talmage White, already resident for nearly 40 years. Besides the Villa Valentino where he lived, he owned the Villa Mura in Strada Nuova (Via Roma), Villa Alba and Ca' del Sole in Via Castello; all the land between Villa Valentino and the Castiglione; and other properties in Anacapri and Amalfi. He established a gallery and museum in Cà del Sole, where there was open house for his French Impressionist friends.

The American contingent was joined in 1894 by William Page Andrews and his wife Edith, a lively and attractive woman, much younger than himself. Born in Massachussetts in 1848 and educated at a variety of schools and by private tutors, William had been prevented by illness from going to university. A semi-invalid and hypochondriac for the remainder of his life, he was looked after by Edith, who sometimes sighed for

Foreigners watching the procession of San
Costanzo, 14 May 1891, by C. W. Allers

Raffaele Federico, by C. W. Allers

Boy posing for C. W. Allers in the 1890s. *Courtesy of Centro Caprense Ignazio Cerio*

romance, but remained faithful to William. She was very proper, had no money of her own and, as another American remarked gravely: 'it's mighty difficult to commit adultery when you have to give your husband his medicine three-quarters of an hour before every meal'[3] – so she guarded him 'with a kind of half-resentful devotion'. William's life work was the metrical translation into New England American of Goethe's *Faust*, and he could talk about nothing else. He could hitch the wagon of any conversation to the star of *Faust*, and no one in Capri ever succeeded in diverting his talk away from the subject for more than five minutes at the utmost.[4]

In 1895, three young Englishmen, who may have felt the need for a change of air after Oscar Wilde's trial and sentencing in May and were certainly attracted by Capri's reputation for sexual permissiveness – which had been enhanced in 1891 when sexual relations between men were legalised in Italy – arrived independently in the island – William Somerset Maugham, Edward Frederick Benson and John Ellingham Brooks. Brooks remained almost permanently in the island until his death in 1929; Maugham and Benson returned many times in later years.

The senior member of the trio was Brooks, who, after reading law at Cambridge, was called to the Bar, but soon left it, decided to become a writer and went to Heidelberg to learn German. Here he had a brief love-affair with the young Maugham, who after a short public-school education at the King's School, Canterbury, was sent at the age of sixteen to complete his education in Germany. Brooks, then twenty-four, was in the vanguard of the aesthetic movement and well-read in the authors of the *fin-de-siècle*, to whose books he introduced the impressionable young Maugham. Brooks's dilettante approach to life was well matched by his handsome, finely-cut features, curly hair, pale blue eyes and a hesitant, wistful expression – perfection marred only by his shortness of stature. He arrived on Capri in or shortly before 1895 and found it much to his liking; later he told a friend that he 'came for lunch and stayed for life'. Although Capri was very cheap, it was still too expensive for Brooks, who had no money at all, simply wanted to pursue unhurriedly his literary and musical aims, and otherwise do nothing except enjoy what Capri had to offer. He had a gift for friendship and indeed was able to tolerate almost anyone; he lived on what he could scrounge.

After Heidelberg, Maugham studied medicine in London and, although successful in his final examinations, decided to turn to literature. By 1895 he had already reacted against the dilettantism of Brooks and recorded this opinion of his first lover: 'He can discover nothing for himself. He intends to write, but for that he has neither energy, imagination, nor will. . . . He has a craving for admiration. He is weak, vain and profoundly selfish.'[5]

Last of the trio was E. F. Benson, third son of Edward White Benson, future Archbishop of Canterbury, who had been educated at Marlborough and King's College, Cambridge. After gaining First Class honours in both parts of the Classical Tripos, he wrote his first novel *Dodo*, which was published in 1893. It was 'thought to be based on Margot Tennant, who next year married the future Prime Minister, H. H. Asquith. It had immediate and resounding success', which so encouraged Benson that for the rest of his life he became 'uncontrollably prolific', producing at least 93 books, many of which 'suggest that he had a generalised dislike of women'. He was also a considerable athlete, particularly as a skater and winter-sportsman. Three years at the British School of Archaeology in Athens were followed by this first visit to Capri in 1895.[6]

For part of 1896, while his friend Wilde was languishing in prison, Lord Alfred Douglas came to Capri and rented the upper floor of the Villa Federico in Via Pastena, where for two months he had as his guest another of Wilde's friends, Robert Ross, an amiable Canadian, who claimed to have been Wilde's first male lover. In May 1897 Wilde was released and immediately crossed to Dieppe by the night-boat. After some months in France he took up again with Bosie, and the two moved south to Naples, where they rented the Villa Giudice ('lovely villa over the sea') at Posillipo. They spent three days together in Capri, where Bosie stayed on after Wilde's return to the mainland:

> *Letter to Reginald Turner*, dated Friday 15 October 1897.
> 'I have extracted after three weeks of telegrams, £10 from Smithers! It is absurd. However, with it we go to Capri for three days. I want to lay a few simple flowers on the Tomb of Tiberius. As the Tomb is of someone else really, I shall do so with the deeper emotion.'
> *Letter to Robert Ross*, dated Tuesday 19 October.
> 'Bosie is in Capri. I came back yesterday as there was scirocco and rain. He dines with Mrs Snow. We both lunched with Dr Munthe, who has a lovely villa and is a great connoisseur of Greek things. He is a wonderful personality.'[7]

The visit was not without embarrassment. When Wilde and Douglas entered the Quisisana for a meal, all the English guests rose from their tables and threatened to leave the dining-room if the two remained; Federico Serena, who had become *sindaco* in 1895, considered it prudent to escort them from the hotel.

Mrs Snow, with whom Bosie dined, was an American with a 'booming voice and invincible optimism', who had left her husband in London and come to Capri with her son to build up a new life. She occupied the top

floor of the Palazzo Ferraro and entertained generously. Norman Douglas, writing many years later, noted that a vision of her helped him to
portray the Duchess in *South Wind*, 'with her handsome profile and
towering grey hair inducing her to cultivate an antique pose, with a view to
resembling La Pompadour'.[8]

The 'wonderful' Dr Munthe was enjoying phenomenal success in
Rome. 'New and exclusive patients flocked around the door of his
consulting room and the trusty old guard of his neurotic patients, whom
he thought to escape now, also sought him out afresh. He was doctor to
the British Embassy and the French colony, and even Roman society
yielded to the foreign doctor. The famous Professor Kraft-Ebbing sent
him from Vienna his neuropaths "of both sexes and of no sex", and the
American Professor Weir Mitchell "his surplus of dilapidated millionaires and their unstrung wives". In Rome's poorest suburb he opened
a free clinic for the destitute, which increased his popularity still more, at
the same time as he thereby made more enemies among his colleagues.' In
1892 Crown Princess Victoria of Sweden encountered Munthe in Rome
and asked him to become her doctor. Thus began a long relationship
which brought Victoria to Anacapri and continued until her death in
1930.

Munthe's Roman triumphs went to his head. Björnson, the Norwegian
who had known him in Paris, describes how Munthe paraded round the
city in a carriage with a coachman and footman, both in livery; in his house
was a prodigious dish full of visiting cards. 'Gladstone's card lies upper-
most; one assumes, of course, that he was with Munthe yesterday. . . . He
mentions without reason that he had been to the Queen, the Crown
Princess, Princess Ruspoli, the American millionaire's son, or relates the
consultation which preceded the death of the British ambassador and at
which he alone was acknowledged to be right and all the other doctors
were wrong.' Björnson ends: 'I have been once at Munthe's and on that
occasion he had my visiting card placed in his dish; since then he has not
had any use for me, and I have had none for him either.'[9]

Munthe had a yacht always anchored in Anzio harbour, so that he could
visit Capri at short notice. The building of San Michele progressed, as did
the collection of antiquities excavated either on his own land, or elsewhere
by the peasants, or bought from antique dealers in Naples. In the hunt for
Roman marbles and ceramics, there was a jealous rivalry between Munthe
and Mackowen in Anacapri, and Coleman and the Cerio family in Capri.
The peasants did their best to keep pace with this increasing demand, as
did the dealers and fakers of Naples. In giving free treatment to the poor,
Munthe as often as not had an eye on their land and any antiquities found
on it as eventual rewards for his services. Always a lover of animals and
extraordinarily sensitive in his relationships with them, he was already

Capri Index for Munthe

Federico Serena, surrounded by political supporters and municipal officials, after his election as *sindaco* in 1895. *Courtesy of Centro Caprense Ignazio Cerio*

beginning to develop a campaign against the snaring and shooting of song-birds, and this was to arouse much hatred against him.

In 1872 the German zoologist Dr Anthon Dohrn had founded the Aquarium at Naples and within 20 years developed it into a station of international importance for the investigation and display of the marine biology of the Mediterranean. Here, in its tanks, could be seen the world's finest collection of cuttle-fish, electric rays (which visitors could actually touch and experience a shock), numerous brilliantly-coloured fish, many different kinds of living coral, jelly-fish, crabs, crayfish, eels and so on. While the Aquarium was mainly financed by Dohrn himself, other countries, including the United States and Italy, contributed to its upkeep, so that their own scientists could join in its work. When, therefore, Friedrich Alfred (Fritz) Krupp, head of the great armaments firm and fabulously rich, wrote from Essen that he wanted to offer his help, Dohrn was at first sceptical, but, having established that this rich amateur was sincere and that yachts specially equipped for marine research would be provided, he relented and prepared to welcome the 'King of Guns'.

Fritz, born in 1854, the son of Alfred Krupp, owner and head of the firm, had been a disappointment to his father. Fat, myopic and placid, his only real childhood interest had been natural science. As a youth he spent much time labelling samples of flora and fauna – and weighing himself. He was removed unwillingly from school to become literary assistant to his prolific and very demanding father. In an attempt to escape him, Fritz joined the Army, but was quickly discharged on account of 'short-sightedness, asthmatic attacks and corpulence'. As a defence against a hostile world, he cultivated the talents of craftiness and intrigue, which, combined with a good brain, enabled him to survive. In 1882 he married Margarethe (Marga) Freun von Ende, by whom he had two daughters – in 1886 Bertha (who succeeded him and became famous as head of Krupp), and Barbara in 1887, the year in which Alfred died. Fritz now took charge of the firm. Although unimpressive in public, he inherited his father's business sense and managerial ability, which, combined with his own sly and serpentine nature, ensured a period of great prosperity for the firm.[10]

His most profitable stratagem was what the amused Kaiser Wilhelm II called the *Schutz- und Trutzwaffen Schaukeln* (the defensive and offensive weapons see-saw). This arms game, in which about thirty governments were enmeshed, worked as follows. Having perfected nickel-steel armour, Fritz advertised it widely; armies and navies bought it. Then he unveiled chrome-steel shells that could pierce the nickel-steel; armies and navies invested again. Next he appeared with a high-carbon armour-plate that would resist the new shells. But just when every general and admiral thought he had equipped his forces with invincible shields, Fritz

once more produced good news for the advocates of offensive warfare . . .
the improved plate could be pierced by "capped shot", with very expensive explosive noses. . . .'[11] Fritz himself became vastly rich and a member
of the Kaiser's privy council, but he still found time to fuss about his
weight and, in order to reduce it, had a gymnasium installed at his home,
where after rigorous workouts he would ascend the weighing-machine
and record the results.

This was the man, who early in 1898, at the age of 44, arrived in Naples
with his two yachts – *Puritan*, commanded by Capt. J. McCallum, a
Scotsman, and *Maia* – ready to make his contribution to the work of the
Aquarium.

Krupp made Capri his headquarters and took an entire floor of the
Quisisana for himself and his entourage. This was a great triumph for
Serena, but a source of bitter envy in the Pagano camp. When not at sea,
Krupp's yachts were moored off Marina Piccola. A man of simple tastes,
he was delighted to escape from the formalities of Germany; and he was
glad to be free, for the summer at least, from a shrewish wife. Amidst the
beauties of Capri and its welcoming inhabitants Krupp relaxed and
expanded. He had unlimited money to spend, not only on his marine
researches but also on the people and the place where he quickly became
so happy, and he was a kind and generous man. He was also a German and
a sentimentalist. He knew little or nothing of the indigenous population of
Capri, and in particular that it fell into two distinct classes. Commenting
later on the Krupp affair, Norman Douglas defined these two classes as:
'the real natives who own property on the island, whose ancestors were
born there, and who ask for nothing save to be allowed to go on with their
work in peace; and a race of newcomers, immigrants from the mainland,
who settle there for longer or shorter periods, attracted by the tourist-
traffic. The majority are decent folk – officials, tradesmen, professionals;
others are the reverse, a disturbing element of impoverished adventurers,
unscrupulous and malicious, with no reputation of their own to lose, and
no respect for that of others. It was Krupp's misfortune not to realise the
fact that, while the native of Capri, however humble, is a man of position,
who had been brought up by his parents under patriarchal rule, those
others, though speaking the same language, are often the scum of the
province and of the Naples pavements, living on their wits. . . . In his
romantic eyes the inhabitants of Capri were children of nature, one and all
of them'.[12]

Krupp had his pet barber, Adolfo Schiano, 18-year-old son of the
former owner of the *caffè* Zum Kater Hiddigeigei; he took a great fancy to
the young man, and lavished money on him. Adolfo also played the guitar
and with his brother Francesco and Giuseppe Massa would sing and play
the latest Neapolitan songs for Krupp – either at his shop in Via

Hohenzollern or in the Costantina restaurant, in Via Fuorlovado, where Krupp and his entourage would go to eat German sausages. This aroused great envy amongst other barbers and musicians. A group of untalented immigrant artists persuaded him to buy their paintings for far more than they were worth; others whose work remained unsold were furious. He also neglected to drink beer with his fellow-Germans at Zum Kater Hiddigeigei, and thus made an enemy of Serena's political and business rival, Giuseppe Morgano. But he was widely popular on account of his unfailing generosity and willingness to tip anybody who did him a service. Thus Serafina, who delivered telegrams for the Ufficio Telegrafico, having received three telegrams for Krupp, brought them at intervals throughout the day and received a tip for each one.

One Caprese who did particularly well out of Krupp was Eduardo (Tuardino) Settanni, brother of Mrs Maria Binyon and Principessa Emilia Caracciolo, who was employed by the *municipio* to keep records of the various land-parcels of the island. Although not qualified as a land-surveyor, Settanni was a competent draughtsman, and it was on this account that he got the job. He knew in advance which land was coming up for sale and those parcels on which the owners had neglected to pay their taxes. He thus had opportunities of acquiring land for himself ahead of everyone else.[13] Having learned that Krupp was planning to acquire an extensive piece of land between Castiglione and the Certosa, with the intention of creating at his own expense a *parco-giardino* for the people of Capri, Settanni bought this and some adjacent land, sold Krupp all he wanted, which included a farm around the Certosa, and, keeping the remaining piece of hillside for himself, in 1900 built a house, which he called Villa Blaesus.[14]

For the construction of the *parco-giardino*, Krupp's friend Ugo Andreas, a rich banker from Frankfurt, who had just built himself a spacious villa at the north end of Tragara, recommended Luigi Ruggiero, a young landscape-gardener from Naples, who was laying out the garden of the Villa Andreas. Luigi was too busy to do the work himself and sent his brother Domenico (Mimì), a cheerful and energetic young man, who tackled his important commission with skill and enthusiasm.[15] Immediately below the garden Krupp had a tennis-court built and made it available to foreign residents free of charge.[16]

Marina Grande was already linked to Capri town by a carriage-road. Travel to and from Marina Piccola was still on foot or by pack-animal up and down the Via Mulo. Construction of a carriage-road, however, was in progress by 1900. Meanwhile Krupp, feeling the need of a convenient route between his suite in the Quisisana and his yachts at Marina Piccola, offered to finance the construction of a road from the marina, eastwards along the southern slope of Castiglione, then in a series of loops up the

E. F. Benson in the early 1890s.
*Photo: Radio Times Hulton
Picture Library*

Friedrich Alfred Krupp in
1901. *Courtesy of Centro Caprense
Ignazio Cerio*

sheer face of the mountain to the new *parco-giardino* and finally, skirting the Certosa, into Capri town. In May 1899 his proposal was accepted by the *comune* which entrusted the work to the veteran engineer Cavaliere Emilio Mayer,[17] who had built the Anacapri and Marina Grande roads and was in charge of the new road to Marina Piccola.

Half-way down the vertiginous route chosen for his road, Krupp came upon and bought the Grotta di Fra' Felice, named after the hermit who had once inhabited it. Shown on some maps as *carcere antico* (old prison), the place consisted of two caves. In front of the larger cave, there was a small terrace with stone bench, which was linked by stairs to a smaller cave below. Krupp had the larger cave converted into a simple living-room, and in the smaller a stove was installed for cooking or heating up dishes from the Quisisana. Here he found seclusion where he could relax privately with his *capresi* friends.

*

In 1899 Filippo Trama became *sindaco* again, but Serena was back again in 1900 and remained in office until 1909. The flow of visitors continued to increase. Sailings from Naples were more reliable and comfortable. At the head of the list was the Norddeutscher Lloyd luxury ship, the *Nixe*, which ran daily from February to May and provided a massive lunch of sausages and beer for the many Germans who visited the island. A variety of mail-boats and other local steamers were available all the year round; small boats could still be taken on the shorter crossing from Sorrento and Amalfi. But there was still no breakwater at Marina Grande, which remained completely exposed to the north and west winds. When these blew in force, the rowing boats refused to come out, and all the trippers got from the excursion was a very rough and unpleasant round-trip and only a distant view of Capri. When the north wind (*tramontana*) blew, it was, however, calm at Marina Piccola and the steamers sometimes disembarked their passengers there instead.

The season was now spread over the whole year, with the emphasis still on the autumn, winter and spring, but with the hot summer beginning to attract some northern visitors, as well as Neapolitans and foreign residents of Naples who wanted a change of air. There was good bathing at both the Marinas. There were seven hotels at Marina Grande, six in Capri and two in Anacapri – with a growing number of lodgings, apartments, restaurants and *caffè*. Most of the visitors were German, and the Kaiser's birthday on 27 January was celebrated with far more gusto than that of the King of Italy.

There was one German who considered that, although Capri catered admirably for the physical needs of German visitors, their spiritual welfare was neglected. Moritz von Bernus, son of a rich merchant family of Frankfurt, had been sent to London to study British mercantile practices, but instead became deeply religious and devoted the rest of his life to the German Evangelical movement. Because he suffered from asthma, he could not be a preacher himself and every winter for the sake of his health went to Italy, but nowhere could he find an Evangelical Church. He decided, therefore, to build churches for the benefit of Germans visiting Italy – and the first was in Capri. He bought a piece of land at the north end of Via Tragara and with Ugo Andreas financed the building of a church, which was opened on Christmas Eve 1899 and completed in 1901. Andreas was also building a chapel dedicated to his namesake St Andrew for the fishermen of Marina Piccola. He entrusted its design and supervision to Riccardo Fainardi, a poverty-stricken painter from Parma, who had gravitated to Capri; Fainardi also painted an altar triptych with scenes from the life of the saint. The chapel was dedicated in 1900 and gratefully received by the fishermen, but when Andreas discovered that Fainardi was having an affair with his young wife Emma, he could not bear to remain any longer in the island and took her back to Germany, where he died of shock or by suicide in 1901. Emma inherited the villa and married Fainardi, but they too found it painful to live in Capri and, after renaming the house Villa Capricorno, left the island.

By 1900 Mackowen felt that he had had enough of Anacapri and decided to return to the States, Yankees or no Yankees. He had lived with but never married Mariuccia Cimino, and he left her behind in the Casa Rossa in Anacapri, with their two *naturali* children – a son, Tiberius, and daughter, Julia. He packed up his papers, the fruits of long research, removed some of his portable treasures and returned to his estates in Louisiana, which during the years of absence had been managed by his brother. Here he was shot dead by a freed slave.[18] Apart from a few bequests to nieces and nephews in America, he left everything to Julia, but nothing to Tiberius, whom he had always disliked. Julia took the name of Cimino and later married Giovanni Maresca, whose family had made money in Sorrento from *mozzarella* and butter. Today their son Mario Maresca manages a small hotel in Mackowen's old house at Marina Grande.

If Capri lost one American eccentric, there were others to take his place. Thomas Spencer Jerome,[19] born in 1864 at Saginaw, Michigan, graduated as a lawyer in 1887 and began a successful legal career in Detroit. After twelve years he suddenly retired, left the United States, and in 1900, with his close friend Charles Freer, who had made a fortune in car-building in Detroit and was devoting his wealth to the collection of works of art, bought the Villa Castello in Capri, with its large garden and seven street doors. After a year as US Consular Agent in Sorrento, Jerome settled in Capri, became Consular Agent there, and in 1906 bought Freer's share of the villa. The US authorities seem not to have minded that Jerome was living with, but not married to, his beautiful mulatto housekeeper Henrietta (Yetta) S. Rupp, who had come with him from the States, being no doubt content that American interests were being handled by a person of brains, legal knowledge and integrity. In these early days Jerome was 'a big brawny fellow, with thick black hair and a black beard, of a powerful physique', and every afternoon during the summer months would take Yetta out from Marina Piccola in an Indian canoe, which was the envy of every local boy, paddle round to a tiny beach at the south-west corner of the island, to swim and lie in the sun, until evening brought them back to shore.[20]

Nearby Charles Coleman, a distinguished, tall, Bohemian figure, with flowing white beard, usually dressed in a white suit and wide-brimmed hat, was still painting pictures of Vesuvius in all its moods, depicting the girls of Capri in oriental and classical draperies, seducing them, and entertaining visiting artists and friends from America. He had grown tired of 'Serafina baroque' and redecorated the villa with arches and twisted columns in the Hispano-Mauresque manner then fashionable in the United States. Later he reorganised the interior in a Pompeian manner and called the house Villa Narcissus.

In 1901 Elihu Vedder, who, though based in Rome, had often stayed with Coleman, decided to have a house of his own in Capri. He wanted a view of both the Bay of Naples and the Gulf of Salerno, and for this purpose bought a piece of land on the saddle between Monte Solaro and the Castiglione. Imagining that as an artist he was also qualified to design a building – and indeed in those days there was no architect in Capri to whom he could turn for advice – he drew his own plans, with a strong Hispano-Mauresque element, which the builder Giovanni Desiderio and his cousin Luigi Desiderio, both 'Marzianielli' descendants, did their best to follow. After much chopping and changing the house was completed in the summer of 1903; the outside resembling 'a miniature of the Alhambra . . . the inside . . . not like anything except a number of very small square rooms and a maze of unusable staircases'. The Villa Quattro Venti had a tower, the corners of which were aligned to the four points of the compass and certainly earned its name, being 'directly exposed not merely to every wind that blew except one, but also to their concentrated force tearing between the precipices of Monte Solaro and the Castiglione. The west wind, which was the only one from which he had supposed it would be sheltered, was in fact the worst of the lot, because it rushed up the slopes of Monte Solaro from the Anacapri side and charged down on the Quattro Venti from above'. Vedder lived there for a few years; after that he came only for a few weeks in the summer and then only when he had been unable to let it to some gullible northerner.[21]

Amongst visitors to the Quattro Venti was the American novelist and playwright, Booth Tarkington, who had teamed up with Harry Leon Wilson, another writer; and together these two made a high-spirited and bibulous progress around Europe, writing plays. Whenever Tarkington's alcoholic excesses landed him in the Capri jail, the Morgano family would come to the rescue with sheets, food and wine. In the party at Quattro Venti was Rose O'Neill – beautiful, witty and ebullient. She had taught herself to draw and achieved some success as an illustrator of American magazines. Already once married and divorced, she took Wilson as her second husband, but they were ill-suited, and in 1905 Rose moved on to become Coleman's lover and favourite woman, which she remained for the rest of his long life.

By the beginning of the century, Ignazio Cerio's three sons, all agnostics like their father, had now reached maturity. Giorgio, the middle brother, combined a rather desultory practice of the medical profession with an eagerness to acquire land and property, and for this latter purpose was on the look-out for a rich foreign wife. His first wife, however, Marchesina Jenny Ungaro, daughter of Marchese Enrico Ungaro, Member of Parliament, was Italian. Jenny, who was already, but unhappily, married, fell in love with Giorgio and he presumably with her. At this time no divorce was possible in Italy and she could obtain release only if the marriage was annulled. The Vatican, therefore, was petitioned for an annulment on the grounds that, because of a congenital malposition of Jenny's uterus, the marriage could have no progeny and, therefore, had not been consummated. The annulment was granted, but later a second petition was submitted requesting permission for a new marriage to Giorgio Cerio, on the grounds that the uterus defect had been cured by surgery and Jenny was able to bear children. While all this was going on, Giorgio was practising medicine in America. As soon as the second petition had been granted, he returned to the island, married Jenny on 18 October 1902 and, having built a house (Villa Jenny) at the end of Via Camerelle, continued his medical career in Capri.[22]

Edwin, the youngest son, trained as a naval architect and engineer, and graduated shortly before Krupp's arrival in 1898. After making friends with Ignazio Cerio, Krupp recruited Edwin as a collaborator in his marine researches. Later Edwin was given a job with the firm and worked for them in Germany and in South America. Edwin was intelligent, astute and, like Giorgio, very acquisitive; he also prided himself as a seducer of *contadine*.

Arturo, the eldest brother, was a bit strange (*un po matto*). He suffered

from asthma, was often in poor health and never embarked on a professional career. Something of a misanthrope, he lacked the hard and greedy
natures of his two brothers, appeared to have no interest in women, and
amused himself with painting and amateur photography. Amongst the
subjects of his camera was the Certosa. In 1901, following pressure by the
Caprese authorities, the unpopular Disciplinary Company was withdrawn
from the Certosa where it had been since 1860; and, apart from a few
squatters, the monastery buildings were completely abandoned. The
Company's last medical officer, Dr Pasquale De Gennaro, transferred
to private practice and became panel doctor (*medico condotto*) of Capri.
One of Arturo's diversions was to dress up as a monk and take photographs of his friends, similarly attired, in the deserted cloister of the
monastery.

On 29 September 1902 the Cerio brothers lost their mother, Elisabetta. She had gone mad soon after Edwin's birth and lived at home.
She always slept in an old-fashioned bed adorned with quantities of metal,
and in one of the destructive thunderstorms to which Capri is prone was
blasted by a thunderbolt which hit the Palazzo Cerio and quickly found its
way to her bed.

For four seasons, from 1898 to 1901, Krupp came south to enjoy
himself in Capri and pursue his research aboard *Maia* and *Puritan*. His
standing in the island became so high that on 28 April 1900 he was
declared an honorary citizen of Capri. The same privilege was conferred
on Dr Huethe, formerly a senior medical officer of the German Navy, who
had retired to the Albergo Pagano in Capri in 1895 and once had been
instrumental in saving the life of Manfredi Pagano.[23]

In 1901 Dohrn, conscious of Krupp's value to science, placed all the
resources of the Aquarium at his disposal and lent him the services of its
curator, Dr Salvatore Lo Bianco, to superintend the work of the two
yachts. Lo Bianco, 'the white one', was a Sicilian with pronounced negro
strains. As curator 'he was in charge of the bottling, despatching and
classifying department of the Aquarium. He knew all sea-beasts by name,
down to the humblest and rarest, where they lived, when to catch them
and how to preserve the frailest of them in their original bright tints. . . .
The *Puritan* dredgings brought to light 68 marine forms new to the
Mediterranean, nine of which were altogether unknown to science.
Krupp had intended to carry on these investigations in 1903 with a larger
yacht and a still more complicated outfit'. But this was not to be. His happy
life in Capri came to a sudden end in the summer of 1902, and he died in
Germany on 22 November of that year.

What went wrong? For Krupp, Capri was a revelation not only of a
life-style which greatly attracted him but also of his own nature. If he had
not realised it already, he discovered in Capri that he was homosexual and

that homosexual relationships, so severely inhibited in Germany, could be enjoyed in the island. Under paragraph 175 of the German penal code, anyone who practised or was associated with sexual perversion was liable to be given a severe prison sentence. Nevertheless, in the 'nineties, male homosexuality was widespread in the German government service, the General Staff, the armed forces and in high society. Prince Phillipp zu Eulenberg, who was a close personal friend of and adviser to the Kaiser, was leader of the homosexual element at Court, and it was rumoured that the Kaiser himself had homosexual inclinations; Eulenberg was also having an affair with Count Kuno von Moltke, the military commandant of Berlin. What Fritz Krupp, married and with two daughters, thought about all this is not known. Perhaps in Germany he was too busy worrying about his weight and manipulating the 'weapons see-saw'. But in Capri he could forget Essen and Berlin, and, when not on his yachts, was free to do what he liked on this beguiling island. In respect of another foreigner who exceeded the limits of prudence, Donna Lucia considered that 'the Mediterranean climate, the beauty of the island, and the amiable manners of Capriot youth, were apt to cause men from colder northern climates to lose their heads'.[24] Krupp was very fond of his musical barber, Adolfo Schiano. Another favourite was Antonino Arcucci, son of Giuseppe (nicknamed 'Ciccariello' – 'nice little thing'), a net-fisherman at Marina Piccola. There were others, fathers and grandfathers of today's citizens, who made love with Krupp for money. Attractive but poor, they did not mind obliging Europe's richest man, who enjoyed their company and paid them so well for their services. Many years later, Edwin Cerio remarked to another islander that some families, if not actually launched on the road to success, at least benefited substantially from his donations to their willing young ancestors.[25]

Extraordinary stories have been woven around the Grotta di Fra' Felice, beside the Via Krupp. Its caretaker, it was said, wore the habit of a Franciscan monk and thither, also dressed as monks, came Krupp's friends, among them Arturo Cerio and the sycophantic artists. Such parties sound harmless enough, but, in *The Arms of Krupp*, the American author, William Manchester, drawing on a number of sources, gives a more colourful and damaging account. The 'grotto was transformed into a terraced, scented Sodom. Favoured youths were enlisted in a kind of Krupp fun-club. Members received keys to the place and, as token of their benefactor's affection, either solid-gold pins shaped like artillery shells or gold medals with two crossed forks,[26] both designed by him. In return they submitted to sophisticated caresses from him, while three violinists played. An orgasm was celebrated by sky-rockets, and now and then, when the boys were intoxicated by wine and Krupp by his passion, the love play was photographed. That was careless of Fritz. Prints were hawked by a local vendor of pornography. He was guilty of other lapses. From the pictures it was clear that some of his companions were mere children.'[27]

Manchester also quotes from German sources, which suggest that Krupp was already being investigated for goings-on in the Hotel Bristol, where he stayed whilst in Berlin, but always sent his wife to a different hotel. Krupp had asked the proprietor, Conrad Uhl, to accommodate and employ, at his own expense, a number of his young Italian protégés (*Schützlinge*), on the understanding that they would be released from their duties whenever he was in town, to provide him with companionship. Uhl was surprised 'but he supposed that a great industrialist must be indulged. At the outset he had no idea how much indulgence Fritz expected. The boys who came were very young, spoke no German, were insubordinate, and lacked the dexterity to serve as porters, pages or cook's helpers, let alone wait at table. That was when Krupp was away. When he checked in it was worse. The entire stable of handsome youths would crowd into his suite, and the hosteler, listening to the giggles and squeals echoing within, drew the obvious conclusions. He spoke no Italian . . . but he did not need an interpreter to understand *that*.' Afraid that he might be answerable under paragraph 175 of the penal code, he reported the matter to Kriminalkommissar Hans von Tresckow of the Berlin police. Thus began the Krupp case (*Fall Krupp*) in Germany.[28]

The chain of events which brought Krupp to public notice in the summer of 1902 started in Capri and in a manner which he could not have foreseen. Sometime during his stay he had taken Italian lessons and chose 30-year-old Luigi Messanelli, one of the island's two schoolmasters, who was married to a cousin of Federico Serena and was delighted to be able to supplement so substantially his miserable income in the local school. The other schoolmaster, Ferdinando Gamboni, was bitterly envious. A native of Massa Lubrense, just across the water, he had for a time taught in an elementary school on the mainland. Dismissed from this post on account of improper conduct with school-children and the violence of his disciplinary methods, he migrated to New York, where he supported himself by organ-grinding and picked up a little English. Returning to Italy in the early 'nineties, he managed to get a job in Capri from the then *sindaco*, Manfredi Pagano. Both because the parish priest had played a part in getting him sacked on the mainland and because he was himself a rationalist, he was fervently *anticlericale* and pro-Pagano, and had this added reason for detesting Serena's star-guest at the Quisisana. Also ranged against Krupp were the barbers, musicians, artists, restaurateurs and *caffè*-owners whom he had not patronised.

Gamboni is widely credited with having taken the first active steps to interest the Naples press in scandal about Krupp. Following this initiative,

Eduardo Scarfoglio, a journalist who specialised in scandals, tried to blackmail Krupp's secretary into buying silence about the matter. When he was rebuffed, Scarfoglio published a venomous article entitled '*Il Capitone*' about Krupp's alleged activities. The title was skilfully chosen, for *capitone* is also the common name of *anguilla vulgaris* – the eel which all Neapolitans eat on Christmas Eve and whose shape has an obvious obscene connotation. The left-wing paper *Propaganda* followed with details of how the German armaments-king, capitalist, exploiter of the working-class, was using his ill-gotten wealth; the tale was taken up by Rome's *Avanti*; accompanying editorials deplored the corruption of children.[29]

The story broke while Krupp was in London. He returned to Essen completely *bouleversé* and not knowing what to do. On 8 August he wrote to Ignazio Cerio:[30]

> Essen a.d. Ruhr,
> le 5-VIII-1902
>
> Mon très cher et honoré Docteur!
>
> Vous m'avez beaucoup touché par votre amiable lettre du 19-vii. Je vous remercie sincèrement pour les bons mots, pour les marques de votre sympathie et d'amitié que soulagent un peu mon coeur. Vous qui savez comme j'étais heureux à Capri parmi les bons Capresi, comme Capri était ma seconde patrie, me sentant moi-même Caprese, et j'en étais même fier, vous comprenez bien quelles ont été mes douleurs.
>
> Je n'oublierai jamais ce que vous et vos fils ont été pour moi. Du premier moment vous m'avez traité en ami, sans que je n'eusse jamais senti qu'en effet j'étais un 'maledetto forestiere.'
>
> Cet évènement triste pour moi a peut-être, le bon qu'il me rapproche encore plus à mes vrais amis de Capri.
>
> Le jour le plus heureux sera quand je pourrai retourner parmi vous, après que l'affaire triste ait trouvé une solution satisfaisante.
>
> Mille remerciements encore ecc.
> Toujours votre devoué
> F. A. Krupp

But there was to be no happy ending. Krupp considered legal action against *Propaganda* and *Avanti*, but did nothing. German papers took up the tale, cautiously at first. In October anonymous letters with clippings enclosed were sent to his wife Marga, who went straight to the Kaiser. Fritz, at his wits' end, agreed to the advice of friends that she should be declared not responsible and had her bundled off to an asylum in Jena. No paper dared use Krupp's name until 15 November, when the Socialist

Vorwärts published a long article under the headline KRUPP AUF CAPRI. Fritz immediately sued for libel and appealed to the Government to help him. The Chancellor agreed to charge *Vorwärts* with criminal libel, and the Imperial police were ordered to confiscate every copy they could find.

Meanwhile Krupp had asked Salvatore Lo Bianco to dispose of the farm around the Certosa and the tennis-court beside the Villa Krupp, both of which he had originally intended to present to the *comune*. 25-year-old Costanzo Vutto, who was one of Krupp's circle, bought the farm, while the *sindaco*, Federico Serena, acquired the tennis-court for a ridiculously small sum. Serena also wanted to get his hands on the wooded hillside above the Villa Krupp, but Lo Bianco refused and instead gave it to the *comune*, to enlarge the public park, and Serena's greedy conduct came in for harsh criticism.[31]

The tragedy drew quickly to its close. Krupp was sensitive and vulnerable, and no fighter. Neither the Kaiser's Government nor the Kaiser himself was prepared to intervene on his behalf. The appalling prospect of his wife being unjustly committed to an asylum and of acting out a lie with his two daughters was too much for him. He would rather die; and so he did. The actual cause of death is uncertain. His enemies said it was suicide; others that he died of an existing heart-condition, which had been aggravated by the strain of his last months. The official German news agency reported without comment: 'Villa Hugel, November 22. Exzellenz Krupp died at three o'clock this afternoon. Death was due to a stroke which he suffered at six in the morning.' There was no official autopsy, and the corpse, inaccessible to relatives, friends and the Krupp board of directors, was placed in a sealed casket, before being buried in the presence of the Kaiser, who acted as chief mourner and in a short oration said he had come 'to raise the shield of the German Emperor over the house and memory of Krupp', and castigated all those who had assailed Krupp's honour.[32]

In Capri Krupp was mourned by his many friends, and in his honour Arturo Cerio organised a memorial ceremony in the Villa Krupp, with fireworks, amidst a great concourse and with all the school children participating. Krupp left 15,000 *lire* (£588) each to Antonino Arcucci and to the Schiano brothers, and 12,000 *lire* (£471) to Mimì Ruggiero. Arcucci used the money to construct four magazines on the beach at Marina Piccola, which he rented to fishermen for the storage of their boats, nets and tackle, and behind the magazines later built a small house.[33] Krupp's legacies to the people of Capri, for which countless islanders and visitors have been grateful, were the *parco-giardino* and the wooded hillside above it, which reformist officials renamed 'Giardini di Augusto', but which everyone else continued to call 'Villa Krupp'; and the splendid scenic route of the Via Krupp down to Marina Piccola. Not inappropriately, the Via Krupp and the hillside of the Villa Krupp became and still remain a centre for male prostitution.

CHAPTER FOUR

Heyday of the Foreign Colony

It will be remembered that in 1902, the year of Krupp's death, another German, Wilhelm Allers, departed unwillingly and in a hurry. His villa was bought by an Englishwoman, Emilia, Lady Mackinder. She suffered from tuberculosis and in 1899, because the climate of Kenya was thought to be beneficial, had been taken there by her husband, Sir Halford John Mackinder. In 1900 the Mackinders returned to England but soon parted company. He was appointed Professor of Geography in the University of London, and she made for Capri, another resort for tubercular cases, with her mother, Mrs Ginsburg, and her two married sisters, Mrs Hinde and Mrs Spottiswood – 'all of whose husbands found them impossible to live with'. According to her sisters, Emilia 'was worn out by her husband; she put up with him too long. She tried her best; but he was continuously and steadily unfaithful to her.' On account of her tuberculosis she bought a strip of level ground all the way from the villa to Punta Tragara, so that she could take the air and enjoy the view without the exertion of descending to Via Tragara and ascending to the villa on return. Apart from this promenade she seldom left the house and delegated the running of it to Mrs Hinde.

All four ladies were dreadfully shocked by what went on in the rest of Capri. They looked hopefully for 'a steady injection of well-to-do English residents – nice people with families who played golf . . . they were so glad when the tennis-club was formed, because they hoped it would link the English people together in good healthy sport and be the prelude to golf-links. Mrs Hinde was sure that it was the absence of golf, more than anything else, which made Capri so bad for people's morals.' Meanwhile they maintained high standards in the Villa Tragara (no longer Villa Allers), made hay of other people's reputations, and each afternoon at 3.30, when everybody else was enjoying *siesta*, took afternoon tea in their summer-house. They were keen supporters of All Saints Church, which since the end of 1894 had ceased its wanderings from villa to villa and settled down in its own building on Via Pastena. Among regular church-goers was Mrs Fraser of the Villa Discopoli, and the Misses Calvert, who rented the Villa Croce (Wreford's old home) from the Scoppa family – 'a pair of massive old maids, with hips that swung to and fro like immense satchels, who wandered round Capri grunting at the bright colours worn by presumably respectable women, grunting and routing about in olive-groves for suitable views to paint'. Neither the Misses Calvert nor the Tragara ladies, however, cared for their churchwarden, Harold E. Trower.

Born in England in 1853, Trower had been a rather spoilt only son, who was educated at Harrow and then Balliol, where he read Law, but he never embarked on a legal career and drifted to Australia. Next he went to Belgium, and then Florida, where he grew oranges. In America he met and married Bertha Peck, who was already a widow with two daughters. Harold had very little money and relied on remittances scrounged off relations in England; Bertha had a modest income from a life-annuity derived from property in New York. When, therefore, they arrived in Capri in 1895, they could not afford to buy a house of their own and, after two short lets, settled down in the Villa Cesina (Wreford's other house) as tenants of the Scoppa family. Trower was not popular in Capri either with the foreign residents or the islanders. He combined an air of officious rectitude and a boisterous British-bulldog manner with a pair of unex-pectedly shifty eyes. Always rather pompous, given to making feeble jokes, he would never talk to passers-by, and on his walks about the island was usually to be seen with a parasol. Conscious of failure in early life, he was determined to enjoy what authority he could in Capri, as self-appointed leader of the English colony, as churchwarden and treasurer of All Saints, and, from 1900, as British Consular Agent. As well as being disliked by most of the congregation, Trower was usually at loggerheads with successive chaplains sent out year by year by the SPG to take services from November to May.

Trower grew fond of the island and, as a means of earning a little money, compiled *The Book of Capri*, which was a guide-book, 'not for the specialist on Roman remains and architecture, but for that larger class, the average traveller, who necessarily possesses little exact knowledge on these points'.[2] He extracted details of Capri's past history from earlier writers and enlisted the help of Jerome on Roman history and antiquities; of Ignazio Cerio, on geology and botany; and of Arthur Silva White, Secretary of the British Association, on climate.

Trower was concerned about the cruel practice of blinding quail to lure migrant birds into the nets. He was distressed that the Society for the Prevention of Cruelty to Animals had so far been unable to convict, since by Italian law the mere possession of a blind quail was not sufficient evidence; the owner of a bird had to be taken *in flagrante delitto* in the act of blinding it – and in Capri this was most unlikely to happen. Trower also thought that the islanders' treatment of their donkeys left a lot to be desired and started a competition for the best-kept donkey.

While Trower was working on his book, a fellow-countryman of very different character and as full of charm as Trower was without it arrived in Capri, partly in order to get away from his wife and partly to devote his wide-ranging and scholarly mind to meticulous research on an island which fascinated him. Norman Douglas, as he later liked to be known, was born in Austria in 1868, George Norman Douglass, three-quarters Scot and one-quarter German. His ancestry was noble, and the family derived a respectable income from ownership of local cotton-mills. Norman's father was killed in an accident when the boy was only six. His mother married again, and he spent his early years variously in Austria, Germany, Scotland and England. German was his nursery tongue and, at this time, English only his second language. After a brief spell at an English preparatory school, he went to Uppingham, which he loathed – 'herd-system and team-life . . . a mildewy scriptural odour . . . ; the masters struck me as supercilious humbugs; the food was so vile that for the first day or two after returning from holidays I could not get it down.'[3] In 1882 he delivered an ultimatum to his mother that, if she did not remove him from school, he would arrange to be expelled. The threat worked and the family moved forthwith to Karlsruhe, so that Norman could be installed in the Gymnasium. Here he remained for six years, taking a course in Classics, learning Italian, beginning Russian and becoming an accomplished pianist. At Karlsruhe too he developed his lifelong interest in natural history, botany and geology. In March 1888, with his elder brother, Johnnie, he visited Italy and, after passing through Naples, crossed over from Sorrento to Capri 'chiefly to procure the blue Faraglione lizard'. They were 'rowed out in a tiny boat in a rough sea by Carlo Spadaro, who, while they were feeling seasick in a tossing boat, climbed slowly to the top of the Faraglione rock and brought down six blue lizards which were added to Norman's collection. Next day Norman was on top of Monte Solaro, looking for Alpine swifts, but found none. It was too early in the season.'[4]

He left the Gymnasium in 1889 and at the age of twenty-one, with an income of some £2,000 a year, derived from his share of the cotton-mills in Austria, and enjoying the social life of London, decided to prepare for the Foreign Office. He entered it in 1893 and in the following year was posted to the British Embassy in St Petersburg. Russia was not a success. He had an affair with a Russian girl, whom he made pregnant, and to escape the vengeance of her parents was sent swiftly back to London. This was the first of his many quick skips across frontiers ('Burn your boats! This has ever been my system in times of stress'), and shortly afterwards he resigned from the Diplomatic Service.

In 1897 he went south again, bought the Villa Maya at Posillipo and resolved to become a writer. He had enough money to employ servants and lead the life of a gentleman, and in 1898 carried the notion of a settled life still further by marrying his first cousin, Elsa Fitzgibbon, who in February 1899 presented him with a son, Archibald. They visited Capri together in the autumn of 1901. He went there alone for part of 1902, and in August their second son Robert (Robin) was born in Austria. Douglas was in Capri again from February to May 1903, when he began a deep study of the island. The delights of Capri and Naples, where he still had the Villa Maya, demolished any thoughts he may have entertained of leading a conventional life. Not only did they induce a desire to be free of social restraints, but also encouraged his, so far latent, pederasty. In the summer of 1903, on a visit to Austria, he told Elsa that he would have to divorce her. In the autumn he returned to establish himself firmly in Capri and absorb himself in his researches, the first product of which emerged in 1904 in two monographs – *The Blue Grotto and its literature* and the *Forestal conditions in Capri*. Douglas had to work hard for his raw material. He acquired what books he could and sought out living sources. There was no available library or archive on the island apart from individual collections assembled by Ignazio Cerio and Thomas Jerome. Naples was his main source of material, and here he sometimes spent weeks at a time making extracts from 'worm-eaten books and chronicles and manuscripts not to be found save in this or that library in Naples'.[5]

For a short time Douglas rented part of the Villa Monte San Michele from old Prince Caracciolo, who occupied only the ground floor of what was still a humble villa, 'superintending his vines . . . and painting images of Madonnas and Saints for churches'.[6] Emilia, his wife, fat, untidy but still beautiful, and their ten children lived apart in the Villa Caterina, near the Quisisana. Unfortunately Prince Caracciolo was addicted to gambling. For this reason and because he also had a large family to maintain, he became progressively poorer. Whereas the elder children had been brought up by governesses and were tolerably well educated, the younger children's upbringing was sketchy. One day he was gambling in the Villa Monte San Michele with a visiting Englishman, Lord Algernon Gordon-Lennox, and lost a large sum of money which he was unable to pay. Being a gentleman, he felt that he had to honour the debt and offered Gordon-Lennox the whole of the property in lieu of payment. Gordon-Lennox accepted the bargain, and the Prince had to retreat to the Villa Caterina. The family was furious, tried to hush up the facts and branded Gordon-Lennox as a rich, harsh English aristocrat who had wronged the poor, helpless Principe.[7]

Gordon-Lennox the second son of Charles Henry, Duke of Richmond and Gordon, had been an officer in the Grenadier Guards, ADC to the Duke of Cambridge, and seen service in Egypt and South Africa. In 1886 he had married Blanche Maynard, a London beauty of the 'eighties, who fell in love with the property in Capri and, firmly installed there by the autumn of 1904, resolved to build a new and larger villa and create an extensive garden around the mountain. In 1905 they held a *festa* to celebrate the *vendemmia*, with a wine press made for them by Rolls-Royce.[8]

A notable addition to the foreign colony at this time were two American spinster friends, Kate and Saidee Wolcott-Perry. Kate's father Colonel Perry had commanded one of the forts in the north-west territories of the United States in the days when Indians still occasionally went on the war-path. He had become a widower, and his only daughter lived with him out there, independent of all but the roughest schooling, from the time she was 14 until she was close on 20. In 1860, when Kate was 23, her father adopted the daughter of a distant cousin who had died in poverty. Saidee Wolcott was nine when she entered the Perry family and forthwith she became the absorbing concern of Kate's life. The two cousins became totally devoted to each other, and, not wanting to be considered anything but actual sisters, hyphenated their names as Kate and Saidee Wolcott-Perry.[9] Before his death Colonel Perry had acquired a large tract of farmland in Iowa. At first it produced no worthwhile income, and the two friends had to get on as best they could. It was rumoured that Kate had opened some sort of school so that Saidee's education could be carried on without their separation; that they had managed a store; that they had run a brothel in New Orleans. Some of the Iowa land was sold, and with the money Kate and Saidee decided to explore Europe, leaving Mr Garfield, a trustworthy lawyer, to manage their affairs.

In 1897, in the course of their European trip, they set foot at Marina Grande and immediately knew that they had reached journey's end. They stayed at the old-fashioned Hotel Continental (later Metropole; now Palatium), which stood on the cliff-top at the west end of Marina Grande and commanded a fine view of the surrounding country. One day from the *terrazza* of the hotel their eyes fell on a small house with three shallow domes set in the middle of a vineyard above the marina, and decided that this must be their home. They sold enough of the Iowa property to buy the *casetta* and the attached land, which occupied the whole of the last bend down to the marina.

They started to build over and around the *casetta*, which was soon submerged under the new structure, and were able to move out and up into the new rooms and install the household staff (*famiglia*) below. The foundation stone of 1902 records that the builder was Luigi Desiderio, who was also currently building the Torre Quattro Venti for Elihu Vedder. It was not surprising, therefore, that the Hispano-Mauresque style was applied to the new construction, but in a unique manner. Between them, the two ladies and the contractor conjured up an extra-

Villa Torricella, home of Kate and Saidee Wolcott-Perry, c. 1910

Stammtisch at Caffé Morgano (Donna Lucia Morgano on left, Don Giuseppe Morgano in skull cap), by C. W. Allers

ordinary hotch-potch of Doric and Moorish columns, Romanesque and Renaissance arches, Gothic windows, and finally on top of the second floor, which was completed in 1907, Moorish towers and minarets. They called it 'Villa Torricella'. Mimì Ruggiero was commissioned to lay out borders, plant oranges, lemons, shrubs and trees, make paths, marble seats and flights of marble steps up and down the slope. At the bottom of the garden a door through the garden-wall gave access to the final stretch of Via Marina Grande and over it was built a terrace from which on 14 May they could sprinkle petals over San Costanzo, as he passed in procession between his church and the port. A small number of vines were preserved so that they could have the amusement of making two or three barrels of wine from their own grapes.

A guest-house (*foresteria*) was built away from the house, so that both hosts and guests could feel free to do as they liked. Over the fireplace of the guest-house were put tiles of *putti* riding dolphins and the inscription '*amore marittimo*', to flank a central design of two hearts entwined with the monogram WP. On the other side of the villa was their summer-house – a pretty version of the Temple of Vesta, which they had seen and admired in Rome – surrounded with newly-planted cypress trees. They devised a bogus Wolcott-Perry coat-of-arms, which was carved here and there in the house and used for a book plate. They took as their motto a line from an Epistle of Horace: 'Not bound to swear at the dictation of any master.'[10] And indeed they were completely independent. Thanks to the good management of their lawyer, they were already rich and growing richer. With the house built and furnished and the garden laid out, they were free to spend their money as they loved, on the entertainment of their friends – in the big *salone* and spacious loggia, which looked out over the bay, or on the porcelain-paved terrace. There were luncheon parties, dinner parties, dances which went on into the small hours and, when the guests at last reluctantly took their leave, Kate commenting 'Oh my, I do hate to have folks go. Isn't it too bad we can't keep it up for ever?'

Every Sunday afternoon members of the American and English colonies forgathered there for tea. There were, it is true, a few absentees. None of the Tragara ladies was among the guests, nor, any longer, Harold Trower. Kate had quarrelled with him 'over a commission she accused him of taking when she bought an extra piece of land for the villa', and had told him 'that she never wanted to see his mean, shifty, lying face inside her house again. This was her way when she quarrelled with anybody. She did not intend to be reconciled and she never was.'

Although Kate, 'with her ivory eagle's countenance and eternally fluttering fan', was considered by most people to be the more ruthless of the two – and it was she who did the open fighting – those who knew Saidee well, 'with her tight intolerant mouth and high cheekbones, her defiant smouldering eyes and her Quaker air', regarded her as more unforgiving than Kate and as the provider of 'fuel for the older woman's flames'. Their ruthlessness was not confined to the foreigners. On one occasion they had entrusted a large sum of money to a local lawyer to transact some business for them in Naples. He proceeded to lose the entire amount in one night's gambling. They remained deaf to the pleas of his friends and insisted on prosecuting him. He was found guilty; the money, however, was repaid and he was spared jail. Merciless to their enemies, they never refused a peasant or fisherman who appealed to their charity, and, like Krupp, generously bought a host of bad pictures from bad painters and hung them in the villa.

For Sunday tea, most of the elderly folk took carriages from the Piazza and down the meandering Via Marina Grande. For energetic guests there was the more direct, if steeper, route by steps and paths through the vineyards and lemon groves. After an enormous tea of éclairs, cream cakes, ices and finally *crème de menthe frappé*, the guests could take a walk round the garden and when they returned sink into wicker chairs on the terrace and consume as much whisky and soda as they wanted.[11]

On these palmy Sunday afternoons at the beginning of the century you would have found the American colony, which outnumbered the English, in full strength – Thomas Jerome, Charles Coleman, Elihu Vedder and his granddaughter Anita, Edith Andrews, and sometimes even her husband William, if he had grown tired of being an invalid and wanted to talk about *Faust* to a captive audience.

There was Alice Tweed Andrews (no relation of William), a rich 60-year-old widow from Cincinnati, with her daughter, Edith, and son, Vernon. They had spent some years in Europe, done a world tour, and Vernon's cosmopolitan education had been entrusted to a variety of tutors, including a half-caste Hawaiian engaged in Honolulu, from whom he learnt to dance the hula-hula. The family reached Capri in 1897, when Vernon was eighteen and decided to put down their roots in a friendly environment, where this tall, slim, good-looking and effeminate young man could live his life without embarrassment.[12] He is remembered by an elderly resident as one of the earliest wearers of tight trousers.

Mrs Nathan (Annie) Webb, short, dumpy and grey-haired, and with 'eyes that protruded from her head in a fixed stare like a *poulet effrayé*', was a rich New Englander from Portland, Maine, with no brains but that restless American temperament which is entirely dependent on other people and keeps its owner in perpetual motion. She flitted from country to country, always travelling by car because she could not endure the formalities and delays of crossing frontiers by train. She had a mania for doing kindnesses – giving money away, buying things she did not want from people who needed ready cash, and looking after protégés. She would choose and assemble her protégés in America during the winter and bring them over to Europe in the spring – one year it was deaf and dumb girls taken on a tour of Italy, and the next young singers with little talent but a burning desire to sing in opera, who were given singing-lessons at her expense. These visits usally took in Capri. Finding the Villa La Certosella just what she wanted for her flying visits to the island, Annie Webb bought it and had it enlarged and furnished for her benevolent purposes.[13] Eventually she presented La Certosella to Jan Styka, a Polish painter who came with his family from Paris. ('Clever people', wrote Norman Douglas, 'I never extracted a villa from her.') Styka renamed it '*Museo Quo Vadis*' and hung fifteen paintings on the *Quo Vadis* theme and some enormous canvases illustrating Homer's *Odyssey*. Entry to the museum was free to all Capresi and to artists of any nationality; others had to pay. Booming at them in French with a metallic Polish accent, Styka was merciless in waylaying victims of the Via Tragara and dragging them reluctantly into his gallery; people had 'even been known to leap walls and conceal themselves in thickets of prickly pears until he had passed'.[14]

Of the English colony, there was William Wordsworth, great nephew of the poet, who, after a career in the Education Department of the Indian Civil Service, had built himself a villa in the Moneta district, halfway between Capri town and Tiberio, where he was looked after by Miss Kennedy and her niece Isabel. 'Wordsworth' was impossible for the Capresi to pronounce, so they called him '*Vota e svota*'. Later he was just ' *'U Barbone*', on account of his long beard, and 'Barbone' is still the familiar name of the district around his villa.[15] There was Horace Fisher, who, after studying at the Royal Academy and winning a medal, settled in Anacapri in 1887 and year after year sent home Capri scenes for exhibition. 'Nebulous and deferential', as a fellow-Englishman described him, Fisher was glad to escape occasionally from his studio and had hopes of a commission to paint the Wolcott-Perrys' portraits. John Ellingham Brooks, penniless but a welcome guest, a good talker and a good listener, was seldom absent from their Lucullan luncheons and dinners.

There were two former Army officers living in Capri – Godfrey Henry Thornton and Colonel Bryan Palmes. Thornton's army career had been very short indeed. Starting as a second lieutenant (equivalent of ensign) in the Hertford Militia, he had been commissioned in the Life Guards in October 1877, but he resigned eight months later, while still only 21. Supported by a very substantial private income, he embarked on a largely aimless life, drifting about the Orient and the West Indies, climbing in Switzerland and living it up in London. He had musical talent and, after taking piano lessons with Clara Schumann, became an accomplished performer of the works of Chopin, Brahms and Liszt. Having spent most of his fortune on young men or on paying blackmail, he made for Capri, with his Bechstein grand, a wardrobe of the 'eighties, photographs and other mementoes, bought a cottage in Anacapri and did little else but practise the piano and spend what was left of his money in the same way as before. He was a very lonely man, not yet 50, and the tall handsome young officer with wavy flaxen hair and fair moustache had degenerated into a monumental, gross figure, with white moustache and globular light blue eyes. He enjoyed the Torricella tea-parties and, when asked, would play for the guests.[16]

Colonel Palmes had served with the Somerset Light Infantry in England and India from 1872 to 1883. In the Army, according to Douglas, he had been a notorious rake, using 'black silk sheets to show off the snowy amplitudes of the female form'. Well over six feet tall, with sparse sandy-coloured hair and walrus moustache, he arrived in Capri with his wife, Maimie, who was barely five feet high, and proceeded to build the Villa Mezzomonte at the east end of Via Sopramonte. He was excessively mean, and the builder of his villa, which turned out to be far too big for his needs, assured Douglas that he had 'never met a more close-fisted man to deal with'. Palmes was reputed to weigh out the sugar for the kitchen each morning and to sell water to the *contradini* at 10 *centesimi* a bottle. Once, when letting his villa, he cut off the water from the bathroom, and the tenants, finding no other use for it, kept chickens there. In the summer he would go to Switzerland where he paid for his meals by milking the Swiss peasants' cows. But Palmes was far from being what 'at first sight he seemed, the stock half-pay officer that haunts the continent for the sake of cheap living'. He was intelligent, an entertaining talker, with 'a rich, cynical, sesquipedalian wit . . . a good Russian scholar and possessor of a noble erotic library'. During their long years in Capri neither he nor his wife ever learned to speak Italian.[17]

The Wolcott-Perrys employed a young Neapolitan lawyer, Giovanni Galatà, who had married Gwenddolen Wickham, a Welsh woman, for the sake of her money and accepted the degree of subservience this situation demanded. Born in 1873, Gwen had been brought up in a conventional 'shooting-and-hunting' world of a Welsh county family – 'Go over anything', she said later. 'Take any gate anywhere. Just the same when I loved a man. Dozens of men in love with me. When I was a girl, no man could be in the room with me for two minutes without trying to make love to me. Upset tables and chairs.' Having forsaken this environment, she spent an adventurous period in the 'Nineties, which included a stay in Paris. There was an element of mystery about her which, had she wanted to, she was unable to dispel, because she was incapable of stringing together a long enough sentence to be intelligible. She had been married before, but whether they had divorced, or he had died, and how she came to marry Galatà, nobody in Capri ever discovered. They lived in the Villa

Farnesina, (later called Esperia), on Via Sopramonte, not far from Brian Palmes. Gwen, now in her early thirties, was a 'handsome woman. . . . ample in the style of feminine beauty that was so much admired when Edward VII was Prince of Wales', with auburn hair, classic features and luscious mouth. In character rather masculine and often overbearing, she could, according to her moods, be spiteful, cynical, amusing, eccentric, or hospitable; and in speech she was usually incoherent. Giovanni (John), two years younger, small, neatly-dressed, in her opinion an honest lawyer, would shrug his shoulders and let the tide flow over him when Gwen in one of her overbearing moods taxed him with infidelity. He certainly had other women and, being Neapolitan, liked them fat. 'Can't resist fat girls. Can't help it. Too excitable. Pants. Always know. Went to Mrs Andrews's last week. Thought he was pinching her Carmela. Pinched me instead. How I laughed! Serve him right. All Neapolitans the same. Come back to Capri black and blue after a day's shopping in Naples. . . . John made love to my dear Assunta. Turned her out at once. Wouldn't stand it. Caught him kissing her and he said he was sponging the statue of Venus. Such lies. Hate lies!' – was Gwen's summing-up on John. She never mastered more than a few words of Italian and even then mangled them terribly. John knew little English and had to learn Gwen's idiosyncratic version of elementary French in which she was accustomed to order him around – 'John! John! Vous venn ici. Vous dance with Sophie Grahame toute la swore. Vous comprong bang, John?' And when John protested that he had other assignations – 'Nong! Nong! Moi toojer raisins. Vous dance with Sophie Grahame, John. Dont argue. And her skirts – vous comprong – her gonnas must rester bass. Nong dwar kick her legs on haut. Vous fais comme see, or moi furious.'[18]

In these days at the beginning of the century the resident foreigners and the Capresi lived in separate worlds. The foreign residents did not talk Italian, and the Capresi did not speak English. Among the few 'natives' who met the foreigners were Roberto Serena, Costanzo's eldest son, a rising young lawyer who was respected for his brains and integrity and who dealt with their legal problems; doctors Vincenzo Cuomo and Pasquale De Gennaro, who attended to their medical needs; and the indispensable Don Giuseppe and Donna Lucia Morgano.

The Caffè Morgano had become the hub of the island's social life. Giuseppe Morgano was usually to be found outside seated by his crowded show-window of groceries, bottles and 'florid paintings of Capri turned out half a dozen at a time to attract Germans, to whom they sold like early tomatoes' – and these items also lined the walls inside. The main part of the *caffè* contained one big long table, seating 18 to 20 people; three smaller ones; a few square tables; a round table and settee in the corner; and, near the counters at the back, the *Stammtisch*, which was reserved for customers who wanted to talk to Donna Lucia or her son Mariano. Donna Lucia always sat at the counter beside it and by 10 o'clock in the evening and sometimes during the day too would doze off and snore quite loudly. Mariano was also inclined to nod over his ledgers, in which he recorded the loans which had been made to foreigners and the bills they had run up in the *caffè*. It was he who drew the beer from the keg which was imported direct from Munich and was handed round in beer-mugs by two maids and by Anna (Nannina), Giuseppe's daughter by his first marriage. To the right of the main saloon was a terrace raised a few feet above the level of the street, having a number of square tables with cast-iron frames and marble tops, and covered by a wistaria vine and pergola to give shelter from the noonday sun; and beyond this another terrace with billiards-table and more small tables. As well as meeting for conviviality, the foreigners bought groceries, drink, bottles of seltzer-water, pictures and even toys; and, as always, sought and usually received help and advice from Donna Lucia, Giuseppe and Mariano about their needs and problems.[19]

Giuseppe Morgano's brother Enrico continued to run an art gallery at the end of the Via Roma, just off the Piazza where local artists could exhibit their paintings. Among the more successful was Augusto Lovatti, who had emigrated from Rome many years earlier and specialised in marine subjects. A handsome and distinguished figure with a moustache and Van Dyck beard he was know as *Il signore della coppola rossa*, on account of the red beret which he habitually wore. He had been a friend of Krupp in the 1898–1902 period and through him had exhibited paintings at Essen. Soon after the completion of the Marina Piccola road in 1903, Lovatti built a large 'classical' villa – the Villa Flora (now Villa Mastrillo) – above the road just before the first hairpin bend. He took as his wife a girl who had been his model, and they had three daughters – Flora, Italia and Olga.[20]

The majority of Capresi were still poor and uneducated. Only the boys received any elementary education and would go to school only when their parents felt they could be released from work in the fields or helping with the fish. There was a handful of educated people like Giorgio and Edwin Cerio and Roberto Serena. The priests had an education of a sort in the seminary, but it was narrow and superficial. Don Giuseppe De Nardis, *parroco* since 1900, took a wider view of life than most of them. He made friends with English and American *anglicani*, usually with the aim of enrolling them into the Catholic Church. He did a good deed in 1906 by introducing half-a-dozen elderly Sisters of S. Elisabetta, with their superior, a handsome Prussian baroness at least twenty years younger than any of the Sisters, and established them in a house near the Certosa, where they did excellent work among the poor.[21]

Foreigners were looked up to by the islanders, first because they were rich, secondly because they were well-educated, and thirdly because they were usually worthy of respect. A certain prestige surrounded any foreigner, regardless of his morals and possible low-standing in his own country. In the eyes of the foreigners the islanders were welcoming and attractive people who provided them at very little cost with an agreeable life-style. As the number of foreign residents grew, so did the supporting services. New buildings sprung up. There were no architects in the strict sense of the word, but a number of contractors and builders, like Maestro Vito[22] and Luigi Desiderio, who built houses for foreigners, or for well-to-do Capresi, either to live in themselves or let to visitors. There was Mimì Ruggiero,[23] cheerful and energetic, who was pre-eminent as designer of attractive small gardens. He opened a nursery on Via Tragara and from it stocked the gardens he built, and ran a flower and plant-shop in front of the Quisisana. Carlo Ferraro, son of Don Giacinto, started the Farmacia Quisisana in Via Hohenzollern, opposite Hotel Pagano. There were rumours that he had obtained his diploma fraudulently, but nevertheless he was recognised as a *bona fide* pharmacist. The nearest (and first) approach to being an established jeweller was made by Filippo Lembo, a former *commissioniere* who had gone over to Naples to buy jewellery for young men to present to their *fiancées*. Later, wearying of these daily trips, he bought a stock of jewellery in Naples and set up business in his house in Via Madre Serafina.

A non-Caprese undertaking was the Anglo-Saxon Company, housed in the Villa Massimino in Via Camerelle[24] and, as the name implied, run by an Englishman – Alfredo Green, oldest son of Henry Thompson Green, the benevolent English doctor of Anacapri. Alfredo Green stocked English goods and stores for tourists and residents, developed and printed photographs, ran a circulating library and acted as house-agent. He had a wife in Naples, but lived over the shop with a beautiful *caprese* girl, Cristina Di Stefano. Two-thirds of the ground floor were occupied by the shop; the remaining third was a tea-room run by Cristina, where young Capresi met to play cards and talk to Cristina. Alfredo was 'a shrivelled-up little man with a grey-green face the colour of the faded prints which visitors who took their snapshots to be developed by him found that most of them had become a few months later. . . . Able to gossip with equal facility in English and Italian, he was the chief clearing-house of Capri scandal'. Whatever they may have felt about his liaison with Cristina, Mrs Hinde, her mother and sisters, found him useful both as a source of household supplies and of the gossip on which they thrived. Socially they regarded him as 'something between a dentist and a shop-keeper of the old-fashioned type'. Cristina too was useful because she was willing to escort old Mrs Ginsburg on her shopping expeditions to

Naples, where transport would be provided by one or other of Cristina's lovers.[25]

Cooks, servants and gardeners were readily available, and most foreigners recruited them through the Morgano family. Trower found local servants 'obliging and anxious to please ... superstitious, jealous and quick-tempered, but not malicious ... not very honest'. It was customary for foreigners to allow cooks to buy food and provisions for the household. This enabled the less honest to feed their own families as well as their employers. Household books tended to soar during religious festivals and whenever any unusual or scandalous event agitated the island.

Transport, if not on foot, was by donkey or carriage. There were one-horse carriages and carriages-and-pair, which plied between the Piazza, Anacapri and the two Marinas. In summer the horses were regularly freshened with sea-baths. Coachmen (*vetturini*) were a favoured race and were usually ready to drive foreigners up to Anacapri, if required, for amorous purposes beyond the actual journey.[26]

*

In April 1904 Kaiser Wilhelm II paid a visit to Italy. Beginning at Rome, he called on King Victor Emmanuel III and the Pope. After these formalities he boarded his gleaming white and gold yacht, the *Hohenzollern*, and cruised south to Sicily. The Sicilian visit gave members of his entourage a chance to call on Baron von Gloeden at Taormina. The Baron, although intended by his father for politics, had turned instead to the arts. Suffering from consumption, he forsook Germany for Southern Europe and in the mid-'eighties established himself at Taormina, first as an artist and then in the early nineties as a photographer. He began with landscapes for postcards, but soon turned to the much more lucrative subject of nude boys, mainly Sicilian, but also from other parts of Italy, including Capri. He sold the prints to tourists visiting Taormina and to a homosexual clientele all over Europe.[27] Amongst those who signed the Baron's visiting book on this occasion were the Kaiser's second son, Eitel Friedrich; his cousin, General Graf Hohenau; General von Moltke; and the Kaiser's close friend, Prince Phillipp zu Eulenberg. Having finished with Sicily, the Kaiser sailed north to Capri, curious to see the island which had caused the downfall of Fritz Krupp; he also wanted to call on Crown Princess Victoria of Sweden in Anacapri. He was met at Marina Grande by the *sindaco*, Federico Serena, and conveyed in the Quisisana's VIP carriage, not to Capri town but straight up to Anacapri to pay his respects to Victoria. The party then returned to Due Golfi, where young Giorgio Weber, who was watching the event with his parents, remembers how startled the Kaiser was to be hit on the right shoulder by a bouquet of flowers thrown by an over-enthusiastic girl. Again avoiding Capri town, he descended to the Marina and was away on the *Hohenzollern*.[28]

The doctors of Rome had become increasingly jealous of Axel Munthe's continuing success with the resident aristocracy and rich neurotics of all races. In 1902, unwilling to face their hostility any longer, he gave up his Roman practice and retired to Anacapri, where the Villa San Michele was all but complete. He had already bought Castello Barbarossa and the whole of the hillside between it and the Villa San Michele. One of his first acts was to remove the poles on which the peasants hung nets (*parate*) to ensnare the quail. Crown Princess Victoria of Sweden, who was tubercular and also suffered from ozæna ('smelly nose'), had been Munthe's patient since 1892 and spent every winter on the island. Initially she lived in a hotel but, wanting a permanent home, bought some land in Caprile, a hamlet south of the village, and commissioned a large villa. Munthe supervised the construction, which, however, proceeded slowly. Access was primitive and rough, and the village sewer ran along one side of the property. A peasant who had land bordering the site announced his intention of starting a pig-farm there, and had to be bought off.

The year 1904, with the hospitable Villa Torricella firmly established, seemed set to usher in halcyon days for the foreign residents. Everything was changed by the arrival of a young Frenchman, who precipitated a train of squabbles and misunderstandings from which the Anglo-American colony never recovered.

Jacques Fersen-Adelswärd,[29] was born on 20 or 21 February 1879, the son of Baron and Baronne d'Adelswärd, of mixed Swedish and French descent. The family was rich, thanks to the steel foundries established by his grandfather at Longwy, where the frontiers of France, Belgium and Luxembourg meet. In 1896 or 1897, on a family visit to Naples, Fersen met and made friends with another, older, Frenchman, and together they made a sortie to Capri.[30] They stayed at the Quisisana and during their sight-seeing visited the Villa Iovis. Here surmounting the ruins of the imperial villa they found the Church of Santa Maria del Soccorso[31] and the resident hermit, Fra Giovanni Serena, who showed them round the antiquities and told them of a plan to erect a statue of the Madonna in order to purge the memory of Tiberius; the donor was the Count of Caserta, a member of the Bourbon family.[32]

In 1898 Jacques inherited his father's title and a considerable fortune. He fancied himself as a poet and moved in the literary as well as social circles of Paris. In 1901 he formed an attachment with an aristocratic girl of seventeen and at the end of the year began his military service, which he did not enjoy. Soon afterwards he fell ill and during his convalescent leave

The Piazza, c. 1900

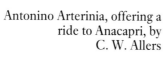Antonino Arterinia, offering a
ride to Anacapri, by
C. W. Allers

contrived to visit Capri again with his friend. On Tiberio they found the gilded statue of the Madonna already erected on its pedestal and due to be dedicated later in the year by the Archbishop of Sorrento. Near the Roman lighthouse and on the edge of the cliff was a new *caffè*, owned by an attractive young couple, Carmela Cerrotta and Raffaele Salvia. Carmela, then twenty-seven and as 'La Bella Carmelina' to become famous as an exponent of the *tarantella*, was already a skilled dancer, as was Raffaele. It was apt that two dancers should be living and performing near the hermit-chapel, because every year on 7 and 8 September, the eve and morning of the Nativity of the Blessed Virgin Mary, it was the custom among Capresi to spend the whole night on top of Tiberio and hear mass at dawn in the chapel, while Anacapresi did the same in the cliff-top church of Santa Maria a Cetrella. Ostensibly a religious occasion, it was more akin to Dionysus and vintage-time than to a festival of Our Lady. The furniture and cooking facilities of several *caffè* would be transferred *en bloc* to the darkness of Tiberio, to sustain the revellers on this very special *caprese* occasion – 'a night of fireworks and feasting, of drinking and dancing and music and love'.[33]

Fersen completed his military service in the autumn of 1902 and returned to his family in Paris. By now he was busily in pursuit of young boys and acquired a *garçonnière*, where he conducted himself with a marked lack of discretion. After evidence against him had been given to the police by a servant he had sacked, Fersen was arrested and the flat searched. In November 1903, together with a friend similarly involved, he was put on trial and charged with 'outrage to public morality' and 'incitement of minors to debauchery'. The first charge was dismissed. Both men were found guilty of the second and condemned to six months' imprisonment, a fine of 50 francs and five years' deprivation of family rights. As Fersen had already served his time and did not choose to appeal against conviction, he was released.

Abandoned by friends and relations, he returned to Capri in January 1904 and started a new life. He elevated himself to Count, dropped 'd'Adelswärd', the name under which he had been sentenced, called himself 'de Fersen', took a room at the Quisisana and decided to build himself a villa. He sought 'some romantic spot on a cliff . . . overlooking the sea', not too near the town, 'something remote and solitary'.[34] The place he chose was a bare stretch of rocky ground, supporting only a few carob-trees, on a cliff-edge below Tiberio, at the north-east tip of the island. From it there were magnificent views of Marina Grande and the Sorrentine peninsula – and the site was near his hero Tiberius. He bought it for 15,000 *lire* (£600) from the owner Salvia – one of the many citizens of that name who still inhabit the north-east corner of the island – and made plans to build a house and garden. He summoned the Parisian architect,

Chimot, to design the house, engaged the contractor Maestro Vito to build it and Mimì Ruggiero to lay out the garden. Chimot advised a villa in the local style, but Fersen wanted something that would be unique in Capri and chose the style of Louis XVI. As the land was on a slope, the architect decided to place the villa at the higher end, at the very edge of the cliff, with enormous rocks as its foundations. As it was also barren, large cisterns had to be excavated, to supply the house with water and nourish the profusion of trees – pine, ilex, bay and mimosa – which were to be planted.

Having set the wheels in motion, Fersen left Capri and visited Ceylon. He was enchanted by the beauty of the young Cingalese and was initiated in the pleasures of opium. Returning to Capri he lived in a rented villa, while his new home was being built. He engaged a valet, cook and gardener, and entered the social swim of Capri. Nothing of the Parisian scandal was known, and everyone was charmed by his good looks, prodigal hospitality and apparently limitless wealth. In June 1904 there was an unfortunate accident at the new villa. One of the workmen was killed by a fall of stone. Realising that Fersen, as initiator of the work, could be held responsible, Donna Lucia whisked him across to Sorrento before the *maresciallo* could collect himself and report the matter to the judge for a decision.[35]

From Sorrento Fersen went to Naples and then on to Rome. Here by chance he encountered and fell desperately in love with a 15-year-old building worker, Nino Cesarini.[36] The boy's family were very poor and, in exchange for a substantial payment, allowed Nino to become Fersen's 'secretary' and live with him in Capri. Having been assured that the matter of the dead workman had been settled and that he was no longer in danger of prosecution, Fersen returned to his rented villa and awaited completion of his new home on Tiberio. Although he and Nino were accepted enthusiastically by the Wolcott-Perrys, there was some reserve amongst other foreigners, and positive hostility on the part of Fersen's locally-recruited staff, who resented being subservient to a pampered young labourer, and furthermore a Roman.

The Christmas party of 1904 at the Torricella marked 'the culmination of Fersen's popularity; it marked also the end of an epoch, being as it was the last occasion on which all the foreign residents on the island met with goodwill to enjoy themselves together'.[37] In the early spring of 1905 unease about Fersen's relationship with Nino, mutterings about his vanity and ostentation, and vague rumours of a scandal in Paris, gave place to definite information that he had been in prison for offences against young boys. At first there was some confusion between 'miners' and 'minors'. Colonel Palmes observed that there was 'a fortunate paucity of mineral deposits on Capri, on which we may congratulate ourselves', and, when enlightened about Fersen's propensity, criticised the 'embarrassing state of amphibology' in which the English language exists.[38] As the real facts emerged, members of the foreign colony began to adopt attitudes, but cautiously at first. Many waited until Kate and Saidee Wolcott-Perry had taken up their position – and they were in something of a quandary. As lesbians themselves they understood male homosexuality and, whatever protestations of disbelief they may have voiced about the Paris reports and rumours about Fersen's activities in Capri, cannot have been ignorant of his true nature or shocked by it. On the other hand, they loved entertaining their friends and must have foreseen that, if they supported Fersen, they would alienate many of their usual guests. Later it was said that Saidee had romantic feelings about 'Count Jack', as she called him. Kate certainly did not; her attitude was entirely unsentimental and, once resolved on a course of action, she was ready to carry it through. Kate and Saidee let it be known that they did not believe any of the reports and gossip, that Count Jack had their unqualified support and that anyone who criticised him openly would immediately be struck off the Torricella list. This hurt, and many who enjoyed their hospitality kept quiet; some tried to enlighten the old ladies and suffered appropriately. Amongst the first casualties were Elihu Vedder and his granddaughter, Anita, who had been considered by hopeful match-makers as a possible partner for the Count. She was a self-assured young lady and, hoping to make the old ladies feel small, went down to Torricella armed with press-cuttings from Paris. She was bundled out and, with her 'grubby, dusty, fusty old grandfather', banned for ever from the Torricella. Next to suffer was Charles Coleman who, although outraged by Fersen's sex-life, also greatly enjoyed Torricella hospitality. Faced with the threat of being excommunicated by the Vedders if he continued to visit the Wolcott-Perrys, he dressed himself dandily for the occasion and went down one afternoon to remonstrate with them. All he got in return was a tirade about his own scandalous behaviour with young girls, and the slashing there and then with a tea-knife of a picture he had painted of Kate and Saidee 'in vestal contemplation of the Bay. . . . He pulled himself up from his chair, bowed ceremoniously to the two old ladies in turn, and, such an old man himself, walked very slowly and a little unsteadily over the pale blue porcelain tiles of that big *salone* for the last time.'[39]

The next person to play a part in the Fersen affair was Mrs 'Adelaide Edwardes', who in the spring arrived with a French maid and English butler and rented a villa for the season. She had known Kate and Saidee long before their arrival in Capri. Like Kate she was in her late sixties, 'but she had caulked all her wrinkles so carefully and painted her face so cleverly that at fifteen or even ten yards away men involuntarily straightened their ties when they saw her coming. . . . Besides being extremely rich, Mrs Edwardes was not in the least likely to covet Fersen for herself. She was extremely fond of young men . . . and she spent a great deal of her large income on them . . . but she liked men to be men . . . and her habit of presenting the handsome young mariners of Capri with gold watches was not entirely due to her anxiety that they should know the right time.' Her friends in Capri begged her to speak to Kate and Saidee and do what she could to enlighten them about Fersen. When she had accumulated enough gossip about Fersen's behaviour, she 'dressed herself in her brightest satin and longest plumes to pay her visit of remonstrance'. It so happened that Saidee was up at the Villa Lysis with her dear Count Jack. So she found Kate alone and told her frankly and in detail of Fersen's mode of life in Capri. If Saidee had been present, Mrs Edwardes would have been bundled out of the house in two minutes. Kate, however, listened, and for the first time her opinion of Fersen wavered. Soon after Mrs Edwardes had departed, Saidee returned, accompanied by Fersen, who, on being taxed with the accusations, swore by the memory of his dead father that all were untrue – and next day Adelaide Edwardes received one of those letters which Kate and Saidee 'wrote when they intended to make a quarrel perpetual'.[40]

The hard core of the opposition to Fersen lay with members of the Anglican congregation – Mrs Ginsburg, Mrs Hinde, Mrs Spottiswood, Lady Mackinder, Harold and Bertha Trower, and the Misses Calvert – but, as none of these was a member of the Torricella circle, this made little difference to social arrangements in the island. Although Giovanni Galatà was amazed that a man could be interested in anything except fat girls, he kept quiet, because he acted legally for both Fersen and the Wolcott-Perrys; Gwen took the view that Fersen could not help being 'one of those', and disapproved of the upset caused to Capri society. Vernon Andrews, who was thrilled that Fersen 'had been sent to prison as a martyr to temperament, saw more and more of him, did translations of his French poems and sat in Fersen's makeshift opium den listening to his unending rhetoric; but, to his great humiliation, Vernon could not smoke opium without being sick'.[41]

The affair had a stimulating effect on Thomas Jerome, who had by now abandoned his outdoor life and all other interests and activities, in order to devote himself to a monumental history of Roman morals – which was to include a rehabilitation of the Emperor Tiberius and be part of a larger study of the psychological causes which led to the downfall of the Roman Empire. Jerome rarely left his roomsful of books and notes in the Villa Castello, where Yetta kept a jealous eye on him, made herself so objectionable over his female friends that he stopped asking them, was capricious about admitting his men friends, and steadily ruined his health with her appalling cooking. One wonders how she dealt with American tourists who sought Jerome's help in his capacity as United States Consular Agent. On account of his official position and reputation as a widely tolerant person, he had no need to take sides and would discuss with members of both factions 'the niceties of the moral problems involved'. Douglas considered that the whole business was doing Jerome 'a great deal of good. Even the bawdiest passages in his authors were getting dusty, and one by one they're turning as fresh and rosy as the day they were written'.[42]

Douglas himself found Fersen extremely tedious – with his rambling poetry about his tortured emotions, his fluent but shallow talk, his passion for living 'on stage', his vanity and total inability to laugh at himself. Douglas, while deploring the division of the foreign colony into 'cantankerous little cliques', amused himself by stirring the pot. He would visit Coleman and 'relate the most appalling scenes of debauchery alleged to have taken place at the Torricella ... then, chuckling all the way to himself, would hurry down to the Torricella and regale the old ladies with an outrageous account of what went on daily at the Villa Narcissus'.[43]

Among Fersen's friends who remained faithful to him were Count Vitoldo and Countess Ephy Lovatelli, who lived in Via Roma in the Villa Weber, where the *pretura* now is. On one occasion, in order to escape his creditors, the Count had taken refuge in the island of Corfu, where he met and married Ephy, daughter of a Corfiot barrister. They came to Capri, where 'Ephy installed a big loom in her house at which she wove woollen cloth to Greek designs. She wore the material herself, and also sold it. . . . Her jewellery was copied from some of the treasures found at Mycenae and on her feet she wore sandals like those which shod the Victory of the Acropolis. Finally, an adept in theosophy, she corresponded with a leader of that sect who resided in America.'[44] A contemporary[45] describes Ephy as 'a very strange woman, eccentric, extravagant, with very little money, but she had rich friends and directed them in the spending of their cash'. She and Fersen took to each other immediately and she remained a friend until his death. Count Lovatelli is remembered as quick, clever and amusing. Carlo della Posta Duca di Civitella recalls seeing him in Morgano's giving a Fascist-style salute (long before Fascists had been thought of) to a lady of easy virtue and saying: 'I salute you as the only honest woman in Capri;' all the other women present were very shocked.

Maintaining the age-old tradition of Capri's hospitality, the islanders took Fersen in their stride, and welcomed the fact that he was building a sumptuous villa with local labour and spending money in the island; in consequence they were extremely polite to him. The Morgano family continued their role as guardians and helpers of foreigners and did not hesitate to speak in favour of the Count. Mariano, although only 25, was already fatter than his substantial father. Like all Morganos he was very greedy about food; in his case it was *pasta*, of which he ate enormous quantities. Various foreigners would appeal to him 'for help and advice, which he gave with a quizzical brusqueness that was compounded of insolence, condescension and goodwill'. The clue to his character was that, while he had inherited from Don Giuseppe 'cunning and cynicism and greed, his mother had mitigated those qualities with her own wisdom and benevolence'.[46] Federico Serena was friendly; Fersen had stayed for a short while in the Quisisana and was always a welcome guest there. Giorgio and Edwin Cerio, who prided themselves on their normal sexual appetites, privately disapproved of Fersen as a pederast, but so far had no reason to quarrel with him publicly.

By July 1905 the house on Tiberio was ready for occupation and at the north-east corner Nino, a building-worker again for a moment, laid the dedication-stone, on which was cut:

L'AN MCMV
Cette villa fût construite
par Jacques
Cte. Adelswärd Fersen
et dédiée
á la jeunesse d'amour.

He called his new home first 'La Gloriette', then 'Villa Lysis', after the young friend of the philosopher Socrates, who is commemorated in Plato's dialogue of that name. On the white marble architrave of the Ionic peristyle of the entrance was inscribed in large black marble letters AMORI ET DOLORI SACRUM. On the façade were the coats of arms of both Fersen and Adelswärd families, which gave him the excuse to assume a variety of titles – Count Fersen or de Fersen, Count Adelswärd-Fersen, Count Fersen-Adelswärd, or simply Fersen – he never made up his mind what his name really was, though in fact he was no more than a Baron.[47] In the autumn Fersen and Nino made a short visit to Paris, where they selected and sent back furniture for the villa.

In July and August 1905 Somerset Maugham was back in Capri with a friend Harry Philips. They stayed at the Villa Valentino, where Talmage White's son, Alberto, had just started a *pensione*, which he called 'The White House'. Maugham wrote of this visit: 'One does nothing from morning till night, yet the day is so short that it seems impossible to find a moment. . . . Capri is as charming as ever it was, the people as odd: everybody is very immoral, but fortunately not so dull as those who kick over the traces often are. Each foreigner has his little scabrous history, which far from being whispered into the willing ear, is shouted from the rooftops. . . . All the morning I bathe; after luncheon I sleep till tea-time, then wander among the interminable vineyards, in the evening read or look at the moon.'[48]

By 1905 tourism was bringing more than 30,000 visitors a year to Capri, still mostly Germans, and still mostly from autumn to spring and tending to avoid the hot summer months. Each visitor paid a small tax (*tassa di soggiorno*), which was divided between the Municipality, the poor, and the two Marinas. Part of the Municipal share was spent on the formation of the 'Pro Capri Society', which advised visitors how to spend their time, gave information about tariffs for carriages and donkeys, and collected data on tourism. The Society had an office, staffed by its clerk Anna ('Putti') von Rahden, at the corner of Via Hohenzollern and the short street which leads into Via delle Botteghe. Anna was the daughter of Baron Edward von Rahden, who had been an officer in the Kaiser's Imperial Guard – until he broke the rules by marrying a commoner. Forced to resign, he left Germany for Capri where with his family he spent the rest of his life. At first he and his wife tried to run a hotel. Unsuccessful in this he became the concierge of the Quisisana and in this capacity was a great success. Putti and her sister Maria (Nukkè) earned what they could as nannies to foreigners' children.

Since 1892 an organising committee (*comitato promotore*) had been supervising the construction of a funicular railway between Marina Grande and Capri town. There was pressure for the railway from all quarters. First, there were the islanders, who wanted quick and easy transit for themselves and what they carried between the town and the port. For day-trippers the visit to Capri was all too short. Steamers left Naples at 9 a.m., stopped first at Sorrento and reached Marina Grande at about 11 o'clock. After a short pause to disembark passengers, steamers moved on to the Blue Grotto, where small boats were waiting to take tourists into the cave. They returned to Marina Grande a bit after midday and left again for Naples at 4 p.m. Allowing time for disembarkation and re-embarkation in small boats to and from the short pier, visitors had barely three hours ashore, much of which time would be needed for a carriage to take them up to the town and back. For hotel visitors the Quisisana usually sent down a stage-coach; for Royalty and other VIPs there was a magnificent victoria. Visitors to other hotels, who in the summer included many Neapolitans, took carriages as available. Building materials, food and supplies were still carried up mainly by hand or on women's heads.

The *funicolare*, which was built and managed by an Italo-American company, the Società Imprese Pubbliche e Private Ischia e Capri (SIP-PIC), formed mainly for this purpose, ran every half-hour during the day, was driven by its own electricity-plant, which had been installed at the Marina Grande end. Electricity was soon extended to the town itself, the

Young Capresi, 1898, photographed by Baron von Gloeden. *Courtesy of Carlo Knight*

'Count' Jacques d'Adelswärd-Fersen, c. 1907. *Courtesy of Concetta Salvia and Manfred Gräter*

The statue of Nino Cesarini in the garden of the Villa Lysis. *Courtesy of Centro Caprense Ignazio Cerio*

first building to get it being the Hotel Gaudeamus in Via Fuorlovado, where the director of the SIPPIC was living; bit by bit current was extended to hotels, houses and streets, to replace candles, kerosene lamps and acetylene gas. There was an agreement that after 25 years (i.e. in 1932) the *comune* would take over the *funicolare* and the electricity plant.

As the flow of tourists increased, Serena decided to enlarge the Quisisana, where pension terms had risen to 9–15 *lire* (7–12 shillings) a day, and in 1907 began to build a long west wing. At the same time his political and business rivals, Manfredi and Michele Pagano, converted the nearby Villa Romana, which they had bought at the beginning of the century, into an annexe of the main hotel. Giuseppe Morgano continued to prosper and added the Hotel Continental, in what is now Via Croce, to his holdings. He already had plans to double its size and from the new building, which was to be called Tiberio Palace, to be able to 'piss' on the flat roofs of the Quisisana below.[49]

As yet there were no banks in Capri and money-lending continued to be done privately by Capresi with cash to spare, like the Ferraros, Morganos and the Cerio brothers. Since every moneylender was on the look-out for acquiring new property, borrowers had to watch their step, or they might find themselves signing away their houses and land. The only foreign *usuraio* was Frederick Wedekind, rumoured to have been the black sheep of a German banking family and exiled by his relatives to Capri. First he bought and lived in the *fortino* at Marina Piccola; later he moved up to more spacious quarters in Villa Speranza at Due Golfi. He would lend small sums of money to anyone in need who could be trusted to repay his debts in small weekly instalments at interest of 12 to 15%. He took as his common-law wife an Anacaprese girl and as an agent used a relative of hers to undertake the daily rounds of his debtors.[50]

In January 1905 Joseph Conrad arrived in Capri with his wife and son, completely exhausted by the writing of *Nostromo* and seriously embarrassed financially, hoping that a few months in Capri would restore his health and speed his pen to write a Mediterranean novel. Ignazio Cerio gave him access to papers about the French and English struggle of 1806–8. Conrad also toyed with the idea of a book about Naples, Capri and Sorrento, aimed at English and American tourists. Everything, however, went wrong. He suffered from influenza, bronchitis and an obstinate insomnia, hated everything about Capri, and wrote nothing but querulous letters to his friends. At the beginning of May, three days before he departed, he told Ford Madox Hueffer:[51]

This climate, what between Tramontana and Scirocco, has half killed me in a not unpleasant languorous, melting way. I am sunk in a vaguely uneasy dream of visions, of innumerable tales that float in an atmosphere of voluptuously aching bones. *Comprenez-vous ça?* And nothing, nothing can do away with that sort of gently active numbness. The scandals of Capri, atrocious, unspeakable, amusing, scandals inter-national, cosmopolitan and biblical, flavoured with Yankee twang and the French phrases of the *gens du monde*, mingle with the tinkling of guitars in the barbers' shops and the rich contralto of the *buona sera, signore* of the big Mrs Morgano as I drag myself in an inwardly fainting condition into the café to give some chocolate to *ma petite famille*. All this is a sort of blue nightmare traversed by stinks and perfumes, full of flat roofs, vineyards, vaulted passages, enormous rocks, pergolas, with a mad gallop of German tourists *lâchés à travers tout cela* in white Capri shoes, over the slippery Capri stones, Kodaks, floating veils, strangely waving whiskers, grotesque hats, streaming, tumbling, rushing, ebbing from the top of Monte Solaro (where the clouds hang) to the amazing rocky chasms of the Arco Naturale – where the Lager beer bottles go pop. It is a nightmare with the fear of the future thrown in.[52]

Norman Douglas on the other hand, who met and made friends with Conrad during his visit, was enjoying the island and hard at work. In July 1906 he published four more monographs – on *Fabio Giordano's Relation of Capri*; *The Lost Literature of Capri*; *Tiberius*; and *Saracens and Corsairs in Capri*. In addition to all this he was accumulating material about Suor Serafina, San Costanzo, the Faraglioni lizard, Capri as viewed by writers of the Romantic period, the Anglo-French occupation, the Arcucci family and the Certosa, the change of place-names, the Sirens, and various archaeological matters.[53] He thought he might 'browse a lifetime away among such literature as might be expected to deal with the island, producing every now and then some fresh monograph illustrative of its historical and other curiosities'. He was running short of money, however, and learnèd monographs had no popular appeal. If, for the sake of some cash, he had intended to produce a tourist-guide of Capri, which he would have done very well, he had been anticipated in 1906 by Trower's *The Book of Capri*, which covered well enough for the average visitor most of the meat of Douglas's published or projected papers. He had other reasons for disliking Trower. In character they were completely opposite, and Trower, who disapproved of Douglas's pursuit of young boys, sided with Elsa in the divorce proceedings which were grinding on. Douglas took his revenge ten years later by portraying Trower as 'Mr Freddy Parker', the seedy British remittance-man of *South Wind*.[54]

On 4 April 1906 Vesuvius erupted with great violence and ejected an immense amount of material. Naples was plunged into darkness and ashes even reached Capri. The action continued for several days and was assiduously recorded by Coleman from his studio.[55] When the eruption subsided, he saw that the volcano was considerably reduced in height, and the symmetry of its cone, which had collapsed into the mouth of the crater, completely shattered. Moreover, in place of its robust billowings, it had become almost lifeless, giving out no more than pathetic little wisps of white smoke. He never painted Vesuvius again.

CHAPTER FIVE

Maksim Gorki and Compton Mackenzie

The revolutionary movement in Russia, which had been smouldering for many years, flared up after Russia's defeats in the Russo-Japanese war of 1904. Agitation culminated in the general strike of September 1905 and the Moscow rising of December, which was, however, quickly crushed. Amongst those arrested was the 38-year-old writer Alexey Maksimovich Peshkov, known as Maksim Gorki. Born in Nizhni Novgorod in 1868, he had suffered a wretched childhood and adolescence, keeping himself alive with a variety of odd jobs, until he discovered that his gifts lay in literature. He adopted the pen-name Gorki (meaning 'bitter') and soon became a successful writer, drawing his material from the hardships of his early years. He was invited by the publisher Pyatnitskiy to join his firm 'Znaniye' (Knowledge), and this further increased Gorki's standing. He became a Marxist and a member of the Social Democratic Party. When the party split in 1903, he joined the Bolshevik wing and regularly gave it a part of his earnings. His arrest after the Moscow rising caused an outcry both in Russia and abroad, and a petition secured his release. In the summer of 1906, with other dissident 'intellectuals', he sought refuge abroad.

Gorki left his wife and son in Russia, and took with him his mistress, Mariya Feodorovna Gelabushkaya (known as 'Andreyeva' and also married) and his 22-year-old natural son Zinovi Peshkov. They paid a brief visit to England, then crossed to the United States, where he and Andreyeva were deported back to Europe, as double adulterers guilty of 'moral turpitude'. In October 1906 they arrived in Naples, where, as a distinguished writer of the left, Gorki was welcomed by the Italian Socialist Party. On 6 November they crossed to Capri, lodged for a time at Marina Piccola and then rented Eduardo Settanni's Villa Blaesus on the hillside above Krupp's *parco-giardino*. Gorki found in Capri both a climate which was kind to his lung complaint and congenial surroundings in which to write. The royalties from his earlier writings and money from Pyatnitskiy's business enabled him to live comfortably and to subsidise the penniless Russian refugees who followed him to the island. The Gorki trio – Maksim, with his sallow, grave, resolute face, high cheek bones and bushy moustache; Andreyeva's seductive beauty; and the boy's good looks and charm – were an immediate success in the island. The Russians were frequently to be seen in the Caffè Morgano, where they drank endless cups of coffee, talked incessantly and played game after game of chess – often outnumbering the German princelings, bankers, writers and romantics, who for so long had dominated the *caffè*. Gorki did what he could to pay the Russians' debts at Morgano's and in their lodgings, and put them up at his own home when their local credit was exhausted.

Among the Russian refugees was Dr Wigdorchik, a dentist, who escaped from Siberia and arrived in Capri with 5 *lire* in his pocket. At this time the only dentistry practised in Capri was that of Enrico Morgano, who combined politics and a picture gallery with an ability to extract teeth; and Wigdorchik was welcomed as the first qualified dentist. Later his family – wife, son and daughter – joined him, together with a musical cousin of Mrs Wigdorchik, Rosa Raisa. Rosa, born in Bialystok in 1893, had fled from Poland when only fourteen years old, to escape a pogrom, and found her way to Naples. She had a promising voice, and Wigdorchik paid for her training in Naples. After successful concerts in Rome and Parma, Rosa appeared at Covent Garden, and in Chicago where she sang year after year. In 1924 Toscanini engaged her for La Scala, Milan, and she became one of the great dramatic sopranos of the day. Rosa remained devoted to the Wigdorchiks and often, when opera commitments allowed, came to Capri to see them.[1]

The Italian authorities were worried about the security aspects of this mini-invasion and instructed the Commissioner of Police, Domenico (Mimì) Tiseo, to keep tabs on the Russians. He already had the task of safeguarding Crown Princess Victoria in Anacapri, a commitment which assumed added importance when she became Queen of Sweden in 1907. For a short time Tiseo's life was further complicated when Queen Alexandra of England paid a short visit to Capri and also had to be protected from the spectre of Bolshevism. Tiseo, one of the very few locals who frequented the Caffè Morgano, had no objection when his surveillance duties took him there. He considered that the Russians were an economic rather than a security problem, and he was more interested in earning from Queen Victoria the order of chivalry which she had promised him as a condition of being left in peace.

In 1907, feeling the need of a larger house, Gorki rented the Villa Behring, so named because for several years it had been the home of Emil von Behring, the German bacteriologist, who became famous for his work in devising immunity to tetanus and diphtheria. Painted a rich deep red, it was renamed by Gorki Casa Rossa, and here he produced a stream of novels, short stories, plays and critical studies; housed destitute Russians; and took Italian lessons from the schoolmaster, Luigi Messanelli. A 'people's tribunal' was set up and amongst the cases which it investigated was that of Fedor Ivanovich Chaliapin, Russia's most distinguished operatic bass, who, although already a member of the movement, had unwittingly joined the chorus of *Boris Godunov* in kneeling before the Tsar at the Marie Theatre, and was charged with betraying his revolutionary ideals. After a moving defence by his friend Gorki, Chaliapin was acquitted and continued to delight the island with his singing.

In Capri, Federico Serena was still *sindaco*, and the Quisisana increased in size and prosperity. His namesake, Fra Giovanni Serena, hermit of Santa Maria del Soccorso on Tiberio for many years, died in 1904. No hermit could be found to replace him, and care of the chapel was entrusted to yet another of the clan, Don Costanzo Serena, a fat, jovial *bon vivant* and gossip, who liked the pleasures of Capri town, and whose duties on Tiberio were confined to saying Mass there on Sundays, usually combined with a bibulous picnic. Don Costanzo's father was *commissioniere*, in which capacity he visited Naples daily and carried out errands for islanders and foreigners. Filippo's nickname, which was inherited by the priest, was 'Sciabolone' (long sword).

In the winter of 1905 Fersen and Nino returned to Capri, to arrange the furniture, screens, rugs, pictures, porcelain, sculptures and books which had been sent from Paris. His staff had been augmented by a French chef and a former housekeeper at the French Embassy in Turkey, who quickly imposed her will on the unruly boy-servants, who now included two Cingalese.

Some months earlier Fersen's sister, Germaine, had become engaged to the Marchese Bugnano, a Neapolitan who was Member of Parliament and junior Minister in the Government. The marriage was fixed for October 1906 in Paris, and the honeymoon would be spent in Naples. Taking a hint that a visit to China during this period would be beneficial, this is exactly what Fersen and Nino undertook. He did not come back empty-handed. In Tientsin he bought a collection of 300 opium pipes – in gold, silver, ivory, rock crystal and hard stone – said to have belonged to an emperor of China and to be the finest of its kind in the world. In paying a very large price for the collection, he was encouraged by the fact that by now Nino had also acquired a taste for the drug.

Shortly after the wedding Germaine, with her mother, the Baronne d'Adelswärd, and her younger sister, Solange, visited Jacques at the Villa Lysis, and, to save embarrassment, Nino was temporarily boarded out. Nino was *au fond* a normal and vigorous youth, who was beginning to chafe at his exotic life in Fersen's gilded cage, and, when opportunities occurred, tried his luck with the girls. He was very good-looking, with straight nose, large chestnut-brown eyes, curled lips and long lashes, which were black like his hair; and at 17 he was physically well-developed. Fersen thought that the time had come to immortalise his youthful beauty in sculpture and commissioned Francesco Ierace, a leading Italian sculptor and fortunately working in Naples, to make a life-size bronze of the boy, nude and seated on a triton shell, which was placed in the garden of the villa.[2]

In November 1906, the 31-year-old German writer, Rainer Maria Rilke, who was striving 'to become a real poet, a pure poet, an absolute poet at whatever cost', accepted an invitation from his friend Frau Alice Faehndrich, owner of Villa Discopoli in Via Tragara, to visit Capri, where he hoped to concentrate on serious work. Living alone in the guest-house of the villa, he worked at his poetry and wrote copious letters to his wife Clara and a few friends – his aim being to remain 'unnoticed, unseen, invisible'. The Capri which he found did not appeal to his introspective and fastidious nature – 'the tourists are for the most part gone, but the marks of their stupid admiration . . . are so blatant and cling so tenaciously that even the tremendous storms that occasionally take the island in their jaws cannot sweep them away. Always I grow melancholy in such beauty-spots as these, faced with this obvious, praise-ridden, incontest-able loveliness. . . . But that says nothing against the people; they were at all events sincere and industrious. . . . But have you ever seen, when men acted or let themselves go in the direction of pleasure, relaxation and enjoyment, that they came by any pleasant results?' Going hopefully to the Piazza on New Year's Eve, for midnight mass, he found the church closed, 'as though it had been shut for centuries'. At a local wedding he 'saw the *tarantella* danced three times. What a dance! as if devised by satyrs and nymphs, old and somehow rediscovered and rearing up all behung with primordial memories: cunning and wildness and wine, men with goats' hoofs again and girls from the clan of Artemis'. He found happiness walking in the wilder parts of Anacapri – 'that ultimate Anacapri . . . really lovely and wild . . . and it is something to see even a shepherd. And the houses fall behind and where the few stony paths stop there is sea once more . . . no landscape could be more Greek, no sea more brimming with ancient horizons'. At the beginning of May he spent an evening with Gorki – 'The melancholy lamp-light fell upon everything equally without picking out anybody in particular. him, his present wife and a couple of morose Russian men who took no notice of me. . . . As a democrat Gorki speaks of art with dissatisfaction, narrow and hasty in his judgements; judgements in which the mistakes are so deeply dissolved that you are quite unable to fish them out. At the same time he possesses a great and touching kindness . . . , and it is very moving to find on his completely unsophisticated face the traces of great thoughts and a smile that breaks through with an effort, as if it had to pierce a hard unsym-pathetic surface from deep within. Curious, too, was the atmosphere of undefinable, anonymous egalitarianism which you entered as soon as you took a seat at the round table. It was like a limbo where these exiles lingered, and their eyes seemed to turn back towards the earth which is Russia, and which it appeared so utterly impossible ever to revisit. . . .'[3]

By the end of 1906 Norman Douglas had wearied of his antiquarian researches and was very short of money. His brother had sold the Austrian property and in place of an income from the mills Douglas had received a lump sum, which soon vanished with his wife's extravagance and his own mismanagement. In 1907 he published the last two of his monographs – *The Life of Suor Serafina di Dio* (which 'had called for an absurd amount of research') and *Some Antiquarian Notes*. He was still charmed by the island and anxious to establish a base on it.

The evidence relating to his property ventures in Capri is scanty and confusing.[4] He made three attempts to make a home for himself. The first was probably the Caterola property bought at a public auction in Naples for 5,000 *lire* (£200). It consisted of a small derelict farmhouse, set in several acres of olives and vines above the steep cliffs on the north-east side of the island. Here he planted oaks, ilexes, cypresses and pine, and buried seeds of the native palm, which, once common, had by this time almost vanished from the island.[5] He did nothing to improve the building, however, never lived in it, having become aware of the disadvantages of the cold and damp which affect north-facing houses in Capri, and sold it to William Andrews, who in turn let it to a peasant. Next, probably in 1904, he started to build a house on the east side of Castiglione. When only the lower floor of the Villa Daphne was complete the builder, whom he had recruited on the mainland, was arrested, taken back to the mainland and charged with the double murder of a mother and daughter. No further work was done on the house. Soon after this set back and certainly before October 1904, Douglas bought an inaccessible, cup-shaped hollow, high up on the sheer south-west face of Castiglione and graced by an attractive cluster of Aleppo pines, which he had seen and admired from the Marina Piccola road. The site, perched high above the marina, could only be reached by scrambling down from the top of the Castiglione or across the boulder-strewn tract on its western slope, called Petrara. As soon as he had bought the site, he had a causeway built from Due Golfi along the west side of the hill to his property. Across the causeway he set a gate to block access and hired a builder to begin work on a simple villa. The Petrara property was his main preoccupation in 1907, the year in which his divorce proceedings were approaching finality.[6]

In August 1907 Douglas made his first visit, lasting a week, to Calabria. It was a case of love at first sight, and he was to revisit the region many times; he was particularly taken by the Sila, the mountain-block east of Cosenza, which reminded him of his native Scotland. He had already divested himself of responsibility for his two young sons, Archie and

Robin, and in March 1908 obtained his divorce in the High Court of Chancery. Forty years old, overjoyed at his freedom from domestic entanglements and no longer having to watch his behaviour for the sake of the Court proceedings, he became a professional writer – as much for financial reasons as any – and embarked on the unconventional way of life which he was to follow until the end of his days. Douglas was not only homosexual, but also pederast in the true sense of the word. 'A child,' he wrote in *Alone*, 'is ready to embrace the universe. And unlike adults, he is never afraid to face his own limitations.' His favourite age in boys was 12 to 14. His attachment to these children was often heartfelt and genuine, and, if the relationship involved love-making, he saw nothing wrong in it. With an understanding of the young, to whom he never 'talked down', able to charm them, possessing much worldly wisdom, and gifted as an educator, he exercised a beneficent influence on the boys he liked, and some remained friends in later years. His own verdict on himself was: 'No boy I have cared for has failed to profit from our relationship.' Other adults, apart from his homosexual friends who tended to be reticent about his pederasty, usually regarded things differently; and there were inevitable clashes with the law, which on occasions compelled Douglas to move quickly and involuntarily from one country to another.

In May 1908 Douglas moved to Nerano, a hamlet of Massa Lubrense, perched above the Gulf of Salerno. Here, attended by a peasant-boy, 'a laughter-loving child', whose surname was Amitrano, he began to write his first book, *Siren Land*, and made plans for a second book – on Calabria. Thanks to the friendship of Joseph Conrad, Douglas also began to gain a foothold in the literary circles of London, with articles in the *Cornhill* and *English Review*.[7]

At 5 a.m. on 28 December 1908 an earthquake of appalling severity shook southern Calabria and the eastern part of Sicily, completely destroying Reggio and Messina, eight smaller towns and many villages; in Messina the horror was augmented by a tidal wave. The catastrophe was the greatest of its kind ever recorded; about 150,000 people were killed and countless numbers injured. Isolated in Nerano Douglas did not hear full details of the disaster until he visited Capri in May 1909. To supplement the help that was flowing in from all over the world, he decided to collect money privately in Capri and hand it over in person to some of those who had suffered. He approached only the foreigners, 'since the Italians had their own channels for rendering aid, if they cared to do so'. Most of the foreigners gave something, the 'poorer folk . . . more generous relatively speaking than the wealthy ones', but the total was not impressive. Annie Webb, touched by his account of the catastrophe, 'gave twice as much as the rest of them put together. No doubt she could afford to give it. But the point to note is that she did afford to give it.' Having assembled the money, he set out to deliver it. To his surprise, he was joined at the last moment by Vernon Andrews, who did not seem at all the type for a wild tramp in Calabria, and at the beginning of June the two set off for Reggio and Messina. Having distributed the money to victims on the spot, they explored the deep valleys and pine-clad hills of the region. Vernon 'proved a good companion; he could walk; he could tell improper stories about his life as a boy in Honolulu; he could eat things swimming in grease'. At one point, after a picnic lunch, he 'drew forth from his bag a mysterious box and began, mirror in hand, to powder his cheeks and touch up his lips with rouge'. The muleteer was speechless; as a rough mountain-fellow he had never seen women do such a thing, let alone a man.[8] Returning to Capri, Douglas wrote an eye-witness account of the devastation in Messina for *Cornhill* and continued to work on *Siren Land*. He was now very short of money and all work on the Petrara site had to be stopped, but, hoping for better times, he held on to the property.

Gorki meanwhile developed his revolutionary campaign, which aimed especially at increasing 'the cultural forces of the masses'. More and more Russians came to Capri to debate how these aims could be achieved. One Bolshevik, however, thought that Gorki was too reasonable and too soft, and that there was altogether too much talk. Vladimir Ilyich Ulyanov, known as Lenin, had left Russia in the winter of 1907 and in April 1908 accepted an invitation from Gorki to visit Capri. Lenin had discussions with Gorki and his companions, played chess and tried his hand with a fishing line. He enjoyed the fishing but found it difficult to judge the right moment to pull up the line – the moment, that is, when the fish takes the bait and gives two or three tugs on the line to announce its presence. After Capri he visited Pompeii, Vesuvius and the Naples Museum. Later his wife, Krupskaya, records that Lenin had little to say about this visit and talked of the beauties of the sea and of the local wine rather than discussions about sensitive topics. Gorki naïvely treasured the memory of 'another Lenin, an excellent companion, a happy man, lively and tireless in his interests', and completely failed to detect the yawning gulf between the 'intellectuals' in Capri and Lenin's absolute commitment to the 'proletariat'.[9]

Although he never mastered the Italian language, Gorki was held in high esteem by the islanders, who presented him with some valuable parrots, of which he was very proud. In the middle of 1909 he left the Casa Rossa and rented two houses beside the Via Mulo, half-way down to Marina Piccola – the Villa Pierina, for himself, and the Villa Serafina next door, to accommodate destitute Russians. To feed and pay these refugees and act generally for him, Gorki employed Cataldo Aprea, member of a family, originally Sicilian, which had migrated to Capri from the Sorrentine peninsula. In August, at the marina itself he rented the house which young Antonino Arcucci had built with Krupp's legacy, and established in it a 'School of Revolutionary Technique for the scientific preparation of propagandists of Russian Socialism'[10]. Leaders of the school, with Gorki, were Anatoliy Lunacharskiy, Alexander Malinovskiy (Bogdanov) and Gregori Aleksinskiy. Lunacharskiy was preoccupied with the problem of fitting religion into the new revolution, had a feeling for art and antiquities, and liked to conduct parties of Russian exiles round Pompeii, Herculaneum and the Naples Museum. Bogdanov was wrapped up in 'empiriomonism', and Aleksinskiy, a doctor and philosopher, in the 'ultimatists'. Gorki himself espoused a religio-philosophical trend called *Bogostroitelstvo* ('God-building'). Lenin, now in Paris, had no time for all this high-flown nonsense and the academic emphasis of the school as a whole. Nevertheless he was able to increase his own influence in the revolutionary movement, when five students and one organiser walked out of the Capri school and, as convinced Leninists, joined him in Paris. The school itself was closed down in December.

Russians of a different kind were Barbara Riola, a rich aristocrat, and her daughter Olimpia ('Lica'). Cav. Gennaro Riola, who was in the Italian Consular Service, had met Barbara in Russia and taken her to live in Naples, where Lica was born in 1890; a second girl, Olga, followed in 1895. Barbara was very suspicious of Italian hygiene and in particular of its milk, and used to keep a pet cow which travelled with the family wherever they went. In 1908 Olga died of typhus in Naples. Her mother was distraught, and relatives advised a change of scene, but she loved the area and, as a compromise, went to live in Capri and rented the Villa Blaesus. Lica, eighteen years old when they settled in Capri, was a strikingly attractive girl, with deep blonde almost red hair (*bionda tiziana*) and vivid green eyes – fresh, trim, debonair and full of life. She liked tennis and skating and found Capri rather restricting. She was also unlucky in love. She had an affair with a rich young man on the mainland,[11] until one day she read in the newspaper that he had killed himself for another woman's sake, who in turn had taken her own life. All Lica could do was to arrange for both to be buried decently, and to grapple with her sorrow.

Across the water, but not unknown to Capri, was the Principessa Helène Soldatenkov, who lived in opulent splendour in the Villa Siracusa at Sorrento. Great-grand-daughter of Prince Alexandr Gorchakov, the famous Chancellor who handled Russia's foreign policy in the middle of the nineteenth century, she had married Soldatenkov, a rich commoner. Her mother had bought the villa from Queen Margherita di Savoia, wife of King Umberto I, who was assassinated in July 1900. Soon after the birth in 1901 of a daughter, also christened Helène, but known to all as 'Baby', her marriage broke up and henceforth she lived at Sorrento in

Lenin playing chess with Bogdanov, watched by Gorki and Andreyeva, 1908. *Courtesy of Constanzo Vuotto*

The Weber family, summer 1914. Back row: American tourist, Vincenzo Desiderio, Lucy Flannigan, Giorgio Weber, Minnie Egener. Middle: Raffaella Weber, Augusto Weber, American tourist. Front: Maria Weber, Carol Mather, Matilde Weber. *Courtesy of George Weber*

great style attended by a large indoor and outdoor staff; the Tsar often spent part of the summer there. The Principessa was uncompromisingly lesbian. 'The mere contour of a man affected her mind as unpleasantly as the contour of a mountain affected the old Roman mind.'[12] As often as not her girl-friends became part of the household under the cover of governesses for 'Baby', and no doubt they were impressed by her bedroom, which was paved with hand-made tiles topped with rose petals.

Through all the excitement of this decade – Fritz Krupp, the Wolcott-Perrys, the Fersen imbroglio, Russians of all kinds – the English Church maintained a steady presence under difficult conditions. The SPG, although responsible for finding Capri a chaplain each season from November to May, would not contribute towards the upkeep of the church and expected the emoluments of the temporary chaplain to be met from offertories at services and donations by local residents. For the season 1900–1, for example, total receipts from collections were £34 1s 8d. As the chaplain was to receive a remuneration of £45 for 30 Sundays, this left a deficit of £10 18s 4d, which had to be made up by the congregation. Collections, therefore, were scrutinised with particular care. Service records include the following entries by the chaplain of the day: 11 Dec 1898, 'collection included half a *lira* note (of course useless) and a Swiss coin'; 18 Dec, 'collection included a Greek coin (out of course)'; 16 Nov 1902, 'out of a collection of 5.20 *lire*, 1 bad *lira* – not counted. 1 doubtful *soldo is* counted'; Whitsunday 1903, 'a *lira* of Vittorio Emanuele *re eletto* was in the offertory, of course being out of date I cannot count it in the amount'. In 1903 the chaplain recorded that there were 'very few English in Capri now. Many Germans'.

The situation of the English Church was complicated by the fact that after the death of its owner in 1899 the SPG had to go to law over possession of the church itself and the land on which it stood. After a lengthy battle, costing £669 4s od in legal fees, the church and site were at last sold for £600. The fittings and furniture were kept for a new church, which had been authorised at the end of 1907. In April 1908 a piece of land at the Tragara end of Via Pastena was bought for about £80 from Giovanni Esposito, one of the three brothers who owned much of the land on the east side of Tragara. The new church, with a capacity to seat about a hundred people, was built of tufa with a vaulted roof of brick and iron. Until it was complete services were held either in the Palazzo Cerio, or in the villas of well-wishers or in hired rooms. The harmonium had a rough time being moved from place to place and not surprisingly, on 14 February 1909, it broke down in the *Te Deum*. The first reference to a choir at All Saints is in January 1909.

Axel Munthe, who had divorced his first wife in 1888, married again in May 1907. His bride was Hilda Pennington-Mellor, daughter of a

Scottish businessman. Munthe had met her in Rome, when she was only 17, at the British Embassy's turn-of-the-century ball. After resistance by her father had been overcome and a church wedding in London, Munthe took his wife to Sweden.

In December 1907 Gustav and Victoria became King and Queen of Sweden and in the following year set out on a round of visits to the Courts of Europe. Munthe was in attendance when they visited Berlin. Here Queen Victoria received the news that Prince Phillipp zu Eulenberg had been convicted of perjury and sent to prison. In 1893 Eulenberg had visited Stockholm with the Kaiser, enlivened the stuffy Swedish Court with his wit and musical talents, and made friends with the young Crown Princess Victoria. In 1907 he and other members of the Kaiser's entourage had been named in a newspaper article as suspected homosexuals. When at his trial Eulenberg swore that he had never committed an offence under paragraph 175 of the Penal Code, he was confronted by a witness who deposed on oath that he had been intimate with Eulenberg a quarter of a century earlier. The Kaiser abandoned his old friend, and for reasons of etiquette it was impossible for Victoria to visit Eulenberg in prison. So she sent Munthe, who found him in the prison hospital, reduced to a nervous wreck by his ordeal. It is clear from Eulenberg's own account of the visit that Munthe helped to restore his self-confidence. Meanwhile the Kaiser had been asking for Munthe and, when the Doctor at last arrived for his audience and explained why he was late, he was treated to a cold stare, a change of subject and abrupt dismissal.[13]

At the end of 1908, Fersen, feeling neglected and aware that he had achieved no fame as a poet, decided to try his hand at prose. Having returned to Paris with Nino, he began to write a novel about Capri and at the same time launched an *avant-garde* review. The first number of *Akademos*, described as *Revue mensuelle d'Art libre et de Critique*, emerged on 15 January 1909. The fact that Gorki had promised to write for *Akademos* brought an enthusiastic response from French writers of the left. Subsequent numbers appeared monthly, until October, and then ceased.[14]

The hero of Fersen's novel is a young Frenchman who cuts himself off from his family and goes to live in Capri as a sculptor. Here he marries a boyish-looking English girl, who later deserts him for a Russian prince. The sculptor is comforted by another Frenchman, who talks enthusiastically of the charms of boys. Finally he mutilates the statue of his wife on which he has been working, and casts it from a cliff into the sea, with imprecations against the island and a torrent of invective against women, and then hurls himself to follow the statue to its watery grave. The last page of the book consists mainly of dots. Entitled *Et le Feu s'éteignit sur la Mer. .* (one of his friends suggested that the two dots after *Mer* might be misinterpreted), the novel was reviewed enthusiastically in *Akademos*, which also carried a caricature of the author. It was *dédié respectueusement à Mesdemoiselles Wolcott-Perry*, who, while delighted to be honoured in this way, did not understand a word of French and engaged a penniless multilingual Russian exile to read it to them in translation.

The plot – built variously around himself, Nino, Anita Vedder, and a woman who had seduced Nino while Fersen was temporarily out of the island – was interwoven with mockery and criticism of everybody and everything in Capri. Fersen drew recognisable portraits of leading Capresi and foreigners. He made fun of the Church and, worse, lampooned the *carabinieri*. 'He denounced the tradesmen of Capri as a pack of voracious wolves . . . called the hotel-keepers brigands, the doctors assassins, accused the law of blackmail, and the civic authority of corruption. He suggested that the youth of the island, both male and female, existed on vice. He even declared that the bathing in summer was bad and the climate in winter much exaggerated.'[15]

Complimentary copies of both the book and the review had already been sent to Capri, so that, when in the summer of 1909 Fersen and Nino returned to the island, they found themselves in a hornet's nest. All the island's early feelings of benevolence vanished. One reader of the book (possibly Edwin Cerio) noted in his copy that it had been written by *uno squilibrato* (deranged, insane). Donna Lucia, who disapproved of the character-assassination of any foreigner and was usually ready to offer support, for once was baffled and could do no more than assure the Wolcott-Perrys that Mariano would do all he could to help *il signor conte*. Mariano himself, also at a loss, 'bowed before the storm and, entrenched behind his ledgers, declined to discuss the crisis with anybody'.[16]

By running down Capri's bathing and winter climate, Fersen had put a ready-made weapon into the hands of its rivals, Sorrento, Amalfi and Ischia. The Church was incensed that *Akademos* had published articles by Gorki and 'other enemies of the throne and the altar', while natural disasters like the eruption of Vesuvius and the Messina earthquake had gone unmentioned. On top of all this, Fersen, a Protestant living in a Catholic island, was known to disapprove of the statue of Santa Maria del Soccorso, and to be an admirer of Tiberius. Nino, a Roman *ragazzo*, was unpopular, because he was favoured over local boys.[17]

Compton Mackenzie wrote in *Vestal Fire*: 'Carlyle once said that Herbert Spencer was the most unending ass in Christendom. He had not met the Count.'[18] Nino, now rising twenty, was about to begin his military service. Fersen decided that before his departure Nino should be ceremonially flogged, with suitable Mithraic rituals, to consecrate him as a soldier. The ceremony, which took place in the Matermania cave, was attended by Kate and Saidee Wolcott-Perry, two other friends, and the Cingalese boys from his household, who, with two of the Torricella maids, acted as 'slaves'. Elaborate Mithraic rites continued throughout the night until at sunrise the naked Nino was given twenty lashes with straps by the Cingalese. Unluckily the culminating act was observed by a *caprese* girl, who was out very early cutting grass on the hillside below the Arco Naturale. Her father lodged a complaint with the authorities that an indecent spectacle had been witnessed in a public place. For the *municipio*, still smarting from Fersen's book, this was the last straw. Out of respect for his rank, they referred the matter, not to the *questura*, which would have led to public deportation and press publicity, but to Fersen's brother-in-law, the Marchese Bugnano, who was still a member of Parliament. Fersen was summoned to Naples and told that, unless he wanted to be deported, he must leave Italy at once. He retreated to Paris, and Nino began his two years of military service.[19]

In 1909 Talmage White, the English water-colourist, who had lived in Capri and Amalfi for more than 50 years, died in Poland. His considerable properties passed to his son Alberto, who married, dabbled as an artist in the shadow of his talented father, conceived unsuccessful schemes for making money, and gradually squandered much of his inheritance. The *pensione*, called 'The White House', which he had started in the family home at Villa Valentino, proved a failure and he sold it to Damiano Arcucci.

In his early years Damiano, an Anacaprese, had driven one of the horse-drawn carts which carried imported goods up from Marina Grande to Capri and Anacapri. He spoke some English which had been picked up on a visit to America. It was rumoured that the money with which he bought the Villa Valentino was provided by an elderly American lady whose lover he was at the time. Although Damiano's formal education had ended at the elementary stage, he had acquired good manners and dressed well. He was handsome in a *macho* way, charming and an insatiable womaniser. His friend Giorgio Weber considered that, if Damiano had been a Muslim, he would have acquired half-a-dozen wives and kept them all satisfied and happy. He was a good businessman and, after putting the Villa Valentino *pensione* on its feet, bought the ailing Hotel Capri in Strada Nuova (now Via Roma). In spite of its cold and damp north-facing aspect, he was successful there too and managed to keep its 25 or 30 beds occupied for most of the year.

At the end of 1909 Federico Serena, who had become an invalid, bowed out as *sindaco*. He was followed by his political rival Nicola Pagano, who by his marriage to Giacomina Morgano, sister of Giuseppe, had reinforced the political alliance which existed between the two families. Manfredi Pagano, Nicola's elder brother, however, was in difficulties. In 1910 the famous hotel, which since 1826 had accommodated and enlivened countless visitors, went bankrupt and was closed. Manfredi and his family moved to the *dipendenza* at Villa Romana, renamed it Hotel Manfredi Pagano and enlarged it.

Nicola Pagano gave up office in 1911. The new *sindaco* was Carlo Ferraro, the pharmacist, son of the late Don Giacinto, and now head of the family. This, the first and only occasion that a member of this very rich but remote family held high office in Capri, was brought about by a political reorientation in the island. Vincenzo Desiderio, who as a young priest had defied his father's wrath and conducted the marriage of his sister Raffaella to Augusto Weber, had for many years been a political supporter of Serena. Intelligent, a good administrator and with a flair for politics, he was trusted because he had no personal axe to grind and was always willing to help other people. It was he who had undertaken the preliminary negotiations with the SIPPIC which led to the opening of the *funicolare* and the introduction of electricity in 1907. When Serena retired from politics, Vincenzo Desiderio formed an alliance with Carlo Ferraro. He managed Ferraro's election campaign and on grounds of merit could have become *sindaco* himself. The Vatican, however, was still at war with the House of Savoy and, as a priest, he was forbidden to swear loyalty to the King of Italy, which the office of *sindaco* required. So Ferraro became *sindaco*, and Desiderio, *assessore delegato* and *vice-sindaco* – responsible, in effect, for the day-to-day administration of Capri.

As a bachelor priest, Vincenzo lived with the Webers at Marina Piccola. After his marriage in 1893 and the birth of Giorgio in July 1894, Augusto Weber, although still receiving an allowance from his mother in Munich, decided that he ought to do something on his own account to support his family – to which two daughters, Maria and Matilde, had been added in 1896 and 1900 – brushed up his languages and gave lessons in German, English, French and even Latin. He also added six rooms to the house and started a *pensione*, which he called 'Strandpension'.

Giorgio Weber describes his father as follows: 'My father was a very unusual man, his personality being so simple and at the same time so complex. He had utter disregard for social standing, for money and especially for conformity. He was honest, compassionate, abhorred violence and cruelty of any kind, and never thought or spoke ill of anybody, being a firm believer in the innate goodness of his fellow-men. As for his religion, he simply followed the moral code on which all religions are founded. Perhaps, if a religion were to be attributed to him, Buddhism would be the one to which his mode of life and thoughts conformed. He had no great desires and, therefore, never experiencnd great sufferings. He had found his Nirvana in the Piccola Marina, where he could spend his days free to do what he wanted, and to act as he felt, loved by his family and respected by all.'[20]

After the establishment of the Strandpension, Augusto's zest for painting gave way to literary expression, in the form of poetry, including rhyming proverbs, which he wrote down in notebooks, on the walls of the pension and even on his linen shoes, of which he had many pairs; many of his poems were illustrated by line-drawings.[21]

The first person to occupy one of the new rooms was Miss Lucy Flannigan. Although she stayed for over thirty years, the Webers discovered very little about her past or indeed her present. They knew only that she was a native of Boston, Massachusetts, and had been awarded a scholarship by the Boston Art Academy to study in Rome. How long she remained in Rome, why she came to Capri, how long she was in Capri before she turned up at Marina Piccola in search of a room, was not known. At first, she paid the rent out of what was left of the scholarship money, but after a few months her money ran out. Then luck appeared in the form of the Mather family (direct descendants of Cotton Mather, famous for his persecution of witchcraft in Salem, Massachusetts, at the end of the seventeenth century), who in 1903–4 were staying at the Quisisana. Miss Flannigan made friends with the Mather girls, Margaret and Carol. She seemed to have a beneficent influence on Carol, who was already showing signs of the streak of insanity which ran through the family, and was moreover interested in art. When the Mather parents returned to their home in Florence, the two girls took rooms at the Strandpension and remained there for several years. They also rented the studio by the beach, so that Miss Flannigan could give Carol lessons. The rent for the studio was paid by Margaret, and Miss Flannigan gave the Webers small sums of money on account, for her own board and lodging. Augusto, however, never exerted any pressure on her, or indeed on any other defaulters, most of whom paid up when they were able to do so. She seemed less concerned than anyone about not paying her bills. She had no hesitation about ordering extras, like wine, tea and coffee, and would complain if the service was not as it should be. No member of the Weber family was ever allowed in her room. After lunch she would go to the studio and remain there until late, sometimes not returning to her room until 2 a.m. She never sold any of her works, mostly landscapes, impressionist in style, violent in colour and usually in pastel or water-colour – not so much for lack of prospective buyers, but because she hated to part with them. Although she was an attractive woman, with a slender figure and a rich mane of golden hair, she appeared to have no suitors, no obvious sex-life of any kind, and to be totally absorbed in her art. She died in 1934 and was sent to Rome for cremation. Her ashes were buried in the 'suicides' corner' of Capri's Catholic cemetery, because in those days it was not respectable for a Catholic to be cremated.[22]

When Gorki moved to the Villa Pierina in 1909 and rented the Villa Arcucci for the 'School of Revolutionary Technique', the Webers saw much of the Russians. Gorki was fascinated by the skill of the fishermen and engaged one of them, Luigi Lembo, to be his boatman. Luigi was the youngest of four sons of Costanziello (' 'A Sorechella') Lembo – direct descendants of King Ferdinand's skilful retriever of quail in the eighteenth century. Although living up in Capri town, their days were spent at Marina Piccola, where, for storing their tackle, they rented one of the four magazines which Antonino Arcucci had built with Krupp's legacy. The Lembo family disdained the use of nets and employed only lines, either those which they fashioned themselves from horsetail-hair, or *coffe*, which were long lines of strong twine to which shorter lines, ending in hooks, were attached. They also used *nasse*, beautifully woven conical traps made of split canes. When the sea was calm and clear, they used a long four- or five-headed spear and with amazing precision could spear an octopus or fairly large fish 15 or 20 feet down. If the water was not smooth enough they would use olive oil to calm and clarify it. Their life was harsh and at the lowest rung of poverty.

After the School closed in December 1909, Gorki turned to open-air meetings, which were often held on the *piazzetta* in front of the Chapel of Sant' Andrea, but under the Capri moonlight and beside the shimmering sea they would soon tire of ideology and turn instead to Russian choruses, and Chaliapin would sing.

In June 1910 Lenin paid a second visit to Capri. He wrote to his mother: 'Dear Mama, I send you cordial greetings from Naples. I have come here by steamboat from Marseilles. It was cheap and pleasant. It was like the Volga.' After visiting the Blue Grotto, Lenin told Gorki: 'Of course the grotto is beautiful, only it is so theatrical, as if it were scenery in a theatre. On my way here I thought about the Volga all the time. The beauty there is of a different sort, it is simple and dearer to me.' Lenin wandered over the rocky, sun-burnt paths of Capri; tried his hand again at fishing; admired the grubby children of the fishermen; gave Russian lessons to a young Caprese girl, Maria Aprea, niece of Gorki's factotum, Cataldo Aprea; played chess; and argued with Gorki and his companions.[23] In November he was back in Paris and feeling the cold. He wrote to Gorki that there had been no news of him and Andreyeva 'for a very long time. I have been looking forward eagerly for news from Capri. What's wrong? Surely you don't keep count of letters as some people are said to keep count of visits. . . . Brrr! It must be nice on Capri.' And in January 1911, still in Paris, after Gorki had written to him from Capri complaining about the cold ('my hands are shaking and freezing'): 'What wretched houses you have on Capri! It's a disgrace really! Even we have central heating; and "your hands are freezing". You must revolt. All the very best, yours, Lenin.'[24]

By 1910 the population of the island had risen to 6,400, of whom about

4,400 lived in the commune of Capri. Foreigners, more than half of them German, were visiting at a rate of about 40,000 a year. The tourist industry had become by far the most important factor in the island's economy. In his revised edition of 1912, Baedeker included for the first time a plan of Capri town. A formal bathing establishment, administered by the SIPPIC, was set up at Marina Grande ('50c, including towels'), followed by others at Bagni di Tiberio, Marina Piccola and Spiaggia Saracena. Baedeker lists five hotels at Marina Grande; seven hotels and four *pensioni* in Capri town; and three hotels in Anacapri, where furnished rooms were 'abundant'; most hotels had electricity. Drinking-water, which was 'limited in quantity and of doubtful quality', remained a problem, and visitors were advised that mineral water was preferable.

The increasing popularity of Capri was welcomed by Alberto Lembo, who made his living as *commissioniere*, a job which had greatly increased in scope. With a cousin, Costanzo Lembo, Alberto operated from an office-cum-store in Via Hohenzollern, opposite Hotel Pagano. In the store he sold liquor, coffee, sugar and confectionery. From his office he provided a service for those who needed legal documents from provincial offices in Naples; obtained goods from the mainland which were not available in Capri; bought rail-tickets and made *wagon-lits* reservations; and arranged the transport of luggage and even of dead bodies. There was no tourist office, and residents and visitors alike availed themselves of his services. At the beginning of the century people who travelled for pleasure were invariably rich and always had quantities of baggage in which to transport the dresses, petticoats, voluminous coats and large hats of the women; and the heavy woollen clothing, starched shirts, bowler-hats and leather footwear of the men. All this provided good and steady business for the Lembo cousins. Not content with his success as *commissioniere*, Alberto Lembo, having persuaded the *parroco* Don Giuseppe De Nardis to break into the massive wall of the parish-church and excavate a space for two stores at the south-west corner of the Piazza, took the lease of one and started the Caffè Tiberio. The other went to a barber. Later, when the barber died, Lembo took that too and doubled the size of the Caffè.

All the old shops and stores prospered, and new ones started business. In 1906, a clothes-shop, 'La Parisienne', was opened on the Piazza by Maria and Michele Di Fiore, to combine Paris fashion, which was then the rage in Italy, with local craftsmanship. In 1910, Gennaro Canfora, whose father Giuseppe already made shoes, opened a shop in Via Camerelle, to sell shoes of a quality which would attract foreigners; and in 1912 Pietro Lamberti established an antiques business in Via Hohenzollern.[25]

Thanks to the initiative of Edith Andrews, the island's shoe-industry was born. She and William had taken a lease of the top floor of the Villa

Federico in Via Pastena – and here William nursed his health and translated *Faust*. The villa was owned by Michele Federico, who by marrying Carmela Strina had united two old Capri families. Their son Costantino, aged about 20 and apprenticed to a shoe-maker in Via Hohenzollern, attracted the attention of Edith Andrews, and she conceived the idea of manufacturing by machine the popular rope-soled canvas shoes (*scarpe di Capri*), which were then still made by hand. She sent Costantino for training to Spain, where the machining of this type of shoe was already widespread, and when he returned she gave him the money to set up a small industry. With 12 to 15 workers and his sister as book-keeper, Costantino started a factory in Via Acquaviva. He was intelligent and industrious, and by 1910 was not only satisfying the Capri market, in which he had a virtual monopoly, but was also exporting part of his output; the business lasted until 1962.

Costantino's sister Giulia married Adolfo Patrizi, whose father, the Marchese Ettore Patrizi, had brought his family from Siena to Capri in 1900. Ettore became agent in Capri for a Neapolitan wine distributor named Rouff, who produced large quantities of so-called Capri wine and had a shop in Via Hohenzollern, next door to Schiano the barber, where a few barrels and shelves of bottles were displayed. Although sold with a Capri label, the bottles contained very little Capri wine but mainly a mixture of wines from Ischia and the mainland, considered perfectly suitable for sale to tourists. Ettore had three daughters, who were very religious and lived the simplest of lives. His son, Adolfo, however, was different – vivacious, good-natured, intelligent, extravagant, addicted to gambling, and one of the leaders of a small group of lively young Capresi. On one occasion he sent Vittorio Emanuele II a donkey as a present; when after a time he had received no word of thanks, he posted the King a registered letter with prepaid reply asking if his present had reached its destination. Elegant in both dress and manners, Adolfo was famous for his prodigious appetite, and was variously reputed to have eaten at a sitting: several chickens; 16 veal cutlets, with other courses; 36 stuffed peppers; 500 thrushes; and 5 metres of sausages.[26] He was hopeless with money, always spending whatever he had and 'if given the chance, could easily have run through the reserves of the Banco D'Italia'.[27] In 1911, while they were in Benevento, where Adolfo had property, Giulia bore him a son, Ettore.

Details of English Church activities during 1910 are lacking, because the Service-book was mislaid among a pile of magazines and no record kept until its rediscovery in February 1911. By now the new Church of All Saints was almost ready, and the churchwarden, Harold Trower, had the unenviable task of collecting the furniture and fittings which were scattered about the town and installing them in the new building. The

Service-book contains his despairing commentary underlined in red and blue chalk: 'Owing to moving of Church furniture etc etc by ignorant Capri *facchini* many difficulties and inconveniences suffered by the Warden in his devoted work.' The first service in the new church was held on 12 March 1911, and the building was consecrated on 16 April 1912 by the Bishop of Gibraltar.

At the end of 1909 Douglas went to Tunisia with £50 in his pocket, in order to collect material for a book about it. After three months he returned to Capri with the fruits of his observations and experiences, a large collection of prehistoric flint implements, but no money. Mrs Webb stepped into the breach and bought the flints for £50. Thanks partly to the influence of John Mavrogordato, one of Dent's readers, that firm made an offer for *Siren Land*, which in a somewhat reduced form was published in March 1911. Seven of the original twenty chapters were omitted as being 'too remote from human interests'. The thirteen chapters which comprised the book included the already published monograph on *Tiberius* and a résumé of the *Life of Suor Serafina*; thoughts on *The Philosophy of the Blue Grotto*; discursive musings about the Sirens; and accounts of various aspects of the Sorrentine peninsula. Meanwhile *Fountains in the Sand*, which dealt with his visit to Tunisia, began to take shape, and he was working hard on *Old Calabria*. Apart from a small advance on *Siren Land*, his writing had so far brought him only trivial sums of money. To his great grief nothing could be spared for the development of the Petrara site and Douglas was forced to sell what had been the apple of his eye.[28] He still owned the Villa Daphne on the eastern slope of Castiglione but took no further steps to finish it; there is a photograph of him on its balcony taken in 1912. It was in this year that his fortunes improved. Offered a post as sub-editor of the *English Review*, he accepted it and returned to London. He held on to the Villa Daphne, until in 1915, just before the entry of Italy into World War I, he sold it to a German engineer, who had barely got it, before he had to leave Italy, and the villa was confiscated as enemy property.[29]

Amongst those who were impressed by *Siren Land* was the 30-year-old writer Compton Mackenzie, who had recently done well with his books *The Passionate Elopement* and *Carnival*. His father was Edward Compton, an actor-manager, and his mother Virginia Bateman, an American and Edward's leading lady. The families of both parents had long connections with the stage, and from his earliest years Mackenzie (the family's actual name) met many stage and literary celebrities. In 1905 Monty married Faith Stone. Faith, a little older than Monty, was already on the stage, but achieved no success, and her health suffered from the arduous and uncertain life of trailing round the provincial theatres. As well as being an actress, she was a talented pianist and, in deciding to marry Monty, had to abandon any prospect of making a musical career. They married secretly and caused great shock to their respective families. Monty had very little money, but resolved to make some as an author. Faith's first and only child, a son, was born dead in May 1908; she resolved never to have another. Throwing herself bravely into Monty's world, she found common ground with his actress sister, Fay Compton, whom she already knew from her acting days, and felt that her own career on the stage, unsuccessful though it had been, had not been wasted – 'I had unconsciously laid a pretty good foundation for the peculiar structure of my future life,' she wrote later, 'I was proof against surprises. I knew from the first that I didn't want a nice conventional marriage, and I was justifiably sure that I had avoided this. . . .'[30]

In the spring of 1913 the Mackenzies left England and made for Naples, partly because his doctors advised Monty, who was prone to excruciating bouts of sciatica in periods of nervous exhaustion, that he ought to winter in a kinder climate than England, and partly because they were attracted by *Siren Land* and Douglas's own oral account of the region. After a few days in Naples they went to a cheap hotel in Sorrento, while they looked around for a small villa. They visited the end of the promontory, looked across to Capri and decided to spend a weekend there and use some of the letters of introduction which Douglas had given them. When the boat called next day on its way from Naples to Capri, they boarded it with a couple of suitcases. 'The moment we emerged from the funicular in the Piazza,' Monty wrote later, 'we felt that nothing must prevent our living in Capri.' For Faith, it was 'falling in love, irrevocably. Its magic sank into my heart.'[31] They were so perfectly happy immediately that, before any further exploration of the island, they sent across to Sorrento for the rest of their belongings.

They stayed first at the Hotel Faraglioni, 'an old white building with plenty of terraces and Banksia roses and pink geraniums climbing about the walls'. Nicola Ferraro, not always successful in his management of the hotel, which he had opened in 1894, was having a good season in 1913. Most of the residents were 'gurgling German tourists', who plunged enthusiastically into their sight-seeing on the aromatic slopes around Matermania, at the Villa Iovis, and up Solaro 'with cabbage leaves under their hats, to drink "Capri wine" on the summit'. At the end of the day they would bargain in the shops for garish pictures of their favourite views and of old Spadaro in his red cap and long pipe. No German returned to the homeland without a 'huge collection of olive-wood boxes, paper-knives, castanets, book-stands with swallows on them, reversible knitted caps in splendid colours, rope-shoes, striped Sorrento umbrellas, yards and yards of lovely *filet* lace made by the Capri girls, coloured baskets, shawls and scarves'. There were also a few English old maids in the hotel, who spent the day botanising and came back triumphantly to lunch with their latest floral treasures. It was the fly-orchis season, but they were rare enough to cause excitement when found.[32]

Fersen's exile had now lasted four years. He had lived in France during Nino's military service, so that meetings could be arranged during the soldier's rare leaves. After his release in 1911, they joined forces again, and this was a comfort to Fersen in more ways than one, for Nino was a conscientious and practical young man, who managed their day-to-day business, as they toured the world – Greece, Constantinople, Algiers, Japan and China. At last, after some string-pulling by Giovanni Galatà and Fersen's sister Germaine, the authorities agreed that the exile had been punished enough. The decree of banishment was rescinded and in April 1913 he returned with Nino to the Villa Lysis.

To celebrate his home-coming Kate and Saidee Wolcott-Perry prepared a grand dinner to which all their 'real friends' were invited. They let it be known that those who accepted the invitation would remain welcome guests at the Villa Torricella; those who declined would never be allowed to enter it again. And so it was. Although the table for this dinner of welcome was as long as it had been for the Christmas party of 1904, when all was sweetness and light in the foreign colony, it lacked the spirit of the earlier gatherings. Many of those present were in Capri only for the season and were, therefore, semi-strangers to the scene. For them jokes and allusions to past events had to be laboriously explained. To stamp the hallmark of respectability on the occasion, the old ladies invited several inappropriate people – a retired Indian civilian, the wife of a rural dean, the cousin of an American senator, a decayed German baroness, and one of the Italian officials who had helped to secure Fersen's return.

In spite of the expulsions and defections, Sunday afternoons at the Villa Torricella were still a feature of Capri life, while the gaiety of the evening parties was enhanced by the advent of electricity. 'Salons and loggias blazed with fairy lamps; long pergolas were lit by coloured bunches of glass grapes among the vines. Till dawn they would speed the dancers, ply the band with wine, Kate fanning herself vigorously, her tall figure held upright in its lace dress till the last guest went. . . . Saidee more sober . . . went quietly among her friends seeing to food and drink, her steadfast eyes fixed often on their hero, their Count Jack. . . .'[33]

While the old ladies had not become reconciled to any of the former friends with whom they had quarrelled, there were some newcomers to fill the gaps. The Mackenzies, armed with a letter from Norman Douglas, were soon enrolled. Another new guest to the Torricella, but by no means new to the island, was Mrs Emelie Fraser.[34] A pillar of the English Church since the early 'nineties and now a widow, she had long forgotten that her maiden name was Smith and in every sense had adopted the pedigree of her late husband, William Langland Fraser. Her cards were engraved with his family's crest and motto. The motto happened to be 'I am ready', and this caused great delight amongst the ribald islanders. Her nickname was 'Bonny Sarah', owing to a report that when, soon after her arrival in Capri, passers-by wished her *buona sera*, she had supposed them to be commenting on her good looks. Although not particularly tall or imposing, she was rarely seen in anything except trailing gowns of silk and satin, of some crude shade of pink, and enormous picture-hats, built up with sham flowers and coloured streamers. Except in the depths of winter, she went for a swim every day at Marina Grande, wearing hat and gloves as well as a bathing-dress, because she did not wish to become sun-tanned. She was stingy, proud, vain, gaudy and renowned as a gossip, but her tittle-tattle was malicious and self-righteous, rather than scandalous or witty.

For the spring and summer of 1913 Mrs Fraser had staying with her a niece, Doris, a slim, clean-cut girl of eighteen, with sunburnt boy's hands and rose-brown cheeks, who was, however, in her aunt's opinion, most unsatisfactory. She was consistently late for meals, accepted invitations to go bathing with young men without asking her aunt's permission, smoked in the street and (except at the Villa Torricella) was always a much more welcome guest than Mrs Fraser. Kate and Saidee Wolcott-Perry adored Mrs Fraser, who was an unwavering supporter of Fersen and with her venomous propriety provided a weight of respectability to the French-man's cause. Gwen Galatà could not abide her, but had to keep her opinions to herself, since anything approaching a rift with the Wolcott-Perrys would have imperilled Giovanni's position as their legal adviser.

Alexander (Sandie) and Sophie Grahame had arrived in Capri in the autumn of 1910.[35] Alexander was a Scot of good family who, after Cambridge and a few years of administrative work in the Far East, had taken to drink, cut adrift from his family and become a peripatetic schoolmaster. Sophie's origins were obscure. According to her own account, she had been found on a door-step and adopted by virtuous but strait-laced people. She ran away in her early 'teens, met Alexander in London and wandered around the world with him until they ended up in Capri. By now he had abandoned all pretence at a profession and was drinking away the rest of his life. Sophie was devoted to 'Tot', as she called him, and did her unsuccessful best to control his alcoholism and cope with him after parties. Fortunately both had small remittances from their respective relations and were able to support a modest existence in their *villino* on Via Sopramonte, and to keep Alexander in drink. Sophie became a friend of Gwen Galatà, gained access to the Torricella, where on Sunday afternoons Sandie could sink into a comfortable chair on the terrace and drink all the whisky-and-soda he wanted. He was a well-liked member of the Anglo-American colony and in February 1912, in spite of his addiction to the bottle, was elected People's Warden of All Saints Church.

The chaplain of All Saints for the 1912–13 season was the Rev. Francis Burra, Curate of St Alban's, Fulham, and in his late twenties. He soon found himself out of sympathy with the church congregation and attracted to the people whom they warned him against. Thomas Jerome gave him access to his library and instructed him about Roman morals. Burra made friends with Fersen, attended Torricella parties and in the spring of 1913 conceived a romantic passion for Vernon Andrews. Although the official season ended on Whitsunday, his offer of voluntary ministrations throughout the summer was accepted, but to the horror of Trower and the congregation he appointed Vernon as his churchwarden. After a happy time passed mainly in bathing, picnics and parties, the chaplain returned regretfully to another curacy in London. He wrote several letters to Vernon, but Vernon forgot to answer them, and all too soon Francis Burra became a Capri legend.[36] His successor as chaplain in the following winter was the Rev. Henry J. Gepp, a rural dean in his mid-seventies, married and accompanied by his wife. 'He had a beard so long and so thick that he was never upset by the hoops of the little Capresi being driven between his legs, for it served as a sort of cow-catcher, and it was generally believed that he used it as a most efficacious mosquito-net.' While the Tragara ladies were reasonably confident of avoiding scandal during his tenure of office, Harold Trower, the churchwarden, quarrelled with him over the collections, so that 'by early spring they were not on speaking terms except during the responses at Morning Prayer'.[37]

Newcomers also to the Torricella were what Kate and Saidee called 'our dear Baker girls'. These were two Quaker sisters from New England, whose forenames are not known and so are referred to by Mackenzie's pseudonyms 'Rachel' and 'Hannah'. Rachel, the elder, 'was about fifty and looked it ... pleasantly colourless and flabby, the sort of pasty old maid one sees by the dozen on steamers crossing the Atlantic, by the thousand when one lands in America'. Hannah, the younger sister, was thirty-three, thin, with a plume of grey in her dark brown hair and a fine profile. Her blue eyes were lit up not with the purity of her Quaker ancestry, but with a practical and unsentimental approach to sex, which had an immediate appeal to the libertine. She did not throw herself at men, and in public was 'demure enough, and one of her most precious thrills was the way she could surprise a dancing partner, who was supposing that he held in his arms a prim Quakeress with the realization that he held instead an accomplished wanton'. Gwen Galatà 'wouldn't trust her with a man on top of an iceberg'. Although Hannah was too thin for Giovanni's taste, he discovered that 'what she lacked in acreage she made up for by accessibility'; and for the sake of an amorous encounter in the garden at one of the Torricella all-night parties, he was prepared to risk Gwen's wrath when they returned home at half-past four in the morning. Although everyone else knew what she was like, Hannah had succeeded in impressing herself on the Wolcott-Perrys as what they did not hesitate to call their ideal of a young woman . . . 'and it was understood that Kate had done more than remember the sisters in the ultimate disposition of their property, that in fact she had forgotten everybody else.'[38]

Compton Mackenzie was just in time to meet Gorki and often accompanied him to the tiny cinema-theatre of Capri below the Terrazza Funicolare, which Gorki found a restful contrast to the incessant babble in his own house. In April 1913 the Tsar proclaimed an amnesty to celebrate the 300th anniversary of the founding of the Romanov dynasty. Gorki and Andreyeva returned to Russia. His adopted son, Zinovi Peshkov, stayed behind and later joined the French Foreign Legion. With no one in Capri to pay their debts, the other Russians quickly dispersed. Their departure was genuinely regretted by the Capresi. Even the tradesmen felt a sense of loss that they were no longer being called upon to give them credit. Donna Lucia, who had been particularly generous to the *habitués* of her *caffè*, said that they had promised to pay their debts as soon as they had overthrown Tsarism.[39]

It was again the *festa* of San Costanzo, which off and on lasted for a fortnight. On 7 May, a picture of the saint was suspended from a rope stretched between the Church of Santo Stefano and the Palazzo Cerio, to the accompaniment of bells, and bangs (*botti*) from the surrounding hills. On the evening of the 13th, Pontifical Mass was celebrated by the Archbishop of Sorrento, the silver effigy of the saint was taken from its cupboard and, surrounded by candles and heaps of flowers, displayed on the high altar, while the people looked anxiously to see if he was pleased or angry, his apparent mood varying with the angle from which he was viewed and the light, or lack of it, which struck his face.

Later the Piazza and streets were illuminated, the good citizens celebrated and the city band played. These were the days when it was as important for an Italian town to have a, mainly brass, band, which performed at all the secular and religious *feste*, as it is today to possess a football team. The day was brought to a close with fireworks, Bengal lights and more *botti*. Capri was fortunate in having Don Giovanni (nicknamed 'Cicione'[40]), *il pirotecnico*, and his son who were masters of their trade – flaming wheels, grenades that soared in the air and lines of petards each louder than its predecessor – and had spent weeks and months preparing for the great day. Such was Cicione's importance that in 1922 Edwin Cerio, then *sindaco*, presented him with a gold medal.

Dawn on the 14th, which opened serene and clear, was greeted by *botti* from all over the lower part of the island. In the morning, after high mass, the procession set off from the church to escort the saint to his church at the Marina. At the head of the procession, as it emerged from Santo Stefano, was Montrasti, the *guardia municipale*, unaccustomedly sober, and two *carabinieri*, 'displaying marvellous coolness on a hot day in spite of their uniforms', followed by the Capri band 'blowing away like billy-oh at a jolly southern march'; then the young *figlie di Maria*, in white frocks with blue sashes and veils; the old *figlie di Maria* in black; boys of the Guild of San Luigi Gonzaga ('Luigini') trying to look as pure as their patron on his white silk banner; representatives of various other guilds and fraternities; a crucifer and acolytes in scarlet cassocks and white surplices; and finally the clergy of Capri and Anacapri, with lighted candles, preceding and surrounding the silver effigy of the saint, which was carried on the shoulders of six fishermen. Behind the saint were the leading citizens of Capri, and behind them all others who wanted to join the procession. The people of Anacapri were still aggrieved that their clergy were compelled to take part in the *festa* of San Costanzo, whereas no such obligation required the priests of Capri to attend the annual celebration of Sant' Antonio da Padova in Anacapri on 13 June. Moreover, it had rained during the *festa* of 1912 and the paint had run down Sant' Antonio's face, much to the pleasure of the Capresi onlookers.

The procession moved from the Piazza down Via Acquaviva to Via Marina Grande, then, showered from housetops, balconies and garden walls with genista and rose petals, wound slowly down to the Church of San Costanzo. After a brief rest in his church, the saint set off again in the early evening for a tour of the port and then returned to his church for a day's repose before the journey back to Capri town. On this particular occasion in 1913, as the procession retraced its steps up the road from the sea-front, a grey squall came suddenly across the blue sky and drenched the lower part of the island. The Wolcott-Perrys and their guests on the terrace above the road paused long enough to empty several baskets of sodden petals over the procession before dashing into the Villa Torricella. This was too much for the bearers of the effigy who broke into a trot and with the leading citizens of Capri, San Costanzo streaming with rain and rollicking along, hurried on to the shelter of the church.

Not a drop of rain fell that day in Anacapri. Two wet but happy Anacapresi watched the disaster contentedly. '*Ecco*,' said one of them, '*nostro padre Sant' Antonio ha dato un buon pugno a quel porco di San Costanzo*' (Our father St Anthony has given a good punch to that pig St Costanzo).

On the 16th the saint returned in procession to the parochial church, to rest again until the *ottava*, or eight days later, when he made an extensive tour of Capri town. As a final act the *maestri di festa* polished the statue and returned it to the cupboard for another year of repose.[41]

The Mackenzies were now determined to make Capri their home. They asked William Andrews if they could rent La Caterola, which was still let to a peasant, and its farm-house inhabited by the tenant's two cows. Andrews received a certain amount of milk and olive-oil as part of the agreement, but the oil was always slightly rancid and the milk had recently become suspect. He was, therefore, delighted to get rid of the peasant and his two cows and to let the property to the Mackenzies for £6 a month. He promised to do some repairs to the building, but asked to be allowed to retain one of the rooms as a study where in summer he could lie down and rest between sessions with *Faust*. Having made these arrangements they departed for England.

Capri continued to be visited all the year round. For foreigners, late autumn, winter and spring were still the most popular, but there was a steady increase of summer visitors for bathing and sunshine. The main spurt to the summer season came not from Northern Europe and America, but the Italian mainland. In 1910 an epidemic of cholera in Naples and the surrounding regions drove the Neapolitans, who had been accustomed to take their holidays in the Sorrentine peninsula, to Capri. Having 'discovered' Capri, their numbers swelled, until in 1913 William Andrews commented that Capri was in danger of becoming 'a sort of debased Trouville'. Gwen Galatà hated 'these Neapolitans who come over for the summer. So dirty. The old woman at the bathing-place told me the sea's quite black every morning.'[42] Nevertheless the visitors were welcomed by many islanders for the new business they brought. The Quisisana imported the first automobile to be seen on the island, to shuttle its clients to and from the bathing-establishment at Marina Grande. One day disaster struck the *funicolare*. While the cable was being inspected or changed, it slipped, and the car that was at the upper end ran down and hit the car at Marina Grande, killing both attendants.[43]

In the late summer came the startling news that Fersen was to conduct Kate, now 76, and Saidee, a mere 62, on a tour of south-east Asia – Siam, Cambodia, Cochin-China, Annam and China itself – and then return by way of Japan, Honolulu and the United States. 'Even those most bitterly prejudiced against the Count admitted that the proposed trip did him credit. Whatever his behaviour might have been in the past, he was showing most unmistakably his appreciation of the battle the old ladies had fought for his name.'[44] The party, consisting of Kate and Saidee, Fersen and Nino, and the Baker girls, set off in October.

A week earlier Charles Coleman had sailed in the opposite direction to see Rose O'Neill, who was too busy with her drawing and writing to pay her usual visit to Capri; to visit some of his old friends before they died;

and to mount an exhibition of his work in New York. Only three years younger than Kate and just as lively, he was attended in the Villa Narcissus by three young maids with ribbons in their hair, who might have stepped straight out of one of his pictures, and he never tired of entertaining his friends to wine parties in the studio. The rest of the house was crowded with uneasy little chairs, dark tables loaded with bric-a-brac, tapestries, church vestments, Roman bits and pieces, his own pictures and pastels everywhere – and, leaning forlornly against a wall 'large canvases sold or given in the good old days to the Wolcott-Perrys, scornfully returned without a word of explanation during the crisis'.[45]

In America, Rose was enjoying phenomenal prosperity, thanks to her 'Kewpies' (diminutive of Cupids), drawings of which first appeared in the December 1909 issue of the *Ladies Home Journal* and which she patented in March 1913. Kewpies became the rage on both sides of the Atlantic – not only the dolls themselves, but also Kewpies used as decorations on nursery china, wallpaper, stationery, inkwells and figurines on the radiator-caps of cars. As fast as she made money, she spent it or gave it away, and Uncle Charley was high on the list of her charities.

It was a quiet winter for many of the foreigners with the two main centres of hospitality closed down for many months. To console the Wolcott-Perrys' friends, postcards arrived at intervals describing their progress round the 'gorgeous East'. A few favoured friends, like Mrs Fraser, received long letters describing their tour – 'dear Count Jack is a mine of information . . . our beloved Baker girls grow nearer and dearer to us every day. We are proud to show them to the dear natives as the best type of our fine American womanhood. . . .' Mrs Fraser 'was so proud of these special letters that she gave tea-parties with really expensive cakes, for the pleasure of sitting in a conflagration of cerise and carmine silk and rolling them out in public'. Postcards from Cambodia were followed by postcards from Macao and Shanghai, and then there was silence until the following arrived from Yokohama:

'Here we are with our dear boys amid the fairy blossoms of lovely Japan. The Misses Baker left for San Francisco yesterday.

Kate and Saidee Wolcott-Perry.'

No one in Capri had any doubt that Hannah had been caught out at last, and wild rumours circulated about her likely sexual exploits with hospitable potentates, Chinese coolies, Nino and even Fersen. The trouble in fact was that both she and Nino were finding the tropics too much for their feelings – in Nino's case the pace of the tour left little or no time for opium-smoking, the anaphrodisiac effect of which might hve kept his virility in check. Fersen told the old ladies that, having successfully seduced Nino, Hannah was now trying to seduce himself. Kate's action was swift and typical. Taking her will, in which Rachel and Hannah were named as the sole beneficiaries, she tore it up in small fragments in front of them, told them to take the next ship to San Francisco and 'never let me see either of your shameless faces ever again'.[46]

The Mackenzies had returned to Capri and in November took up residence in La Caterola. They made friends with William Wordsworth, now nearing eighty, and his companion Miss Kennedy, who lived a little further up towards Tiberio. Great-nephew of the poet, whom he had known as a boy, the old man delighted Monty by reading the poems in what must have been near to the accents of their writer, while Miss Kennedy, who always took the gloomiest view of everything, regaled him with her pungent comments on Capri society, about which she was very well informed.

Faith was much impressed by Axel Munthe, who would walk down from Anacapri to see them, and she returned the compliment by lunching at Materita and playing his piano. Munthe had lost the sight of his right eye altogether, and the left was over-sensitive to strong light. He could no longer stand the glare of the sun on the white walls of San Michele and in 1913 retreated to the subdued light of the Materita tower. This apparent remoteness from the life of the island was deceptive, for he took particular care to keep abreast of local gossip and know about the private lives of the island's inhabitants. Monty's neuritis was very bad at the beginning of 1914, and his condition was not helped by the cold and damp of Caterola. Munthe offered them a lease of San Michele, which was now empty, but the Mackenzies felt that it had the same defects as Caterola – it faced north, was cold and damp, and had no heating arrangements. In March Edwin Cerio, back in Capri and no longer employed by Krupp, asked them if they would like to look over a new house he was building on the south side of the island. This was 'La Solitaria', which was reached by a cliff-path from the south end of Via Tragara. The house stood on the edge of the cliff, looking out over the Faraglioni rocks. It was protected from the north wind by the towering heights of Monte Tuoro. A few yards beyond it was a tall phallic shaped rock called Pizzolungo, which was also the Caprese name for the area. They had no hesitation in accepting Cerio's offer of a 10-year lease at £50 a year. Until it was ready and furnished, he offered them 'Il Rosajo', a cottage he had in Anacapri, which was just a sitting-room, bedroom and kitchen, under a domed roof and opening into a small rose-entangled garden. 'Except for the barking of wandering packs of dogs on moonlight nights, utter tranquillity reigned. The view was equally tranquil, a wide silvery-green slope of olive groves stretching gently down to the lighthouse.'[47] Here Monty could escape from Capri society and concentrate on volume II of *Sinister Street*, whose first part,

Charles Coleman and Rose O'Neill in the garden of Villa Narcissus, c. 1910. *Courtesy of Centro Caprense Ignazio Cerio*

John Ellingham Brooks

published in the previous year, had been widely acclaimed by the critics as a penetrating study of an attractive boy's childhood and adolescence, but, because it dealt explicitly with an amorous school friendship and other sexual topics, was banned by some of the circulating libraries and by many headmasters, which of course greatly helped its sales. The ban imposed by Eton created a comic situation, because Monty had dedicated the book to his father-in-law, who was an Eton housemaster.

Norman Douglas returned to Capri that spring and, having injured his ankle, went about like Silenus on a donkey. He succeeded in distracting Monty from his writing and took him and his wife to the best eating-places in Capri and Anacapri. The Mackenzies were also able to enjoy the singing of the tenor, Bertram Binyon, son of Edward and Maria, who, only two years old when his father died in 1876, had after college in Naples trained as a singer in London and Paris, and was now taking leading tenor parts in opera. Splendid musician and excellent company, he was visiting Capri to see his mother Maria and sister Bianca, who lived in the Villa Bianca built on their plot of land in Via Pastena.

Giorgio Cerio, finding Capri too small for his ambitions, had moved with his wife Jenny to Rome, where his ability, neat appearance and polished bedside manner, combined with Jenny's social connections, enabled him to develop a thriving practice, particularly in the foreign colony where his fluent English gave him the edge over Roman doctors. It was thus that Giorgio met Mabel Norman, a rich American artist with a studio in Rome, whose family had large property and business interests in Newport, Rhode Island. For Giorgio, this was the long-sought prize, and he set about divesting himself of Jenny, so that he could marry Mabel. He applied for annulment on the grounds of lack of progeny and, when this had been achieved, he went again to the United States. Jenny tried to commit suicide by throwing herself into the sea. Although she was rescued, she developed pneumonia and died in 1913. Giorgio commemorated her by building a porphyry tomb, inscribed JENNY and *PACE*, which still stands, ostentatious and indestructible, in the Catholic cemetery of Capri.

Death also took its toll in other fields. Federico Serena, for long an invalid, died in October 1913, leaving his sons and widow to carry on the Quisisana. In April 1914, Thomas Jerome, plagued by stomach ulcers, which Yetta's cooking did nothing to help, and 'not much thicker than a two-cent stamp', died of a gastric haemorrhage in his fifty-second year. During his many years of research in Capri he had made a few contributions to learned journals; provided material for Trower's *The Book of Capri*; lectured in Rome, Capri and London; and, shortly before his death, published *Roman Memories in the Landscape seen from Capri*. By 1914, however, he had at last assembled the material for his *magnum opus*, dealing with the causes of the fall of the Roman Empire, and was poised to complete his work. In the eyes of Somerset Maugham, Jerome's 'life was success . . . he did what he wanted and he died when his goal was in sight and never knew the bitterness of an end achieved'.[48] He was buried in the *cimitero acattolico* under a tombstone recording, in Latin, details of his birth (wrongly given as 1854) and death, and with a quotation from Tacitus (originally applied by the Roman historian to the Emperor Tiberius) – 'that . . . their praise and kindly thoughts may still attend my deeds and the memories attached to my name'.[49] Jerome left some money to Yetta and granted her a year's tenure of the Villa Castello. She stayed on for ten months, bought a new hat every week and a variety of gaudy clothes, and then returned to America. The Villa Castello was bought by Alice Tweed Andrews as a home for herself, her son Vernon and daughter Edith. Jerome was succeeded as US Consular Agent by Giovanni Galatà, who was now *vice-pretore* of Capri.

Coleman returned to Capri in May 1914. His exhibition in New York had been successful, with his pastels of Vesuvius selling very well – in particular one entitled *What the painter saw*, in which smoke from the crater is filled with the shapes of female nudes. This was in such demand that he sat in Rose's studio and did fifty more on commission. The big canvases did not do so well – which he attributed to 'this darned life they lead nowadays in apartment houses. By gad, they've no time to look at a large canvas.' Many New Yorkers visited the exhibition to admire not so much the pictures, as Coleman himself. They 'had no idea that they possessed such a fine Tennysonian antique . . . and with the slightest encouragement would have put him in the Bronx Zoo'.[50]

Everyone revelled in the glorious summer of 1914. There was bathing and basking at the two marinas and the Bagni di Tiberio; expeditions to the Villa Iovis; walks to the top of Monte Solaro, where even in the hottest weather the air was fresh and cool; dinners under vine-pergolas; drinking and cards in the *caffè*; and at night strolling on the Piazza and Strada Nuova, to look at the shimmering sea, and in the distance the lights of Naples with the sultry glow of Vesuvius behind. Whatever the foreigners may have thought of the Neapolitan intruders, they provided excellent business for those hotels which were prepared to accommodate them – not all were – and for the restaurants and *caffè*. Perhaps the Neapolitans too temporarily forgot their grubby and overcrowded city under the spell of this lotus-land.

As in many past years, E. F. ('Dodo') Benson came to Capri that summer to stay with John Ellingham Brooks. Since his arrival in 1895, apart from occasional visits to Naples, Brooks had lived permanently in Capri, where he had devised for himself an inexpensive life of idleness – translating Greek epigrams and the sonnets of the French symbolist poet

Hérédia; struggling with the piano; playing with his dogs and cats; bathing and boating; meeting and scrounging off his friends; and observing the Capri scene. There was an extraordinary interlude in 1903 when he married Romaine Goddard, an American portrait-painter. They had met first in 1899, when Romaine, with very little money, spent the summer in Capri and with the help of Mrs Snow established a small studio. Having entered Capri society, she made friends with Brooks and got some minor commissions to paint portraits. At the end of 1902 her mother died in Nice, leaving Romaine a large fortune and valuable properties in France. In the spring of 1903, aged 29, she returned to Capri to find Brooks in worse financial state than usual, living in squalor and slowly selling his possessions to buy food. She paid off his debts, put his house in order, gave him enough to live on and, surprisingly, in view of her own lesbian inclinations and his homosexuality, accepted his proposal of marriage. Mackenzie, who later made friends with Brooks, suggests that he was captivated by Romaine's boyishness; her biographer, Meryle Secrest, considers that Romaine wanted an undemanding companionship with someone who shared some of her interests. The marriage lasted no more than a year. Leaving Brooks in Capri, Romaine retreated to London, where she purchased a studio in Chelsea. She bought Brooks off with an allowance of £300 a year and the proviso that she never saw him again. Although not a generous settlement, it helped him to survive as a lotus-eater in Capri – 'Enough for meat, but not enough for pickles,' commented Maugham's friend, Alan Searle, 'she screwed him down to the last half-penny.'[51]

In earlier years Benson had shared Brooks's lodging for his summer visits, which usually lasted until the two became exasperated with each other and Benson returned to London – Benson irritated by Brooks's amateur music-making and dilettante translations, Brooks loathing Benson's endless stream of sentimental novels. In 1913, however, they and Somerset Maugham took the lease of the Villa Cercola, where Brooks could live all the year round, and the other two could come and stay as they pleased, usually at different times. The villa stood a little above the eastern edge of the town, 'white walled and cool and covered with morning-glory and plumbago. A garden in terraces lay below it with a pergola above the water-cisterns, and a great stone-pine whispered with the noise of the far-off sea whenever there was the faintest breeze astir.'[52] Instead of the usual warning to visitors about the dog, 'CAVE HOMINEM' was inscribed on the doorstep. Brooks's piano, furniture and books occupied only a small part of the villa, which had once housed a retired Indian Army general and his housekeeper.[53]

Benson was busy throughout June furnishing the empty rooms with cupboards, tables and chairs carpentered in the island, and with linen, crockery and cutlery bought in Naples. He had visions of spending three or four months every summer there, and in July planned to return to England, to assemble books, bookcases and summer clothes from his London house, and return with them by sea to Naples before the end of August.

The murder on 28 June of the Archduke Franz Ferdinand, heir to the Austrian throne, by a young Bosnian fanatic at Sarajevo, and the Austrian ultimatum to the Serbian Government which followed, meant nothing in terms of geography or politics to the islanders and little to most of their visitors. It certainly could not disturb the enjoyment of a halcyon summer. Maugham arrived with his friend, the portrait-painter Gerald Kelly,[54] and joined in the leisurely routine. They were all still there when, at the end of July, Austria-Hungary declared war on Serbia; Russia ordered general mobilisation against this threat to its south-western flank; Germany declared war on Russia and France, and by invading Belgium brought Great Britain into the war on 4 August.

CHAPTER SIX

World War I

The outbreak of war had no immediate effect on Capri. Italy was neutral, and foreigners, whatever their nationality, could come and go as they pleased. Maugham and Kelly saw no reason to change their plans for a summer holiday in the island, until one day a telegram arrived from Mrs Syrie Wellcome, a married woman with whom Maugham was having an affair, to say that she was in Rome and on her way to Capri. Brooks and Benson were horrified at the prospect of having a woman in the house, and Maugham wired back immediately telling her not to come, since he was about to leave. She ignored his message and arrived. A few days later all except Brooks returned to England.[1]

The Italian authorities took their neutrality seriously and, when what appeared to be a coded telegram, was sent to London by Alfredo Clark, the Italian Secret Service in Naples, having spent a fortnight trying to unravel it, sent the *carabinieri* to investigate Clark as a suspect spy. He cleared up the mystery by explaining that it was a telegram to a commission agent in London, putting a sovereign accumulator on three horses at Newmarket. It was a revelation to his friends that the worthy but dim Mr Clark, pillar of the Pro Capri Society, with his *contadina* wife Sara, whom nobody ever saw, was a gambler. Two Russian exiles also came under suspicion of espionage, and their samovar, thought to contain wireless equipment, was removed for investigation.[2]

The English and German residents, however, were uneasily aware that they were guests in a country, which, while temporarily neutral, might at any moment emerge as a combatant. Those, like Augusto Weber, who had married Italians or had dual nationality, and their families were also in an uncertain position. As the son of a German father and Italian mother, Giorgio Weber's birth had been reported to the German Consulate in Naples, as well as to the *municipio* of Capri. In the winter of 1914 he was summoned to report for medical examination by the German Consulate and by the Italian military authorities. It was agreed by both that he need not opt for his nationality until his 21st birthday in July 1915.

Axel Munthe, married to an Englishwoman, sided with the Allies. The Queen of Sweden, who was descended from the Grand Dukes of Baden, sympathized with the Germans. Munthe resigned from the Swedish

Court, sought naturalisation as a British subject and applied to serve as a doctor in France.[3]

One neutral who did well was Gilbert Clavel, a Swiss, who, suffering from tuberculosis, had come to the island for his health and established himself in the Villa Saida in Anacapri. A friend of Fersen, whose sexual outlook and addiction to narcotics he shared, nicknamed ''O Scartelluzzo' ('little hunchback'), he was described by Douglas as 'a deformed young Swiss, with pushful and almost offensive manners, unhealthy complexion and a horrible rasping voice', but he was intelligent, widely read, fancied himself as one of the avant-garde, and had a love of natural history, which in Douglas's eyes mitigated but did not redeem his vulgarity. Clavel had a wine-business in Anacapri, a tower in Positano, which he had bought for 150 *lire* and later converted into a house, and an import/export firm in Naples. Already rich from his father, who had made money in textiles, he prospered throughout the war, by selling to both sides.[4] In 1927 he returned to Basel, where he committed suicide.

In 1914 the Capresi elected a new *sindaco*, Carmĭně Vuotto, to replace Carlo Ferraro, the pharmacist. Vuotto was a good choice. Upright and endowed with common-sense, he was always ready to seek advice if he needed it. Although modest by nature, he also knew how and when to assert his authority. He had married Anna, daughter of Michele Pagano, and worked in the Manfredi Pagano Hotel. Politically he was independent, and with him disappeared for good the already largely meaningless *clericale/anticlericale* distinctions of Capri politics. He remained in office until 1920.

In October, Monty Mackenzie, considered at 31 to be too old for an infantry commission, returned from England with Faith and took up possession of Casa La Solitaria. They found it 'quaintly furnished by Edwin Cerio with a set of ceremonial Venetian armchairs of surprising discomfort, Gorki's writing table, which was about seven feet long and covered with green baize, a divan the size of a small room, also from Gorki's Capri house; an enormous baroque mirror in the *salone*, which, although oblong in shape, covered nearly the whole of one wall. Such necessities as beds and chests-of-drawers had been supplied with an obvious lack of enthusiasm. Our furniture and curtains were already on the way, so what did it matter?' Their household consisted of Carolina, 'a wisp of a woman just over fifty'; her nephew Antonio, who, although only fifteen, was already an excellent chef; and Carolina's youngest daughter – who was housemaid. Faith discovered that, unless she was having a party, it was useless ordering meals in advance, because nobody knew what the daily boat would bring and what would be found in the shops. It was the chef's job to get to the Piazza as early as possible and pick the best. Although chefs did their own shopping, they were not to be seen carrying the smallest parcel, and every morning Antonio would return from his shopping followed along Tragara by an old *facchina* heavily laden and with a full basket on her head. In due course Antonio in white cap and coat would receive Faith in the kitchen, show her the *spese* book and what he had bought and tell her what they were going to have for lunch and dinner.

Soon after the Mackenzies were installed in La Solitaria, Fersen returned from his world tour, bringing cases of new treasures and enough opium to last for years. He also had charge of all the trunks which Kate and Saidee had filled with anything and everything that had taken their fancy. They themselves returned a few days later to celebrate with a series of prodigal parties. As well as masses of new things for the Torricella, they had presents for all their friends and for sometime to come on Sunday afternoons the guests had to admire the trophies of their tour, while Fersen whispered that they were all of very inferior quality and bought against his advice.[5]

Although the United States was busy 'waging neutrality'[6], there was not a vestige of it in either the Villa Narcissus or the Villa Torricella. Charles Coleman, now 74, still received a few hundred dollars a year from Washington for his part in defending the Union over fifty years earlier. He declared that he was 'darned near ashamed' to draw his pension, and considered that for President Wilson ('blasted college professor . . . big-mouthed Democrat') to stand by while 'these filthy German brutes are slaughtering women and children every day . . . is dragging The Stars and Stripes in the dust'. The Wolcott-Perrys were equally vehement, but time had not softened their feelings about Coleman, particularly as 'dear Count Jack' was assuring them that he would soon be off to fight for France. They thought it outrageous that some Englishmen should not also be leaving for the Front – and sent postcards to Godfrey Thornton, aged 58, whose career in the Hertford Militia and the Life Guards in 1877–8 had lasted less than twelve months, and to Horace Fisher, one year older, who for more than 25 years had pursued his life as a painter in Anacapri, urging them to volunteer, and promising them a farewell lunch. Thornton's view was that if he *did* go to the Front he jolly well wouldn't go with Fisher, who would *bore* him to *death*. Fisher, while ready to 'do his bit', if his services were required, did not see eye to eye with Thornton on sexual matters and would rather have gone with somebody else. Colonel Bryan Palmes, for many years a soldier in India and now 62, offered his services to the War Office 'for any kind of obscure employment' and, when told that there was nothing useful he could do, remarked that England was embarking on a 'war against the most powerful military nation in the world like a lot of old women fighting to get on an omnibus'. Of course, it was reported all over Capri that he was pro-German. But the French Government showed no eagerness to call Fersen to the colours, and he spent the winter in Capri dreaming away the time with opium, while Kate became increasingly impatient about his situation.

At La Solitaria Mimì Ruggiero created and stocked the garden. Monty and Mimì had become friends soon after his arrival in the island, and Monty was having an affair with Mimì's brother Luigi. Mimì's appeal was summed up by Faith: 'There was something about him, his wiry movements, the intelligence of his flashing brown eyes, and the rakish angle of his straw hat, worn at the back of his head and yet over one ear, that proclaimed him a personality not to be passed by. . . . '[7] He was the undisputed creator of gardens – at Villa Torricella for the Wolcott-Perrys; Villa Lysis for Fersen; the enlarged Quisisana; Villa Regina Svezia (Casa Caprile) in Anacapri for Queen Victoria of Sweden; Villa Cercola for Brooks, Maugham and Benson; and several others.

The second volume of *Sinister Street* appeared in November and 'without the help of being banned in England by the circulating libraries, sold nearly as well as the first volume' – which enabled Monty to pay off all his debts and feel confident about his literary future.

Earlier in the year, after instruction by the *parroco*, Monty had been received into the Catholic Church and a week later was confirmed by the Archbishop of Sorrento. In the week before Christmas the *parroco* obtained permission to say Mass at La Solitaria. The house was blessed beforehand and, while the *parroco* was sprinkling the room with holy water, two *zampognari*, shepherds from the Abruzzi – one with an instrument having bellows of goat's hide and resembling a Scottish bagpipe, the other with a kind of oboe – played a haunting, age-old tune of the mountains. It was, and still is, the custom for the *zampognari* to bring their music to Capri, for the ten days leading up to the Feast of the Immaculate Conception (8 December) and again, truly in their role as shepherds, from 16 December until Christmas Day. They play at roadside shrines in the island and in private houses, where, after they have been complimented on their playing and given food, wine and money, they may present the donor with a spoon of olive wood as a token of gratitude. For the celebration of Mass Mimì erected an altar with an eight-foot cross of irises. Also in the week before Christmas Monty gave a dinner-party at Marina Piccola for thirty fishermen and coachmen.

Fersen had brought back a pair of cats from the Royal Palace of Siam. The male had died during the voyage, and on arrival in Capri the little princess consoled herself with a ginger tom who lived on Tiberio. Two tortoiseshell kittens were born and, because they were a threat to his carpets and disturbed his opium-dreams with their mews, he gave them to the Mackenzies. They were christened Guy and Pauline, after the title of a new book which Monty began on New Year's Eve 1914, dealing with his own experiences in an early love affair.

In the middle of January 1915 there was a violent earthquake on the mainland, which destroyed the town of Avezzano and did much damage in Rome itself. Monty noted that the only trace of the earthquake in Capri was 'the quiver of hanging perches in bird-cages'.

In early spring he bought for £400 almost the whole of the southern face of Monte Solaro – a property of some 60 acres called Ventroso, a range of wild uncultivated promontories and ridges. The mountain-side was inhabited only by birds, wild flowers, lentisk, myrtle and rosemary. There was a tiny beach which could only be reached from Marina Piccola, and from it Monty commissioned Mimì Ruggiero to make a long winding path through the thick *macchia* to the cliff-top 1,600 feet above.[8]

On 19 February the Dardanelles were attacked by a British fleet and at last Monty saw the possibility of joining in the war. Thanks to some string-pulling he was given a commission in the Royal Marines and awaited his summons to go east. In his honour Kate and Saidee Wolcott-Perry gave a farewell lunch party at which his health was proposed by Fersen, who was still in Capri and no nearer the Western Front. Somerset Maugham, who was in the island again, and Brooks came to dinner to say goodbye. Finally, orders arrived that he should proceed immediately to Alexandria. To catch the steamer from Naples, he had to leave very early the next morning. Capresi of every age and station were already assembled to kiss his hand and cheeks, give him bouquets of flowers and wish him '*buon viaggio e presto ritorno!*', before he disappeared down the *funicolare*.

On 23 May 1915 the Italians, eager to seize Trieste and the Trentino – those 'unredeemed' parts of Italy which Austria refused to concede – declared war on Austria. Bohemians in Capri were dragged off to internment, but, until 23 August, when Italy also declared war on Germany 'Prussians continued to strut about the island without the mildest invigilation'.[9] Out of respect for his great contribution to medicine, the property of Emil von Behring, consisting of the Villa Behring (Casa Rossa) in Capri town and the *fortino* at Marina Piccola, was exempted from confiscation; but he died in 1917 before he could return to enjoy them.

The tourist industry had completely dried up, and the effect on hotels was very severe. The younger males were called up for military service, but many other people went hungry, and for them Vincenzo Desiderio, appointed head of the 'Congregazione di Carità', Capri's welfare agency, set up a soup-kitchen where people in need could get at least one hot meal a day. His brother-in-law Augusto Weber wrote OGGI PATATE, DOMANI NO! on a pair of his linen shoes.

Not all young Capresi relished the idea of serving with the colours in some distant part of Italy. Two, who wanted to stay at home, bought a

Compton Mackenzie, 1915

Faith Mackenzie and Norman
Douglas, c. 1925. *Both courtesy of
William Collins Son & Co Ltd.*

motor-boat, recruited a friend to act as seaman, and offered their services for the anti-submarine war. They were assigned to the protection of the Capri boat on its twice-a-day run of the Gulf. How they would have dealt with a German submarine, had it appeared, is not known.

After Italy's decision to join the war Giorgio Weber was again called to the German Consulate and, when he refused to go, was declared a deserter from the German Army. On his 21st birthday on 13 July, the *sindaco*, arrayed in tricolour waistband, presided over the ceremony in which Weber opted for Italian citizenship. He was immediately called up and assigned to the Infantry. Some months later he was transferred to the Medical Corps as a medical student and sent to Rome.

Nino was soon enlisted, and Fersen, whose income had been drastically reduced by German occupation of the family steel-works in Lorraine and the coal-mines which supplied them, spent every franc he could collect on bribes to secure Nino a position in Naples. For a while he was successful, but at length Nino was sent off to the Front and his health was greatly improved by the hard régime and lack of opportunity to smoke opium. The Allies began to call up each other's nationals, and Fersen was summoned to report for medical examination at the French Consulate in Naples. He was found unfit by reason of his addiction to narcotics and ordered to enter hospital for detoxication. Deprived of his opium he sought desperately for another drug and, unknown to the doctors, managed to procure a supply of cocaine.

War frenzy gripped the women of the English colony. Mrs Hinde of the Villa Tragara 'rushed about the island in a convulsion of loyal hydro-phobia' and wrote letters to the War Office denouncing other English residents as 'pro-Germans, spies and traitors'. The competitive denun-ciation by Emelie Fraser and Gwen Galatà of one person after another 'emptied the hospitable rooms of the Villa Torricella far more successfully than the social war over Count Fersen ever did'. Gwen became patho-logical about Margarete, German wife of the artist Goffredo Sinibaldi, 'a comfortable, blond, middle-aged Prussian whose two sons were already on their way to the Trentino with their regiments'. She succeeded in rousing the whole colony against this inoffensive woman, who lived in the Villa Quattro Colonne on Via Tragara and, when not in the house, 'spent much of her time sitting on a seat outside La Solitaria, where she was away from the crowd and its cruel or cold looks'. Here she was befriended in her loneliness by Faith Mackenzie.[10]

A group was formed under the Italian Red Cross, headed by Dr Vincenzo Cuomo, health officer of Anacapri, and run by the ladies of Capri, to knit sweaters and socks, make shirts and roll bandages. Promi-nent on the committee were Emelie Fraser and Gwen Galatà, who hated each other and struggled for the leadership. Committee members included the beautiful Lica Riola; her cousin Natasha, who later became Dr Munthe's secretary; and Lady Mackinder, from the Villa Tragara. The workers were mostly local girls: among them, Maria (Marietta) Russo, daughter of the philanthropic Antonino Russo, who ran the Banco Lotto and was prominent in the Società Operaia; Lellina, daughter of Emiddio Trama, carpenter and picture-frame maker; Elena, daughter of Manfredi and sister of Teodoro Pagano; Matilde, daughter of Augusto Weber and sister of Giorgio; and Maria Gamboni, daughter of the schoolmaster who had helped to secure Fritz Krupp's downfall. Kate and Saidee Wolcott-Perry occasionally came up from the Villa Torricella to lend a hand. Faith Mackenzie joined the group but, disliking the air of tension which prevailed on the committee, left a donation and retired from the fray. In July she went to London and, for something to do, served in a canteen near Victoria Station and packed parcels of books for the troops. She frequented the company of Norman Douglas, whose ribaldry appealed to her; he told her that he was also looking for war work of some kind.

After a short period on Sir Ian Hamilton's staff at Gallipoli, Monty was transferred to the British Secret Service in Athens. In November he asked Faith to join him for a short leave in Capri. They found the island in the depths of gloom – '*O signore mio, che miseria! Questa brutta guerra quando finirà?*' By now life was at a complete standstill, and to Faith it seemed that the impossible had happened – that the 'ghosts of revelry and amorous sports of all descriptions', which had haunted the island for countless years, had at last been laid to rest.

Mrs Fraser, apprehensive that Italy might be overrun by the Austrians, decided to spend the rest of the war in Scotland. Her departure was warmly welcomed by Gwen Galatà, who hoped whe would be torpedoed, and by Sophie Grahame, whose scornful opinion was that 'a torpedo wouldn't touch her with a barge-pole'. After Mrs Fraser's departure Kate and Saidee Wolcott-Perry came to depend increasingly for company on Giovanni and Gwen Galatà. Fersen's continued skulking increased Kate's lack of confidence in him, and 'there began to dance through Gwen's mind . . . the richly attired possibility of inheriting one day the whole of the old ladies' splendid fortune'.[11] Towards the end of 1915, depressed by the dreariness of Capri and the emptiness of the Torricella, Kate and Saidee went off to spend the winter in Rome.

Capri shed a little of its gloom in the New Year, everybody being convinced that the war would be over in a few months. In the spring there was a rumour that the British Government had decided to send hundreds of convalescent officers to the island, and for a fortnight the Piazza was cheerful. But the officers never arrived and were sent to the French Riviera instead. The Capresi blamed the French, but later discovered that the culprit was Mrs Hinde, who had written to the War Office, to point out that Capri was not a fit place for convalescent officers, on account of the temptations to which they would be exposed there at a time when they would, as she put it, 'just be feeling their legs again'.[12]

Douglas did not persevere in his search for war work. Instead, encouraged by the success of *Old Calabria*, which was published in February 1915, he embarked on what was to become his most successful book. *South Wind*, to quote the author, 'was my craving to escape from the wearisome actualities of life. To picture yourself living in a society of such instability, of such "jovial immoderation" and "frolicsome perversity", that even a respectable bishop can be persuaded to approve of a murder – this was my aim'. Douglas expressed much of his own philosophy of life through three of the characters – Keith, Count Caloveglia and Eames. Although some of the other characters owed their creation to people he had known in Capri – Freddy Parker (Harold Trower), The Duchess (inspired by Mrs Snow) and the red-haired judge, Malipizzo (Pretore Pestalozza), for example – it would be an error to identify 'Nepenthe' with Capri. If one is to be topographical about Nepenthe, it would be accurate to call it a conflation of Capri, Ischia and Sorrento, with details drawn also from the Ponza and Lipari Islands.[13]

Douglas started *South Wind* in London at the beginning of 1916 and continued it in Capri, where in May he took two rooms in the empty Villa Behring. Faith typed his manuscripts – not as fast as Douglas wanted – and found him an old piano on which he rendered Chopin, Bach, and English hymn tunes played with great feeling.[14] He returned to London in August to complete the book.

Lord Kitchener's death at sea on 5 June sent a wave of hysteria through the English colony, some members of which thought that the war was now as good as lost. Faith Mackenzie expressed the view that Kitchener's work was done and that his death would make little difference, but in Capri there were howls of rage from Gwen Galatà and others, who already disapproved of her kindness to the lonely Margarete Sinibaldi. After branding her publicly as pro-German, Gwen persuaded the Wolcott-Perrys to ostracize Faith from the Villa Torricella. Munthe, who had finished in France and was back in Capri, asked Faith to lunch and lightly chided her with her 'serious offence.' After the meal he opened an untidy parcel of German ribbons, decorations and medals, and announced that he was returning them forthwith to the Kaiser, who had personally given them.

The summer of 1916 passed quietly, with visiting Neapolitans bringing some comfort to the hotels. Harold Trower resigned as British Consular Agent. Giovanni Galatà became *pretore*. William Andrews died of cancer on 20 September, at the age of 67, his translation of *Faust*, to which he had devoted 22 years of his life, completed but unpublished.[15] In the absence

Red Cross group, 1915, on the terrace of the Quisisana, led by Dr Vincenzo Cuomo. To his left are Lica Riola and Gwen Galatà (with ribbon); to his right, Mrs Fraser (in bonnet) and Lady Mackinder. Above Lady Mackinder, in white hats, are Saidee and Kate Wolcott-Perry. *Courtesy of Signora Nina Stabile*

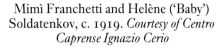

Mimì Franchetti and Helène ('Baby') Soldatenkov, c. 1919. *Courtesy of Centro Caprense Ignazio Cerio*

rincipessa Soldatenkov, c. 1919. *Courtesy of Centro Caprense Ignazio Cerio*

of a resident Chaplain, the Chaplain of the English church at Palermo visited the island to bury him in the *cimitero acattolico*.

Relations between Fersen and the two old ladies remained cool. Communication between his villa up on Tiberio and theirs by the sea was indeed made difficult by his own opium-weakened heart condition, which deterred him from walking to and from Marina Grande, while they, in the absence of all the island's donkeys on active service, were unable to make the ascent to Tiberio. In the autumn, again depressed by Capri, they shut up house and moved to Rome for the winter. In mid-December Saidee was knocked over by a tram and severely shaken. As soon as she was strong enough to travel, they returned to Capri in time for her birthday-party on 21 January. With only the Galatà pair as guests, Saidee did her best to be festive, but her heart was hardly beating, and she died in her sleep twelve days later. After Saidee had been buried, Kate was taken back to the villa in a state of collapse. Fersen was in Naples at the time and, although news of Saidee's death and the time of the funeral was telegraphed to him, he did not return in time for the ceremony. Instead he hurried to the Villa Torricella, where his arrival roused Kate from her stupor of despair into a passion of hate, which may well have saved her own life. After telling him what she could never have done while her friend was alive, that he was a liar, a slave to his vices and a coward, she drove him out of the house for ever.[16]

In the cemetery, over Saidee's grave, she put the replica of a Moorish-Gothic Torricella window, with the Wolcott-Perry coat of arms and motto carved in its spandrel. On one side of the grave she placed a tablet inscribed with her friend's favourite poem:

SAIDEE
Warm summer sun,
Shine kindly here!
Warm southern wind,
Blow softly here!

Green sod above,
Lie light, lie light!
Good night, dear Heart,
Good night! Good night!

and on the other side a blank stone for herself. She bought the adjacent plot, had it paved with broken Roman *tessarae* and fixed on it a small marble seat. Here she sat every day and all day gazing out at the marina and the blue sea, and dreaming that Saidee was beside her. But, back in America, her family decided that Kate must return home and sent a cousin, to bring her back. The Torricella was closed and left in the care of Giovanni and Gwen Galatà. All the valuables were put under lock and seal in cupboards and chests, and the keys left with Giovanni. In mid-summer Kate and her cousin sailed for America; she was now 80, and nobody expected to see her again.[17]

*

On 15 March 1917 the Czar of Russia abdicated, and the revolution rolled slowly forward. Kerensky, the social revolutionary, tried to stir the army into activity against the Germans. Lenin and Trotsky, however, who had returned from abroad (the former's passage having been facilitated by the Germans), organized the Bolsheviks, called for an immediate peace and set out to undermine the discipline of the army. By the end of July the Russian front had crumbled, and in November the Bolsheviks gained power. Notable among the Capri exiles who obtained positions of authority was Lunacharskiy, who was appointed Peoples Commissar for Education, and with his civilizing influence did much to preserve works of art from destruction by the rabble. Gorki founded *Novaya Zhizo* (New Life), in which he openly attacked the dictatorial methods of Lenin and later had to be silenced by censorship.

On 6 April the United States entered the war on the side of the Allies amid general rejoicing amongst the foreigners. The only American in Capri to be directly affected was 35-year-old Morgan Heiskell, who since 1910, with his wife Ann and two young children, Andrew and Diana, had rented the Villa Discopoli. Morgan received a generous allowance from his parents, who also lived in Capri, had no need to earn his living and was able to pursue his hobbies of painting and photography. His wife Ann, a great beauty, was a West Virginian from Wheeling and had completed her formal education at Vassar. After an enthusiastic send-off from Charles Coleman and a farewell lunch at the Torricella before Kate's own departure for the States, Morgan went to Paris to join the American Red Cross.

The only other American of military age was Vernon Andrews, who was now 38. He made no effort to join up and there appeared to be no request for his services. Coleman's opinion was: 'Gad, he and that skulking brute Fersen ought to be tied together and shot.'

Early in June *South Wind* was published in London. It was an immediate success. It would have been a hit at the best of times, but, coming as it did in the midst of a desperate and dreary war, its high spirits, its amoral devotion to fun and its urbane presentation caused a sensation – even though there were some who disapproved of Douglas's attack on accepted customs and beliefs at a time when England had its back to the wall. Many critics thought it had no plot, and this annoyed Douglas, who later retorted: 'How to make murder palatable to a bishop; that is the plot. How? You must unconventionalise him, and instil into his mind the seeds of doubt and revolt. You must shatter his old notions of what is right.'[18] The book brought him not only fame but a good deal of money – though less than he deserved. Whereas his English publishers treated him fairly, in America certain houses availed themselves of a loophole in the copyright laws of that country, in order to avoid paying him a royalty on the great number of copies that were sold.[19]

Unfortunately Douglas was not in England to witness his triumph. At the end of November 1916 he had been arrested and charged with an offence against a 16-year-old boy, whom he had picked up in the Natural History Museum and persuaded to go back to his flat. He was remanded in custody for a week, but at a second hearing was released on bail. At a third hearing he was charged with further offences in July against two brothers aged 10 and 12, also at the Natural History Museum. At a fourth hearing on 9 January 1917 Faith Mackenzie appeared as a witness and testified, what was in fact true, that Douglas had been in Capri in July 1916. Discharged on this count, he was ordered to await trial on the other. He decided to skip the country as soon as possible and made his way to Italy. Eventually he settled down in Florence to deal with the proofs of *South Wind*, which duly made its triumphant appearance in the summer.

In Capri, following the Kitchener episode, Faith turned against all the English and American expatriates. She found solace in her piano, took lessons in sculpture and went on lonely walks. For friendship she sought out Bianca and Isabella Caracciolo, the fifth and sixth daughters of old Prince Caracciolo, and their cousin Bianca Binyon. Giulia, the eldest Caracciolo girl, who had been brought up when the Prince still had enough money to afford governesses for his children, and was fluent in German, French and English, ran a small circulating library, and was popular in the English and American colonies. By the time Bianca and Isabella were beginning to grow up their father had gambled away most of his money, and their education suffered accordingly. They spoke no English and on this account reacted against the cosmopolitan environment of their elder sister. They were thus good companions for Faith in her self-imposed isolation. Through the two girls, she met their youngest brother Marino (Nini), who was showing promise as a painter. With her own interest in sculpture as a common bond, she made friends with and fell in love with the young man; she was nearing 40 and he just turned 22. Throughout the summer of 1917 Capri society watched the love-affair develop and wondered what would happen when Monty returned from Greece.

Monty was regarded by the Head of the British Secret Service as a successful intelligence officer. Arrogant, no respecter of persons and unorthodox in his methods, he nevertheless, or perhaps because of these qualities, achieved useful results. But his support of the republican Venizelos was severely frowned upon by the British and Italian political authorities, and at the end of August he was recalled to London. In October, on the verge of a breakdown, he was given indefinite leave, and, returning to Europe, he made his way south to Italy. His arrival coincided with the disaster of Caporetto, when on 24 October 1917 the Italian army, destined for the capture of Trieste, was routed by the Austrians, who had been stiffened by six German divisions, and driven back with huge losses of men and equipment, and in total confusion, to the River Piave. Here they rallied, morale was restored and, reinforced hurriedly by French and British divisions, they held the river-line successfully throughout the winter.

When Monty reached Capri at the beginning of November, Faith told Nini that the affair was at an end and he must not visit La Solitaria again. In a state of despair he wandered about the countryside through the savage weather, caught rheumatic fever and, with a congenitally weak heart, collapsed and died. Faith, who thought that his weak heart was a broken heart and blamed herself for his death, suffered a serious breakdown. Monty silenced the gossip by attending Nini's funeral and then, in order to occupy Faith's mind, asked her to type the scripts of his new book *Sylvia Scarlett*, which with a great effort of will, she agreed to do. He had set himself the task of completing the 300,000-word novel by February 1918, but, after unremitting work in which 280,000 words were written in 80 days, he too cracked and told the publishers that there was no chance of finishing the book on time.[20]

Throughout the winter and early spring Capri continued to be gripped by depression and shortages of all kinds. The authorities interned 71-year-old Augusto Weber and his daughter Matilde, in spite of the fact that his wife was *caprese* and his son Giorgio serving in the Italian Army; they feared, it seemed, that he might signal to German submarines from his *pensione* at Marina Piccola. They also interned the German Sisters of St Elizabeth and some other German women, but allowed Margarete Sinibaldi to go free. In January 1918 the internees were sent to Sant' Agata de' Goti, a walled town near Benevento, where they were confined until the end of the war.

Unless they had invested their money in munitions, or as neutrals like Clavel done business with both sides, many natives and foreigners alike were feeling the pinch. Gwen Galatà, who had put much of her money into Belgian railways and lost it all, was now very hard up and reduced to taking paying guests at the Villa Esperia. Fortunately she was an excellent cook and added a touch of jollity and eccentricity to an otherwise drab scene.

Fersen, discharged from hospital as an incurable drug-addict, took up residence again at the Villa Lysis, where he allowed the thickets of casuarina and mimosa to grow denser and denser, and forbade the gardener to cut so much as a twig. Fersen compensated for his lack of war activity by awarding himself the Legion of Honour, but plucked it hastily from his button-hole whenever he saw anyone he knew.

The Mackenzies were pulling themselves up from their respective collapses. They were greatly helped by Axel Munthe, who came down to the Solitaria one day in March and analysed their situation. He spoke of the sacrifice of her career as a pianist, which Faith had made in marrying Monty; her encouragement of his work as a writer and care for him during his bouts of neuritis; her loneliness and difficulties in Capri; the trauma of her affair with Nini Caracciolo; and altogether the basic incompatibility of their two characters. Munthe persuaded them to abandon a conventional marriage and to make a pact of friendship whereby each could henceforth be free to live his and her own life.[21] Accepting at last that Nini's death was due to a weak heart and not heart-break, Faith renewed her friendship with Bianca and Isabella Caracciolo, and became absorbed again in her sculpture, while Monty tackled the final chapters of *Sylvia Scarlett*. He and Mimì Ruggiero added to the garden of La Solitaria and often visited the path which under Mimì's guidance was being cut up the southern face of Monte Solaro. Mimì prudently used any cut wood for making charcoal – the staple fuel for cooking in Capri. Monty had the idea of building a house beside the Ventroso landing-place and as a first step made a small square cistern. No sooner had it been built and lined, than an enormous rock from the side of Solaro crashed into it, and that was that. Later in the year Monty bought a four-roomed cottage on the plain of Cetrella, together with two acres of land, where he and Mimì planted tulips, narcissi, hyacinth, anemone and iris. He used the cottage for private meetings with his boy-friends and lent it to others for this purpose.

As 1918 wore on, the resistance of the Italian Army, with its Anglo-French reinforcements, became stronger. British officers from the front took their leave in Capri and got boringly drunk in Morgano's. The summer brought over the usual Neapolitans. Disquieting was the news that representatives of a group of Milanese war-profiteers (*pescecani* – 'sharks') had been enquiring about the possibility of buying up the main hotels.[22]

With the certainty of victory ahead, optimism grew apace. Characteristically the island, so deeply versed in the arts of pleasure, anticipated the rest of Europe in the hedonistic spree which elsewhere waited until the intolerable years of war were finally at an end. Faith Mackenzie, who witnessed the phenomenon at first hand, wrote:

> Life at Capri in the last year of the Great War and after might well be described as highly spiced. ... Capri, dedicated for centuries to first-class bacchanalia, still excelled in that hectic aftermath; she was the queen of pleasure and light pursuits. No wonder disillusioned and exasperated people flocked to her shores. They usually found what they wanted in the beauty of the island or in its superficial air of gaiety. For there was a desperate quality in that gaiety, and everyone was either a little bit or extremely mad.[23]

As usual, it was the foreigners who made the running. In the forefront was Van Decker, a lighthearted Dutchman with plenty of money, who gave wild parties, and, as the villa he rented was in a conspicuous part of the town with a large window and terrace, visible to the public, there was a good deal of talk about them. At one party Van Decker danced a *pas seul* wearing nothing but a small bunch of roses. At another, Nadegin and Mariescas, two Tsarist officials, who had lost their jobs to Bolsheviks at the Russian Embassy in Rome and hopefully made for Capri, stripped for a wrestling bout and were much admired by Oscar Wilde's friend, Reggie Turner, who was on a visit from Florence. Don Luigi Lembo, who had succeeded De Nardis as *parroco*, wrote to Mackenzie, unavailingly it seems, asking him to use his influence as a Catholic to 'discourage such painful orgies'.[24] Italo Tavolato, a 'futurist' born in Trieste and of German culture, came to Capri, where he felt instantly at home and published the first and only number of a monthly magazine entitled *Eros*, in which he inveighed against the social conventions and taboos of the time.[25]

The last year of the war also saw the sudden flowering in Capri of a lesbian coterie, which is amusingly described in Mackenzie's *Extraordinary Women*. The ground was already well prepared. Across the water in Sorrento was the Principessa Helène Soldatenkov (Gortchakov). In spite of losing all her Russian assets in the Revolution, she had plenty invested abroad and was still rich enough to live in style at the Villa Siracusa and to stay in Capri when she wanted. Her entire staff – gardeners, chauffeurs, sailors and grooms – were female. The Princess herself, a substantial woman in her forties, had a 'finely cut profile, the slight hardness of which was accentuated by her dark complexion and sharp arrogant eyes'. She was usually dressed in jacket, leather belt and long white skirt, and sported a monocle hung on the end of a cord. Her daughter, 'Baby', was a beautiful, if somewhat doll-like, girl of seventeen, who to her mother's displeasure had fallen in love with Luigi Gargiulo, the good-looking son of the local barber. In order to separate them the Princess sent Baby over to Capri with her governess 'Missi', to stay in the Quisisana and, she hoped, recover from Luigi.[26]

Staying as guest of the Princess was another Russian, Olga de Tschélis-cheff, who had fallen on bad times. Daughter of a diplomat, she had been compelled as a girl to marry one of her father's colleagues, and had a son who died very young. In 1914 her husband sent her out of Russia for safety, and after living first in Paris and then in Egypt she arrived in Capri at the end of 1916 with little else but her jewellery, on the gradual sale of which she lived. Her husband was killed in the Revolution, and what was left of her property in Russia was swallowed up. Olga was *non bella*, but *molto elegante* and well-dressed, with grey eyes and chestnut-brown hair. Intelligent, and fluent in several languages, she had perfect manners, a sense of humour, and astonishing tolerance of all and sundry. She was not hostile to men, as the Princess was, and, if men 'did not greatly trouble her passions any longer, they were by no means displeasing to her intelligence'. But she kept her distance, was 'all things but one to all men, and, as she purred her approval of whatever they told her, would murmur: 'how wonnderful . . . I do find that so wonnderful'. In spite of their different situations and characters, the Princess and Olga were real friends, and Olga was well-liked by the staff, who considered her *una buonissima signora*.[27]

In Capri was the pianist Renata Borgatti, daughter of Giuseppe Borgatti, the great Wagnerian tenor. At her coming-out dance just before the war Renata had been decked out in her finest clothes, but given shoes that were much too small and agony to wear. After a dance or two she refused to go on, and this catastrophe seems to have marked the beginning of her revolt against a conventional life. She took up the piano as a career, made her way to Capri and rented a studio at Punta Tragara. Renata had a straight Grecian nose, jutting brows and finely carved chin; a shapeless, ungainly body on which she carelessly flung her clothes rather 'as curtains hung up to exclude the night'; and large feet like a man's. Except anatomically, she was to all intents and purposes a man, and she treated all women accordingly. 'She suffered as women of her temperament are condemned to suffer from passions which are not returned . . . the masculine side of her nature was so dominant that she sought women as she found them, without waiting for those who were temperamentally akin to herself.' It was thus at the age of twenty-four that she fell in love with the slightly older Lica Riola. Their encounter coincided with the Revolution and the loss of all the Riolas' assets in Russia. Lica had a warm heart, but she was not lesbian. Fond of Renata though she became, she did not have time to return much of her friend's affection, because she was perpetually engaged in making dresses and rushing about as commission agent, in order to keep herself and her now impoverished family off the breadline.

Faith Mackenzie was enchanted by Renata and, according to one source, in love with her. She would often go to Renata's recitals at the Punta Tragara studio and invite Renata to La Solitaria, where she would play Wagner operas for hours on end, now and then singing in her deep, hoarse, masculine voice. Clotilde Marghieri, the writer, remembers creeping into La Solitaria during one of Renata's recitals as she performed Beethoven's last piano sonata, *opus* 111, cigarette hanging out of the corner of her mouth, her pale face wreathed in spirals of smoke, playing with the whole of her body, swaying over the keyboard, her raised arms quivering after a chord, and from time to time laughing, spellbound.[28]

Living at the Quisisana were Mrs Francesca Lloyd (known as 'Checca' or Frances), a rich Australian of the family Edersham, whose marriage had broken up, together with her friend Mimì Franchetti. Checca was masculine in outlook, but inconveniently feminine in shape – which made it something of an ordeal to don full evening dress, with white tie and stiff shirt, which she liked for grand occasions. Mimì was the daughter of Baron Alberto Franchetti, Italian opera composer, and of a beautiful mother who had bequeathed her good looks to her daughter. Mackenzie remembered her arrival at the Quisisana in May 1918 with 'short accordion-pleated skirt . . . rifle green jacket and waistcoat, her double collar and black satin tie with coral pin, her long jade cigarette holder and slim ebony stick and . . . rippling hair lustrous and hatless'.[29]

Checca was hopelessly in love with Mimì, but so were other women, like the bedraggled 'Contessa Giulia Monforte' who traipsed around Europe in pursuit of her and was also staying at the Quisisana. Unfortunately for all concerned Mimì was an accomplished 'bitch-girl', who loved only herself and used her charms to play off one woman against another and create general havoc. *Extraordinary Women* is mainly about the chase she led poor 'Rory Freemantle', a composite character in the novel, but based on Checca Lloyd. There were frequent quarrels – Carlo Civitella remembers seeing them at the Quisisana throwing bottles at each other – and separations, interspersed with reconciliations and rare periods of harmony.

Mimì could not be expected to refrain from intervening in the friendship between Renata and Lica, and for a time Renata in her frustration succumbed to Mimì's charms. The one person who puzzled Mimì was Olga de Tschélischeff, who seemed not to care at all when the Principessa Soldatenkov became temporarily infatuated with Mimì and for a time abandoned Olga, who withdrew gracefully to a remote cottage on Tiberio.[30] Her inability to wound Olga infuriated Mimì, and what she found even more offensive was the fact that Olga appeared to be laughing at her.

Baby Soldatenkov, described by one of the set as *'jeune fille . . . fourbe, mais au fond innocente'* – the imputation of innocence reduced her to tears – was soon conquered by Mimì. Baby's affair with Mimì was warmly encouraged by her mother who felt that 'it struck as hard at the whole male sex as it had at one presumptuous youth'. Baby, however, soon got tired of Rosalba and took up with another boy. Mimì then found herself burdened with far too much of the Princess's company. In the autumn they returned to Sorrento, where Baby joined a group of young people who passed the time in playing poker, drinking cocktails and making love. All this reduced 'Missi' to a breakdown and she was sent on a long holiday. Her place as governess was taken by the 'Baroness Drenka Vidakovich', 'a handsome young woman of about thirty with a hard mouth, coarse hands and bright bitter eyes which always seemed to be looking as if she had not been given the correct change'; the Princess was confident that her daughter would learn something of the world from the Baroness.[31]

Lesser characters flitted in and out from other parts of the world. 'Mrs Royle', a rich American living in Rome, old and ugly 'like a squat cracked little gilded bronze', came to the Quisisana with her daughter 'Janet', 'tall and slim and olivine, with graceful mind and body, and gentle melodious voice, fastidious and intellectual'. Janet was serenaded and temporarily won by Mimì.[32] There were 'Principessa Flavia (Bébé) Buonagrazia', disingenuous, urbane, with a serpent's tongue and a 'laugh which tinkled and pricked like broken glass';[33] 'Dicky Freemartin', Gloria, Lola and Lydia[34]; Aretusa, Titi and Zenaide.[35] Faith Mackenzie summed them up: 'The fair ladies, and some were very fair indeed, put pretty noses out of joint and monopolised attention with little apparent effort. They had but to walk on the Piazza or Funicular terrace, swinging military capes, or wearing feminine little frocks as the case might be, fingering interminable cigarette-holders, to be immediately the objects of popular interest. Their kaleidoscopic changes of companionship were enough to keep the gossips amused.'[36]

In October the Italian Army went on the offensive and in the victory of Vittorio Veneto routed the Austrian army. Austria sued for peace, by early November the War was over, and Italian troops entered Trento and Trieste in triumph.[37] The bells of Capri rang out with the joyful news. There was a High Mass and Solemn *Te Deum* in Santo Stefano. In the evening Vernon Andrews emerged from seclusion and threw a champagne party in Morgano's for the island's notables. 'Drinks and speeches, tears and raptures, toasts and panegyrics, culminated in a short Italian speech from Monty Mackenzie, after which the notables rushed at him to embrace him and he was lost in half a dozen stifling beards. . . . '[38]

A week after these celebrations came news of the Armistice in France and the German surrender, which at last brought the *brutta guerra* to an end. For the island it had not been without sacrifice – 31 Capresi and 12 Anacapresi killed in the fighting, and as many again who died as a result of the war.[39]

CHAPTER SEVEN

The Post-war Pursuit of Pleasure

In spite of 'Spanish 'flu', which caused much illness and several deaths, the outburst of spending and the pursuit of pleasure increased by leaps and bounds. 'Not merely profiteers,' wrote Mackenzie 'but soldiers home from the war, English people showing their daughters the continent now it is once more available, Neapolitans with pasty-faced, sweet-smeared children, Americans looking like the supernumeraries in a film, Germans swigging and guzzling and paying for it in Swiss francs, Russians who have decided to turn Bolshevik and so have money to spend, French artists who have won travelling scholarships, Dutch intellectuals, Scandinavian eccentrics, central Europeans flushed with self-determination, and of course pederasts and pathics of every nationality. This is the post-war harvest, the thought of which had sustained the island through all those dreary winters when Capri life seemed to be dissolving utterly away.'[1]

One particular Neapolitan had started at the beginning of the War as a porter in a small fireworks factory. Somehow he managed to become owner of the factory and there made explosives. 'By the time the War was over he was almost literally rolling in money, a large fat man with a retinue of parasitic flatterers. While the finishing touches were being put to his new *palazzo* at Posillipo, he was staying in Capri; he had already acquired the other two essentials for a Neapolitan *pescecane* – a larger solitaire diamond than most of his rivals, and a secretary.' The secretary he chose was Prince Ruffo, a small, spritely but penniless octogenarian with an immense lineage, who could not afford to refuse the salary which subservience to this vulgar upstart demanded. His master, of course, 'felt that in engaging a prince of ancient lineage as his secretary, he had made the secretaries employed by other *pescecani* look small fry'.[2]

All this sudden boost did not save the Quisisana from going bankrupt, and in 1919 Federico Serena's widow had to sell it. The original Hotel Pagano was also sold, but the family held on the Manfredi Pagano annexe. Both hotels, together with the Hotel Villa Igea, were bought by the SIPPIC, the prosperous, mainly Milanese, company which owned the *funicolare* and electricity plant at Marina Grande; and a separate company, the Società Italiana Alberghi (SIA), was formed to run them. Under the energetic management of the SIPPIC the Quisisana quickly re-established itself as the principal hotel and, with the daily pension less than one pound sterling, was crammed with foreign visitors. Outside the hotel there were always donkeys available to carry tourists up to Tiberio or Monte Solaro or indeed anywhere in the island. To arrange sea-trips, there were Panza, 'Giulione', 'Boccanfuso' and other members of a small group of sailors with no steady occupation and owning nothing except a small rowing-boat, which would carry a couple of sightseers from Marina Grande or Marina Piccola to the Faraglioni or one or other of the grottoes. Although it was hard work for Panza and the others, it was the only job they knew and liked; most lived in small apartments in town with their women-folk and a flock of children; Panza himself was a noted *meteorologo* and usually right about the weather.[3]

Giuseppe Morgano came out of the war in reasonable shape, and instead of selling the Tiberio Palace, which he had built before the war as a rival to the Quisisana, for a pittance, was able to lease it to the SIPPIC, giving them the option of buying it before a fixed date. The hard-headed Milanese had the idea of rescuing Capri 'from the unpleasant bohemian-ism of manners and morals for which the island had long been notorious' and converting it into a health resort. The Tiberio Palace became a sanatorium, and a clinician was brought from Milan to manage it. A clinic with laboratory and x-ray apparatus was set up nearby in the Villa Igea and an English Sister recruited to head the nursing staff. The sanatorium was not a success and, when on the appointed day in 1922, the SIPPIC had not exercised their option to purchase, Morgano moved in immediately to repossess it and re-establish his hotel.

Many lesser old-style buildings were bought up and demolished by the Milanese, 'whose sense of beauty did not extend beyond the notion of a fat woman in bed'. Meanwhile their wives and daughters 'in guaranteed Parisian models hobbled about the roughly paved alleys with high heels. The air seemed heavy with large hips and rice-powder and the languors of Latin vulgarity.' If they bought 'an hotel surrounded by a fair old wall over which sprawled a tangle of roses and wistaria they pulled down the wall and put up iron railings in the convulsive Munich style'; and prices went up at the same time.[4]

Ing. Emilio Vismara from Milan bought the land around the end of Via Tragara, one of the fairest spots in the island, perched high above the Faraglioni rocks. Carmela's *caffè* and Renata Borgatti's studio were swept away and in their place rose a palatial villa. Carmela's daughter Maria, however, was not defeated and established another *caffè/ristorante* a little way up Via Tragara and as near as possible to the original site, but without the stunning view which the end of Punta Tragara provided. The Villa Vismara rose massive, but not out of harmony with the rocks on which it perched, earning the praise of Le Corbusier, which in those days was

2 Anacapri, Marina Grande and Eastern Capri

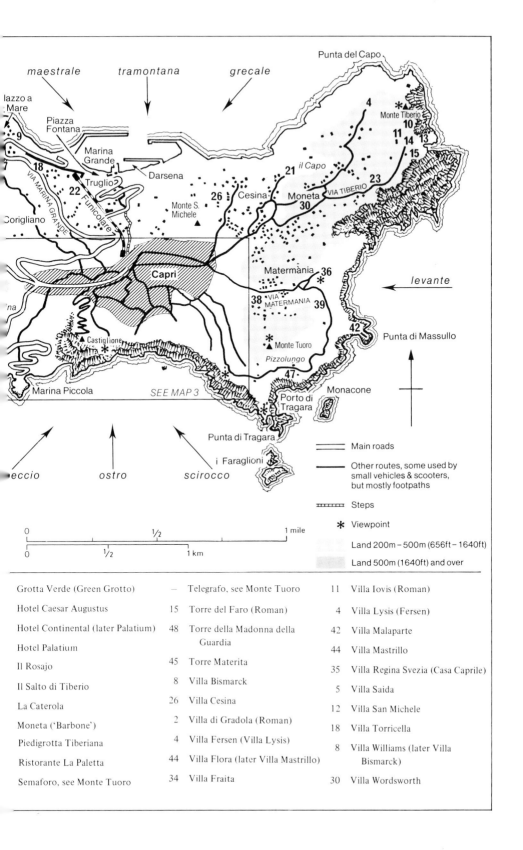

maestrale   tramontana   grecale

Punta del Capo

lazzo a
Mare

Piazza
Fontana

Marina
Grande

Darsena

4

Monte Tiberio

10

11   14   13

15

9

18

Truglio

22 Funicolare

il Capo

21

23

Corigliano

26   Cesina

Moneta   VIA TIBERIO

Monte S.
Michele

30

Capri

Matermània   36

38 VIA
MATERMANIA   39

levante

Castiglione

Monte Tuoro

Pizzolungo

42

Punta di Massullo

47

Marina Piccola   SEE MAP 3

Monacone

Porto di
Tragara

Punta di Tragara

i Faraglioni

eccio   ostro   scirocco

═══ Main roads

─── Other routes, some used by
     small vehicles & scooters,
     but mostly footpaths

⊞⊞⊞ Steps

✱ Viewpoint

     Land 200m – 500m (656ft – 1640ft)

     Land 500m (1640ft) and over

0   1/2   1 mile
0   1/2   1 km

praise indeed. It was rumoured that Vismara planned to turn it into a *casinò*.[5] As with buildings, so with land. Many hard-up Capresi sold their land to profiteers for as little as £10 a square metre and later had the mortification of seeing vast profits made by the buyers, as well as by those Capresi who had been able to hold on to their properties.

A new class of Russian descended on the island. Before the war most Russian visitors had been revolutionaries, and many of them now held power in Russia. Now they were all refugees from the Revolution, and exiles for life, or not yet sure what their future was to be. Nadegin and Mariescas, who in the previous summer had enlivened one of Van Decker's parties with their wrestling bout, stayed on, uncertain what to do. Both had fine voices, and after a while Mariescas left Capri to embark on a career as a professional singer. As a student, Nadegin had been mildly revolutionary and spent two years in Siberia, but was now certain that he never wanted to see Russia again as long as the Bolsheviks were in power. He remained in Capri, made friends with Faith Mackenzie and for a time was her lover. Michele Katz, a Russian sculptor, who before the Revolution had come to Italy with a travelling scholarship from the Academy of Fine Arts, arrived, gave lessons to Faith and made busts of her and Monty. Two young brothers Florenski made a brief appearance, gave some wild parties and then returned to Russia, where one became an important official.[6]

Mytilene was in full swing. Checca Lloyd bought the Cà del Sole and the Villa Alba next door in Via Castello, and moved out of the Quisisana.[7] At the beginning of August 1919 the lesbian dovecotes were fluttered by the arrival of Romaine Brooks, now in her mid-forties.[8] She turned her husband out of the Villa Cercola, where the Maugham/Benson/Brooks triad had already dissolved, and set up a studio in it; Brooks retreated to a *villino* in Via Matermania. To Faith Mackenzie, Romaine was a 'figure of intriguing importance . . . a woman complete in herself, isolated mentally and psychically from the rest of her kind, independent in her judgements, accepting or rejecting as she pleased movements, ideas, people. To be loved by Romaine for even five minutes gave any young woman who cared about it a cachet not obtainable since the days when young women could boast of being loved by the mighty Sappho herself. The arrival of this striking personality was a sensation. A heat-wave, hot even for Capri in August, sent temperatures up. Feverish bouquets of exhausted blooms lay about the big studio, letters and invitations strewed her desk, ignored for the most part, while she, wrapped in her cloak, would wander down to the town as the evening cooled and sit in the darkest corner of Morgano's terrace, maddeningly remote and provocative.'[9]

Mimì Franchetti set out to conquer her, but found this a daunting and uphill struggle. Partly in order to annoy Mimì and partly for her own

Mimì Franchetti and Checca Lloyd, c. 1919. *Courtesy of Centro Caprense Ignazio Cerio*

Romaine Brooks, c. 1923

Harold Trower, c. 1926

Edwin Cerio, by his sister-in-law Mabel Norman Cerio. *Courtesy of Donna Laetitia Cerio*

pleasure, Romaine invited to Capri 'Zoë Mitchell', a young American friend who was the mistress of a Parisian shirt-maker. Knowing that Romaine disapproved of the way girls let themselves get sunburnt, Mimì countered by encouraging Zoë to bathe until, much to Romaine's displeasure, she had turned from 'a lovely rosy thing . . . into the colour of an old flute'.[10] On the night of the September full-moon – the vintage-moon – Checca gave a long-delayed house-warming party at the Cà del Sole/Villa Alba, to which she invited all her friends, enemies and acquaintances.[11] October brought the summer to an end. Zoë was summoned back to Paris by her impatient lover. Romaine too went to Paris, taking with her Faith Mackenzie, who, after a short stay with the painter, went on to London.

What of the familiar *dramatis personae?* Munthe had begun to write *The Story of San Michele*. He was back again as doctor to Queen Victoria of Sweden. For many years past he had lived in Torre Materita, and San Michele became partly a show-place and partly a house which he could let. The *lire* paid by visitors were given to a fund for the protection of birds in Sweden.

Munthe's tenant at San Michele for the summer of 1919 was the Marchesa Luisa Casati – a fiendish woman, already renowned throughout Europe for her eccentricities, tall and lean, with make-up in black and white, hung around with rings and bells, and usually attended by a black servant and a retinue of animals. After her departure at the end of the summer Munthe went to inspect the ravages inflicted on the villa – the most serious being 'French quotations and proverbs . . . written in black paint on the whitewashed walls. In the writing desk she had left a photograph of a painting of herself by Romaine Brooks, showing her lying nude on a bearskin rug. Munthe was indignant. "What do I want with a picture of the Casati stark naked?," he said'.[12]

Giovanni Galatà was still *pretore*. Gwen continued to survive by taking paying guests at the Villa Esperia – 'Young Neapolitan married to an Egyptian princess. Jealous. Frightfully jealous. My God, you don't know how jealous that woman is. Beats him on the head with the heel of her shoe when he comes home late. Making love all over the house. Can't help it, poor boy. Beats him if he won't. Never mind. Pay their bill every week. Couldn't live otherwise.'[13] After the death and burial in January 1917 of her alcoholic husband Sophie Grahame had astonished the mourners by leading them straight from the little cemetery to Morgano's and treating them all to three rounds of hot rum.[14] From that day onwards, shedding her image as a dull commonplace little woman, she blossomed into a 'character', and no party was complete without her. Godfrey Thornton, 63 and in poor health, was 'living in a cottage in Anacapri, with a tyrannical housekeeper and a Bechstein grand on which he used to play all day, with intervals of attending to the geraniums on his little terrace. He was never to be seen without a dark blue cricketing cap on his bald head; he even wore it in bed.'[15] Charles Coleman had his beloved Rose O'Neill staying for the summer. For Rose, who drank like a fish, the enforcement of prohibition in America which had began soon after the war was an added inducement to visit Capri. Vernon Andrews, who had once been compared to the Naples Narcissus, grew a beard, not, as some suggested, 'to assume a masculinity he did not possess. . . . A double chin, not a double life, was the inspiration of the change.'[16] Morgan Heiskell, who had been awarded the Legion of Honour for distinguished service with the American Red Cross in France, spent some time in Paris with the American peace mission and then returned to a great welcome by Coleman, but estranged from his wife and feeling altogether lonely and unwanted.[17]

Kate Wolcott-Perry, now 82, was still in America and no one expected to see her again. In the autumn of 1919 various oriental pieces – shawls, kimonos, robes and rugs – made their appearance in Lamberti's antique shop in Via Vittorio Emanuele, as Via Hohenzollern had been renamed. Although 'people had the uncomfortable notion that they were extremely like some of the fabrics and embroideries they had seen in the Villa Torricella, they could not resist buying them. What they felt was that, if they did belong to Miss Kate, the old lady was never likely to come back and miss them and that, if they did not belong to her, they were being sold much too cheaply to let strangers take advantage of such bargains.' Lamberti told customers that he had 'bought them from a wandering Indian who wanted to pay his fare back to Ceylon'. Inevitably the finger of suspicion pointed at the Galatàs, who had charge of the Villa Torricella and its contents. When informed of this gossip by Sophie Grahame, who met her one day in Via Tragara, Gwen sat down on one of those seats thoughtfully provided by the Pro Capri Society to deal with crises of this sort. 'Oo! Oo! What disgusting lies! Oo! Everything locked and sealed. John keeps the keys in his safe.' The oriental pieces vanished into private houses or were bought by transient visitors, and by Christmas the affair was forgotten.[18]

Nino Cesarini, who had won the Croix de Guerre, was demobilised, but at first lingered on the mainland unable to face a return to the Villa Lysis and Fersen. He was now 30 years old and as a soldier had gained a strength and self-confidence which enabled him at last to look the world in the face. He was a conscientious young man, and it was from a feeling of compassion for his friend, whom he now regarded as a madman, that at last he decided to return. Although he resumed a comfortable and agreeable life in Capri, he also had to endure Fersen's alternate reproaches and self-abasement; they were now 'just friends', and Fersen's attempts to revive the old sexual relationship were rejected.

For three months in the summer of 1919 the composer, Ottorino Respighi, famous for his 'Pines' and 'Fountains of Rome', with his wife, Elsa, who was a singer, rented 'Il Rosajo' from Edwin Cerio and had a piano sent over from Naples. 'A shy, delicate little man, who could never be persuaded to come to parties', Respighi and his wife greatly enjoyed Anacapri, where they could live *in armonia con quella stupenda natura, completamente isolati dal mondo*. He got up very early, took breakfast in the garden, walked or read a bit and before eight o'clock was hard at work.[19] To this period belong his musical settings of four poems by the poet Gabriele D'Annunzio – hero of the fledgling Fascist movement, for the part he had played, supported by mutinous elements of the Italian Army, in the successful raid on Fiume that September. Among the musicians who visited Respighi was Claude Debussy, who recalled the episode in his prelude 'Les collines d'Anacapri', full of southern lightness, tarantella rhythms and flattering harmonies.[20]

Respighi was followed as tenant of Il Rosajo by Francis and Jessica Brett Young. A doctor and writer of novels, Francis had joined the Royal Army Medical Corps and served with the 2nd Rhodesian Regiment in East Africa. The campaign took a heavy toll of his health and after the war he was not well enough to resume his medical practice. He decided to live entirely by writing and with his wife, who nobly gave up her career as a singer, tried Capri as an escape from the English winter. They arrived with very little money and for several weeks lived at Weber's 'Strand-pension', promising to pay as soon as Francis's writing had brought something in. Then they took II Rosajo for a winter-rent of 60 *lire* a month.[21]

At the end of 1919 D. H. and Frieda Lawrence, decided to exchange England for a mountain village in southern Italy but, finding that too cold, also sought refuge in Capri and rented two large furnished rooms and the use of a kitchen on the top floor of the Palazzo Ferraro. At this stage of his erratic career Lawrence was working on *Fantasia of the Unconscious* and obsessed with the notion that people ought to 'think with their genital organs instead of their minds'. One day he surprised strollers in the Piazza by pointing at his fly-buttons and announcing in his high-pitched Midlands voice: 'What we have to learn is to think *here*.' This incident and other curiosities engendered the usual Capri gossip, which got on the Lawrences' nerves, and after two months they decided to move. To the writer Catherine Carswell he wrote on 5 February 1920: 'I am very sick of Capri; it is a stew-pot of semi-literary cats. . . . I can't stand this island. I shall have to risk expense and everything and clear out; to Sicily, I think.' Writing to Mackenzie on 8 March, he said: 'I hope you won't scorn us too much for moving to Taormina. It was chiefly, I think, the arid sort of dryness of the Capri rock; a dry, dry bone. But I don't know, I feel a bit of a stranger here – feel the *darkness* again. There is no darkness in Capri. . . .'[22]

During the war Edwin Cerio's wife Elena had contracted tuberculosis and been sent to a sanatorium in Switzerland. Immediately after the armistice he went to collect her and his daughter Laetitia, and was shocked to find that she had fallen in love with a fellow-patient at the sanatorium and wanted a divorce. He promptly divorced her and returned with Laetitia to Capri.[23] Although only 45, Edwin decided to abandon his profession as architect and engineer, and devote himself entirely to Capri – where he began to write copiously about the island; acquired land, property and antiquities; and seduced the women. A few Capresi, including Giorgio Weber, now demobilised and starting a medical career in Capri, asked Cerio to run as *sindaco* in the 1920 elections. Carmĭnĕ Vuotto, who had held office creditably through the difficult years of the war, graciously stood down, and Cerio was elected.

Cerio cared very much for the island and, in particular, its architectural traditions, to which he had made some distinguished modern contributions in houses like Il Rosajo and La Solitaria. He sought to save it from the insistent ravages of the Milanese developers; to preserve the simple buildings, which he and others loved, from being razed to make way for pretentious palaces. 'Businessmen from the north,' wrote Faith Mackenzie, 'ignorant of the subtleties of Capri, dared to think they could transform the paradise of lovers and poets into a profitable resort for smart people, with therapeutics as a side line. It was curiously depressing to see these egregious strangers poking about the place with an air of possession, to hear the smart uneasy heels of their womenfolk on the cobbled streets, and it was with a sense of deliverance that one watched the handsome home-spun figure of Edwin Cerio striding along, his arms full of papers, his mind firmly fixed upon the project he had evolved to save Siren Land from vandalism.'[24]

More Capresi were being educated to European standards and entering the professions. Of Costanzo Serena's sons, for example, Roberto was a successful and trusted lawyer, and when the first bank opened in Capri he became its manager. He was Munthe's lawyer, and the doctor held him in 'the greatest respect. He used to say of him that not only was he clever – nearly all Italians are cleverer than North Europeans, especially in business – but that he was absolutely straight – in other words a gentleman.'[25] The second son, Carlo, who had entered the priesthood in 1905, did well and was recommended by his Archbishop to the Vatican; later he became a Nuncio, first to Czechoslovakia and then Colombia; and in 1935, Archbishop of Sorrento. The third son, Giovanni, also became a lawyer and banker.

Augusto Weber, released from internment, celebrated the fortieth anniversary of his arrival in Capri, and a banquet was given in his honour. Augusto's brother-in-law Vincenzo Desiderio, who had run Capri's soup kitchen during the lean years of war, was still head of the Welfare Agency, which administered small pieces of property bequeathed over many generations for the benefit of the poor. The rent from these properties, which was minimal, would have been insufficient to help any poor had there been poor in need of help. On the other hand Desiderio felt that Capri badly needed a hospital. So, immediately after the war, he sold most of the little parcels of land and for about £500 bought the Villa Scoppa at Due Golfi. Thus the present hospital was born and, because much of the land sold was from the estate of Guiseppe Capilupi, his name was given to it. Having arranged for the German Sisters of St Elizabeth to administer the hospital, he set about the long and intricate process of obtaining permits from the mainland authorities to allow it to function. In this task he was helped by Lady Mackinder, who introduced him to the Duchess of Aosta, then living at the Royal Palace of Capodimonte. With the Duchess's influence the necessary permits were obtained and a working hospital established.[26]

Morgano's survived, was still a focus of what remained of the old foreign colony and became the haunt of the 'extraordinary women'. Don Giuseppe was now 70 and Donna Lucia 57, and a lethargy gradually descended on the *caffè* – 'Mariano slept over his ledgers and Donna Lucia's head nodded and nodded behind the counter'. The *stammtisch*, no longer needed, was put in a corner and reserved for bridge – a four usually being formed by Edwin Cerio, Edna Blake, Dr De Gennaro and Damiano Arcucci, who played for a couple of hours in the afternoon and again after dinner until the *caffè* closed.

In 1920 a new *Bierstube*, called 'Tip-Top', was opened by Michele (Mimì) Pagano, eldest son of Manfredi, opposite the Quisisana. It had permission to stay open all night and was much used by people from the hotel who wanted supper or even breakfast after a dance. It was also frequented by English homosexuals like Compton Mackenzie and Hugo Wemyss. Member of an aristocratic family, brother of an Admiral of the Fleet, Hugo had been sent by his family as a 'remittance-man' to Capri, on the understanding that he never returned home. Described in Debrett's as 'hon. attaché in Diplomatic Service', Wemyss, who was now in his sixties, lived in a villa on Tragara, where he entertained, and had a cottage on the way up to Tiberio where he met his boy-friends. He also gardened at the cottage and was often to be seen commuting between it and Tragara 'with a basket of garden tools over one arm and a tropical umbrella hooked over the other, his silver hair and red-spotted tie brilliantly surmounting his deliberately unkempt attire' of sky-blue trousers and white shirt, or tussore suit, and sandals on his feet. He made few friends in Capri, and depended mainly on the visits of people he knew and any stranger who seemed interesting enough to be cultivated for a short time.[27]

In February 1920 there was a severe epidemic of influenza. One of the victims was Vernon Andrews, in his forty-first year. 'Considering his reputation of effeminacy, he behaved in a sportsmanlike fashion on that occasion. They had told him that there was very little chance of his recovery. "Well then," he said, to his mother and sister, "we'll just have one more bottle of champagne together, we three." '[28]

In the spring came the astonishing news that Kate Wolcott-Perry was returning to the Villa Torricella. She arrived, accompanied by 'a pleasant, colourless, woman called Miss Hazell', looking no different from when she had departed three years back. Although in her eighty-third year 'she carried herself as straight as ever . . . her eyes were not less keen . . . her fan cleft the air not less sharply.' Her first act was to visit the cemetery, and once again in the April sunshine she sat on the marble stool beside Saidee's grave, gazed out over the azure bay and dreamed of her lost friend. Then she drove down to the villa and took back her keys from Giovanni Galatà. All the cupboards and chests had their seals intact and were securely locked, but when opened were found to be empty – all the family silver and all the treasures they had brought back from their world tour of 1914 were gone. There were plenty of people to say that the Galatàs had removed the seals and unlocked the cupboards, and Mrs Fraser, who arrived back in Capri at about the same time, was quick to fuel the flames of suspicion against Gwen. Fersen, who suspected the Galatàs of having roused Kate against him in 1917, gloated over their misfortune. Charles Coleman had a theory that Fersen himself 'had committed the burglary. "Why it's as clear as daylight," he croaked, "a mean-spirited skunk like that, why it's just the very way he'd be revenged on that poor old woman down there." But, attractive though this theory was for an afternoon, general opinion condemned the Galatàs.' The crime was traced to Costanzo Federico, a member of the household staff, who had always been Kate's special favourite. According to Mackenzie he had become enamoured with a woman in Naples, 'who had instructed him how to remove the seals with a hot knife, who had supplied the skeleton keys and who had disposed of the silver for him'; other members of the Federico family were suspected of having helped to dispose of the orientalia through Lamberti's shop. As much of the loot as had been acquired by local residents had to be disgorged, but none of the silver was recovered. Found guilty and for a time imprisoned, Federico was paroled to the Italian Navy. When his service was ended he returned to Capri and started a restaurant at Marina Grande; he was nicknamed 'The Thief'. The suspicion that Giovanni Galatà was implicated in the theft persists, however, to this day.[29]

In the early summer Marchesa Casati, having written to Munthe that she again wanted to rent San Michele and been refused, turned up at Marina Grande with a mountain of luggage and the usual assortment of staff and animals. She sent a message to Anacapri announcing her arrival and then ascended to the Piazza to await her reluctant host. Even though the Capresi affect to be surprised at nothing where foreigners are concerned and one or two may have muttered '*puverella, è furastera*' (poor woman, she's a foreigner), Casati's sudden emergence from the funicular was not an everyday occurrence. 'She wore an astrologer's hat, from which depended long veils enveloping her person. Her face was plastered like a mountebank's, her eyes surrounded by large black circles, and her hair was red. She wore bells in her ears. Her make-up melting in the heat ran in streams down to her dusty shoes . . . escorted by an effeminate *cicisbeo*, on whose arm one of her own rested. In her other arm was a gilded gazelle, and the *cicisbeo's* other arm encircled its gilded companion. . . . Presently an enormous buck negro appeared carrying a blue parrot in a cage.'

Once again she turned San Michele upside down. 'The walls were hung with black draperies and the stone floors covered with black carpets. She herself wore black, with black pearls and jet rings. Her hair which had been red at first and later green, was now likewise black.' She celebrated black masses in the chapel of San Michele, where the hide of a black sheep was pinned on the wall, and slept in a coffin. The negro, however, was no longer black. She had had him gilded from head to foot. One day he collapsed. Fortunately the doctor was present and by scraping his skin was able to save his life. The negro's daily diet included two fowls, and day by day Munthe had to ensure that they were provided.

What Munthe hoped might be just a summer visit turned into an indefinite stay. As an opium addict, the Marchesa found a kindred spirit in Fersen, and was often at the Villa Lysis. Munthe, who linked a deep sympathy with and understanding of animals with a hatred of zoos and menageries, disapproved strongly of Casati's use of animals as ornaments and adjuncts to her already bizarre appearance. To the gilded gazelles, which were usually standing on either side of the entrance, she added two greyhounds, and these were dyed different colours to match her clothes. Once, when dining with the Principessa Gortchakov at the Villa Siracusa, she not only took the negro, stripped to the waist, to stand behind her chair, but also a large snake which was coiled round her arm throughout the meal.[30]

Munthe was still living at Torre Materita; the Queen of Sweden at Casa Caprile. The two often took their dogs for walks in Anacapri, setting a brisk pace, which the Queen's two ladies-in-waiting, Countess Taube and Countess Andlau, dressed whatever the weather in white Capri wool, had to maintain – cursing the Queen under their breath for dragging them up and down every *kloake* (sewer), as they termed each narrow, stony ravine.[31]

On 25 April 1920 Coleman celebrated his eightieth birthday. Although he had become very deaf and was sometimes in an invalid chair, he was still a dandy and still loved to entertain, especially so whenever Rose was over from America. Her Kewpie doll continued to be successful on both sides of the Atlantic. Money poured into her lap and was dispersed with equal speed to the many obscure poets, artists and musicians whom she kept off the bread-line. Faith Mackenzie who met her at one of Coleman's parties wrote: 'Rose was indeed adorable, of that shining type of American which fascinates men and is apt to repel certain English women, who jealously wonder what on earth it is about these brittle creatures that gets and keeps a man.'[32]

Rose was back in 1921 for his next birthday. 'We had the garden lighted with lanterns again,' she wrote, 'the long carved monastery table in the dining room rich with a feast, the three maidens in their native dress, and boys playing mandolins and guitars. Carlo was in his blue velvet dinner jacket with his snowy curls and beard shining in the candle-light. He was very gay and danced the *tarantella* with his long thin legs flying.' Coleman had long intended to leave her the Villa Narcissus, and, in order to circumvent the Italian laws of inheritance, sold it to her for a nominal sum, on the understanding that he and his three maids, Maria, Assunta and Paolina, could occupy it during his lifetime.[33]

Ignazio Cerio died on 1 May, having just passed his eightieth birthday. His life in Capri had been varied and highly individual. Possessed of a fine brain, a resolute and generous character, and robust health, he had devoted himself to the welfare of others in a manner rare amongst the islanders. Professionally a doctor, who practised for fifty years, he made valuable contributions to geology, botany, zoology and archaeology, and assembled material on these subjects in the Palazzo Cerio. He was also a competent draughtsman. As *consigliere* he had been involved in the administration of the island. A free-thinker in matters of religion, he had played a leading part in founding the *cimitero acattolico* in 1878 and had always been ready to help the struggling English Church. Finally it was as a man that Cerio was greatly admired. 'Very human, everyone liked him' was the verdict of a contemporary, and at his funeral a weeping peasant woman said simply: '*Era la più bella figura di Capri*'.[34] The Cerio mausoleum in which he was buried was remote from the other non-Catholic graves, in the extreme southern corner of the cemetery, beside the steps leading up to the Catholic cemetery – virtually in no man's land.

Lord Algernon Gordon-Lennox died in October during one of his very rare visits to Capri and was buried in the *cimitero acattolico*. On the *stele* at the head of his grave was inscribed THERE ARE NO DEAD, and it was topped with a bronze figure of St Michael (subsequently stolen), pointing with his sword towards Monte San Michele across the valley. Lord Algernon's widow Blanche, tall, slender and youthful, had created around the mountain, previously uncultivated except for Prince Caracciolo's vines, 'one of the loveliest gardens in the Mediterranean', and she was still adding to it. As a rule she visited Capri in the autumn for planting and returned again in the spring to enjoy the fruits of her labours. Monte San Michele had a notable advantage over all other gardens in Capri – plenty of water – for the Romans had endowed the mountain with cisterns to support the villa which once crowned its summit. Blanche loved animals and instituted a competition for the best-kept horse, presenting a prize to the winner at a *festa* held each spring in the Piazza.

Those who thought that Kate Wolcott-Perry had come back to die and find eternal rest beside Saidee were mistaken. Just as in February 1917 her fury against Fersen had aroused her from what might have been fatal despair, so now the outrage of being robbed by her cherished servant sustained her. Staying for much of the time at the Villa Torricella were Edward B. Hitchcock, her cousin from Decatur, Illinois, who had escorted her home after Saidee's death, and his wife Myrna Sharlow, an American opera-singer. These two, who had been married in the Torricella's Temple of Vesta, shielded her from the loneliness of her vanished world. On 13 August 1921 the Hitchcocks called on Charles Coleman, and on the last day of March 1922 all three went together to the Villa Narcissus, to pay their respects to the old man and sign his book. It is difficult not to see this as a reconciliation manoeuvred by the Hitchcocks and on Kate's part a most uncharacteristic burying of the hatchet after seventeen years of enmity.

By the beginning of 1922 the Milanese developers had already done much irreparable damage. In his capacity as *sindaco*, Edwin Cerio put up a last fight for tradition by organising a '*Convegno per la Difesa del Paesaggio*', which was to urge on the Italian Government the need to protect the domestic architecture and countryside of Capri from further destruction and disfigurement. To the Convegno he invited officials from Rome and Naples, together with an assortment of artists, architects, writers and musicians from all over Europe.

As principal speaker Cerio chose 45-year-old Filippo Tommaso Marinetti, poet, novelist and playwright, who in 1909 had created the 'Futurist' movement. When Italy declared war in May 1915, Marinetti volunteered for service, fought bravely and was decorated for valour. Immediately after the war he led his group of futurists in 'defence of victory', which for them meant the defeat of socialism. Thus the Futurists were drawn into the Fascist movement and were the predominant element in the Milanese *fascio*. On 15 April 1919 in Milan, Marinetti helped to organise the destruction of the office and printing-works of the socialist newspaper *Avanti*; he rose rapidly in Mussolini's hierarchy. Futurism had already planted a dainty footprint in Capri when the artist Fortunato Depero organised an exhibition of Futurist art in the Caffè Morgano for a week in September 1917. There had also been the one and only issue of Tavolato's monthly magazine *Eros* in March 1918. And on the Piazza were to be seen bevies of owl-eyed young men, with solemn faces and dank hair, who scoffed at romantic passion, looked askance at humour and cared only for Truth.[35]

With Marinetti came many other leading futurists. 39-year-old Alfredo Casella, composer and pianist, who for many years had been trying to interest the Italian public in the music of Stravinsky, Ravel and other moderns, came with his friend Gian Francesco Malipiero, a Venetian aristocrat, who had once gained sudden notoriety by entering five works each under a different pseudonym for a musical competition in Rome and winning four of the five available prizes. Of Futurist artists, the most notable was 27-year-old Enrico Prampolini, a brilliant painter and draughtsman, who had already visited Capri in 1919, and in a series of paintings and drawings, which he exhibited at the Convegno, gave his *interpretazione futurista del paesaggio di Capri*. His pictures were clean and geometrical and just sufficiently representative to suggest that they had been inspired by the landmarks and buildings of Capri.

The *Convegno* opened on 9 July 1922 in the Giardini di Augusto (Villa Krupp), under a full moon and with plenty of electric light, so that the 500 or so people attending, grouped informally about the grounds, seemed to the onlooker like parts of a tapestry. The dynamic and ebullient Marinetti was at his most futuristic. Ignoring the whole point of the *Convegno*, which was to protect the past, he clowned and pranced about, denouncing romanticism and *cinquecento* sentimentality. He praised skyscrapers and metallic bridges five miles long. He demanded a *caffè* on top of the Faraglioni Rocks, with an elevator to it, and an aerodrome on Monte Solaro. Apostrophising the island, he cried: 'You are the refuge for indispensable disorders, the cosy asylum for every hygienic fantasy. Even better you are a blow against European order and its bureaucratic moral duty.'

Thus the *Convegno* got off to an exhilarating, if unpractical, start. Next evening, under a full moon, the distinguished guests piled into the *Principessa Mafalda* for a trip round the island, while Giorgio Weber and a team of boys ignited firework powders of various colours, but without the bang, to indicate different points of interest as the ship sailed by. Later, there was a grand supper at the Quisisana, at which Compton Mackenzie replied to the toast of the '*Stranieri*'.

In the following days everyone revelled in the perfect weather, the seductive moonlight and all the varied pleasures which the island had to offer. Marinetti, Casella and Prampolini went bathing together. Casella gave a moonlit piano recital on the terrace of the Mackenzies' La Solitaria, and during a Chopin nocturne a young French intellectual, in agony, was heard to mutter to his neighbour: '*Mais Chopin! Chopin, vous savez. C'est dur! C'est dur!*' Prampolini did some more pictures and when the *Convegno* was over mounted an exhibition of his work at Salerno, with a foreword by Cerio in the catalogue. Marinetti confessed: 'Much as I love this island, I distrust its effect on my art.' He succumbed, however, to its charms and, having married the poetess and painter 'Benedetta' in 1923, often brought her to visit Capri in later years. The Futurists as a whole must indeed have retired unstrung by the timeless magic of the island.[36]

Cerio followed up the *Convegno* by creating a commission, which vetted and had to give its approval to any new construction, and continued his efforts to preserve the traditional style of architecture.

Both Manfredi Pagano and Giuseppe Morgano died in 1922. In the following year Mariano succumbed to life-long gluttony, after an enormous meal of ravioli, and followed his father to the Morgano mausoleum. Donna Lucia, 'who had wept in sympathy with so many, weeping now for herself, watched the *facchini* staggering under the burden of that twenty-stone corpse; the immense laurel wreaths, some of which took a couple of men to carry; the long trail of empty carriages with their hoods raised in token of grief'. She sold the *esercizio* of the *caffè* to an Italo-American in Anacapri who tried hard to maintain its character, but with no Donna Lucia the magic was gone; it quickly became a very ordinary *caffè* and then vanished.[37]

Before he returned to Milan, Marinetti remarked to Mackenzie, who was arguing in defence of the past and against Futurism, 'This Government is already dead.' If not dead, it was certainly dying, as Mussolini's forces steadily gained support. The *Fascisti* came to Capri that summer and demonstrated on the Piazza. Their leader in the island was 29-year-old Teodoro Pagano, second son of Manfredi, who had joined them because he admired Mussolini and sincerely thought that the movement would save Italy from Communism and ruin. He took part in the March on Rome at the end of October and, with the King dithering about whether or not to declare an emergency, saw Mussolini become the twenty-seventh Prime Minister of Italy.

Mackenzie had grown tired of Capri. The first step in uprooting himself had occurred in 1920, when he took a sixty-year lease of two of the smaller Channel Islands – Herm at £900 a year and Jethou at £100. Faith, who was still devoted to the island, remained at La Solitaria, where the lease from Cerio still had three years to run. By the autumn of 1921 she had recovered from a long illness – caused mainly, according to Munthe, by having too little to do – and made friends again with Gwen Galatà.[38] Monty had returned to Capri in July for Cerio's *Convegno*, but not for long. As he walked with Mimì Ruggiero through a grove of young pines they had planted on the side of Ventroso, Mimì, sensing his mood, said: 'Ah, *signore mio*, you are here, thank God, walking with me as we used to walk, but your heart is no longer here.' In September he was back in England.[39]

If Capri lost one old face, it recovered two others – at least for occasional visits. Maksim Gorki, who had never been happy with the Revolution, continued to publish articles against the Bolshevik leaders. He was in poor health with his chronic lung complaint, and in a letter of 9 August 1921 Lenin told him point-blank to leave Russia and go south again: 'I'm tired, so tired that I can do absolutely nothing. And you spit blood and don't go away. I assure you that it is neither conscientious nor reasonable. Here, there is no possibility of being looked after or of doing anything useful; nothing else but agitation, vain agitation. Go away, you will get better. Don't be obstinate. I implore you. Your Lenin.'[40] By this time Gorki had been compelled to give up his mistress Andreyeva and return to his lawful wife. In 1922, together with his own son and daughter-in-law and Moura Budberg[41] as secretary, he went south, found a house at Sorrento and settled down to write *My Universities*, the last part of the autobiographical trilogy, which had begun with *My Childhood* and *My Apprenticeship*. When in Capri he frequented 'Tip-Top'.

The other returning exile was Norman Douglas. After his hasty exit from London in January 1917, he had lived mainly in Florence, with intervals in Rome, Paris, St Malo, Menton and Greece. In Florence, where he settled in 1922, he made friends with the vastly rich Sir John Ellerman's daughter Annie Winifred, who by this time had changed her name by deed-poll simply to 'Bryher'. A warm-hearted person – critic, poet and novelist – she used her money to encourage *avant-garde* literature. She was drawn to Douglas by his books *South Wind* and *They Went*, and they began a friendship which lasted all his life. It was Bryher who was at Marina Grande to meet him in March 1923: 'Let nobody tell me he was not loved there. The news of his arrival spread from mouth to mouth. I have never seen a political leader enjoy so great a triumph. Men offered him wine, women with babies in their arms rushed up so that he might touch them, the children brought him flowers. I slipped away as he walked slowly through a crowd of several hundred people, shouting jokes in ribald Italian, kissing equally the small boys and girls and patting babies as if they were kittens. The *signore* had deigned to return to his kingdom and I am sure that they believed that the crops would be abundant and the cisterns full of water as a result.'[42]

Cerio's term of office as *sindaco* ended in 1923. He was very protective of his teenage daughter Laetitia and asked Giorgio Weber's sister Matilde, who was in her early twenties, to be Laetitia's companion and chaperon. Edwin himself, freed from the constraints of marriage, anxious to begat a male heir, and an inveterate womaniser, had a number of amours in Capri. Some of these affairs resulted in pregnancies. One involved the daughter of a retired judge. She refused an abortion and, when her time came, Cerio arranged for her to be delivered at a clinic in Naples. The agreement was that, if the baby was a boy, Cerio would marry the girl and legitimize his son; if a girl, the child would be given out for adoption. Although a girl was born, the mother would not let the child go and brought her back to Capri. No whit disconcerted when Cerio refused to marry her, she wheeled the child's pram around the town and, whenever anyone stopped to admire, would say, 'Doesn't she look like her father?' – and everybody knew who the father was.[43] Cerio also coveted Lica Riola, who was in her thirties and still very attractive. On one occasion he knocked on her door and asked her to go to bed with him and, failing that, to be allowed to sleep under her bed; Lica was not impressed.

In medical care the island had advanced a long way since the nineteenth century, when there was only one ill-paid municipal *medico*, supplemented on a voluntary basis by foreign residents like Giorgio Clark, and Henry Green and John Mackowen; Dr Huethe, the retired German Naval doctor; and Axel Munthe. By the turn of the century things had improved, with Ignazio Cerio and Pasquale De Gennaro practising full-time in Capri and, Vincenzo Cuomo in Anacapri. In the early 'twenties the system was expanded, so that there were five full-time doctors in the island.

While they all had their share of private patients, most of their work, for which they received an official salary from the *municipio*, was done for nothing or for a very small fee. The islanders entertained the pleasing notion that a doctor's services should be free, or, if not, that doctors' bills should be haggled over to the lowest amount possible. On the other hand many would compensate the doctors with presents of fruit, vegetables and fish, and Weber remembers being brought a lamb during Easter week by one of his patients.[44]

Fersen, more dependent than ever on cocaine, continued to live his futile existence in the Villa Lysis. He still wrote poetry about his tortured emotions, still begged Nino to become his lover again, took part in the new social life of the island and liked to join Marchesa Casati for a pipe of opium. One day at the Quisisana in the summer of 1921, he met some rich citizens of Sorrento and fell in love with their schoolboy son, Manfred. The boy was flattered by Fersen's attentions, the parents raised no objection to their son being left in his company, and throughout 1922 and much of 1923 they met in Capri and on the mainland. In spite of long addiction to opium and cocaine, Fersen's outward appearance at 43, with slender figure and clear complexion, was astonishing, 'but the glance of his eyes was now frequently dull and stupid . . . eyes deeply sunken in his head, and their pupils dilated. He was no longer satisfied to sniff cocaine, he mixed it in his drinks, but he knew that he could not without immediate danger exceed the massive dose of three grammes.' In October 1922, in his loneliness, he sent Edwin Cerio a collection of photographs of the Villa Lysis, inscribed '*pour Edwin Cerio d'un ami et d'un solitaire accordé au balcon des souvenirs*'. In September 1923 he visited his sister Germaine, and she considered his condition sufficiently alarming to summon their mother from Paris. In mid-October he took Manfred to Sicily and there, in Taormina, renewed his acquaintance with Baron von Gloeden, who, after spending the war in Germany, was back in his studio. Still hale and hearty at 67, he 'was now at his third generation of boy models and in a position to show portraits in the nude of grandfather, father and son, all photo-graphed at fifteen years of age and all crowned with flowers. He had been awarded a medal at the Milan exhibition in 1911, the accompanying diploma specifying that it was for his "propaganda promoting tourism". That he had earned it was apparent from the signatures which still continued to cover page after page of his visitors' book, from the crowded hotels and the booming activity in the building of new villas.'[45]

At the beginning of November they returned to Naples, where Nino met them, crossed over to Capri, walked up from Marina Grande to the villa to what everyone thought was joyful homecoming. After dinner that night, in the presence of the unsuspecting Nino and Manfred, Fersen committed suicide by taking an overdose of cocaine in a glass of wine. Since he had asked to be cremated, which could not be done in Capri, his body had to be 'embalmed', conveyed to the mainland and sent to the crematorium in Rome. Preparation of Fersen's body was undertaken by Dr Weber. Having arrived at the villa, Weber found Fersen's Greek friend Ephy Lovatelli, who wanted the face of the corpse to be made up with rouge and lipstick. When Weber refused, she did the job herself and then sealed Fersen's lips with a gold Macedonian coin, to pay Charon's fee across the Styx. A long funeral cortège followed the body to the *cimitero acattolico*, where many *contadini* put flowers on the coffin – but none of the Catholic priests walked in the procession or attended the funeral.

The contents of Fersen's will 'came as a surprise to everyone except Nino. Fersen had given Nino to understand . . . that he had certain obligations to his family and to society; that a man might live his life as he pleased, but must die as he had been born'. Thus Nino was left 300,000 francs and the usufruct of the Villa Lysis, with power to let it. Ownership of the villa and its contents went to Germaine; everything else was left to his mother, the Baroness d'Adelswärd.

The lawyers acting for Fersen's relations procured an autopsy of the body in the hope of substantiating a suspicion that Nino had poisoned him. The body lay for a time in the cemetery chapel, but as soon as it arrived in Naples was seized by the police and taken to Rome – where the post-mortem examination vindicated Nino. In due course the ashes were returned to the cemetery and still rest in a white marble chest set on a block of granite – the forename misspelt (JAQUES) and without the nobiliary particle before ADELSWÄRD.

After a number of unsatisfactory tenants Nino sold his rights to Germaine, who gave the villa to her daughter, the Marchesa del Castel-bianco. Ierace's statue of Nino seated on a triton shell and a painting of him in the nude on horseback were sold to an antiquary, together with the furniture of the Chinese room. On his return to Rome, Nino took up his father's trade of newsvendor and for many years was to be seen in charge of a newspaper kiosk. He died, middle-aged, in a Roman hospital.[46]

Kate Wolcott-Perry survived Fersen nearly a whole year; and until two months before her death visited Saidee's grave every day, sitting beside it on that small marble stool fixed to the path she had had paved with fragments of marble tesserae. 'She sat there to tend for a little while yet the fire she had tended for so many vestal years, dimly though to her clouded eyes the flames seemed to be burning now. She never flinched from her pagan creed. She never paltered for a moment with the fancy that she might meet Saidee in another world.' She died on 28 August 1924, a month short of her eighty-seventh birthday. Beneath KATE on her stone was carved her verdict on life:

> Happiness
> Is the Only Good
> and the Greatest Happiness
> consist [sic] in
> Making Others Happy.[47]

Kate left everything to the Hitchcocks, who for a time lived in the house and then, having removed the best of the furniture and Kate's personal belongings (including, it is said, a collection of dildos), sold the property and its contents to Barone Alfredo Gargiulo of Naples, whose grandsons Alfredo and Raffaele (Ralph) are the present owners.

Emelie Fraser, still wearing enormous hats and trailing gowns, bathing every day, changing for dinner every night, holding tea-parties with cucumber sandwiches on Thursday and sometimes playing the organ in the English Church, appointed herself leader of the English colony, but had few followers. Gwen Galatà now lived apart from Giovanni, who was having an affair with the daughter of an elderly Czech couple who managed the Pensione Esperia for Gwen. Giovanni moved up to his villa on the Anacapri road, while Gwen continued to run her hotel. Eventually the girl became pregnant by Giovanni and in 1928 committed suicide. Good-natured Sophie Grahame was her usual 'bright self'. She could never drink more than a glass of wine without feeling the effects, and then she would dance on the table, or kiss some sober and startled stranger, use 'her slippers as castanets or beat time with them on the bald heads of grass-green gentlemen'. On one occasion, having been escorted home to her *villino* in Via Tiberio after an all-night party, she 'had let herself into the wardrobe and slept cosily among her dresses until it was time to keep a luncheon engagement at the Quisisana'. Her verdict on herself was: 'Why, my past would make a jolly good future for some woman.'[48]

Godfrey Thornton was very ill and bed-ridden in Anacapri. Bryan and Maimie Palmes, still sticking it out in the Villa Mezzomonte, usually threw a children's party at Christmas time, which gave temporary life to a house that was much too big for them. Harold and Bertha Trower, with a bevy of maids, who cost very little, lived contentedly at the Villa Cesina on her annuity and what he was able to scrounge from his relatives in England. Bertha, who was now very deaf, seldom went out and, according to his nieces who stayed with them, spent much of the time 'floating about in tea-gowns'. Harold, proud of his status as 'Bishop's Churchwarden', worked hard to maintain and beautify the English church. On the other hand, he did nothing to help towards the Chaplain's stipend, considering that this was the responsibility of the SPG – which it was not. Chaplains, therefore, who still came for the winter season, were entirely dependent on church collections for their pay – and these were unpredictable.[49]

While Charles Coleman continued to hold court at the Villa Narcissus, the most lively member of the American colony was Edna Blake. Widowed and resident for nearly twenty years, though past her prime, she was still a handsome woman and capable of attracting men. A Russian exile, who claimed to have been a member of the Imperial Ballet, shot himself on the doorstep of her home, because she would not return his love.[50] She herself was attracted by Damiano Arcucci and, when she became his mistress in the 'twenties, moved to the Villa Erminia, which was part of Damiano's Hotel Capri in Via Roma. While for her the relationship was a serious love-affair – the last fling of a woman who had little else to look forward to – for Damiano it was only one of the several sexual affairs that he always kept going.[51]

In July 1923, owing to financial difficulties, Mackenzie gave up the lease of Herm and established himself on the much cheaper island of Jethou. He and Faith were in Capri again in the spring and early summer of 1924 – the year in which their lease was due to run out. At the end of April Mimì Ruggiero took them and a party of friends to see Cetrella, where his work had progressed *ermeticamente* (Mimì's invariable adverb to stress a point) and wondered whether they would ever come and live in the *casetta* on which he had lavished such care. The party included Norman Douglas, who was on one of his many short visits. He had no money, and, as no hotel was willing to take him as their 'guest', Edwin Cerio lent him a villa for the occasion.[52] They all made a picnic of cheese and wine in the hermit's room adjoining the little church – 'poised like a swallow's nest upon its windswept limestone crags' – and gazed down on the white and green mosaic of eastern Capri and the dimpled sea far below. The day ended with a descent down Ventroso to see how the cliff-side paths were progressing and finally by rowing-boat to Marina Piccola.[53]

Carmĭnĕ Vuotto, whose administration during the war had commended itself to the islanders and who had stood down in 1920 to allow Edwin Cerio a term of office, became *sindaco* again in 1924 – the last to be elected by popular vote before Mussolini abolished all local self-government in Italy at the end of 1925. In this year, also, control of both the SIPPIC and SIA was acquired by Barone Alberto Fassini. Born and bred in Piedmont, Fassini had been first a naval officer, then, before the war, had made a fortune from artificial silk. He married a Sicilian aristocrat and early on became an important Fascist and contributor to Party funds. Vuotto's term of office was brought to an end at the beginning of 1926. He was followed for a short period by a Fascist *commissario prefettizio*[54] appointed from Naples, until in the middle of 1926 Marchese Marino Dusmet de Smours, employee of a shipping firm in Naples, was appointed *podestà* – mayor, that is, nominated by the Central Government and not elected by the local council.

CHAPTER EIGHT

Prosperity under Fascism

When Dusmet was appointed *podestà*, he was unknown to the islanders. A Neapolitan aristocrat – his father Luigi was a duke – and in his thirty-second year he was married to Marian (Polly) Power, a well-to-do American from California, who at 22 was already a leading light in the Christian Science Church. Although it is likely that Fassini had manoeuvred Dusmet's appointment to Capri, in order to protect his business interests there, Dusmet soon made his own mark as an efficient administrator. Unencumbered by a town council and with no family ties, he gave orders which he could expect to be obeyed and was able to devote personal attention wherever and whenever it was needed. One of his earliest decisions was to put the whole island under a single administration, though subdivided into three inhabited centres of Capri, Marina Grande and Anacapri. After Dusmet's arrival Teodoro Pagano's position changed. Although, as secretary of the local Fascist Party, Pagano held an independent authority in parallel with the *podestà*, who was chief agent of Government, Dusmet quickly established a dominating position. He let Pagano keep the appearance of power by leaving him to do the tedious work of keeping the islanders in line with Party policy – and this Pagano did energetically from his headquarters (now the Ristorante al Campanile) in Via Roma, while his *amica*, Anna (Putti) von Rahden, set about organising the female members of the Party. There were frequent parades in black shirts. The bells in the Campanile summoning this or that Party gathering were rung so frequently, that the *parroco*, Don Luigi Lembo, finally locked the bell-tower and set up an electric control, so that the bells could only be rung from his office in the parish church.

Whatever their real feelings about Fascism may have been, local officials, professionals and leading citizens enrolled as Party members, simply in self-preservation and for the sake of their careers. In Rome such people were known as 'PNF' – 'Partita Nazionale Fascista' or 'Per Necessità Familiare'. The Cerio brothers, Edwin, Giorgio and Arturo, were early members, but refused to exhibit the Party insignia in their lapels; in addition Giorgio, now married to the rich American, Mabel Norman, gave the Party a donation. Amongst others who joined were the lawyers Roberto and Giovanni Serena, and Giovanni Galatà; doctors Cuomo, De Gennaro, Prozzillo and Ruocco; and the town-engineer Guglielmo Adinolfi. Dr Weber, however, not only refused to join the Party but was also openly anti-Fascist.[1]

In general, unlike many parts of the mainland where fascist-inspired violence was rife, Capri remained peaceful. The islanders were either ignorant of or indifferent to what was happening on the mainland – and they welcomed the news that Mussolini regarded Capri with special favour. *Il Duce*, with a bodyguard of Fascist youth, had visited the island for a few hours in the spring of 1925; had been welcomed in the Piazza by two brass bands which struck up separately and simultaneously the Italian National Anthem and the Fascist hymn *Giovinezza*; and then been fêted at an official luncheon in the Quisisana.[2] Later he recorded his verdict that Capri was '*un isola che si non scorda mai*' (an island which one never forgets).

Mussolini decided to make Capri a show-piece, where he could offer recreation to foreign VIPs. He ordered the Prefect of Naples to supply Dusmet with any extra funds which might be needed for the enhancement of the island. With this assurance of unlimited support, Dusmet launched a programme of public works which included the extension of the harbour-jetty so that ships could enter and tie-up in most kinds of weather; the surfacing with macadam of the roads to Marina Grande, Marina Piccola and Anacapri; and the paving with cement of the principal country tracks. He instituted a *pulizia della montagna* at points where rockfalls were common, particularly at Barbarossa above the top of the Anacapri road and on the south side of Castiglione above the Via Krupp. Suspended on platforms and secured each to a rope, the 'cleaners' poked the rock to dislodge weak and loose material, which cascaded under control into the regions below. Dusmet set a good example by living modestly in a rented apartment in the Villa Mimosa, at the junction of Via Tuoro and Via Cercola. He was often out and about in the early morning, to ensure that the streets were properly swept and everything in good order.[3]

It was decided that Capri's new status also required a moral clean-up of the foreign colony – a process which was energetically supported, if not initiated, by Dusmet's wife. An American pianist who had rented the Villa Lysis from Nino was asked to relinquish his young Roman boy-friend and take his music elsewhere; and Nino's next tenant, a Dutch Baron, who found difficulty in keeping either menservants or gardeners, was also sent on his way. Hugo Wemyss, remittance-man and *doyen* of the English homosexuals, was served with an expulsion order. When the news reached his horrified family in England, they persuaded the Foreign Office to exert pressure on the Italian Government, and by the time

Marchese Marino Dusmet, *podestà*, and Teodoro Pagano, secretary of Capri *fascio*, at the *festa* of San Costanzo, 14 May, c. 1930. *Courtesy of Teodoro Pagano*

Celebration of the 2,000th anniversary of the birth of the Emperor Augustus at Villa Iovis, 1937. Prof. Amedeo Maiuri and Teodoro Pagano in front. *Courtesy of Teodoro Pagano*

Wemyss reached Rome on his homeward journey the order had been rescinded; but he did not return to Capri. Other suspects slipped quietly away to Sorrento, Ischia, Rome and Tunis. After this first outburst of propriety the cleansing fervour evaporated.[4]

At the end of 1924 Faith Mackenzie had packed up at the Solitaria and for a few months lingered on in a two-room *villino* below Via Tragara, which she christened 'But and Ben'.[5] Giorgio Cerio, however, got his hands on it, in order to pull it down, so that he could enjoy an uninterrupted view of the Certosa and Monte Solaro from his new home in the Villa La Pergola di Tragara.[6] Faith, therefore, had to clear out. She sold the house at Cetrella to Edwin Cerio, but kept the surrounding land and the Ventroso property on the seaward side of Monte Solaro, which Mimì Ruggiero promised to maintain in good order. In April 1925 she bade farewell to the island, but with the resolve to return, and joined Monty in Jethou.

In the summer of 1926 Mackenzie at last started to write *Vestal Fire* – a book which he had planned many years back but for two compelling reasons did not start. He felt that the publication of Douglas's *South Wind* in 1917 inhibited a new novel set on a Mediterranean island for some time to come. In that year also Fersen and the elder Wolcott-Perry were still alive, which meant that the true story could not be told without risk of a libel action. By 1926, however, neither of these considerations applied, but there were technical problems to be surmounted. Mackenzie was hesitant about portraying the Wolcott-Perrys as American in case by so doing he ruined 'the book's chance of recognition in the United States by a few inconsistencies of speech which would make them not only ridiculous but improbable'. He took courage, however, from the fact that his mother was American and that from his earliest youth the speech of his American relations had been familiar to him – so the Wolcott-Perrys remained American and were called 'Virginia and Maimie Pepworth-Norton'. Then there was the problem of dealing openly with homosexuality, which he had already encountered in *Sinister Street*. The central theme of *Vestal Fire* was the infatuation of two American lesbians for a French pederast and drug-addict – not at all an easy subject to present explicitly in 1926. Furthermore three other important characters – Vernon Andrews ('Nigel Dawson'), Norman Douglas ('Duncan Maxwell') and Godfrey Thornton ('Anthony Burlingham') – were also homosexual. The book was to cover the period from around 1902, when the life of the foreign colony was uncomplicated and happy, to 1924, when many of its characters were dead and the rest insignificant in the Capri of the 'twenties. Axel Munthe does not feature at all in *Vestal Fire* because Faith made Monty 'promise not to include that great personality. She feared I might present him to the world as a comic figure.' Almost every other person was a portrait*, but Mackenzie used novelist's licence to alter chronology when he felt this necessary†. In portraying events which had occurred before his own arrival in 1913 he relied heavily on John Ellingham Brooks, who had been a shrewd observer of the Capri scene since 1895. Mackenzie dedicated *Vestal Fire* to Brooks in 'memory of the hours you have spent listening to other stories of mine in the making, to many a long talk under the moon and many a long walk in the sun, to the bottles of wine and the glasses of vermouth we have drunk together, to the music and the scandal we have enjoyed, but perhaps most of all to the laughs we have had, of which I hope you will hear a faint echo as you turn over the pages of this book'. In writing *Vestal Fire* he 'hoped that the underlying theme would appear as the tragedy, not the comedy of futility . . . any tragedy of futility must contain more farce than tragedy. . . . I knew that the reading of it would be a waste of time for people without a sense of humour.'

In spite of the difficulty of constructing a book with an unusually large number of characters spread over a period of years, he completed *Vestal Fire* in four months. The manuscript was submitted to several publishers, all of whom admired it but dared not publish. His friend Newman Flower, literary director of Cassells, who was in the process of taking over the firm from the Berry brothers, asked to see it and, to Mackenzie's surprise, wrote to say that he thought *Vestal Fire* one of the funniest books he had ever read and would go all out on it; it was published in the autumn of 1927. The book received a mixed reception in England, and was banned from Italy on five grounds: making fun of the *carabinieri*; making remarks derogatory to the State; mentioning the unmentionable; injuring the *réclame* of Capri; *contra bonos mores*.

As with *Sinister Street* the ban greatly helped its sales and few visitors to Capri failed to read the book. Gwen Galatà was delighted to be identified with 'Maud Ambrogio' ('Thinks I'm a scream. So I am'). Edwin and Giorgio Cerio were furious at the penetrating characterisation of themselves in 'Enrico and Alberto Jones' – and it was largely due to Edwin's perpetual hostility that the book was never translated into Italian.[7]

By the time *Vestal Fire* emerged, its companion, *Extraordinary Women*, had already been written. Started in March 1927 as *The Ladies of Mitylene*, it dealt with the lesbian goings-on in Capri and Sorrento from 1918 to 1920. All the characters except one (Rory Freemantle) were exact portraits; 'Rory' was a composite character which contained a strong element of Frances (Checca) Lloyd.[8] Under the preferred title of *Extraordinary Women – Theme and Variations* and dedicated to Norman Douglas, the book was offered to Cassells in England and Doubleday Doran in

* See Appendix A.
† See Bibliography.

the United States, but neither would touch it. The problem was solved by Martin Secker agreeing to publish a limited edition, at one guinea, of 2,000 ordinary copies and 100 special copies signed by the author.

In mid-August 1928, just before *Extraordinary Women* was due to be published, Radclyffe Hall's lesbian novel *The Well of Loneliness* was suppressed. The attack on it had been launched by James Douglas, editor of the *Sunday Express*, 'who declared that he would sooner give a healthy boy or girl a dose of prussic acid than a copy of Miss Radclyffe Hall's book'. The *Clarion* countered by asking, 'What boy or girl would be likely to read it? And, if a boy or girl did read it, what would they find of an exciting and inflammatory character?' Alarmed by Douglas's attack Jonathan Cape sent *The Well of Loneliness* to the Home Office for an opinion and was advised to withdraw it. *Extraordinary Women* went ahead and was not prosecuted. Some people were upset over the suppression of a serious book about lesbian emotions and the freedom given to Mackenzie's book, which treated the sapphic play-acting in Capri with an amused and cynical tolerance. All this publicity was good for the book, which quickly went out of print and in 1929 was succeeded by a 3s 6d edition, which, to protect the owners of the limited first edition, omitted a few passages.

When *Extraordinary Women* was published, all the principal characters were flourishing. Princess Gortchakov or Soldatenkov ('Countess de Randan'), still rich in spite of having lost all her Russian assets in the Revolution, continued to live in style at Sorrento; her daughter Helène ('Baby') had married Luigi Gargiulo, the barber's son. The Princess's friend Olga de Tschélischeff, who had lost everything in Russia and sold all her jewellery, was penniless. The Princess bought Olga a shop in Via Vittorio Emanuele, where she sold Russian-style clothes, souvenirs and minor antiquities found in Capri; and lived in part of the Casa Lovatti in Via delle Botteghe. In 1923 the Princess of Sayn-Wittgenstein joined forces with her to run the shop, which survived until the end of World War II.[9]

To everyone's surprise, Frances Lloyd began living with a man – Captain Nicholas Borselli, a handsome, much-decorated, former cavalry officer. It was assumed that they were married, but this was not the case. Towards the end of the 'twenties they left the Cà del Sole and moved to Borselli's property at Scalèa in Calabria, taking with them her maid Mafalda, whom Borselli had made pregnant – and in due course two sons were born. Just before Borselli died he married the maid to legitimise the children.[10] After his death Frances returned to Capri with the maid and the boys, whom she always presented as her own sons, and lived there until her death in 1950; she ws buried in the *cimitero acattolico* under her maiden name, Frances Edersham.

Lica Riola, still trim and beautiful, and unfailingly optimistic, contrived to keep herself and her family alive by getting commissions as an intermediary (*mediatrice*) and by making dresses. Her friend Renata Borgatti, also permanently hard up, fell in love with one woman after another. In 1918 it was Mimì Franchetti; in 1919 Romaine Brooks herself. But she did not succeed in engaging Romaine's interest for long, and a year later the latter wrote to Natalie Barney, her lover in Paris since 1915, that 'she was trying to avert another visit from Renata and declining to help her out financially, as in the past'. There is an enduring souvenir of this temporary relationship in one of Romaine's most powerful paintings, in black, white and grey – 'Renata Borgatti au Piano'.[11] Renata's life in Capri was badly upset when her studio at Punta Tragara was pulled down to make way for Vismara's *palazzo*, and she soon left the island. She had a hysterectomy in a cheap hospital in Rome, because she could not afford anything else, and for a time was very depressed, but was soon back again in society, where her striking personality attracted attention. In May 1921, while based on Bologna she paid a flying visit to Capri and called on Charles Coleman.[12] Later in the year she was in London and at a party given by Lady Sibyl Colefax met the painter Sargent, who was so struck by Renata that he asked to be allowed to make a drawing of her. He inscribed it 'all' artista Renata Borgatti' and gave it to her; later she had to sell it in order to live.[13] Most of Renata's time was spent in Paris. Eventually she sickened of 'society', joined a music school in Munich and once more concentrated on the piano.

Romaine Brooks also established herself in Paris, acquired a studio, where she worked hard at her painting, saw a lot of Natalie Barney and entertained her friends. In 1925 Faith Mackenzie met Mimì Franchetti at one of Romaine's parties, 'no longer as slim as a hamadryad . . . said to be writing poetry . . . her charm undiminished'.[14]

A victim of the Fascist régime in Capri was Dr Weber. Although the *podestà* had helped to facilitate Weber's marriage to Julia Hunter, an American – marriage to a foreigner being quite difficult in Italy at this time – and actually performed the civil ceremony in November 1926, in other respects Weber's official dealings with Dusmet were non-existent, and he persisted in his refusal to join the Party. Fortunately, as a long-standing friend of Teodoro Pagano, the Party Secretary, he was not molested or asked to swallow a dose of castor oil. One day in the summer of 1928 he was accosted in the Piazza by a young man in the full uniform of a Fascist officer, complete with high boots and tasselled cap, who introduced himself as Dr Corselli, son of the Provincial Health Officer, to whom Weber reported, and announced that he had been appointed Health Officer of the whole island to replace Weber in Capri and Cuomo in Anacapri. Although Cuomo was a Party member, he was now nearly eighty and almost blind from cataract. From then on Weber noticed that the number of his private patients diminished steadily, especially in the hotels, where most of the employees had become Party members and had been instructed to sabotage his practice. In other respects also his world was disintegrating. His father, Augusto, died in September 1928 and his mother, Raffaella, in the following February. The 'Strandpension' passed to his two sisters, who renamed it 'Pensione Weber', since under the Fascists it was illegal to use a foreign term to indicate a public place. Early in the summer of 1929 Weber took the post of resident physician in the International Hospital in Naples but after several months realised that it would lead nowhere and decided to emigate to the United States. Having given power of attorney to Professor Luigi Messanelli in respect of property at Due Golfi, which he had inherited from his parents, and after a farewell party organised by friends, among them Teodoro Pagano, he and his wife left Capri in December, to start a new life in the United States, where in due course he became an American citizen.[15]

While Dusmet and Pagano sought to extend Fascist influence in the administrative and social life of the island, Barone Fassini, through his control of the SIPPIC, expanded in the economic sphere. In 1928 the company, which since 1923 had been one of the agencies responsible for distributing water in the island, was granted exclusive rights over this vital service. To carry the water, a small water-boat plied between Naples and Marina Grande.[16] Naples was fortunate in having a continuous supply of good water brought by an aqueduct (Acqua del Serino) from the river Serino, near Avellino, over a distance of 52 miles, to be stored in reservoirs and distributed throughout the city. At Marina Grande the water was transferred ashore to the Truglio reservoir, then pumped to three cisterns on Castiglione and from there piped along the principal streets for distribution to any hotels which wanted it, and to a few private houses; in 1934 the SIPPIC were charging consumers 6 to 7 shillings a cubic metre.[16]

In 1929 the company was granted the monopoly of running public transport and set up regular bus services to Anacapri and the two Marinas. Electricity production from the generating station at Marina Grande was increased, and by 1935 there were more than 1,850 users of this facility. The original agreement made in 1907, whereby after 25 years the SIPPIC would hand over the funicular and the electricity plant to the *comune*, was conveniently forgotten and the profits from these undertakings continued to fill Fassini's pocket rather than the municipal coffers. Ing. Raffaele Antonucci, who had directed the funicular and electricity plant for many years, was suddenly and without due explanation sacked by Fassini. A shy and gentle person, much respected in the community, he had little in common with his go-getting boss. He had just become engaged to an

Anacapri girl and was so depressed by this sudden ending of his career in the SIPPIC that in June 1932 he commited suicide by jumping from the *belvedere* at the end of the Migliara.[17]

Death picked off several of the older foreigners. Charles Coleman died on 2 December 1928 in his eighty-ninth year. Resident for nearly 60 years, he had become a unique institution in the island as painter, collector, dispenser of hospitality, and philanderer. His amorous conquests had been numberless, but for many years past, his heart had been set on Rose O'Neill.

In the spring of 1929 Rose, who already owned the Villa Narcissus, came to live in it and worked furiously every day and all day writing *The Goblin Woman*, a tale in which the principal character, after murdering his brother, marries his twelve-year-old niece and finally tries to atone for his sins by mutilating himself. This improbable novel was finished by the end of July, and Rose returned to New York to get it published. Then her luck ran out. During the Great Depression her carelessness about money overtook her. She had to sell all her American property except the family home at Bonniebrook in Missouri. The vogue for Kewpies had passed, but 'ever hopeful, she invented a new doll, a Buddha-like creature called "Ho-Ho", but it never caught on. She died of a paralytic stroke in 1944 and by her own wish was buried without religious ceremony in the family cemetery at Bonniebrook.'[18]

In February 1929 Emelie Fraser died in Rome and was brought back to Capri for burial; she left £50 to All Saints Church, and £10 to its maintenance fund.

John Ellingham Brooks's last years in Capri were lonely and wretched. In his mid-sixties, ill and poverty-stricken, his poetry and translations unpublished, he lived in Via Matermania with his dogs, books and old piano, in two shabby rooms littered with manuscripts. His old friends were either dead or no longer in Capri. It was only at the Brett Youngs' in Anacapri that he could still cadge a meal, talk about literature and listen to the gramophone. The youths who had followed one another as his servant, and had cared for little else but his money, seldom came to see him, although, now grown up, some still lived on the island. A new cross he had to bear was the antagonism of the new régime towards homosexual foreigners. His translations of the Greek epigrams had been sent to a publisher, and he nourished a hope that they would be accepted and bring in some cash. He still had £300 a year from Romaine, given when their marriage collapsed in 1904, but such an income did not go far in 1929 and, with his finances in a desperate state, he became haunted by the fear of being evicted from his home. He took a cab to Caprile, walked wearily down to the Villa Fraita and told Francis Brett Young that he needed £30 to save himself from disaster. The money was given without hesitation, more was promised if it was needed, and Brooks returned home with spirits raised. But he was racked with internal pain and a few days later went over to Naples for a medical check. He was X-rayed and, elated because no operation was recommended, returned very tired after the double journey to find Jessica from Anacapri waiting with food for him. Then a package containing the Greek epigrams arrived by post – with thanks and regrets. He did not feel like sending his life's work off again. The pain grew worse, and on the last day of May 1929, he died of cancer of the liver.[19]

Colonel Bryan Palmes died on 30 January 1930. At his funeral on the following day Sophie Grahame caught pneumonia and immediately succumbed. For Norman Douglas, who was not greatly concerned about Palmes, this 'was a loss of another kind; irreparable! The death of Sophie Grahame extinguished the last spark of the old Capri spirit; it eclipsed the gaiety of nations so far as the island was concerned.'[20]

All were buried in the little cemetery – Charles Coleman under a small Roman altar from his collection; Emelie Fraser below a white marble cross, next door to Vernon Andrews; John Brooks covered by a simple grey slab; Bryan Palmes and Sophie Grahame each overshadowed by elaborately worked angels in white marble, chosen perhaps by Bryan's widow Maimie – Sophie three places away from Archie's grave and the simple cross which she had put over it in 1917.

Although Sophie had passed on, there was still one survivor of those festive days. Gwen Galatà, separated from her husband and hard-pressed for money, continued to run her *pensione* in the Villa Esperia – 'giving her clients an excellent bill of fare, comfortable beds, reasonable charges and perpetual entertainment of one kind and another, often accidental and never organised. . . .' She was still an imposing figure. Her auburn hair was now grey, but she often dyed it orange 'when there was going to be a party or she felt dull'. She would make her appearance while the guests were having breakfast 'already booted, but still in her dressing-gown. "Always put my boots on before anything else. Can't get near my feet after I'm dressed." She wore boots long after they were out of fashion. They were made in Blighty, treasures from a glorious past, and a challenge to those . . . who went about on flimsy rope-soles.'[21]

Faith Mackenzie stayed at the Esperia for a week in 1928 and in the spring of 1930 was again in Capri, but staying at the Quisisana, to wind up her affairs on the island and pay her last respects to the living and the dead. After her departure Mimì Ruggiero continued to keep the garden on Cetrella in some sort of order and to clear the paths on the cliff-side of Ventroso, until early in 1933 he was afflicted by severe pain in his ear; after operations, a long course of radium and an agony of suffering, he died at the end of the year. He sent a last message to Monty through his son

Giovanni 'how he was thinking of him *con grande nostalgia*'.[22] Mimì is remembered for his enduring contributions to the landscape of Capri. It is pleasant to record that his nursery beside Via Tragara and his flower-shop below the German Church still flourish under his descendants.

The English Church was at a very low ebb. In May 1925 the SPG recorded that 'the English residents and visitors are split up into endless little factions and will not mix with one another, and the Chaplain has to stand clear of all such matters'. Chaplains were still sent for the winter/ spring season, and Harold Trower soldiered on as Churchwarden. The last entry in the Service-book is on 15 March 1929, a month after the funeral service for Mrs Fraser. On Easter Sunday 1930, during her last short visit, Faith Mackenzie went to eight o'clock Communion. 'Tubby' Clayton of Talbot House (Toc H), also on a visit, 'was celebrating, and a glow of hearty Christianity warmed its usually vague non-committal atmosphere'.[23] Chaplains continued until the 1931–2 season; thereafter the Chaplain of the English Church in Naples undertook occasional ministrations. Bertha Trower died on 24 May 1934. Over her grave Harold put a sundial with a quotation from Mazzini: 'There is no death in this world, only forgetfulness' – and went every day to the cemetery to leave a visiting card on the grave. After Bertha's death the annuity, which had supported them both in reasonable comfort, ceased, and Harold could no longer afford any rent for the Villa Cesina – but the Scoppa family generously allowed him to remain there without payment for his remaining years.

In the middle 'twenties the health of Queen Victoria of Sweden declined and in 1927 she left Casa Caprile and moved to the Villa Svezia in Rome. Munthe, living in Materita and hard at work completing *The Story of San Michele*, paid frequent visits to Rome in order to sustain his principal patient, and to the Swedish Court in Stockholm. Relations between King Gustav and the Queen were somewhat strained by the fact that the King in his middle sixties took hormone treatment, which made him not only much too frisky but also overtly homosexual.[24] Munthe appears to have been in financial difficulty at this time, due to the expenses of his life at Court and of the constant travelling between Capri, Rome and Stockholm – and in September 1929 at last agreed to be paid for his services, but only on the condition that his pay did not come from the Queen's private income. This arrangement lasted barely five months, for the Queen died in Rome in April 1930.[25]

The Story of San Michele, written in English, was completed in 1928 and in April 1929 published in London by John Murray. It was an immediate success and by November 1930 was in its seventeenth impression – two impressions sometimes following in a single month. Later it was trans- lated all over the world. This is not the place to describe in any detail or analyse the structure of this very well-known book, in which Munthe interwove fantasy with reality and fiction with fact – never quite certain when he was moving from one to the other and then back again. In no sense is it a true account of Capri, but this does not worry the great majority of readers, who know little or nothing of the island and have no independent standard by which to judge Munthe's story. One may best leave the verdict with his cousin Gustaf Munthe, who wrote: 'How and why the book achieved such fame is curiously difficult to answer.'[26]

In a preface to the Italian edition Munthe expressed the hope that his campaign against the snaring and shooting of birds would soon be won. It is related that Mussolini, impressed by the book, asked to see the author and at a private meeting with Munthe in Rome undertook to decree that the whole of Capri would be a bird-sanctuary. Munthe was delighted and as a start designated his property on the pine-covered slopes of Barbarossa as 'The San Michele Sanctuary'. In January 1933 he sent the London *Times* a long letter for English bird-lovers, inviting them to rejoice with him over the new decree. The islanders, who were and still are as avid in their slaughter of song-birds as all other Italians, were furious, and the Anacapresi attacked Munthe where they knew it would hurt most, by poisoning his two dogs.[27]

It was Anacrapri – remote and peaceful, and a place where, if you wanted, you could disappear from view – which in the 'twenties attracted more foreigners than the busy, social, lower part of the island. Most were Germans and a strange lot they were.

Willy Kluck, born in Berlin in 1888, became as a young man one of the leading sculptors of Germany and his studio a meeting place of 'intellectuals' from many countries. He was disabled during service in World War I and was awarded a modest pension. One day in 1920 he landed in Capri as a tourist and remained there for the rest of his life. He gave up all the comforts of civilised life, said goodbye to sculpture, built himself a cottage at the end of the Migliara and, supported only by his war-pension, lived there alone until his death in 1978. Once a week he emerged to buy bread and milk, but otherwise existed on wild herbs cooked over a brushwood fire. He passed the time writing about philosophy and making one drawing after another of a woman he had loved and seen for the last time in 1920. Always dissatisfied with what he wrote and drew, from time to time he cast the pages over the cliff into the blue sea – and nothing of his work survives except a self-portrait.[28]

Less remote was Otto Sohn-Rethel, born in 1877, the son of Karl Rudolph Sohn and grandson of Karl Ferdinand Sohn, both artists of Düsseldorf; his mother was the daughter of Alfred Rethel, also a painter. Before the end of the nineteenth century Otto had established himself as a portraitist of high technical ability and with a meticulous style which was highly regarded in Germany. He travelled far and wide not only in Europe but also in the East, where he visited India, Bali, China and Japan, and widened his interests to include the collection of miniatures and of butterflies and insects. Soon after the war he settled in the Villa Lina near San Michele, and took an Anacaprese as servant and friend. He continued to paint and draw – his favourite subject being naked boys – enlarged his entomological collection and created a salon for local and visiting artists. Another pederast, Hans Berg, a rich German who owned a factory in Brazil, lived close by.[29] Both were friends of Hans Paule, Austrian painter and wood-engraver, who had come to Capri at the beginning of the century and at first lived in the Grotta dell' Arsenale, where he was sometimes marooned by the sea and had to catch fish in order to survive. Later he had taken a room at Palazzo a Mare, near the Bagni di Tiberio. After being sent to a concentration camp in Sardinia during World War I, he returned to his room at Palazzo a Mare, from where he explored every inch of the island and recorded it in a series of brilliant and highly-prized woodcuts.

Baron Ekkehard von Schack, born in the same year as Willy Kluck, came of an old and grand Prussian family . . . and had held a colonel's commission in the German Imperial Mounted Lifeguards. Disgusted by the creation of the Weimar Republic in 1919 and government by Social Democrats ('Sozis'), and attracted by Capri's reputation as a haven for pederasts, he left Germany penniless and with little else except his uniform, including cuirass and plumed dress-helmet, and found his way to Anacapri. Here he took a room above a restaurant in Caprile, but paid nothing for it and for much of the time went hungry. He looked the very epitome of the Prussian Officer, shaven bullet head, sabre-scars and all, and was immensely tall. Every morning he would polish his helmet and every year on the Kaiser's birthday he donned full uniform and drank the Kaiser's health. He indeed drank enormously whenever he had the chance and was fortunate in knowing enough people, like Sohn-Rethel and Berg, who would ask him to meals. But he also had a gentler side, collected wild orchids in the remoter parts of the island and knew more about them than anyone else.[30]

Medical care in the island was reinfored in 1926 by the arrival in Anacapri of Dottoressa Elizabeth Moor. Born in Vienna in 1886, she had a conventional schooling, which was followed by the study of medicine. In 1914 she married Gigi Moor, a Swiss; in the following year she obtained her medical degree and bore her first child, Ludwig. A daughter, Giulietta, followed in 1921, the year in which she and Gigi visited Anacapri for about three months. Both contracted typhoid, and she nearly died. Much of the Dottoressa's time was spent at Positano, where she had an affair with an officer of the Italian Navy, Beniamino Tutino, and in

1926 bore him a son, Andrea. Gigi promptly divorced her. By now she had grown tired of Tutino and refused his offer of marriage. All she wanted were her children. She was allowed to keep Giulietta, but not Ludwig, and with her daughter and the young Andrea she returned to Anacapri, almost penniless, and started to earn what she could as a doctor. With her long training in Austria she had acquired a good general knowledge of medicine, knew her limitations and, if she was unable to cope with a case, said so and referred the patient to someone who could. Thus she gradually built up a practice on the island, which enabled her to survive.[31]

Noël Rawnsley, whose father was Chaplain to King George V and one of the founders of the National Trust, decided to leave England, where he had become bankrupt in 1921, and took his wife Violet, suffragette and poetess, to seek peace and security in Anacapri. His sister-in-law was already living there, and with a little money which Violet had saved he bought a property in the country below Monte Solaro, sent out wood from England to build a house on it, and in 1922, when all was ready, took Violet and his four young children, Una, Conrad, David and Derek to live there. Conscious of the difficulty of obtaining water for a house so far removed from any distribution point, he installed a system to catch the rainwater in the traditional manner and a two-chamber septic tank for recycling the effluent for use in the garden; Noël himself, a practical man of many parts, installed the central-heating, much needed in a house which was very cold in winter. They called the house 'Dil-Aram' (Persian for 'heart's delight'). Noël lost more money in the Slump. He would, no doubt, have found some way of rebuilding his finances, had Violet let him, but she was a strong-willed woman, not much interested in material things, who lived in a world of poetry, painting watercolours and above all the cause of 'Federal Union', which immersed the Rawnsley family in the 'thirties.[32]

Meanwhile, half a mile away in the Villa Fraita, Francis Brett Young, plagued with headaches, worked intermittently at his *Portrait of Clare*. Conceived and written in the exotic surroundings of Capri and beneath a Mediterranean sky, this long novel, set in the West Midlands and reaching to some 270,000 words, was completed in 1926. It was his first real success, and his next book *My Brother Jonathan*, another Midlands novel, also did well. By 1930 he and Jessica were tired of Capri and its inhabitants – the islanders liked Francis but found Jessica very uncongenial (*antipatica alla morte*) – and longed for England again. Fortunately the sales of these two books enabled them to return and buy themselves a house in Worcestershire, in the heart of what was already becoming known as 'Brett Young country', but they retained possession of the Villa Fraita.[33]

Another exile who found the pull of mother-country too strong was

Baron Ekkehard von Schack, c. 1950.
Photo: Islay Lyons

Maria Mellino, belle of Marina Piccola,
c. 1935. *Courtesy of Signora Maria Lembo*

Queen Victoria of Sweden in Anacapri, c. 1926. *Photo: Allhem*

Maksim Gorki. In 1928 he exchanged the sun and freedom of Sorrento for the grim tyranny of the Soviet Union, where he submerged his dislike of the régime, became the undisputed leader of Soviet writers, and in 1934, when the Soviet Writers' Union was founded, was elected its first president. At the same time he helped to found the literary method 'Socialist Realism', which compelled all Soviet writers to become outright political propagandists. He died suddenly in 1936, when under medical treatment, and later the former police chief, Yagoda, confessed to having ordered Gorki's death.[34]

*

By 1929 the new harbour-jetty at Marina Grande had reached a stage at which ships could tie up safely except when a strong east or north-east wind was blowing; then they anchored off Marina Piccola. The great majority of visitors came only for the day. A record number of 133,900 passenger movements in and out of the island, mostly tourists, was reached in 1925. During the early years of Fascist administration numbers dropped to 113,657 in 1926 and 102,738 in 1928, but rose to 121,452 in 1930; they were down to 105,500 in 1931 but rose steadily to a new record of 173,283 in 1934. For visitors who wanted to stay Baedeker (1930) listed seven hotels at Marina Grande; ten hotels and seven *pensioni* in Capri town; one *pensione* at Marina Piccola; two hotels and two *pensioni* in Anacapri.

Amongst the visitors of 1927 was a rising star of British music-hall Gracie Fields, then married unhappily to her actor-manager, Archie Pitt. Born in 1898 in Rochdale, Grace, daughter of Fred and Jenny Stansfield, was fortunate in having a determined mother who recognised her daughter's talents and had no intention of letting her spend a lifetime in the cotton-mills of Lancashire. Instead, she reared Grace on 'clouts, and push and never-give-in'[35] for a career on the stage; the same treatment was meted out to Grace's sisters, Betty and Edie, and her brother, Tommy.

Grace was blessed with a natural singing voice, high spirits, courage, a warm personality and good looks. Her first public appearance was at the age of eight singing in a local cinema. She soon became a successful mimic, danced and sang with a troupe of juveniles – and worked in a cotton-mill or shop when there was nothing for her on the stage. Jenny thought that Grace Stansfield was too long a name for the 'big lights' and made her change it to 'Gracie Fields'. In 1915 Gracie joined a touring revue, of which the principal comedian was Archie Pitt, a Jew who had changed his name from Selinger, and made her first London appearance. Three years later Pitt became actor-manager of his own company and wrote *Mr Tower of London* with Gracie as the star and including Tommy, Betty and Edie; the revue was a great success and ran for seven years. In 1923 Gracie married Pitt, not because she loved or even liked him, but because 'Archie insisted. . . . For nine years, since I was sixteen, Archie had drilled me, encouraged me, driven me, helped and filled my life with work, work and still more work.'[36] In July 1923 *Mr Tower of London* appeared at the Alhambra Theatre in London and here, with her charm and freshness, Gracie instantly attracted the attention of the stars and of the public. Gerald du Maurier offered her the part of Lady Weir in *S.O.S.* With her talent for mimicry, she had no difficulty in adapting her natural Lancashire to the 'posh' accent required for the only straight part she ever played. Although untrained as a singer, her beautiful and flexible voice steadily improved, and her ability to clown her way through operatic arias in a mixture of Lancashire, Italian and French, and get all her top notes, regularly brought the house down – and even attracted the attention of the operatic *diva* Madame Tetrazzini, who tried vainly to woo Gracie from music-hall into real opera. Money poured in. Pitt bought a large house in Hampstead, which he called 'The Towers', and equipped it with lavish furniture, butler, cook and servants. Gracie was totally unused to this sort of thing and hated it all, on top of which she knew that Pitt often went off with other women. One day her sister Betty introduced her to two young men who were friends – Henry Savage, a writer, and John Flanagan, an Irish painter.[37] Gracie fell in love with Flanagan and spent all the time she could in his studio in St John's Wood.

In love for the first time in her life but overworked on the stage and worn out by the tensions of life at 'The Towers', she decided for once to please herself and in 1927 went off for a Mediterranean holiday with John and Henry. Because she had been intrigued by Norman Douglas's *South Wind* and wanted to see 'Nepenthe', they paid a flying visit to Capri. At the very end of their visit they allowed their coachman to take them down to Marina Piccola. Attracted by a notice 'Rooms to let' they followed a path until they came to a broken-down yard and some dilapidated buildings inhabited by a middle-aged man, his wife, and teenage son. This was the *fortino* property which in 1919 Marchese Adolfo Patrizi had bought from the Behring estate and where he now lived in simple style, cultivating his vines, making wine and taking lodgers. They were charmed by the place and wanted to stay. Patrizi, at first reluctant to take in what he thought were *scarparielli* (penniless Germans who walk everywhere), accepted them, and Gracie spent ten blissful days with John, until the two men got restless and Gracie felt she had to return to work. Thereafter, they came every spring for a fortnight and had the same rooms at the *fortino*. Savage made friends with Adolfo Patrizi, who had not a word of English – so they conversed in French. Ettore, his son, who spoke some English, got on well with Flanagan, who one winter went to Capri on his own, took a lodging in the town and with Ettore and others spent much of the time gambling.

Unable to bear 'The Towers' any longer, Gracie moved to a small studio not far from Flanagan. She bought a house, 'The Havens', at Peacehaven, near Brighton, for her parents and here on weekends she relaxed with the family party. Gracie was now appearing in films. The first, *Sally in our Alley*, was a resounding success, and 'Sally' became and remained her most popular song. The sale of her records increased by leaps and bounds, and amidst the gloom and poverty of the Depression, when the average wage was £2 a week and many were unemployed, 'the richest working woman in the world' began to make a fortune with films, live shows and records. But no one grudged success to this great-hearted and versatile entertainer, with her freshness, warmth and fun, who was equally at home in mimicry, burlesque or sentimental ditties – all delivered in an exceptionally beautiful and wide-ranging voice.

Gracie became very fond of Capri and particularly as a place where she could be alone with John. One day in 1933 she received a letter from Ettore Patrizi saying that his father's property at Marina Piccola was to be sold at auction. She bought it for 400,000 *lire* (about £6,000) and became the owner of the *fortino*, some humble buildings, vines, and an expanse of uncultivated hillside; and concessionaire of a stretch of rocky beach. The first person to be told of her purchase was a Rochdale woman with whom she was staying at the time and who admonished her severely – 'A house in a foreign country, over with all them I-talians. Tha' must be oop t'pole, Grace.' Undeterred she went ahead, and in 1934 the Brett Youngs, in Capri on a short visit and asked by Gerald du Maurier to call on Gracie, found her firmly established, with bookcases filled with books, and John and Henry as guests. In 1935 Gracie and John parted company. Accounts vary as to why. According to Gracie herself, when she poured out her heart to Denis Pitts in 1970, Flanagan left her because he did not want to be kept by a rich and famous woman and 'lose the will to work, the need that every artist must have – the need to survive'. Ettore Patrizi, however, says that she left Flanagan, because she had become enamoured with a British *ballerino*. She did not have an affair with the dancer – only sent him passionate love-letters.[38]

Through her work in films Gracie met and became fond of the Italian film-director Mario Bianchi, whose family lived at Cesena, near Forlì. Monty Banks, as he became known, who had started life as a waiter, was warm-hearted, impulsive, an inveterate gambler and womaniser, but for Gracie a welcome relief from the cold, calculating and equally unfaithful Archie Pitt. The dancer blackmailed Gracie and Monty for the return of her letters, which they bought and destroyed.[42] Gracie's family were puzzled by Monty, who kissed all the women and, as Italians are

Monty Banks and Gracie Fields, mid-1930s. *Courtesy of Muller, Blond & White Ltd.*

Norman Douglas and Carmela
Cerrotta ('La Bella Carmelina'),
c. 1948. *Photo: Islay Lyons*

accustomed to do, sometimes kissed the 'fellows' as well. Gracie went from strength to strength, but she was no hoarder of the money which success bought her. Having provided for all her family and relations, she never ceased to give where she felt help was needed. She endowed and maintained an orphanage at Peacehaven; her many donations to hospital charities earned her in 1937 the Order of St John of Jerusalem. In the same year she received the Freedom of Rochdale and in 1938 was created Commander of the British Empire.

In 1936 the *fortino* at Marina Grande also passed into foreign hands. Built during the Franco–British occupation of 1806–15, it lay within the confines of the great sea-side palace (Palazzo a Mare) of the Emperor Augustus. The building itself, with casemates and gun-emplacements, occupied what was probably the actual living-quarters of the Emperor, while a large area to the west of it had been levelled at the beginning of the nineteenth century and turned into a military parade ground (*campo di marte*), which later became Capri's sports ground (*campo sportivo*). All these works had caused great damage to the Roman remains, already despoiled by Bourbon excavations at the end of the eighteenth century.

The buyers in 1936 of this intriguing property were an American couple, Harrison and Mona Williams. Mona Strader was born in 1897 in Lexington, Kentucky, the daughter of a stable-hand on a farm. At 18 she married Harry Schlessinger, who was 37 and owner of the farm. They were divorced five years later, with Mona receiving a settlement of $200,000 and her husband custody of their only child. After a brief second marriage, she married Harrison Williams, a very successful businessman who, amongst other enterprises, was head of the vast Telegraph and Telephone Company of America and a director of the American Gas and Electricity Company. Good-looking, philanthropic and enormously rich, he was liked and respected by all. Mona was a beautiful, attractive and confident woman with wide interests, who, as well as enjoying the high life of New York, liked foreign travel and was passionately interested in gardening. She saw in the *fortino*, with its view of Marina Grande and the Bay of Naples, a site of exceptional beauty, where she could build an idyllic house and create from the wasteland the garden of her dreams. Meanwhile she lived in the Quisisana and here made plans to transform the *fortino*. As companion she had Count Edward (Eddie) Bismarck, grandson of the German Chancellor. They had met in Venice, become fond of each other, and, while Mona planned the garden, Eddie supervised the building of the house. Harrison, who visited Capri rarely, accepted the relationship in a gentlemanly way and indeed thought Bismarck would have a civilising influence on Mona and protect her from predators on her international travels. From the sexual point of view, Harrison had little to worry about, because Eddie was homosexual. It was said that, while as a general rule Eddie contented himself with young men, Mona and he sometimes went to bed together – these occasions being attended by an elaborate ritual of caviar and champagne, but nothing much else seems to have happened. What Mona loved best was her gardening, and during the final years of the 'thirties she began to create her exotic and very private garden – until the onset of war compelled her return to America.[40]

Soon after World War I Giorgio Cerio had returned with his rich American wife Mabel. Flush with her money, he bought from Raffaele Federico a large strip of land between Via Tragara and Via Occhio Marino. For themselves they built the Villa La Pergola di Tragara and, for the staff, the Villa Elena (now site of Hotel La Scalinatella). On the opposite side of Via Tragara they bought a small house which Mabel turned into a studio and linked it with the main property by a tunnel under the street. Arturo Cerio was given a villa which had once been a Federico family home. In addition, Giorgio built himself a work-place and laboratory fronting on Via Occhio Marino.

An extensive park was created, with tennis-court, bowls and archery; and there were peacocks and dogs. The most remarkable feature was a series of aviaries, which was built round several trees. Mabel Norman loved birds and imported exotic species from all over the world. In the centre, according to Edwin Cerio, was the main aviary 'for birds from hot and humid climes, with running hot and cold water, central heating and other tropical comforts, while ranged around were large cages for other species from sub-tropical and temperate zones. In this paradise, with its delightful living conditions, as far removed as possible from those of nature, the birds lived and died happily, enjoying an artificial life and a natural death'. Dead birds 'were replaced by purchases made in Naples, New York, Hamburg and Paris'.[41] A middle-aged Caprese, then a little boy, whose mother was a servant in Arturo's household, remembers him as a nice, rather strange, old bachelor, who was often ill; Giorgio and Edwin, however, varied from being *allegri* and affable one day, to cold and arrogant the next.

Giorgio also acquired the Torre Saracena property at Marina Piccola, and the Grotta del Castiglione, in which he built a small house. At Torre Saracena he amused himself planting trees and building terraces on the hillside. A keen radio ham, he had brought back from America one of the first large radio sets ever to be produced and, when the set broke down, was faced with the grim prospect of taking it all the way back for repairs. A friend suggested getting in touch with a knowledgeable young student, who was then on holiday in Capri. This was Boris Alperovici, a Russian Jew from Bessarabia – that bone of contention between Russia and Romania, which was Romanian when Boris left it to study architecture in

Rome and became Russian again when the Soviet Union occupied it in 1939–40. Fascinated by developments in wireless, he changed from architecture to physics and soon became an inventive radio technician. He successfully repaired the precious set and so impressed Giorgio that he became a friend of the family and was given the run of Giorgio's laboratory at Tragara.[42]

Amongst the workers at Torre Saracena was a beautiful peasant girl from Anacapri who attracted Giorgio's attention, and, in the hope of producing a son, he seduced her and made her pregnant. Whether this was done with the prior knowledge of his wife is uncertain, but, since she seemed unable to have children, it is possible that she consented to the affair. A girl, Amabel, was born – not, alas, a son – the Anacaprese mother was squared, and the child adopted by Mabel Norman and brought up mostly at the Norman home in Newport, Rhode Island, where Cerio himself was a frequent visitor. As nanny to look after Amabel, they engaged a Piedmontese named Irene Bonus. More will be heard of both her and Boris.

Among the activities encouraged by Mussolini during the 'thirties was archaeological excavation, particularly where it was likely to enhance the grandeur of Rome. The southern part of central Italy was fortunate in having Amedeo Maiuri as Superintendent of Antiquities in Campania and Molise, and Director of the Museo Nazionale in Naples. Before the war he had excavated in Crete and Rhodes and after his appointment to Naples in 1924 began a wide-ranging programme of research. Work was resumed at Pompeii and Herculaneum, and investigations launched at Paestum, Cumae, Baia, Pozzuoli and Stabia. In Capri, from 1932 to 1935 he concentrated on the Villa Iovis – the first work to be done on the site since Bourbon excavations in 1827. This was the first time that excavation of a Roman Imperial site in Capri had been undertaken not for the sake of recovering portable works of art but to reveal the plan of the buildings and, to quote Maiuri, 'render accessible one of the most characteristic and impressive examples of joined villa and residential palace that have survived from the first age of the Empire, and thus the most complete and important monument of Roman Capri'.[43] In 1937 he moved to Anacapri and with the same purpose excavated the imperial villa at Damecuta. 1937 was also, the 2,000th anniversary of the birth of the Emperor Augustus, and to celebrate this event Maiuri conducted a group of distinguished persons round the Villa Iovis. Although the site is better known for its association with Tiberius, no doubt Maiuri was right in assuming that Augustus could hardly have failed to build on such a breath-taking spot. Capri was fortunate in Maiuri, who was a good scholar, a capable excavator and, although superintending a wide and archaeologically rich area of the mainland, always had a warm regard for the island and not only worked hard to uncover the imperial past of Capri but also to preserve its later buildings and customs.

Near the Villa Iovis Carmela Cerrotta ('La Bella Carmelina'), famous as an exponent of the *tarantella*, and her husband Raffaele Salvia, also a dancer, still had their *caffè*. Although now in her fifties, she was still an object of pilgrimage for visitors and ready to enliven the *caffè* with her dancing.

Since time immemorial the *tarantella* had been performed by talented individuals and groups of islanders, with accompaniment of guitar, mandolin, percussion instruments and simple hand-clapping. Folk music and song, however, apart from what was peculiar to the *tarantella* and to another intricate local dance, the *tarascone*, performed by four or eight couples, were largely unorganised, until in 1931 Costanzo Spadaro, an itinerant salesman, created a *gruppo folkloristico* which became known as 'scialapopolo' or 'Banda di Putipù' – *scialapopolo* ('let the people blue their money') being the cry with which Spadaro sought to attract attention as he moved round selling his cloth; and *putipù* an onomatopoeic word for the sound made by the *basso* of the group. As the group developed, it successfully combined a mixture of the conventional tools of folk-music – castanets, triangle, tambourine and concertina (*organetto*) – with four home-made local instruments:

1. *Putipù* (*Crò-crò* in Neapolitan) – the skin of an ox or cow stretched across a small wooden tub (*tinozza*) and manipulated by a stick, the skin always kept wet and taut.
2. *Macinino* (*Trà-trà*) – grinder or rattle.
3. *Triccaballache* – three bits of wood, one rigid and two moving, which are banged together.
4. *Sceta-vajasse* (*Grà-grà*) – tops of beer-cans on pins fixed to a serrated wooden bow, which is drawn across a wooden 'violin'.

The instrumentalists of 'Scialapopolo', all male, wear an eye-catching uniform – tight white trousers, dark blue jersey, red cummerbund, light-blue neckerchief and red beret. The group includes *tarantella* dancers, and any concert given by the group usually has this dance – the girls in a blouse, wide swirling skirt, pinafore and cummerbund; the young men, in coloured trousers, shirt, sleeveless jacket, tie of coloured streamers and tasselled woollen cap.[44] They invariably give a public performance in the *piazzetta* on New Year's Day; often in celebration of the *festa* of San Costanzo on 14 May; and otherwise by invitation.

Anacapri, aroused to inspiration by the temporary incursion of artists and musicians during Edwin Cerio's *convegno* of 1922, had inaugurated a 'Festa della Settembrata' – with exhibitions, processions, floats and *feste notturne* of dance, music and song, which happily coincided with the *vendemmia* (vintage). These autumnal celebrations continued until 1930, when inspiration seems to have evaporated, and were not resumed until 1977.

Thanks to the provision of ample funds by the Fascist authorities in Naples, the efficient administration of *podestà* Dusmet and the fascination which Capri continued to exercise over visitors of all kinds, the economy of the island, undeterred by financial gloom and chaos elsewhere, forged steadily ahead. Will Grosz and Jimmy Kennedy's song 'Isle of Capri' of 1934, which became a best-seller in England, no doubt encouraged British tourists to spend their holidays 'somewhere far away, over Naples bay'. In the island itself such propaganda as was needed and basic tourist information was provided by the Pro Capri Society, which since 1914 had been run by the *comune* and was located in the courtyard of the *municipio*, where the police-post now is. It was managed by Antonio Elefante, a handsome man with a long nose and smiling face, who had lived in the island for many years and combined a happy family life with successful amours outside it. The island gained added prestige by becoming a favourite haunt of Galeazzo and Edda Ciano – he, Minister of Foreign Affairs and she, daughter of the *Duce*. She was Mussolini's favourite child and also popular in Capri – 'not *superba*, always very approachable, *simpatica*, *carina*' was the verdict of a contemporary Caprese.[45] They built a large villa on the west side of Castiglione, overlooking Due Golfi and the valley down to Marina Piccola, and Edda prided herself on *not* having a view of the Faraglioni. To serve it, they completed an abortive road up Castiglione begun forty years earlier. The nearby Villa Mura was bought by the Prince of Hesse, who was married to Princess Mafalda, second daughter of King Vittorio Emanuele III. Prince Umberto, eldest son of the King and heir to the Italian throne, and recently appointed commander of the troops stationed in Campania, came with his mistress and entourage to enjoy the delights of the island. Italo Balbo, the Italian Air Minister, was given a *festa* in Capri to celebrate his flight from Italy to North America and back in July 1933, at the head of 24 twin-enginged Savoia Marchetti flying-boats.

It was mainly through the influence of Ciano that in 1938 his friend the journalist Curzio Malaparte obtained – in defiance of all accepted norms for the protection of the countryside – a licence to build a villa at Punta di Massullo, an inaccessible and barren promontory at the south-east corner of the island. Born in 1898 at Prato in Tuscany, the son of a German manufacturer of rugs and blankets, and of a well-to-do Milanese mother, Kurt Erik Suckert attended the school which many years earlier had taught Gabriele D'Annunzio and quickly became an admirer of the poet. In 1915, while not yet seventeen, he ran away from home, enlisted with the

'Legione Garibaldina' and went to fight in France. He distinguished himself, was promoted officer and decorated with the Italian *Medaglia di Bronzo* and French *Croix de Guerre*. After the war he became a journalist, joined the Fascists and with his hero D'Annunzio established himself as one of the leading propagandists for the Party. In 1925 he changed his name to Malaparte and in 1928 became Editor of *Il Mattino* in Naples. During a long visit to France from 1931 to 1933 he came to adverse notice in Rome and on his return to Italy was arrested for 'antifascist activity abroad'. This was not surprising, for Malaparte was completely independent and unpredictable; handsome, vain, attractive to and attracted by both men and women, a compulsive adventurer, tricky (*furbo*) and a bit mad (*un po matto*), he was incapable of conforming to any pattern at all. Banished for five years to the island of Lipari, his release after only one year was secured by Ciano, and he quickly resumed his career as an apostle of Fascism, achieving his greatest success in 1937 with the literary magazine *Prospettive*, which received a subsidy from the *Ministero della Cultura Popolare* and attracted a host of contributors in Italy and amongst sympathisers abroad. During a visit to Capri in 1936 Malaparte's eye was caught by the aforesaid Punta di Massullo, which belonged to a farmer named Vuotto, and he bought it for about £5 – the farmer delighted to sell a useless piece of rock for a sum which then would have kept a foreigner for a week at the Quisisana. In 1938, despite vigorous local opposition, Malaparte got permission to construct a bizarre red villa on an otherwise uninhabited coastline. While it was being built, he ranged round Abyssinia and the rest of Italian East Africa as correspondent of the *Corriere della Sera*.[46]

One of the consequences of Mussolini's plan to make a show-piece of Capri was the 'discovery' of Marina Piccola, already a popular resort for bathing; and during the 'thirties it was much used by the Fascist authorities for entertaining foreign VIPs. Families which owned land and property on or near the marina, in particular Mellino, Cosentino and Albanese, were not slow to profit from this situation.

The Mellino family, immigrants from Nerano, a remote hamlet near the tip of the Sorrentine peninsula, owned the concession at 'Le Sirene', which had once belonged to the Desiderio family, and here they started a *caffè*. Amongst those who patronised it were the hotel staffs of Capri town, who, when the north wind put Marina Grande out of action for visiting ships and they had to unload their passengers on the south of the island, would hurry down to Marina Piccola to receive them, and needed somewhere to have coffee and wine. As the vogue for Marina Piccola increased, the *caffè* developed into the restaurant 'da Vincenzo', and, to make the site still more attractive for visitors, the Mellino family rented part of the beach from the State and set up a few bathing-cabins.[47]

Vincenzo's second daughter Maria rented what was left of the beach, built more cabins and established her own 'Bagni di Maria'.

Maria, a dark, tall and graceful beauty just turned 20, was herself an attraction at the marina, and she was no kill-joy. At Easter 1933 Field-Marshal Hermann Göring, after business with Mussolini in Rome, visited Capri. His visit was not an unqualified success. The authorities arranged for a party of German residents to welcome Göring as he stepped ashore, and Colonel Baron von Schack, as senior resident, was asked to head the reception committee. In declining the invitation he said that he remembered Captain Göring from World War I days. Unfortunately he had a prior engagement, but would be delighted to welcome Captain Göring at his pension in Anacapri any Wednesday afternoon between the hours of four and five; he expressed his wonderment that a man could rise from captain to field-marshal in peace time.[48] Göring was unlucky also in the Quisisana, where a monkey belonging to Lord Tredegar, the Welsh peer and cousin of Gwen Galatà, who was in the adjoining suite, got loose and bit the Field-Marshal's nose. No mishap, however, marred his visit to Marina Piccola where, with the Prince of Hesse and other notables, he took luncheon at 'Le Sirene'. He was enchanted by Maria and promised to send her a present from Germany. Thinking this just a courteous remark, she was surprised when later in the year two Germans arrived with one of the first battery-operated portable radios, accompanied by a note from Göring with his greetings and recommending the radio particularly for enjoyment in a boat.

Göring visited Capri again in 1939 and was much taken by Giuseppe Savarese, called 'Scarola', a sailor who played the guitar and sang Neapolitan songs around the restaurants of Capri. Savarese had obtained his nickname in the following manner. At the beginning of the century his father, an immigrant from Vico Equense, had a *caffè* at Marina Grande. One day 'Ciccio' Cappuccio, an important *camorrista* came in, banged the table for service and, angry at not being recognised, said '*Io sono Cappuccio*'. Now *cappuccio* means 'cabbage', so Savarese replied: '*ed io sono Scarola*' (wild endive, or prickly lettuce) – and the nickname remained with the family. Göring invited Scarola to sing and play in Germany, all expenses paid. Passport and suitable clothes were quickly provided by the *municipio*, and Scarola was whisked off to Berlin. His principal appearance was at the Bristol Hotel, where he performed 'Santa Lucia', 'O sole mio' and the like, before a great concourse of German leaders and foreign ambassadors. In the interval Hitler asked Scarola if he liked Germany. Scarola, not understanding German but thinking that a negative answer was required, said decisively 'No!' He emerged unscathed from the *froideur* which followed and spent a month performing and making records, and returned to Capri with a good sum in his pocket.[49]

Another of Mussolini's distinguished visitors was Sir John Simon, the British Foreign Secretary, who, after business in Rome, was sent off to enjoy himself in Capri. He went up to Tiberio, where 'La Bella Carmelina' danced for him, and on Christmas Day 1933 there was a luncheon party for him and Lady Simon at 'Le Sirene'. Here he met Maria Mellino, was much taken by her and asked her to call on him if she was ever in London. Maria had learnt English from Lucy Flannigan, the mysterious American pastelist who lived at the nearby Pensione Weber. Next year, determined to take him at his word, she discussed the matter with Gracie Fields, now installed at the *fortino*, and with Gracie as escort – Maria had never before left the island – flew to London and turned up at the Foreign Office. Considering the cool state of Anglo-Italian relations in 1934, there was an understandable reluctance on the part of the Foreign Office guards to admit an Italian girl, however seductive, to the presence of the Foreign Secretary. She pressed the point, however, and when the guards telephoned Sir John Simon's office they were told to send her up. He was very hospitable and gave her tea. Before returning to Capri, Maria spent a month with Gracie in London and at Peacehaven.[50]

In November 1933 Maria's elder sister Margherita had married Eugenio Cosentino, the 35-year-old son of a fisherman, who had spent some years as a steward on transatlantic liners. Cosentino, hard (*duro*), very much on the ball (*molto in gamba*) and with the nickname 'Runcillo' (scythe), was shrewd enough to appreciate the great potential of the restaurant and bathing concession at 'Le Sirene' and acquired both from his Mellino in-laws.

The third family which did well at Marina Piccola was Albanese, which by the end of the 1930s had obained concessions for restaurants and cabins at Porto di Tragara (or Faraglioni), at Torre Saracena and Marina Piccola itself.

In 1934, up in Capri town, the *podestà* took a decision, which may have seemed trivial at the time, but was to have profound effects in later years. He gave permission to 26-year-old Raffaele Vuotto, who had recently opened an ice-cream bar on the west side of the Piazza, to put a few chairs outside the bar on the Piazza itself. Until this moment the whole space had been used for walking and talking. Although called grandly 'Piazza Umberto I', after the unlucky king who was assassinated in 1900, it was just known as 'The Piazza', or ' 'A Chiazza' to the Capresi, and measured about 25 to 28 yards. Its diminution by even the small amount of space taken up by the chairs of Vuotto's bar was, therefore, a serious matter.

Raffaele, born in 1908, was the son of Costanzo Vuotto (nicknamed 'Lattaiolo' – dairyman) and Luisa, daughter of Raffaele Federico, who has already been encountered as a land-owner on the lower side of Tragara. In 1902 Costanzo had bought Krupp's farm round the Certosa and kept pigs in the Certosa itself, which after 1901, when the Disciplinary Company was transferred from the island, was completely uninhabited apart from a few squatters. Here he fattened his animals with swill from the kitchens of the Quisisana.[51] By marrying Luisa Federico in 1904 Costanzo Vuotto substantially improved his position. Raffaele left school at the age of 10, and worked on his father's farm. After military service from 1927 to 1929, he started a small business of his own in butter, milk and cheese in Via delle Botteghe. In 1934 he married Teresa, eldest daughter of Antonio Esposito, one of the clan who owned much of the land on the upper side of Tragara, and in 1935 they had a son Costanzo.

From an early age Antonio Esposito, born in 1882 the son of Luigi, had been attracted by gardening and, after working at 'La Floridiana', a villa and public garden in the Vomero district of Naples, became a young gardener at the Villa Discopoli in the days of Alice Faehndrich. It is rumoured in Capri that he was one of Krupp's circle in the 1898–1902 period. In 1907 he married Virginia Strina, member of the ancient and still prosperous *caprese* family. He continued as gardener to Baroness Gudrun Uexküll, who in 1908 inherited the Discopoli from her sister Alice, and in return for his services she let Antonio and his wife live in a *casetta* which she owned just below the villa. Antonio christened it 'La Floridiana' and set up a business of his own as nursery gardener and florist. He worked hard, lived in simple style and with any money he acquired bought land and property. He thus gained a reputation for avarice, but did not mind this label and continued to enlarge his holdings. Between 1908 and 1923 Antonio and Virginia produced three sons, Luigi, Mario and Antonio, and four daughters, Teresa, Maria, Virginia and Venere, and, to accommodate this growing population, gradually enlarged 'La Floridiana'. In 1924 Gudrun Uexküll sold him the house for a small sum, Axel Munthe having begged the Baroness not to charge Antonio too much as he was 'only a poor peasant'.[52] By the time of Teresa's marriage in 1934, Antonio had become a man of substance, and he instituted a system of giving any child of his who got married a piece of land or property; thus, Teresa received a small house on Sopramonte.[53]

Raffaele Vuotto put Teresa to manage the *latteria*, until in 1936 he sold it, and bought buildings on the east side of the Piazza, where the old 'Caffè Scoppa' had once been, and established the 'Caffè Vuotto', with twelve tables, which, as at his *gelateria* on the other side, were allowed to intrude on the cobbles.[54] To have obtained not one but two footholds on the Piazza, hub of the island's social life, was for a self-made man, still in his late twenties, a remarkable achievement, which, combined with his native shrewdness and capacity for hard work, was certain to make him rich.

A new restaurant, 'Ristorante da Gemma', in Via Madre Serafina, was opened in 1935 by Raffaele and Gemma Terrasino. Gemma Lembo, born in 1909, was a member of the Marina Piccola fishing family and earned her keep by selling wood, charcoal and fish. She remembers carrying charcoal with other girls up to the kitchen of the Villa Lysis, where they found Fersen always very considerate and friendly – '*un bell' uomo*' – and Nino also impressed her – '*alto, elegante, bruno*'.[55] Shortly after her marriage to Terrasino, who was an excellent cook, they opened 'da Gemma' and served traditional *caprese* dishes, attractively cooked and at modest prices; the restaurant became an immediate success and still flourishes today.

While throughout the rest of Italy liberal use was made of castor oil and the cudgel, Fascism lay lightly on Capri. One of the few administrations of castor oil had nothing to do with politics. Vittorio Caracciolo conceived the rash idea of courting a girl-friend of Teodoro Pagano and so had to be punished.[56] Things were harsher in Naples. One of its foremost citizens, Benedetto Croce, humanist, philosopher, right-wing liberal and with plenty of money, had first supported the Fascists as a bastion against the political left. But when the brutal character of the régime revealed itself, he moved into opposition and not only repudiated the movement, but also became a bitter and vocal critic. Mussolini was furious and, afraid that the word of this widely respected figure would injure his own position, spent large sums of public money to keep Croce under surveillance. Living mostly in Naples, Croce became within and without Italy a rallying point for the campaign against Fascism. He formed close links with Ian Greenlees, who from 1934 to 1936 was Reader in English Literature at the University of Rome and in 1939–40 Head of the British Council in Italy. Greenlees translated one of Croce's books; visited him in Naples in 1936, when his house was guarded by secret police; and in 1939 started a British Institute in Naples in the same building as Croce in Via della Trinità. For the most part Croce was left in peace as an unassailable figure, and also because his anti-fascist writings published in highbrow magazines had only a small circulation. He was never jailed, like so many of the opposition, but in 1935 his apartment in Naples was ransacked by *fascisti* thugs and his library destroyed.[57]

1936 was Dusmet's last year as *podestà*. He was removed, it was said, because he and Polly left his rented apartment in the Villa Mimosa and built a large house in Via Dalmazio Birago, thereby incurring the Party's displeasure at such a show of wealth.[58] No one, however, belittled his administration, during which the island was efficiently run; widespread public works were carried out; and, thanks to the hospitality of the islanders, visitors came in ever-increasing numbers – all this against a sombre background elsewhere of financial and political turmoil. After 1930 a separate record had been kept of those visitors who slept a night or more in hotels and *pensioni*. The total rose from 9,665 in 1930, with an average stay of 15 days, to 17,721 in 1933, with the same average. After 1933 there were more visitors, but their visits were shorter, reaching 33,085 in 1936, with an average stay of only 5.7 days. The census of 1936 records an indigenous population of 8,042 (3,906 in Capri, 1,499 in Marina Grande and 2,637 in Anacapri). That a people of this size was able to attract four times as many visitors for short stays, as well as a vastly greater number of day trippers, is an impressive tribute to the native skill of the islanders in providing pleasure for all who set foot on their shores.

Dusmet was followed as chief administrator by Renato de Zerbi, official of the *prefettura* in Naples, who came to Capri as *commissario prefettizio* for the year 1936–7. A new *podestà* was appointed before the end of 1937 – Germano Ripandelli, a rich man of good family, an honest and straightforward artillery officer from the mainland, who continued until 1941. In 1938 he had the pleasure of welcoming the Japanese puppet ruler of Manchuria on an official visit to the island.

As the 'thirties drew to a close and moved inexorably towards World War II, the last vestiges of the old-style Capri vanished. Edith Reynolds, widow of William Andrews, the indefatigable translator of *Faust*, and remarried to an English resident died in March 1936 during a visit from America and was buried near William in the *cimitero acattolico* by the English Chaplain in Naples, there being no resident Chaplain in Capri. In January 1938 Gwen Galatà died penniless and alone in a basement room of the Villa Esperia. Her estranged husband, Giovanni, was on hand to arrange her funeral, and she was laid to rest with the Catholics. Although in his eighty-fifth year and in failing health, Trower was still fiercely protective of the English Church and his now shadowy position as churchwarden and representative of the SPG. There was no English congregation, no services had been held for many years and the roof of the church was in need of repair. In March 1939 the SPG in London and their chaplain in Naples were in correspondence about the possibility of keeping All Saints, Capri, alive. The chaplain advised that the building be kept 'always ready for services, using it as a quiet place for devotion'. The SPG wished 'we could see our way to giving them occasional services' and asked the chaplain to do what he could. He wrote to Trower about the situation and this provoked an indignant letter from him, to the SPG. He expressed surprise that they had not written direct to him instead of 'sending a message through a temporary chaplain who has no *locus standi*'; he had represented the Society in Capri since the consecration of All Saints in 1912; the roof-repairs had already been completed and paid for – 'I therefore need not call upon your Society for financial assistance'. An SPG official replied soothingly: 'I am very glad that we have someone like yourself who will willingly look after the church and who has long experience of it . . . and I shall know who to write to in future.'[59]

In May 1939, amidst widespread expressions and sympathy, Gracie Fields had an operation in London for cancer of the neck of the womb – though this was not known at the time – and, since the required surgery involved the removal of the womb itself, she was no longer able to have children. Never much interested in having sex with men, even in her prime, Gracie now at the age of 41 lost all libido.[60] To recover from this traumatic operation she went to Capri with Monty Banks, and there in the *fortino*, amidst the beauties of Marina Piccola, she relaxed.

*

On 15 March 1939 German troops invaded Czechoslovakia. It was clear that Hitler's next victim would be Poland, to which British and French guarantees were given at the end of the month. In April, Mussolini, not wanting to be left behind in the catalogue of aggression, invaded Albania, and Britain and France countered with guarantees to Romania and Greece. On 22 May Germany and Italy signed a formal political and military pact, but Mussolini refused to give any commitment for positive action to match Germany's secret preparations for the invasion of Poland. On 23 August Germany and the Soviet Union signed a non-aggression pact, thus paving the way for the German invasion of Poland and the carving up of its territory between them. Although making 'nonsense of the anti-bolshevist policy for which Mussolini had sent many Italians to die in Spain, he realised that a combination of Germany, Russia and Italy would be invincible and he therefore hailed it as a master-stroke that completely altered the picture'. But in private, among his cabinet and military colleagues, his moods and opinions veered from one extreme to another, and no one knew what he would do. Finally, on 1 September, the day on which Hitler invaded Poland, 'Mussolini told his cabinet that he had decided not to fight and that Hitler's "treachery" exonerated Italy from any treaty obligation. Since the word "neutral" was un-fascist, he coined the term "non-belligerent" to disguise the stark truth. The Cabinet approved unanimously. . . . Most Italians must have realised that he had made the right decision.'[61]

Two days later Britain and France declared war on Germany, and once again Capri faced the bleak prospect of no tourist trade, empty hotels, and shortages of food and supplies; but, unlike 1914–15, with the certainty that, if and when Italy joined the war, it could only be as a partner of Nazi Germany.

CHAPTER NINE

World War II

On the first night of the war all the lights in Naples harbour, where the Italian fleet was at anchor, were extinguished. Gracie Fields decided that she and Monty Banks must return to England, but next day they discovered that all movement of small craft in the harbour had been forbidden. Ettore Patrizi obligingly ferried them across in a speed-boat and, with the whole party looking convincingly like Italian VIPs, they made a safe landing, dashed to the station and took a train to England. Although still feeling 'pretty wobbly' after her operation, Gracie put herself at the disposal of ENSA and with Monty in tow went to France to entertain the British Expeditionary Force.[1]

Some residents took flight. Olga de Tschélischeff left her shop in charge of her partner the Princess Wittgenstein and returned to Egypt, whence she had come to Capri in 1916. Lady Mackinder and her two sisters in the Villa Tragara, their mother Mrs Ginsburg long dead, decided to leave and, having given the documents and keys of the house to their lawyer, Roberto Serena, returned to England. Of the English colony only Harold Trower lingered on, old, ill and poverty-stricken, in the Villa Cesina.

The winter of 1939 brought empty hotels and a growing scarcity of food and supplies. A number of villas, however, which might normally have been let to foreigners, were taken on indefinite leases by well-to-do mainland Italians, who brought their families to Capri as a refuge from Allied bombing to which Italian cities were likely to be exposed if Italy entered the war. A group of Lateran monks, who had been installed in the Certosa since 1936, ran a rough and ready school to provide some education and discipline for the children of these temporary immigrants. Those of the island families who had villas in the countryside tended to stay there rather than in the town.

The spring sunshine of 1940 brought some life to the beaches. The town filled up again from the countryside, and those with time to kill frequented the Sports Club, where they could play tennis, bowls, chess and bridge; and gossiped in the Caffè Vuotto and Caffè Tiberio on the Piazza. In the forenoon the arrival of the Naples boat, with news from the mainland, was eagerly awaited; the few papers it brought sold like hot cakes; and wireless-news circulated round the bars. Small groups of tourists sometimes appeared briefly at one o'clock, hurried round the *boutiques* and vanished again down the funicular to their boat.[2] Barone Fassini lost interest in Capri and sold both the SIPPIC and the SIA, to an Italo–American group; he died in 1942.

Gracie obtained a divorce from Archie Pitt early in 1940 and together she and Monty flew to California, where her parents were living, to get married – to the horror of his family in Italy, who had to abandon any thought of a male heir during Gracie's lifetime. Back in England and then over to France, she gave concerts large and small, until the German invasion of the Low Countries and Northern France led to the evacuation of the BEF and the collapse of France. The now imminent entry of Italy into the war posed problems for both of them. Monty as an Italian citizen could not remain in England without risk of internment, and Gracie had to decide whether to stay at home or accompany him abroad. In the end they reached a compromise, whereby Gracie would give concerts in Canada to raise funds for the Navy League, while Monty would go to America; and then Gracie would return to do her bit in England. Italy entered the war on 10 June, just as Gracie and Monty reached Canada, which was itself the first Commonwealth country to declare war on Italy. Monty hurried on to the United States; Gracie did her concerts in Canada, and then went to California to be with Monty and her parents.[3] Her 'desertion' of Britain in its hour of peril led to a storm of criticism, and 'the national heroine turned overnight into an object of contempt in a nation at bay fighting for its life'.[4] According to her brother Tommy, Gracie's decision to leave had the approval of Winston Churchill, who added, however, that she should not tell the press why she was going.[5]

Giorgio and Mabel Cerio, having given Edwin power of attorney in respect of their properties in Capri, thought it time to leave and duly went to live in the States. They never returned to Capri. Giorgio, always the least *caprese* of the three Cerio brothers, died in Newport on 28 October 1943.

'Mussolini's declaration of war ... seems to have met with more perplexity than enthusiasm among Italians, though he tried hard to convince himself that public opinion was behind him. On the assumption that the war would last only a few weeks, he confirmed his order that civilian life should continue much as usual and people should be protected from being incommoded by a full-scale mobilisation.' Cabinet ministers and leading Fascist officials, however, were sent off at once for military duties, without any proper replacements, and for a time the administration of Italy lapsed into total chaos. One example of confusion 'was that ships at sea and in foreign ports were not warned in time to return home, and a third of Italy's merchant marine was thus lost before any fighting took place at all; no other country made this mistake and its effects were grave. But for Mussolini such details did not matter: he expected to get these back soon in the peace settlement, as well as others belonging to Britain and France that would be due to him by way of reparation.' For a week the Italian armed forces remained inactive, and it was not until the French asked for an armistice, on 17 June, that Mussolini ordered an offensive in the Alps.[6] Early in June Ian Greenlees went to Naples to say goodbye to Croce. He found the philosopher confident of an Italian defeat and certain that at the end of it 'Italia' would become 'Italietta'.[7]

One consequence of Italy's entry into the war was the intensification of measures against the Jews. Since the Fascist 'Charter of Race' published in July 1938, the Jews, together with Arabs and Ethiopians, had been regarded officially as an inferior race; but the Fascists received little or no support for this policy amongst the Italian people. As a fully committed co-belligerent of Nazi Germany, Italy could no longer refrain from instituting concentration camps, but they were benevolent institutions compared to Buchenwald and Auschwitz. One of the victims was Julius Hans Spiegel. Of German–Jewish origin and deaf and dumb since his birth in 1891, Spiegel had left Germany in the late 'twenties and with a large wardrobe of oriental clothes, ornaments and masks had danced and mimed his way round Europe in what purported to be the styles of Bali, Java and Ceylon. He visited Capri first in 1929 and during the 'thirties spent much of his time there – until in 1940 he was removed for internment near Cosenza in Calabria.[8]

The English Church was taken over as 'enemy property' by the Banco di Napoli and thereafter completely neglected. Trower, in his eighty-eighth year and ill with bronchitis, was left in peace until the beginning of 1941. Then, on police instructions, he was transported to Naples for internment. He caught pneumonia and, being obviously near his end, was sent back to Capri, where he died on 21 February; he was buried next door to Bertha in the cemetery, where as churchwarden he had officiated so often. The villa was sealed and his property confiscated, but peasants broke in and ransacked it.

The German Church, however, took a new lease of life, with the prospect of German soldiers based on the island. In addition, concerts were held every Sunday by Paolo Falco, a 32-year-old *maestro di violino*, who ran the Restaurant La Palette in Via Matermania, and his German wife Elizabeth (Rüdorff) of Düsseldorf, who was a professional pianist.

The garrison – the first since the days of Napoleon – was established early in 1941. Anti-aircraft posts were set up at Marina Grande and on the highland of Anacapri at Torre della Guardia. Mines were laid between Capri and Ischia and between Capri and Massa Lubrense; artillery was installed to cover the narrow sea-lanes left unmined for ships plying to and from Naples. The German element of the garrison, which otherwise consisted of ill-clad and ill-equipped Italians, ran a rest-camp for their own forces. Being better supplied than the Italian troops and reasonably generous with their food and payments, they were not unwelcome. A Wehrmacht band played occasionally on the Piazza; and the troops took refreshment in Caffè Vuotto and Caffè Tiberio, sitting outside by day but inside by night for the sake of the black-out, and ate in Gemma's restaurant.[9] Anna (Putti) von Rahden did well for herself by becoming the mistress of the officer who was paymaster of the German forces in Capri.[10] It was not long before *l'aria di Capri* began to work its magic on the garrison. There was nude dancing in the Caffè al Campanile; and, at Bagni di Tiberio, nude swimming-parties and love-making of all sorts on the beach, while spectators watched from the *terrazza* of the restaurant. A few young Capresi were arrested for *atti osceni* with German soldiers and imprisoned for a short while on the mainland.[11]

A new situation was created by Allied air-raids on Naples. There had been a single attack in November 1940. Then, a year later, there were several raids in October and November 1941. There were further attacks in January and June 1942, and on 4 December the Royal Air Force sank a cruiser in the harbour and damaged a battleship and two other cruisers; raids continued until the end of the year. The Neapolitans had a wretched time. There were no effective anti-aircraft defences and few air-raid shelters. Those who lived near the harbour suffered the steady destruction of their homes; food became increasingly scarce; and there were insistent demands by the Germans for forced labour. As conditions worsened, many Neapolitans sought refuge in Capri, itself hard-pressed for food and supplies but untouched by air-raids. Few of the Neapolitan refugees had any money and many were refused leave to land; the lucky ones who were allowed ashore were fed for a while out of charity and then sent back to Naples.[12]

More permanent refuge was afforded in Anacapri to a handful of non-conformist Italian writers, by Antonino and Asta Mazzarella. He, an antiquary and *sindaco* of Anacapri from 1911 to 1924, and she a Dane who had made the island her home, ran a *pensione*, where these literary dissidents were given sanctuary. Notable amongst them was Alberto Moravia, left-wing journalist, short-story writer and novelist who in his 'fictional portrayals of social alienation and loveless sexuality' was anathema to the confident idealists of the Fascist cultural establishment.[13]

In 1941, after four years as *podestà*, during which he proved himself an honest and able administrator, Germano Ripandelli got bored with the job and resigned; for his services he was ennobled as Conte. He was followed by a retired admiral, Stanislao Di Somma, as *commissario prefettizio*. The main problem was the maintenance of food and supplies, which during 1942 became critically short. All rationed and price-controlled goods were bought immediately they appeared in the shops. In order to maintain the crops, the mainland was scoured for fertilizer. Fishing was restricted by an order which prohibited boats from operating out at sea. Life was particularly hard for growing children. One middle-aged Caprese, then a schoolboy, recalls going round the island with his friends, scrounging and stealing, and even eating flowers. The chief spokesman for the island was Giuseppe Brindisi, an able Neapolitan lawyer with a house in Anacapri, who was assiduous in pressing Capri's case with the *prefettura* in Naples and securing what supplies he could. Excellent work in guiding supply-craft through the mine-infested waters of the bay was done by Comandante Marino Canale, a direct descendant of Nathaniel Thorold and Anna Canale (della Noce), who, after a long career in the Italian merchant marine, had become an expert pilot.

On 24 February 1943 a disaster struck the garrison and shocked the islanders. A lorry carrying an Artillery captain and 22 men plunged over the cliff near Sant' Antonio, just as it was beginning the descent from Anacapri. All were killed and were buried with the island's dead in the Catholic cemetery. Capri-based artillery secured its only success on 11 April 1943, when the battery at Marina Grande brought down an American aircraft on its way to bomb Naples; the crew of five parachuted to safety and were taken prisoner. The reality of war struck again on 21 June when the British submarine *Splendid* was sunk by the Germans four miles off Punta Tragara; one officer and ten of the crew survived.[14]

Croce's prediction of 'Italietta' was rapidly fulfilled. In December 1941 the United States had entered the war, and, in spite of initial defeats and losses in the Far East, was bringing its weight of arms and inexhaustible supplies to strengthen British forces in the Mediterranean. In November 1942 a joint Anglo-American Force under Eisenhower's command landed in French North Africa and pushed eastwards. After its victory at Alamein the British Eighth Army pursued the enemy westwards. At the end of January 1943, as the last Axis foothold in Libya was lost and Italian forces retreated with their German allies into Tunisia, Mussolini sacked his Chief of Staff, General Ugo Cavallero. A few days later he removed Ciano from the Foreign Ministry and took the post himself. As well as being Generalissimo, he now had six separate ministerial posts. At a meeting with Hitler in April, Mussolini could not conceal from the Germans that he was in very poor physical shape, had lost his nerve and that Fascism was near its end. Hitler, realising that Italy could seek to break free and make a separate peace, took the grave step of withdrawing some divisions from his hard-pressed Russian front to be ready to occupy Italy if Mussolini's régime should collapse. The last Axis forces in North

Africa surrendered on 13 May, and on the next day the Italian Government announced anti-invasion measures. The first Italian territory to be captured, on 11 June, was the island of Pantelleria, which Mussolini had declared to be impregnable. On 10 July the Allies invaded Sicily and followed up this success with heavy air-attacks on Naples and other mainland targets. On 19 July 700 US aircraft raided marshalling yards on the outskirts of Rome. This was the first air-raid on Rome, where the authorities, confident that the Holy City would never be attacked, had allowed an enormous influx of population; general panic ensued. On 25 July, after an adverse vote in the Grand Council, which indicated that his senior colleagues had lost confidence in his dictatorship, Mussolini visited King Vittorio Emanuele, who informed him that, as the war seemed irretrievably lost and the morale of the Army was collapsing, he had appointed Marshal Pietro Badoglio, a former Chief of the General Staff, to take over as Prime Minister; and, as he left the King's presence, Mussolini himself was arrested. Martial law was proclaimed throughout Italy and a new Cabinet formed, omitting all the Fascist leaders. The Party itself was dissolved; and leading Fascists were put under arrest. On 3 September, after the conquest of Sicily, Allied forces landed on the Italian mainland, and on the same day an armistice was signed.[15]

At first light on 8 September an enormous force of British and American ships was observed from Capri on the horizon south of the island. A little after mid-day the air-raid sirens uttered not five blasts, which would have indicated air-attack, but eight – warning of a naval bombardment, which, however, did not materialise. In the evening the islanders heard on the radio Marshal Badoglio's announcement of the unconditional surrender of Italy. That night a formidable force of German aircraft attacked the Allied fleets, and at a safe distance from the conflict the islanders were able to witness a pyrotechnic display of air-bombardment and anti-aircraft response, more impressive than any fireworks they had ever seen for San Costanzo.

Next day the garrison of Capri was in turmoil. The Italian troops sought to observe the armistice. The Germans, intent on destroying military installations before withdrawing to the mainland, wrecked their own radio station at Punta Carena, but were prevented by the Italians from destroying the lighthouse and from further destruction elsewhere in Capri – and in the evening all the Germans withdrew from the island.[16]

On the 12th an American destroyer arrived at Marina Grande, bringing a plenipotentiary of General Eisenhower, now supreme Allied Commander in the Mediterranean, to take possession of the island. Next day the destroyer sailed away; and in the evening a British warship appeared bringing Rear Admiral Sir Anthony Morse as governor. Having taken up residence in the Villa Ciano on Castiglione, he appointed the senior

Italian officer in Capri as temporary commander of the garrison; and Giuseppe Brindisi, who earlier that year had succeeded Di Somma as *commissario prefettizio*, head of the civil administration. He warned that, if there were any manifestations of Fascism, they would be severely repressed, and various restrictions were placed on the inhabitants. No one was allowed to leave the island. There was to be a curfew and black-out from eight in the evening to six in the morning. Fishing by night was forbidden and during the day limited to one mile offshore. Existing prices for goods and commodities were to be maintained. Sea-bathing was restricted to daylight hours. On 26 September Admiral Morse was joined by a British brigadier, who set about disbanding the Italian garrison, rounding up refugees and housing all and sundry in the spacious confines of the Certosa, for eventual removal from the island.[17]

It was now the turn of Germans in Capri to worry about their future. Willy Kluck, living a hermit-like existence in his cottage at the end of the Migliara, seems to have escaped notice altogether. Otto Sohn-Rethel quickly had his villa registered in the name of the Anacaprese who for many years had been his factotum and friend – a scheme which for a while provided him with security; but after the war the Anacaprese refused to transfer the property back to Sohn-Rethel, and the painter was forced to retreat to Hans Berg's house nearby, where he died in 1949. The Anacaprese compounded his villainy by stealing a number of the Sohn-Rethel's paintings and drawings and selling them surreptitiously in Anacapri.[18] Baron von Schack had a narrow escape. The Americans wanted to arrest him, but he was protected by Giuseppe Brindisi, the *sindaco*, and remained free.[19]

A few Fascists were arrested and put in prison for a while – among them Teodoro Pagano, secretary of the Capri *fascio* since 1923, who had never wavered in his loyalty to the régime, and Curzio Malaparte.[20] The last-named, erratic as ever, had served for a time as war correspondent on the Russian front and on his return published his reports in a book *Il Volga nasce in Europa* (The Volga rises in Europe). Later, drawing on his own experiences, he wrote *Kaputt* – a vivid novel depicting the horrors of war and the ruin of Europe. Marshal Badoglio personally ordered his arrest and imprisonment *'per motivi di sicurezza'*.

With the end of Mussolini's government went the end of the decree against the shooting and snaring of birds in Capri. The gallant hunters joyfully resumed their slaughter; and in Anacapri, according to Edwin Cerio, the hunters' task was made all the easier by Munthe's establishment of the bird sanctuary.[21] The Doctor himself was not in Capri to witness these painful events. In June 1943, unable to cope any longer with his lonely existence in Torre Materita, he had left Capri for ever and returned to his homeland.

On 9 September the US Fifth Army, a mixed force of Americans and British formations under the commmand of General Mark Clark, had landed on the Salerno beaches. At first they made progress, but were soon driven back by German counter-attacks, and it was only after long and bitter fighting that the Allies were able to break out from the beach-head and, still meeting strong resistance, advance over the Sorrentine mountains and down to the Bay of Naples.[22] In the last days of September there was a general uprising of the partisans against the Germans, who evacuated the city quickly and not unwillingly, taking with them most of the sheep, cattle and poultry. The partisans then turned their attention to the liquidation of as many of the *fascisti* as possible. On 1 October the King's Dragoon Guards and US units entered the city. A British Special Forces group which included Major Malcolm Munthe, younger son of Axel Munthe, had rescued Benedetto Croce and his family from their refuge in Salerno and landed them in Capri, where Giuseppe and Ada Brindisi took them into their home in Anacapri and later were instrumental in having the honorary citizenship of Capri conferred upon the philosopher. In early June 1944, after the liberation of Rome, Croce went to the capital to become member of a stop-gap civilian government under Ivanoe Bonomi.

Naples and the Neapolitans were in a desperate state. The writer and traveller, Norman Lewis, then an NCO in the British Field Security Police and attached to the US Fifth Army, found a mood of 'stunned indifference' as he traversed the dismal suburbs of Torre Annunziata, Torre del Greco and Portici, 'through shattered streets, past landslides of rubble from bombed buildings. People stood in their doorways, faces the colour of pumice, to wave mechanically to the victors, the apathetic fascist salute of last week having been converted to the apathetic V-sign of today.' In Naples itself, which smelt of charred wood, there were ruins everywhere, sometimes completely blocking the streets, bomb-craters and abandoned trams. The water-supply had been largely shattered by two heavy air-raids on 4 August and 6 September, and further disrupted by German demolition squads, who had also blown up the sewage and telephone systems. People were experimenting with sea-water in their cooking and trying to distil sea-water for drinking purposes. Universal hunger had led to a desperate search for food. There was an avid hunt for edible plants in the fields around the city. All winkles and sea-snails having been long exhausted, children were prising limpets off the rocks. 'A pint of limpets sold at the roadside fetched about two *lire*, and if boiled long enough could be expected to add some faint fishy flavour to a broth produced from any edible odds and ends.'[23] Owing to the danger of stray mines, no boats were allowed out to fish. All the tropical fish in the celebrated aquarium, founded by Dohrn, lovingly tended by Lo Bianco, and enriched by Krupp, went into the pot – 'no fish being spared, however strange and specialized its appearance and habits. All Neapolitans believe that at the banquet offered to welcome General Mark Clark – who had expressed a preference for fish – the principal course was a baby manatee – the most prized item of the aquarium's collection – which was boiled and served with garlic sauce.'[24] The US forces found no lack of Neapolitans ready to prostitute themselves for the sake of tinned food, of which the liberators had copious supplies. Lewis summed up at the end of October:

> It is astonishing to witness the struggles of this city, so shattered, so starved, so deprived of all those things that justify a city's existence, to adapt itself to a collapse into conditions which must resemble life in the Dark Ages. People camp out like bedouins in deserts of brick. There is little food, little water, no salt, no soap. A lot of Neapolitans have lost their possessions, including most of their clothing, in the bombings, and I have seen some strange combinations of garments about the streets, including a man in an old dinner-jacket, knickerbockers and army boots, and several women in lacy confections that might have been made up from curtains. There are no cars, but carts by the hundred, and antique coaches such as barouches and phaetons drawn by lean horses.[25]

Fortunately the autumn weather was perfect, which made the manifold hardships slightly more endurable, and there was the prospect of an excellent fruit harvest. In north and central Italy and in Yugoslavia the Germans had moved swiftly and efficiently to neutralise the Italian armed forces, the bulk of which were disarmed and sent to Germany for internment and forced labour. The Germans arrested individuals who for one reason or another they considered dangerous, or useful as hostages, including Princess Mafalda, daughter of the Italian King, wife of the Prince of Hesse, and a lover of Capri before the war. She was sent to Buchenwald concentration camp, where she died of wounds received during an Allied bombardment. German troops occupied the main cities, including Rome itself, where they mounted guard in St Peter's Square. They were too late to prevent the Italian fleet from leaving La Spezia, but a German bomber sank the battleship *Roma* before the rest of the fleet reached safety under British guns in the Grand Harbour of Malta. On 12 September Mussolini, who had been incarcerated in an isolated hotel in the Abruzzi mountains, was rescued in a German commando operation and flown off to Munich, from where he announced his resumption of power, and soon afterwards set up a puppet government at Salò on Lake Garda. Early in 1944 he put on trial five members of the Grand Council who had voted against him on 25 July 1943, including his son-in-law

Galeazzo Ciano. All were condemned to death and executed three days later; Edda Ciano managed to escape to Switzerland.[26]

There was a brief wrangle between the British and American authorities for possession of Capri as a rest-camp. The Americans won, and the British had to be content with Sorrento. British rule in Capri, which lasted barely three weeks, was brought to an end when Rear-Admiral Morse was transferred to Naples and early in October his place as governor taken by Colonel Carl E. Woodward, US Army Air Force. Woodward continued in charge of the island until 1945 and before his departure was made an honorary citizen of Capri. Giuseppe Brindisi was confirmed as leader of the *comune di Capri* and was in effect *sindaco*, though not elected in the normal manner by popular vote; he remained in office until 1946.

Capri became a rest-camp for American airmen who had flown enough operational missions to qualify for a break from combat; villas and hotels all over the island were requisitioned to accommodate them, including the Villa Vismara at Punta Tragara, the largest and most magnificent of the Tragara villas, which became the official residence of Colonel Woodward. During the ensuing months, few Allied leaders, in or passing through Italy, neglected the opportunity of visiting the fabulous island, which was an easy journey from headquarters at Caserta. Leading members of Capri 'society' were invited to meals and functions at Villa Vismara, where, having lived for so long on meagre rations, they did their best to conceal the delight with which they tucked into the abundant fare. One leading lady indeed, popularly known as 'Madame de Pompadour', became Woodward's mistress.

Colonel Woodward's headquarters were in the Quisisana & Grand-Hôtel, as it was now styled, and it was from there that the rest-camp was run. While the genial colonel dispensed hospitality, the nuts and bolts of administration were in the capable hands of Captain Leighton, whose father had a well-known restaurant on the highway from New York City to Albany, NY.[27] The Officers' Club was also located in the Quisisana, while in lesser hotels separate clubs were established for NCOs and other ranks. Selected young Capresi, vetted by the civil authorities, were allowed to attend social functions at these clubs. The Caffè al Campanile became a forces' bar; other restaurants and *caffè* were out of bounds. Paolo Falco and his German wife continued their concerts of violin and piano music at the German Church and, after a performance on Christmas Eve 1943, were congratulated by General Morgan himself and asked to tea on Christmas Day at the Villa Borselli. The Americans tried to commandeer the harmonium of the German Church for jazz concerts, but Falco thwarted this plan by hiding the instrument at the Certosa.

The Americans were generous with food and supplies: both personally, with almost forgotten items like white bread, biscuits, chocolate, sweets, cigarettes, nylons and, a novelty in Capri, chewing-gum; and officially, through the United Nations Relief and Rehabilitation Administration,[28] which requisitioned depositories for the storage and distribution of relief supplies. Added to all this were the large pay-packets of the American forces – even the lowest paid had bigger wages than any Italian employee – and their willingness to spend. The islanders, therefore, who numbered a little over 8,000, benefited enormously from the presence of the American forces, of whom there were usually around 3,000 – a mixture of permanent staff running the rest camp and a transient population of aviators resting from combat and anxious to have a good time. One dark spot in this otherwise welcome cornucopia was the introduction of venereal disease, which many Americans had contracted in Algiers and was passed on to a number of local girls; the same thing happened on a much larger scale in Naples.

Another innovation was the jeep, unknown in Capri until this moment. One characteristic which is common to almost all Americans is a reluctance to walk when it is possible to drive. The islanders, therefore, who walked everywhere, were treated to the spectacle of these numerous and versatile vehicles being driven not only on the roads to Anacapri, Marina Grande and Marina Piccola, but also along the footpaths and indeed anywhere in the countryside which was negotiable. The country children, who had never seen a vehicle of any sort before, were scared out of their wits, and there were some accidents to people who did not get out of the way quickly enough. Colonel Woodward regularly commuted by jeep between his office in the Quisisana and his home at Punta Tragara.

Materially speaking, the islanders would have done much less well if they had been saddled with the British, who were paid far less than their American counterparts and, whether fighting or resting, lived more frugally. British personnel did indeed visit Capri from their own rest-camp in Sorrento, but, as far as the Americans were concerned, under sufferance. Aldo Aprea, then a schoolboy, remembers with affection some young British officers who taught him and his friends to play football; later, when he tried to re-establish the link, he found that none had survived the war.[29]

On the night of 14–15 March 1944 there was a German air-raid on the densely populated port areas of Naples, which caused heavy civilian casualties and still more destructon of property. Frantic crowds rushed through the streets, crying 'Give us peace' and 'Out with the soldiers'. Four days later, on a calm and windless day, Vesuvius erupted with great force, blew out all the material which had collapsed into the crater after the eruption of 1906, and sent up a cloud 30–40,000 feet high and several miles across. The cloud hovered for a few hours, then descended on land and sea for miles around – as far away as Sorrento, Ischia and Capri, where several inches of ash were deposited. The eruption continued sporadically for twelve days until in April the main fissure closed – and closed it has remained for 40 years.[30]

During the spring and summer the Naples black market in stolen and 'misdirected' American supplies and equipment – food, cigarettes, clothes, blankets, medical supplies, photographic equipment, vehicles and their parts, weapons of every sort – burgeoned. There was a strong suspicion that the black market process was facilitated by the presence of Vito Genovese, a leading American *mafioso*, on the staff of the Allied Military Government. Born near Naples and well acquainted with its underworld, Genovese was able to harness all the resources of the Camorra (the Neapolitan version of the Mafia) and was helped in his schemes by the connivance of some officials and the simple-mindedness of others. On his recommendation *camorristi* were appointed as *sindaci* of the surrounding towns and villages, and arrangements made for leading black market operators to be immune from prosecution. For the most part, only the wretched minor operators, who could not afford to bribe their way to safety, were convicted and sent to prison, leaving poverty-stricken families to fend for themselves without the bread-winner. The black market was operated so effectively and on such a scale that by the middle of 1944 the Allied forces were themselves beginning to suffer a serious shortage of specialist items like photographic and medical sup-plies, which were readily available to any civilians who knew where to find them and could afford to pay.[31]

On the first of April 1944 Norman Lewis took a day off from Field Security duties and made a trip to Capri. Sitting in the Piazza and observing the scene, he found 'a different world from Naples; escapist, full of make-believe, and almost hysterically concerned to show its lack of interest in the war . . . all the old Capri hands were there; the men dressed to go shooting and the women in sandals and streaming veils, like Isadora Duncan just about to go off on the last fatal trip in the Bugatti. . . . An American major at the next table sat with his arms round the waists of a couple of courtesans singing a blustering version of *Torna a Surriento*, and, when the municipal loudspeakers began to blast out a *tarantella*, one of them was persuaded to hop about in what was supposed to be a dance on the table-top.' Someone pointed out Madame Four-Dollars, an 'expatri-ate, so-called from her fixed price paid to fishermen for sexual services. . . . The haunted face of Curzio Malaparte appeared briefly, and among his courtiers . . . a British officer who, under the spell of his environment, grimaced and gesticulated in all directions.'[32]

Malaparte had extricated himself quickly from prison and found a temporary job as liaison officer between the Allied forces and the newly constituted Italian army. Later that summer, when political activity in

Italy, forbidden for twenty years, was again allowed, and as many as 60 political parties were officially recognised, Malaparte aligned himself with the Communist Party. He began to collaborate with its organ *L'Unità* and wrote an article on his 'political mistakes' in the service of the Fascist dictatorship. When the veteran Communist leader Ercole Ercoli (better known as Palmiro Togliatti), in exile since the banning of the Communist Party in 1926, returned in the spring of 1944 and joined Badoglio's government, Malaparte became one of his close friends and supporters. As soon as he was re-established in his villa, with *Kaputt* now published, much of Malaparte's time and energy were devoted to the composition of *La Pelle*, which described the 'suffering and degradation that the war had brought to the people of Naples, who, as the title implies, had little left but their skins'.[33]

In Capri it was easy to forget that on the mainland fierce battles were raging. Finally, having broken the 'Gothic Line', the Allies paused, regrouped and advanced into the plains. Bologna fell on 21 April 1945 and Allied columns raced ahead to the northern borders of Italy.[34] On 28 April Mussolini, his mistress Clara Petacci and a group of leading fascists, who were trying to escape to Switzerland, were captured by communist partisans at the north end of Lake Como and executed. Their bodies were piled into a truck and taken to be strung up by the heels in the Piazzale Loreto at Milan.[35] Terms of surrender of all German forces in Italy were signed at Caserta and came into effect on 2 May. On the 7th Germany surrendered unconditionally to the Western Allies and Russia.

CHAPTER TEN

Post-war Boom

The American rest-camp was closed, hotels and villas were returned to their owners, and it was not long before tourists and visitors began to reappear. In a very real sense the American servicemen, some of whom stayed on until the beginning of 1947, were the harbingers of Capri's post-war boom. Prices, inflated by lavish American spending, remained high, and much of the available food was only to be found on the persistent black market. The *lira* fared badly against both the dollar and the pound sterling. Fixed at 400 *lire* to the pound when the Allies invaded Italy in July 1943, the rate rose to 900 in the winter of 1946; 1,200 officially and 2,000 on the black market for a pound note[1] in March 1947; and an official rate of 2,317 in November 1948. American visitors came in fair numbers and, as long as Allied forces remained in Italy and Austria, there were service personnel on leave. British civilians, who had only a tiny allowance of foreign currency, were hardly seen; the French did not travel much in those days; and the Germans were confined within their new frontiers. By 1948 the Armies had gone, but the tourist trade had not yet got into its swing. The hoteliers, therefore, kept their prices low, in order to attract any available business, and were optimistic about the future.

The Quisisana & Grand-Hôtel, directed by Signora Ascheri, a strong, honest and capable woman, retained its pre-eminence as the leading and only *de luxe* hotel. It was followed closely by the Tiberio Palace, owned and managed by Nicola Morgano, youngest and only surviving son of Don Giuseppe and Donna Lucia. As a boy, like many other Capresi, Nicola had gone abroad to wash dishes in a German hotel. Thereafter he had progressed up the ladder and in Germany, France and Switzerland carved out a successful career in the hotel trade. The Tiberio Palace, built by his father Giuseppe as a rival to Serena's Quisisana, had remained family property after Giuseppe's death in 1922. In 1934, after many years of letting it to a series of managers and at times closing it altogether, Nicola returned to Capri to manage the hotel himself. His elder brother, Enrico, who had prospered in hotel management on the mainland, died in 1938, leaving a widow Angelina and two sons, Giuseppe and Mario. In 1943, Donna Lucia, in her eightieth year, joined Giuseppe in the family mausoleum. One of the most remarkable Capresi of modern times, she is remembered as *una donna specialissima*. With a good part of the Morgano inheritance now in his hands, Nicola, always very careful about money and already rich, acquired more and more cash. Having renamed the hotel 'Morgano & Tiberio Palace', he worked hard to promote it to the first rank and in 1949 had the satisfaction of accommodating Princess Margaret, who on a short visit lodged there rather than at the Quisisana.

A newcomer to the hotel business was Costanzo De Angelis. His grandparents had migrated from the Sorrentine peninsula to Capri during the latter part of the nineteenth century. De Angelis was among those who did well under the Americans' occupation. After the war he decided to start a hotel and chose a well-placed property which he acquired on favourable terms. This was the Villa Caterina, near the Quisisana, the home of the Caracciolo family, where five of the Principe's large brood were still living. In exchange for being allowed to build his hotel 'La Residenza' in the garden of the villa, he granted them an annuity and the right to live there until the death or departure of the last survivor, whereupon it would become his property.[2] La Residenza came into operation in 1950, and De Angelis also bought the nearly Hotel Semiramis. The Villa Caterina passed to him in 1959.

Raffaele Vuotto, who had done very well with his *caffè* on the Piazza, also decided to go into the hotel business and in 1948 began to build the Hotel La Pineta, on land below Via Tragara which belonged to his wife Teresa.

Gracie Fields returned to her beloved *fortino*. In 1941, after her Canadian tour, which had earned nearly half a million pounds for the Navy League, she had come back to Britain, her reputation largely restored, and sang indefatigably at home and in the Middle and Far East. By 1945 she was again in Europe with Monty Banks, who since the Italian surrender was no longer in danger of internment, and together they celebrated VE-Day at the *fortino*, which had been derequisitioned by the Americans. Her first requirement was to make it more comfortable and she engaged Carlo Talamona, who 20 years earlier had worked in a subordinate role on the Villa Vismara and was now a builder in his own right. Since 1937 he had been married to Pina Francke, a rich, beautiful and cultured German Jewess, who did much to further his career in the island. Talamona, however, started an affair with an islander, whom he married in June 1949, only one month after the sudden end of Pina, who was found dead in her bath with her wrists slashed.[3]

Mona Williams returned to the other *fortino* west of Marina Grande, with Eddie Bismarck, but without her husband. Soon after Williams's death in 1953, by which she inherited an enormous fortune, she married Bismarck and, to her great joy, became a countess. As a rule she spent the winter in Paris; the spring and summer in Capri, developing her garden and increasing her domains. She enlarged the house, created terraces and retaining walls, paths and flights of steps, pergolas roofed with vines and entwined with roses, a labyrinth of small borders filled with imported soil and exotic flowers, and, what was unique in arid Capri, green lawns, kept fresh with water brought at great expense from the mainland in her private water-boat. Whenever she could, she bought up adjoining properties, until she owned much of the Roman palace. If a new piece of land included a building which was not needed, it was removed. Thus she bought the Villa Vivara on the Marina Grande side of her property and razed it to the ground, partly in order to make room for a swimming-pool and partly to spite another resident whose family owned the villa and whom Mona disliked. On the roadside near the south-west corner of her property there was a Roman column which Mona removed and put in her garden; all the women of Palazzo a Mare set up a wail near her house, until she put it back. The one major piece of land which eluded her was the old *campo sportivo*, which, being near the house itself, she tried to buy for the sake of peace and quiet, and to isolate herself still further from the *hoi polloi*. The *municipio* refused, but eventually made a new *campo sportivo* near the Church of San Costanzo. Her builder was Ercole D'Esposito, an Anacaprese, and the supervision entrusted to Bismarck. It is said locally that he always demanded far more money than was needed for the work and pocketed the difference to help his family and friends. Mona was no archaeologist. Roman statues, inscriptions and other *roba*, which came to light, if not destroyed during development of the garden, which some-times involved the use of dynamite, were scattered carelessly about the property. When a German archaeologist, engaged on compiling a corpus of Greek and Roman inscriptions in Capri, asked to see what had been unearthed, she was totally unco-operative and refused him access. Her hairdresser was Tonino D'Emilio, who in his establishemnt in Via Camerelle tended an infinity of celebrities, the Duke and Duchess of Windsor, Queen Soraya, Queen Narriman, Princess Grace of Monaco, Joan Crawford, Jackie Onassis, Onassis himself and his rival Niarchos, to name but a few. But Mona never ascended thither. There was a special room at the *fortino* where she and her guests had their hair done, and D'Emilio came when required. She was hardly ever seen in public and was much disliked by the inhabitants of Palazzo a Mare for her snobbish and exclusive ways. Eddie, who was much younger, was popular. Vivaci-ous, warm-hearted and hospitable, he loved to entertain the rich, titled and famous invited by his wife, and his own friends; sometimes he would ask all the fishermen of Marina Grande. For a time, therefore, the house played a significant part in the social life of Capri.[4]

The other great garden of Capri, established over many years with loving care on the slopes of Monte San Michele, came to a halt in 1945, when its creator, Lady Blanche Gordon-Lennox, died and the property passed to her daughter Ivy, married since 1915 to the 7th Duke of Portland. In 1950 the Portlands gave the property as a wedding present to their daughter, Lady Victoria Margaret Cavendish-Bentinck, who in that year married Don Gaetano Parente, styled Principe, but in fact only the son of a marchese and nicknamed by the islanders 'Prince without property'. In 1952 she bore him a son William, but died in 1955, leaving the Principe a villa which was too big for him and the enormous rambling garden. Parente, tall, elegant and charming, liked the social life of Capri, but was no gardener, and nature gradually regained its hold on the mountain-side, enveloping the trees, shrubs and borders, and all but a few of the walks, terraces, balustrades and flights of steps. Some of Lady Blanche's handiwork, however, remained intact to impart charm to this large private area in the centre of Capri town, which so far has escaped the greedy developers. On the death of the Principe in 1976 the property passed to his son William, who occasionally stays there, but plays no significant part in the life of the island.

Lady Mackinder did not return to the Villa Tragara. Her gardener, who, under the supervision of her lawyer Roberto Serena, was acting as caretaker and wanted to get his hands on a bit of the land and some of her furniture, wrote advising her not to come back. Life in Capri, he said, was now expensive (which it was not for any English person of reasonable means) and the Italians were hostile to the British (which was untrue). Lady Mackinder had been well-liked in Capri. She had been generous to the poor, had looked after the sick and, according to Ettore Patrizi, whom she had nursed when ill, was *una brava signora*. Serena and his niece, Giuseppina Messanelli, wrote strongly in a contrary sense, but failed to persuade her, and she decided to sell.[5] The Villa and its extensive garden were eventually bought by Giuseppe D'Amico, the Italian shipowner, who appointed Cicillo Foresta, a worthy and well-liked Caprese, as his *costruttore*, to convert a house, which was still much as it had been in the days of Allers, and act as *guardiano*.

Harold Trower's niece, Mrs Nancy Sandilands, discovered that she had inherited his furniture and the sum of £86. She went out with a friend in 1946, failed to get hold of the furniture, but had a good holiday on the money.[6]

Norman Douglas, who had spent most of the war in England, resolved to end his days in Capri. In May 1937, after many years of contented residence in Florence, he had been declared *persona non grata* and ordered to leave Italy immediately because of an alleged affair with a little *girl*. Having seduced both her brothers, out of pure kindness he bought their little sister a Scottish outfit, and, when she was asked how she got it she revealed the source – and that was that.[7] From 1937 to 1940 he lived in the

South of France, then moved to Lisbon and in January 1941 returned to London. He had very little money, hated the dull and none too plentiful food, the blackout, the bombs and the general dreariness of life – but he was sustained by his friends and was always adding to their number. Frank Tuohy, the much-travelled writer, then a schoolboy, remembers being taken to dinner at the Royal Court Hotel, Sloane Square, where Douglas talked happily to all the staff and introduced Tuohy to wine-drinking ('Just blackberry juice, my dear').

When after the war Douglas 'first approached an Italian diplomat at the Embassy in London for a visa to return to Italy, he was told that the Italian Government would not grant visas to those who wished to live in Italy, but only those who intended to pay a short visit to the country. To this he answered that he did not so much want to live there as to die there. This reply so moved the Italian attaché that he decided to make a special effort to get an exception made' in Douglas's case and in July 1946 succeeded in obtaining the necessary visa.[8] After a visit to Ian Greenlees, who was then Assistant Press Attaché at the British Embassy in Rome; and having knocked around in Naples and the Sorrentine peninsula during the summer, he went over to Capri in October, hoping to find somewhere to live. He still owned the flat in Florence, but he could not sell it until he had dislodged the tenants and had it repaired and redecorated. Douglas had no money, therefore, to buy anything of his own. Edwin Cerio came to the rescue and lent Douglas one of his properties, a tiny house in Unghia Marina, which looked out over the Certosa towards the cliffs of Anacapri. Cerio also used his influence with the *municipio* to obtain for Douglas, what especially delighted him, the grant of honorary citizenship – a privilege which he thus came to share with Colonel Carl E. Woodward and Benedetto Croce. The winter of 1946, in which Douglas celebrated his seventy-eighth birthday, was, like everywhere else in Europe, exceptionally cold, with snow and freezing temperatures. Solid fuel for heating was almost unobtainable and the supply of electricity uncertain. Warmed only by a charcoal-brazier, in pain with constant rheumatism and living very frugally, he grappled with the problem of existing on next to nothing. But he had the comfort of Maria Grazia, the same cook as he had had in 1903, and a ten-year-old urchin called Ettore, whom he imported from Naples to act as house-boy and run errands. Douglas asked friends and relations in England and America to post him pound and dollar notes, a few at a time, which he changed advantageously on the black market.[9] On New Year's Day 1947 in a letter to Nancy Cunard, Douglas summed up the situation as follows:

Prices are so fantastic here that for the first time in history there was a general strike. It is quite impossible, with the strictest economy and living rent-free, as I do, to manage on less than 35/- a day. Everything is black market, including boys and girls. The Americans are chiefly responsible. They are still here, and their blasted jeeps and camions are the curse of the island.[10]

Help, however, was on the way. In 1927 Douglas's devoted friend 'Bryher' (otherwise Annie Winifred, daughter of Sir John Ellerman), who had witnessed his triumphant return to Capri in March 1923, had married Kenneth Macpherson, author and writer on films. Since both were homosexual, it was an unusual marriage, prompted on her side partly by a desire to escape from her domineering father, and partly to please him by getting married to *somebody*. After the war the marriage disintegrated and was dissolved in 1947, just at the time when Douglas was struggling to survive in Capri. In settlement Bryher gave Macpherson a very large sum from the Ellerman fortune and bought him a substantial house in Capri, with the stipulation that Douglas was to spend the rest of his life in a self-contained flat on the ground floor. This was the Villa Tuoro, with spacious and comfortable rooms, set in a fine terraced garden high above Tragara and with a splendid panorama. About this time Douglas at last got possession of his flat in Florence and was able to have his books, photographs and mementos rescued and sent to Capri. When they arrived he found that many of the best books had been stolen, but there were enough left to fill the long low rooms of his new home. With this secure base and the ever-present help of Macpherson, Douglas's last years were as happy as his ailments and the increasing frailty of old age allowed.

Douglas liked to potter about the town, to eat and drink at his favourite haunts – the Savoia *trattoria* at the piazza end of Via Roma, much frequented by coachmen (now a photographic shop – 'Foto White'); the Caffè Vittoria (now Bar Funicolare), from which he could watch the traffic moving in and out of Marina Grande; and, what he liked best, Peppinella's by the Arco Naturale, where on most evenings he would go to drink some wine and admire the sunset view of Sorrento ('Siren Land') across the water. His sons, Archie and Robin, and many old friends came to visit him – Willy King, a witty and eccentric scholar, and his wife Viva; Faith Mackenzie, who had never lost her love of the island; Alan Anderson, Scottish printer, bibliophile and collector of material about Capri; and Harold Acton, often down from Florence. There was Eric Wolton, whom Douglas had picked up as a boy at the age of 12 at the Crystal Palace fireworks display on 5 November 1910 and who had become a very special object of his affection; Eric, now married and since the end of World War II an officer of the Tanganyikan Police, had never ceased to be a friend.

In or near Capri there were friends within easy reach – Macpherson himself; David Jeffreys, British Vice-Consul in Naples; Ian Greenlees, now on the staff of the British Council in Rome, and temporary resident of Anacapri since 1949, when he bought the Villa Fraita from the Brett Youngs[11]; Cecil Gray[12], musicologist and another *habitué* of Peppinella's; Arthur Johnson[13], an English international lawyer and authority on modern art, who had a house in Anacapri; Somerset Maugham, who still paid occasional visits to the island; and, from 1948, the novelist Graham Greene[14], who had been recruited to write the script of an Italian film of *South Wind* (which came to nothing) and for convenience bought Cerio's house 'Il Rosajo' in Anacapri. Douglas also had the comforting presence of his little friend, Ettore.

The Brett Youngs, in Capri on a short visit to dispose of the contents of the Villa Fraita, found Douglas looking 'older and not well, but just as witty and entertaining as ever. Mrs Thelma Colman, ex-wife of the Hollywood star, was in Capri anxious to give a party, with coloured lights, an orchestra and a singer.' She wanted fifteen men and seventeen women – but all the men would have to be he-men. Douglas, who was asked for advice, thought it would be impossible to find so many.[15]

Douglas made friends with Baron von Schack, who now had a small pension from the new Federal German Republic, most of which he spent on his ruling passions – drink, food and boys. Finally, of the newcomers, there was Gracie Fields, who was an admirer of *South Wind* and had no difficulty in making friends with its author. For many short-term visitors to Capri 'Uncle Norman' was an object of pilgrimage – a cult which he often found tedious but sometimes rewarding. He was liked and respected by Capresi of all ages and walks of life. Islanders, whom long ago he had befriended as boys and to whom he had imparted something of his worldly wisdom, were now middle-aged. His mastery of the Italian language was complete and he could talk to them in their own *patois*, the dialect of Naples. They enjoyed his robust character, his humanity and charm, his genius as an educator, his insatiable curiosity, ribald humour and sheer roguery, and unique knowledge of the island.

During the war Douglas had compiled a commentary on his many books, noting the circumstances under which they had been written, facts about himself and the people whom he had met on life's journey, and what in retrospect he thought about his own writing. He had published nothing since his earlier autobiographical excursion, *Looking Back*, which he put together between 1927 and 1932, and published in 1933. *Late Harvest*, as he titled this somewhat haphazard autobiography, was published in 1946, at 8s 6d, in small but legible type and on paper of the 'authorized economy standard'. Douglas was not pleased with the austerity of its production, and his readers, who had looked for a more substantial and better organised account of his life and work, were disappointed by the book itself. It seemed to him the moment to close his 'little writing-shop for good and all'.[16] He was persuaded differently by seeing a splendid series of photographs of the countryside, buildings and people of Capri and Anacapri, which so inspired him that he composed *Footnote on Capri* – a masterly essay on the island from start to finish, which was illustrated by a selection of these photographs. The talented photographer whose work had roused Douglas was Islay de Courcy Lyons, a good-looking 25-year-old, just demobilised from the Royal Air Force after wartime intelligence work in South East Asia, who arrived on a short visit in the summer of 1947 with letters of introduction to Douglas and Macpherson. After further travels on the Continent, he emigrated to California, but returned in 1948 to settle permanently in Italy and make a career in photography.[17] He became Macpherson's close friend and part of the household at Villa Tuoro. Posterity owes Lyons a considerable debt for the intimate and varied photographic record he made of Capri and its personalities – many photographs are still unpublished – in the late 'forties and early 'fifties.

Elected government returned to Capri. After the collapse of Fascism several Capresi had urged Dusmet, whose disinterested efficiency as *podestà* in the late 'twenties and early 'thirties had gained wide approval, to seek election as *sindaco*; but he refused, because he was not willing to work through an elected council and could only see himself as being in sole charge of the administration. With Dusmet out of the running, there was no post-war politician who commanded sustained popular support. In 1946 Avv. Brindisi, who had steered Capri wisely through the last years of the war and into the peace, was followed for a year by Giuseppe Ruocco, the Marina Grande doctor, who for the sake of his career had joined the Fascist Party in 1926 and was not a Christian Democrat. He was followed in 1947 by Ing. Costanzo Lembo, architect and house-builder.

In this year the island was restored to what it had been before Fascism – the two administrative communes of Capri and Anacapri. While post-war Capri failed to keep anyone in office for very long, Anacapri, where life moved at a slower pace and problems were fewer, chose Dr Tommaso De Tommaso as *sindaco* and was content to leave him in office for 23 years. De Tommaso was determined that Anacapri would not fall behind the lower and richer part of the island. He planned a new road from the centre of Anacapri to Damecuta and the Blue Grotto, and even had visions of continuing it along the coast to Marina Grande; and another, through Caprile and past Materita, to Faro and Punta Carena at the south-west tip of the island. The former would provide an alternative means of access to the Blue Grotto; the latter, by replacing the rudimentary Strada del Faro di Carena would serve the lighthouse and give access to a cove which was Anacapri's only bathing-beach. De Tommaso took the logical view that, as the Blue Grotto lay within the territory of Anacapri, it should be exploited for the benefit of his *comune* and not its rival. Furthermore he considered that Anacapri ought to have its own port and conceived the bold plan of creating one in the Cala del Rio. This scheme was viewed with alarm in Capri town and Marina Grande, and there was relief in the lower part of the island when it was abandoned for lack of funds.

In 1949 the literary scene was enlivened by the publication of Malaparte's *La Pelle*, on which he had been working since 1944. Dividing his time between Capri, Naples and Paris, he reinforced his involvement with the political and literary 'left', made friends with the writers Jean Cocteau and Albert Camus, who with Togliatti, the Italian Communist leader, were delighted to enjoy Malaparte's hospitality at Punta Massullo. The book was first published in Paris as *Le Peau*. After being rejected by several Italian publishers, *La Pelle* was accepted at last and issued early in 1950.

In a series of episodes, in which fact and phantasy were interwoven, *La Pelle* presented every aspect of the degradation and horror which had gripped Naples in 1943 and 1944. It told of the prostitution of young women, girls and young boys; and the eager rush of suitable candidates from the countryside, so that the price of human flesh on the Naples market dropped sharply. Blond wigs for the head and private parts were manufactured and worn to attract black American GIs. *La Pelle* described an elaborate 'flying market' for hiring and enslaving GIs. Ordinary white soldiers were the cheapest; the most expensive were black drivers and white soldiers working in the PX. Hunting negro soldiers was the favourite sport of Neapolitan boys who, having lured a victim, would drag him from bar to bar and from brothel to brothel, selling him in succession for 20, 30, 40 and finally 50 dollars – for the time it took to make the soldier drunk, strip him of everything he possessed and then after nightfall abandon him naked in an alley. Slaves kept by the month were much more expensive, but very lucrative, as they returned daily as honoured guests to a Neapolitan home, bringing sugar, spam, bacon, bread, white flour, nylons, shoes, uniforms, overcoats, bedding and vast quantities of caramels; while drivers, the most expensive of all, would bring their vehicles, and even tanks, all of which were dismembered and dispersed in a matter of hours. *La Pelle* went on to describe the infection of Neapolitans with venereal disease brought by their liberators; of Naples as a centre of homosexuality; of the 'black wind' which affected everyone so unpleasantly; of the eruption of Vesuvius; and of the trial and execution of young Fascists by the partisans.

Naples was outraged by this scabrous account of itself and, on 15 February 1950 at a meeting specially convened for the purpose, the *consiglio comunale* passed a resolution censuring in the severest terms the citizen who had lived and worked in Naples off and on since 1928 – all of which boosted sales of the book.

Malaparte's end was characteristically erratic and extraordinary. After his brush with Naples he set off on a new round of travel to northern Europe, South America and, in October 1956, China, where he made friends with Mao Tse Tung. Here he was stricken with cancer and, after ineffective hospital treatment in Pekin and Chungking, was flown to Rome, where he died on 19 July 1957, but not before making a will in which he bequeathed his villa at Punta Massullo to the Chinese Peoples Government as a cultural centre for Chinese writers and artists in or visiting Italy. Shortly before the end he became religious, burnt his books, all of which were on the Papal Index, and was received into the Church. After Malaparte's death there was a long legal battle between the Italian State, the Chinese Peoples Government, the faction of the Italian Communist Party which followed Mao, and Malaparte's brother and two sisters. The Chinese started paying for the upkeep of the villa, while the relatives contested the will. When Mao fell from favour in 1959, he lost communist support in Italy, and the Italian Government felt bold enough to declare invalid a will made in favour of a Republic which they did not recognise. The villa was handed over to Malaparte's relatives, who in turn founded in it a centre for writers and journalists, but it lacked material to attract researchers, was a considerable distance from Capri town, and was buffeted by sea and weather. So it remained uninhabited and was used only for occasional exhibitions.[18]

While Dr Tommaso maintained a steady presence as *sindaco* of Ana-capri, the administrators of the *comune* of Capri came and went in quick succession. They presided over great changes in the island. Cars and lorries, a rarity before the war but a *sine qua non* for the American forces, began to proliferate. The growing tourist-trade, and the increasing popularity of Capri as a place in which to live or have a second home, encouraged the building of new hotels and villas, and attracted from the mainland growing numbers of immigrants. In 1948, for the first time, the State took a hand in the supply of water, which grew sparser as the demand for it increased. Enough water to provide a free ration of 30 litres per head per day was imported at government expense in military water-boats, while SIPPIC, back in business again after the war and under new management, ran their own water-boats and sold water to those hotels and householders who wanted more than the official ration.

All these changes gladdened those in the island who profited from them, but saddened Norman Douglas. As a postscript to *Footnote on Capri*, which was published in 1952 shortly after his death, he wrote:

At this moment Capri is in danger of developing into a second Hollywood, and that, it seems, is precisely what it aspires to become. The island is too small to endure all these outrages without loss of dignity – the pest of so-called musicians who deafen one's ears in every restaurant, roads blocked up by lorries and cars, steamers and motor-boats disgorging a rabble of flashy trippers at every hour of the day.

Such was Douglas's summing-up of the new Capri. He was not alone in his dissatisfaction. The writer Constantine Fitzgibbon, who was related to Douglas's divorced wife Elsa, had been commissioned to write a life of Douglas and for this purpose lived in Capri from the autumn of 1948 to the end of 1949. In the event the biography never came to be written, mainly because of the difficulties of covering accurately Douglas's long career of pederasty, but Fitzgibbon had a chance to form his own opinion of the island:

The festivals [of San Costanzo in Capri and Sant' Antonio da Padova in Anacapri] were over; the Capri season had begun. Daily, almost hourly, boatloads of perspiring Neapolitans were arriving to see the famous beauty spot, to jostle one another in the crowded piazza, to visit the fake antiquities up on the hill, to be thrust – often, by now, in a state of apparent intoxication – into the Blue Grotto, to eat the uneatable food and pay the preposterous prices of the Capri restaurants, to bawl and yell and quarrel, and finally, if the wind had risen, to vomit their way back to Naples on the evening boat. Other, hardier tourists remained, and the two or three dull little night-clubs did a tremendous business. These people had come from farther afield, from Essen, Chicago, Amsterdam, Glasgow, Lyons, businessmen with or without their wives. And then there were knots of ambiguous, international, mauve young men, cooing or spitting together. And the less equivocal young women – but the poor girls had come to the wrong place. The piazza grew more and more crowded, until the tables of the four cafés almost met in the middle. And still they arrived, the New York chorus boys, the Gothen-burg sardine merchants, the pimply sub-editors of London periodicals, the enormous families of the Engadine. The dirty, rocky little beaches were a mass of almost naked flesh by day – nor has the Mediterranean a healing tide to wash away the refuse – by night the streets of the town re-echoed to strange, barbaric shouts, and in the morning the sad young men whispered together in the piazza as the day's boatload of Neapolitans pulled in at the dock below while the ship's loud-speaker broadcast 'Santa Lucia' across the pellucid waters. I felt that it was time to leave Capri.[19]

Another well-known figure of the past who had become disenchanted with modern Capri and felt that life had no more to offer was Carmela Cerrotta, 'La Bella Carmelina', once the pre-eminent dancer of the *tarantella*. Now in her seventy-sixth year and no more than a legend, she had to endure the polite smiles of visitors to her *caffè* on Tiberio, as she related over and over again tales of her past glory and sometimes, to illustrate what she had been, danced a measure or two and banged her tambourine. On the last day of July 1950, at her home in Via Tiberio, she tore her dress to shreds and, clutching her tambourine, jumped from the window of the upper storey and fell to her death on the terrace below.[20]

What Douglas could not have foreseen – and it would have annoyed him intensely – was that the sort of tourism which he so much deplored was boosted enormously by the death of a man whom he had known since 1897, considered to be a 'portentous fake', and detested – Dr Axel Munthe, who died in the Royal Palace at Stockholm in February 1949 in his ninety-second year.

During the 'thirties, Munthe, based on Torre Materita and basking in the success of his book, had been able to pay frequent visits to his family in London, and every summer he stayed with King Gustav V in Stockholm. Finding life increasingly difficult in wartime Anacapri, he endured Materita until June 1943, when he left it for ever and spent the rest of his days as the King's personal guest in Stockholm Castle. The two men, who were almost exactly the same age – Munthe being the senior by eight months – were similar in appearance, and it was widely assumed that Munthe was the illegitimate child of either the King's father, Oscar II, or his uncle, Charles XV, and thus the half-brother or first cousin of Gustav. As Munthe's health declined, he became increasingly confined to the Castle, unable any longer to undertake minor excursions into the surrounding country. He nurtured a hopeless desire to revisit Anacapri and caused endless trouble to officials who were required to work out painless means of travel to Italy – their proposals and plans always in the end having to be abandoned. Left to himself for long periods, he became increasingly preoccupied with the subject of death. Still yearning for Anacapri, but finally accepting that the journey would be too much for him, his thoughts turned to the future of San Michele.[21] After consultation with the proper authorities he decided to hand over the property to a worthy cause and on 5 January 1948 signed his will, bequeathing 'San Michele . . . with the buildings and grounds appertaining to it, together with all the existing works of art, books, effects and other personal property . . . to the State of Sweden, to be used for the furtherance of cultural relations between Sweden and Italy'. He hoped that charge of the property would be entrusted to the Swedish Institute in Rome. The will continued: 'I am convinced that the Board of the Institute will show itself to have the desire and the ability, with reverent preservation of San Michele's individuality, to allow this my bequest to serve my stated purpose, for instance, by opening the house there for nothing or at a suitable charge to Swedish students, artists, scientists, journalists or other guests who can be supposed to share my affection for Italy and classical culture and also for humanistic research as a whole. I am confident that in the settlement of conditions at San Michele, regard will be paid to the persons who live there and take care of the property.'[22]

Munthe's other properties in Anacapri, some of which had been disposed of before his death on 11 February 1949, went in various directions. The Roman villa and medieval tower at Damecuta, and the surrounding land, were donated to the Italian Government; Torre Materita passed to his sons, Malcolm and Peter. Munthe had sold the Torre delle Guardia during his lifetime for a small sum to his friend, the beautiful Baroness Gudrun Uexküll, who for many years had helped him manage Materita and San Michele, but had never been his lover, as gossip suggested.[23]

In attempting to assess Munthe as a person, one is faced with a bewildering mixture of opinions and judgements by those who knew him. The main difficulty lies in deciding how much of him was pose and how much genuine. There is evidence of a basic sense of insecurity, due possibly to his likely origin as a royal bastard. Already in 1889 he was conscious of himself as a lonely hypochondriac with a weary journey before him. His son Malcolm wrote in 1953: 'Father was utterly lonely to the end.'[24] The Mackenzies, who knew him well during the second decade of the present century, regarded him from different viewpoints and arrived at different conclusions. 'I have met many of the greatest romancers, or to use the more accurate Italian word, *improvvisatori*, of our period,' wrote Monty, 'and I must give the first place to Axel Munthe', and he quotes some examples of Munthe's inventions. Mackenzie cites Lawrence of Arabia, Ford Madox Ford, Frank Harris, Peter Cheyney and others who 'had great gifts of improvisation, but none of them within my observation had quite the spontaneity of Munthe's fairy stories. The immense popularity of San Michele . . . is a tribute to Axel Munthe's skill'.[25] In March 1918, however, Munthe had come down from Materita to the Mackenzies' home at 'La Solitaria' and given them a perceptive account of themselves, why their marriage had collapsed and how they could best continue their life together.[26] For Faith Mackenzie, Munthe had 'a healing presence' and she had made Monty promise not to portray him in *Vestal Fire*.[27]

Munthe was attractive to women and had a deep understanding of their psychology. While, by his skill in mental therapy, he was often able to help and comfort those who were neurotic – in an age when the appropriate drugs, now so numerous, did not exist – the snobbery and taste for rich clients, which he had developed in Rome during the 'nineties, never deserted him. He had little or no respect for most of his female patients, was not interested in them sexually, bullied them and took their money.[28] On the other hand, he would sometimes treat the poor of Anacapri without payment, but as often as not nurtured the hope of a *quid pro quo*, in the shape of a piece of their land or the antiquities found. There can be no doubt that for some people he had the 'healing touch', but others found him forbidding and even frightening.

Some were struck by his self-centredness; to others – and perhaps to himself – he seemed an altruist. Baroness Uexküll wrote that those who wanted to know the 'truth' about Munthe should study the maxim with which he prefaced *The Story of San Michele*: '*Ce n'est rien donner aux hommes que de ne pas se donner soi-même*', which may be read either: 'He who does not give himself up entirely, gives nothing to humanity', or 'He gives nothing to the human cause, who does not sacrifice himself wholly for others'.[29] Norman Douglas considered that Munthe's blindness was exaggerated; and an 'ingenious invention to excite the compassion of romantic readers of *The Story of San Michele*; when it suited him, he could see very well'.[30] This opinion was shared by a contemporary English resident of Anacapri, who knew Munthe well and considered him a 'complete charlatan. Whenever I think of Munthe, I think of Svengali.' An English writer who met Munthe in Paris in 1936, said that 'fraud was written all over him', while his blindness seemed to be false, because he was obviously aware of the identities of the individuals around him. Gudrun's husband, Jakob Baron von Uexküll, called him 'the old sorcerer'. An elderly Swede told the author that Munthe was 'a thoroughly nasty character'; and a Caprese, that 'Munthe loved only himself'.

For more than 30 years past the Villa San Michele had been second only to the Blue Grotto as a magnet for millions of day-trippers. While praised rapturously in the guide-books, the building has been deplored by the few who care about the genuine architecture of Capri. Amedeo Maiuri, Superintendent of Antiquities in Campania until his retirement in 1961, who loved Capri and strove to preserve its buildings and customs, considered that *The Story of San Michele* had 'undoubtedly contributed to set Capri once again in the place that German romanticism had given it in international literature; and for this, and for his loyalty towards his cherished island much praise is due to this great Swedish author.' Maiuri goes on to criticise Munthe's 'ephemeral activity of art lover and art collector', and 'parade of some pseudo-architectural works which have nothing to do with the purity of the Capri landscape'.[31] Professor Roberto Pane, who for many years has been active in protesting against the continuous destruction of the island's traditional architecture, is blunter in his criticism: '. . . the famous Villa S. Michele, the work of Axel

Axel Munthe and King Gustav
V of Sweden in the Villa San
Michele, 1930. *Photo: Allhem*

Dottoressa Elisabeth Moor and
Kenneth Macpherson, c. 1948.
Photo: Islay Lyons

Munthe – a fake as presumptuous as it is offensive; akin to the book of the same name which every day brings up here numerous hordes of visitors to perform a rite which is something between the sacred and the profane.'[32]

Three other foreign residents of Anacapri, less famous than Munthe but, in their humbler capacities, sincere and real people, died beween 1949 and 1952. The painter Otto Sohn-Rethel, swindled out of his property by a dishonest servant, died in 1949 in the villa of his friend Hans Berg. Baron Ekkehard von Schack followed in August 1952, when, having drunk a good deal, bathed at Bagni di Tiberio and walked back up the steps to Anacapri, he had a stroke and succumbed immediately.[33] Three months later Noël Rawnsley died without realising his dream of world unity and left his wife Violet and son David to carry on the struggle. All three were buried in the small area of the Anacapri cemetery which the authorities had thoughtfully reserved for non-Catholic burials.

Douglas's physical condition was slowly deteriorating. He suffered from giddiness, rheumatism, and weakness in his hands and legs – to which in November 1950 was added erysipelas.[34] Under the medical care of Dottoressa Moor, who inflicted on him various medicines, injections and lists of what he could and could not eat and drink, Douglas enjoyed life as best he could. Walking very slowly and always with a stick, he continued to visit Peppinella's, the Caffè Vittoria and, where he most liked to eat, the Savoia. The boy Ettore now lived permanently in his flat at the Villa Tuoro. Ettore's parents in Naples had at first objected to the relationship, but were eventually bought off, and Ettore remained. In the winter of 1951, Robin Maugham, nephew of Somerset, and the writer Michael Davidson made a pilgrimage to see Douglas, because they 'felt he was the last and most distinguished of a marvellous breed of authors'. They found him drinking in the Caffè Vittoria. 'His white hair was parted in the middle, his deep-set blue eyes were soft but searching, his face was surprisingly firm. He was dressed like a clerk on a Saturday afternoon. His baggy grey trousers were unbuttoned at the top, he wore rather frayed braces, an open shirt and a shabby coat.' As they were drinking 'a bearded sailor with a gnarled face approached, knelt in front of Norman and kissed his hand. Norman ruffled the man's grey hair. "You wouldn't believe it," he said, after the sailor had gone, "but thirty years ago he was the prettiest creature on the piazza."' After dinner at the Savoia, at which Douglas drank glass after glass of wine and was in excellent form, Maugham and Davidson staggered up the hillside with Douglas leaning on their arms and deposited him at the Villa Tuoro. Douglas's son Robin, who was visiting the island, warned them that another similar evening might kill his father. But Douglas had already invited them for the morrow and survived another festive occasion.[35] By January 1952 he was bedridden, emaciated, feeling the cold dreadfully and suffering a terrible irritation of the skin.

The end came on 9 February after a three-day coma during which Dottoressa Moor and the German Sisters of S. Elisabetta tried in vain to resuscitate him. Whether his death was caused by a suicidal overdose of sleeping tablets, or was due to old age and disease, remains uncertain.[36]

At sunset on the 10th a great cortège of Capresi accompanied their honorary citizen to the *cimitero acattolico*, where, after giving a funeral oration, Edwin Cerio cast a small branch of an island tree on the flower-covered coffin, in memory of Douglas's concern for the trees of Capri and the many he had planted to keep it green. Then Douglas was buried amongst the Christians and pagans, friends and enemies, who in their time had loved Capri.[37] Over the grave Macpherson placed a slab of dark *verde serpentino* marble and a headstone inscribed with his name, the dates and places of his birth and death, and a line of Horace – *Omnes eodem cogimur* (We are all driven to the same place).[38]

CHAPTER ELEVEN

Reflections on the Last Thirty-five Years

Capri is 3¾ miles long and varies in breadth from ¾ to 1¾ miles. In comparison with three West of England resorts – the population of Anacapri is about the same as Budleigh Salterton; that of Capri and Marina Grande a little less than Minehead; and the whole island, at around 12,500, a bit below Newquay, but with even more hotels.

While many places spend large sums advertising themselves, Capri attracts visitors with little or no effort. The beauty of the island and its admirable climate; its reputation as a place where nobody questions how anyone else lives; its indefinable quality as lotus-land, where worries are shed and the outside world forgotten; the verve, energy and skill with which the islanders make everyone welcome. All these things attract a wide variety of visitors on a gigantic scale.

It is very easy to travel to and from Capri. Naples provides an endless procession of hydrofoils, which do the journey in 35 minutes, and frequent steamers, which take 1½ hours. The island can also be reached from Ischia, Sorrento, Positano, Amalfi and Salerno.

The volume of visitors who have been processed by the islanders can be illustrated by the movement of passengers in and out of Marina Grande (*movimento passageri in arrivo e partenza*), which rose from 726,730 in 1950, to 1,244,021 in 1960, 1,923,334 in 1970, 3,197,272 in 1980, and 3,409,356 in 1982; but fell to 3,188,645 in 1983.[1] Almost all these passengers, of course, had been counted twice. Most were tourists and day-trippers (*pendolari*) from Naples.

Package tours of the Naples area usually devote one day to Capri, and the routine is almost invariable. Having arrived at Marina Grande, most go immediately to the Blue Grotto and back; then by hired buses to Anacapri, where San Michele is visited, and, if there is time, the chairlift (*seggiovia*) taken to and from the top of Monte Solaro – sometimes a problem, because if there is a large crowd on Solaro, it can take up to two hours to get a seat for the return journey; a quick lunch and shopping in Anacapri; buses to Capri for shopping and a visit to the Giardini di Augusto (Villa Krupp); buses to Marina Grande, and off. By the late afternoon peace has again returned to the island.

The 'fifties and early 'sixties saw a worldwide increase in Capri's popularity amongst foreign visitors coming for a holiday, with a peak in 1955, when 53,652 foreigners spent 281,086 nights in hotels – figures which have never since been exceeded. To cope with these longer-term visitors there has been a remarkable increase in both the number and standard of hotels and *pensioni*. In 1950 there were in all 50 concerns (*esercizi*). In 1965 there were 96 – ranging from one *de luxe* hotel (Quisisana) and five category I hotels, through numerous category II, III and IV hotels, to *pensioni* (divided into three categories) and *locande* (inns). The biggest increase was in the number of category II hotels, which rose from five in 1950 to a peak of 30 in 1964 and catered for the numerous visitors of moderate means, who at the same time required reasonable comfort. For most northerners taking a holiday in the south, comfort necessarily includes a bath. While the number of available beds more than doubled between 1950 and 1965 from 1,515 to 3,247, baths over the same period near quadrupled from 364 to 1,265.[2] Whether fresh water was always available for these baths was another matter, because all this precious commodity had to be imported in water-boats from Naples. The number of first-class hotels increased steadily from three in 1950 to nine in 1980.

At first hotel prices remained low, perhaps because there were now so many and because prices had to be competitive to attract clients. The exchange rate for the *lira* – around 1,750 to the pound sterling – remained steady throughout the 'fifties and 'sixties until the devaluation of sterling in 1967 stiffened it to 1,500. Even the Quisisana, with a daily *en pension* rate in 1966 of 9,500/13,000 *lire* (£5.10*s*–£7.10*s*) was within the means of most visitors, and hotels of lesser magnificence were correspondingly cheaper. Capri provided an ideal weekend for NATO personnel based on Pozzuoli, who were also particularly welcome in the island for the American cigarettes which they brought and which were otherwise unobtainable except in the black market; 200 Camel or Philip Morris cigarettes would secure a weekend's board and lodging in a small hotel, and tipping was usually done in cigarettes.

In the 'sixties the supply of enough fresh water for the vast influx of summer visitors became increasingly difficult. More and more trips by water-boats from Naples, bringing the good water of Serino, were needed, and the administration sometimes found it expedient to induce their crews to exceed Capri's ration. In 1971, the SIPPIC came up with a plan to build a desalination plant (*dissalatore*) alongside their electricity generator at Marina Grande, and they persuaded the Cassa del Mezzo-giorno – the State-funded bank for financing public projects in south Italy – to pay half the cost. The plant came into operation in 1975 and began to inject a small amount of water into the system.

The situation continued to be critical until it was decided to adopt the

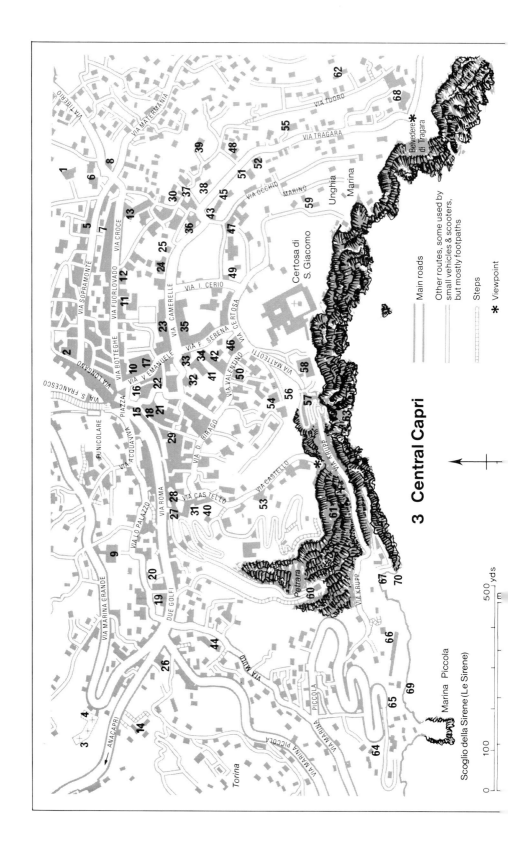

3 Central Capri

VIA TIBERIO
VIA MATERMANIA
VIA TUORO
VIA TRAGARA
Belvedere di Tragara *
VIA CROCE
VIA SOPRAMONTE
VIA FUORLOVADO
VIA OCCHIO MARINO
MARINO
Marina
Unghia
Marina
VIA BOTTEGHE
VIA LONGANO
VIA S. FRANCESCO
Certosa di S. Giacomo
PIAZZA
VIA I CERIO
VIA CAMERELLE
VIA F. SERENA
VIA CERTOSA
FUNICOLARE
VIA ACQUAVIVA
VIA V. EMANUELE
VIA VALENTINO
VIA MATTEOTTI
VIA D. BIRAGO
VIA ROMA
VIA LO PALAZZO
VIA CASTELLO
VIA KRUPP
DUE GOLFI
Petrara
VIA MARINA GRANDE
VIA KRUPP
ANACAPRI
VIA MULO
Torina
MARINA PICCOLA
VIA MARINA PICCOLA
PICCOLA
Marina Piccola
Scoglio della Sirene (Le Sirene)

Main roads

Other routes, some used by small vehicles & scooters, but mostly footpaths

Steps

* Viewpoint

0   100   500 yds
0   m

30 All Saints Church
69 Bagni di Maria
31 Cà del Sole
26 Capilupi Hospital
2 Casa Rossa (Villa Behring)
65 Chapel of S. Andreas
16 Church of S. Stefano
4 Cimitero Acattolico (non-Catholic cemetery)
3 Cimitero Cattolico (Catholic cemetery)
21 Convent of S. Teresa
– Corso Trento e Trieste (later Via Roma)
66 Fortino (later La Canzone del Mare)
36 German Evangelical Church
56 Giardini di Augusto (Villa Krupp)
63 Grotta dell' Arsenale
61 Grotta del Castiglione
57 Grotta di Fra' Felice
12 Hotel 'A Pazziella
49 Hotel Calypso
27 Hotel Capri
24 Hotel Faraglioni
42 Hotel Flora
22 Hotel Gatto Bianco
48 Hotel La Certosella
47 Hotel La Floridiana
17 Hotel La Palma
45 Hotel La Pineta
41 Hotel La Residenza
51 Hotel La Scalinatella
58 Hotel Luna

32 Hotel Manfredi Pagano (Villa Romana)
17 Hotel Pagano (later Hotel La Palma)
34 Hotel Regina Cristina
33 Hotel Sanfelice
46 Hotel Semiramis
11 Hotel Villa Igea
66 La Canzone del Mare
15 Palazzo Arcucci (later Palazzo Cerio)
9 Palazzo Canale
15 Palazzo Cerio
10 Palazzo Ferraro
9 Palazzo Inglese (later Palazzo Canale)
5 Pensione Esperia
64 Pensione Weber
60 Petrara (where Douglas began a house)
19 Pretura
35 Quisisana
68 Residence Punta Tragara
64 Ristorante da Pietro (on site of Pensione Weber)
70 Spiaggia Saracena
– Strada Nuova (later Via Roma)
64 Strandpension (Pensione Weber)
7 Tiberio Palace
67 Torre Saracena
– Via Hohenzollern (later Via Vittorio Emanuele)
– Via Pastena (later Via Reginaldo Giuliani)
40 Villa Alba
55 Villa Allers (later Villa Tragara)
38 Villa Andreas (later Villa Capricorno)
2 Villa Behring (Casa Rossa)

54 Villa Blaesus
59 Villa Borselli
38 Villa Capricorno
29 Villa Castello
41 Villa Caterina (later Hotel La Residenza)
39 Villa Cercola
8 Villa Croce
53 Villa Daphne
43 Villa Discopoli
51 Villa Elena (later Hotel La Scalinatella)
13 Villa Helios
25 Villa Jenny
56 Villa Krupp (see Giardini di Augusto)
52 Villa La Pergola di Tragara
23 Villa Massimino
6 Villa Mezzomonte
37 Villa Mimosa
1 Villa Monte San Michele
28 Villa Mura
18 Villa Narcissus
44 Villa Pierina
14 Villa Quattro Venti
32 Villa Romana (Hotel Manfredi Pagano)
55 Villa Tragara
62 Villa Tuoro
50 Villa Valentino
68 Villa Vismara (later Residence Punta Tragara)
19 Villa Weber (later Pretura)

radical and permanent solution of piping water from the Sorrentine mountain spring of Gragnano to the tip of the peninsula and then pumping it through submarine pipes to Marina Grande. The Cassa del Mezzogiorno, which financed the whole project, gave the contract to the Danish company NKT, which manufactured three flexible armoured pipelines, each about five miles long and in one piece. Before the first pipe (*tubo*) was laid, minesweepers of the Italian Navy swept the course it was to take, in order to remove any World War II mines which might still remain. On the day before the pipe was due to be connected to the distribution point at Marina Grande, a final check was made, and, to the horror of all, a mine, well covered with barnacles and seaweed, was found exactly on the course chosen for the final stretch of the pipe. Although the origin of this mine remains a mystery, it was suspected that it had been planted by the Camorra as a desperate last fling to sabotage the pipe and preserve the waterboats, in which they had a vested interest. The mine safely removed, the pipe was connected with the Capri network and joined the water-boats and *dissalatore* in supplying the island. The second pipe was laid in November 1977 and the third in May 1978, thus providing a final solution to a problem which had vexed the island since Roman times.

With so many visitors, and with a good number leaving their rubbish in the island, the disposal of 'trash' was also a problem for the authorities, which came to a head in an acute and unexpected form in February 1974. Until this time rubbish of all sorts had been taken to an incinerator (*bruciatore*), which was perched on a ledge beside the loop of the first hairpin bend on the road up to Anacapri. Consumable rubbish was burned in the incinerator; the rest was dumped nearby. For years earth and unburned rubbish had accumulated in a largely non-solid mass until in heavy rain, it suddenly collapsed down the sheer cliff, overwhelmed a house below and killed the occupants. Accusations of official negligence were made, but no action was taken, beyond the payment of compensation to the bereaved. New arrangements, however, were made for the disposal of Capri's rubbish. Henceforth it was shipped daily and at considerable expense to Naples, where the island's unwanted but superior clothes, furniture, metal-scrap, food and general oddments, were eagerly 'gone over' by the Neapolitan scavengers, who either kept them for personal use or sold them. The incinerator still stands behind its iron gates, forlorn and weatherbeaten, with its rusting chimney visible to the millions of tourists who are driven to and from Anacapri. It is safe to say that this monument is not included in their itinerary or even given a passing reference by any tour-leader.

To judge from the statistics covering the period (1960–1980), Germans are, as ever, the most numerous visitors, coming mainly in the spring and early autumn. They are followed closely by the Americans, mostly well-to-do, who may have been aroused by an article in *Vogue* of 1 April 1969 about 'play places' in Italy. 'Although in summer', the article advised, 'tourists invade this mountainous island, coming for the day on excursions from Naples, blocking the roads with taxis and buses filled to overflowing, by sunset the confusion is over. . . . Private cars are still not allowed on the island unless one is a resident or can show proof of having rented a house for over 30 days. Swimming is lovely in clear cool water, but since there are no real beaches, renting a small motorboat either at Marina Grande or Marina Piccola is advisable.' The English are a close third, the French fourth, with all other nationalities far behind.

The late 'seventies were marked by astronomical increases in prices of every kind, increases which continued unabated into the early 'eighties. While visitors had to grapple with much more expensive hotels, restaurants and *caffè*, an increasing scramble for property pushed up not only the price of ownership but also the cost of renting. This was distressing to people of modest means who in the past had been able to afford a tenancy but not an outright purchase.[3]

From 1981, spurred on by the earthquake which devastated the Naples region on 23 November 1980, and allured by Capri's apparent immunity from tectonic disasters, Neapolitans with money to spare scrambled all the more for second homes in the island. The buying of land and property by both mainlanders and islanders, either to invest money for a quick profit or as a long-term hedge against inflation – in the latter case properties were sometimes left empty because of the difficulty of evicting tenants – gathered pace, and prices of houses increased at a fearsome rate. Everything else went up as well – rents, hotel-rooms, meals in restaurants, while drinks on the Piazza cost four times as much as in Naples. Visits to the island began to tail off, and some hotel-owners, faced with increasing numbers of empty beds, except in the high-season when Italians flocked over for their holidays, considered the possibility of converting their properties into apartments as a quick means of raising cash. But here the restrictive regulations governing the change of use of premises stood in their way. The conversion of large private villas into apartments, however, which was also very lucrative, was much easier to arrange and went ahead all over the town.

In the summer of 1982 tourism in Capri exceeded all previous records, with 2,395,806 movements through the port in the five busy months May to September, and 3,409,356 for the whole year. By the end of the summer, facilities of all sorts had been strained to and even beyond acceptable limits and most of the islanders involved in the tourist trade were absolutely exhausted. For the first time in its history, Capri was beginning to wonder if it really wanted this kind of thing. It had long been clear that hordes of *pendolari* brought very little advantage to the island's economy, coming usually with picnics, buying little or nothing in the island and leaving tons of rubbish.[4] There were proposals to limit drastically the number of visitors who could come to Capri on any one day, but against this it was realised that it would be difficult, if not impossible, to persuade the ferry companies, who did so well out of the Capri traffic, to reduce their sailings. The richer Capresi had visions of banishing the common herd altogether and concentrating on the 'jet-set', luxury yacht crowd and millionaires generally, who, they hoped, would spend money carelessly in the pursuit of pleasure – and thoughts turned once again to the possibility of establishing a *casinò* in the island. It seemed depressingly clear that many Capresi were totally indifferent to the fate of their island, as long as their pockets were filled to overflowing with money which they could invest in Buoni Ordinari del Tesoro (BOT) – the equivalent of British National Savings Certificates – on which the Government then paid an astonishing 18% interest, tax free (it is now down to about 15%). Enquiries as to where the Italian Treasury found the money to pay such interest evoked only, 'who knows?' As Henry Wreford had noted in 1860, *lucro* appeared to be the 'sole motive power'. In October 1982 Capri-lovers from both inside and outside the island held a meeting at the Certosa to consider the future of Capri and register their sense of foreboding, but apart from one Communist *consigliere*, no local politicians attended.

The elegance of Capri life which was notable in the 'sixties and still evident until the late 'seventies had vanished by the early 'eighties, when vulgarisation, overcrowding, pressure on the island's facilities and assaults on the environment began to turn Capri into a Mediterranean version of Coney Island, while the principal foreigners who before had enriched the life of the island were mostly either dead or departed.

It is clear that, as the island lurches on into the middle 'eighties, all the islanders have got a lot of hard thinking to do about their future.

*

Almost everyone in the island is engaged directly or indirectly in the tourist trade – hoteliers, restaurateurs, owners of *caffè* and bars, and all their staff; shopkeepers; those who transport persons and goods; workers in the utilities and public services; boatmen and fishermen; and workers in the fields.

Tourism has brought vast sums of money to the island. While much is concentrated in the hands of those who own property and tourist facilities, wealth has been diffused in many directions amongst islanders whose families earlier in the century had been struggling peasants. The old-established families, like Esposito, Federico, Ferraro, Lembo, Morgano,

Strina and Vuotto, take great care to keep their property and wealth intact and to prevent intrusion by mainland Italians and other foreigners. Let us consider briefly three of these families.

The children of Antonio Esposito have followed their father in being hard-working, shrewd, practical and careful in their handling of money. The eldest, Luigi, who married the daughter of an hotelier, owns one hotel, a share of another and two shops. We have already encountered Antonio's daughter Teresa, who married the successful Raffaele Vuotto. Another daughter Venere, who married Carlo Federico, *professore* and politician, owns the Hotel Regina Cristina, a category I hotel, which is open all the year round, and another smaller hotel. Another daughter Maria, widow of Domenico Strina, a remarkable Caprese who worked his way from messenger-boy (*fattorino*) to manager of the local branch of the Banco di Napoli, runs the very small and comfortable Hotel Calypso. Antonio's second son Mario, who, unlike the rest of the family, was a happy-go-lucky character (*facilone*), bought the Hotel Capri in Via Roma, which on his death in 1980 passed to his widow and daughters.

Another branch of the Esposito family, led by three brothers, Guiseppe, Giovanni and Tonino, great-grandchildren of Carmela, who ran her celebrated *caffè* at the end of Tragara, have the Gatto Bianco, a category II hotel of great character and excellent cuisine. Their married sister Teresa De Angelis has a share in La Capannina, one of the best restaurants, which has been awarded two spoons-and-forks by Baedeker.

Raffaele Vuotto, who began his business life in 1929 with a *latteria*, selling milk, butter and cheese and in 1934 married Teresa Esposito, has become one of the richest people in the island and is popularly known as 'Il Padrone di Capri'. Amongst his ventures were the Hotels Pineta, Flora and Luna; the Gran Caffè and Piccolo Bar in the Piazza; and the Embassy Bar in Via Camerelle. In 1981 control of the Hotel Pineta and Gran Caffè passed to his son Costanzo, who, by his marriage to Titina Cosentino, had linked himself with the family which has the valuable bathing and restaurant concession at 'Le Sirene' at Marina Piccola. Although some people are jealous of Raffaele's wealth, most Capresi are proud of him as a great success story – a peasant who by his own efforts has become a multi-millionaire, but is still one of the people – who, now in his late seventies, is usually to be seen sloping around the town in casual clothes on a portly frame, and an old blue beret on his head. After dinner he often sits outside the Embassy Bar, talking to friends and waylaying passers-by he knows for a drink.

The Morgano family has continued to prosper and enlarge its domains, on the very solid foundation laid at the beginning of the century by Don Giuseppe and Donna Lucia. The richest, until his death in 1983, was their youngest son Nicola, who ran the category I Tiberio Palace until its sale a few years ago to a Neapolitan. His nephew Mario, proprietor of two hotels, ''A Pazziella' since 1960 and 'La Scalinatella' since 1964, became a very capable hotelier and brought up his sons in the business. In the winter of 1981/82 the Morgano family achieved their greatest *coup* by buying the Quisisana, which was not doing too well, from the German businessman Grundig. In so doing, they outsmarted another bidder, the hotelier Salvatore De Angelis, who was furious and conducted a campaign of threats and blackmail against the Morgano family and sabotage at La Scalinatella. This led to his arrest on 7 May 1983, to face charges of extortion, arson (*incendio doloso*) and the illegal possession of firearms (*detenzioni di armi di guerra*).[5] He was found guilty and sentenced to prison. Impeccably dressed, always calm, affable to the guests, Mario Morgano had made a great success of the Quisisana, the island's one *de luxe* hotel, where in 1984 daily *demi-pension* ranged from about £73 for a single room in the low season to £193 for a suite in the high. It is favoured by rich Americans on holiday and rich Italians on long weekends. On 1 April 1983, just over a month before the arrest of De Angelis, Nicola Morgano died in his ninetieth year. As the offspring of Giuseppe and Lucia, his death severed the last link with those halcyon years at the beginning of the century, when the Quisisana, a flourishing concern, had belonged to Don Giuseppe's rival in business and politics, Commendatore Federico Serena. The effect which the purchase of the Quisisana by the Morgano family had on Serena's ghost can only be imagined.

The De Angelis story is a sad one. It will be remembered that Salvatore's father Costanzo did well during World War II and afterwards invested his gains in hotels. His sons enlarged the hotel empire and by the time he put in his bid for the Quisisana, Salvatore and his brother Costanzo owned four hotels in Capri town and one in Marina Grande – quite an achievement for an immigrant family. A few days after Salvatore's arrest, Costanzo died from a combination of shock, heart-attack and fear, it was said.

Another immigrant family, named Staiano, did much better. They came to Capri in the early part of the century from Fornacelle, a primitive mountain-village north-east of Sorrento, where trade was then still mostly by barter and the inhabitants were supposed by their more advanced neighbours to have rings in their noses (*anelli al naso*). At first the Staiano made a living by transporting goods from Marina Grande to Capri and Anacapri in two-wheeled carts, drawn by horse, mule or donkey. The business, run by the three Staiano brothers, Antonino, Antonio and Giuseppe, was widened to include the importation of coal from Calabria – a grimy occupation, considered *infra dig.* by the Capresi. By the 'seventies their numerous children had spread themselves over a wide variety of lucrative occupations, which included a fleet of buses, taxis and electric trolleys; much of the trade in naphtha and coal; the sale of tickets on commission for the hydrofoils; shops in Capri and a bar at Marina Grande; and a hotel in England. The Staiano are a remarkable example of how by hard work, enterprise and commercial skill a *parvenu* family has managed to infiltrate the tightly-knit structure of the island's business life; the old-established Capresi have little to say in favour of the Staiano family.

This hostility towards outsiders who seek to establish businesses in Capri is deep-seated in all levels of society and not least amongst the boutique-owners and souvenir-shops, who, ever more numerous, compete fiercely to attract custom among the visitors. In 1957 an English-woman, who had recently married an islander and come to live in Capri, opened a boutique in Via Fuorlovado. The Capresi threatened her with dire consequences and persuaded the *municipio* to close down the shop on a technicality. Her husband, a forceful man, went and banged on the door of the *sindaco* and demanded the immediate rescinding of the closure order, which was granted within 24 hours. A talented young French couturier, who was charmed by Capri and came to live there in 1969, opened a shop in Via Camerelle and began to sell fashionable clothes, many of them designed by himself and made up locally. The business prospered and he opened a second boutique. This proved too much for local rivals, who tried to burn down one of his shops, but he survived and continues to flourish.

Having highlighted a few individuals who have done particularly well from tourism, it must be stressed that the continuing viability of the island depends greatly on its administrators – *sindaci, assessori* and municipal officials – and the efforts of those unsung citizens who work hard and cheerfully to create the *vita piacevole* which attracts so many visitors. Too little has been said of them: the porters, boatmen, fishermen and port officials of Marina Grande; the staff of the funicular, which is in constant movement between the port and town; those concerned with the importation and distribution of supplies; drivers who manoeuvre their taxis and buses up and down narrow and twisting roads; conductors of the electric trolleys, who weave skilfully through the milling crowds, to deliver luggage to hotels and supplies to shops, restaurants, *caffè* and bars; the staff of all these establishments, particularly the restaurants, who work very long and exacting hours, serving meals to an endless clientele; and finally the dwindling number of *contadini*, the true salt of Capri, who manage farms, vineyards, olive groves and orchards in the countryside.

Some mention must be made of minority interests – the encouragement of service to the community by a local group of the world-wide Società di San Vincenzo di Paoli; the Società Operaia, the island's 'friendly society'; and the Centro Caprense.

The Società of San Vincenzo, directed by Roberto Alberino, a member of the Marina Grande fishing family, has 275 *confratelli* and *consorelle* organised in 20 *conferenze*, as they are called, who help the poor; are available as blood-donors at the local hospital; run a mini-ambulance to transport the sick from anywhere in the island; visit prisoners (usually Neapolitans) in the tiny gaol of the *pretura* in Via Roma; do what they can to help drug-addicts; type letters for pensioners; and show the addled how to fill in their municipal forms.[6]

The Società Operaia, now 102 years old, dedicated to '*fratellanza e lavoro*', looks after its 190 working members (*operai*). All of them male, they include municipal officials, lawyers, shopkeepers; workers in hotels, restaurants, bars and *caffè*; and *contadini* – who now pay the modest sum of 1,000 *lire* a month (it had been one *lira* in 1883), with extra donations at Christmas and Easter.

The 'Centro Caprense di Vita e di Studi Ignazio Cerio', to give it its full title (usually abbreviated as 'CCIC'), was founded in 1949 by Mabel Norman Cerio, who had bought the Palazzo Cerio from her husband Giorgio and brother-in-law Edwin, in part of which she created the Centro, dedicated to the memory of her father-in-law Ignazio. It consists of a fine hall for concerts, lectures and exhibitions; a small museum of archaeological and geological specimens, including Ignazio's own dis- coveries; and a library, which houses an important collection of books, documents, manuscripts and photographs on the history, architecture, geology, archaeology, topography, botany and social life of Capri. During the last years of his life Edwin added materially to the collection and was fortunate in having Cataldo (Aldo) Aprea as secretary of the Centro and administrator of the Cerio estates on Via Tragara.

Born in 1928, Aldo was the son of Giovanni Aprea and Anna Settanni. His paternal grandfather Cataldo had been factotum to Maksim Gorki – cook, housekeeper, secretary and responsible for making payments to penniless Russians. Aldo's aunt Maria had the brief distinction of being given Russian lessons by Lenin. His maternal grandfather was Angelo Settanni, brother of Emilia and Maria; Aldo was thus related to the numerous Caracciolo and Binyon offspring. As a young man he de- veloped a deep interest in the history, art, architecture, folklore, fauna, flora and iconography of Capri. Precise, accurate and scrupulously honest, Aldo is something of a rarity among Capresi. An epithet com- monly applied to him is *pignolo* (meticulous) – for him and like-minded people a term of respect, but with most of his fellow-islanders mildly derogatory. Practical also and energetic, with a fine sense of humour, and liked by Edwin Cerio, Aldo did much to rescue and arrange precious material and develop the Centro from its earliest days, until he resigned from the secretaryship in 1977. Edwin's daughter Laetitia is now Presi-

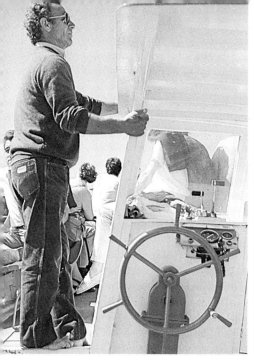

Alberto Sorrentino; an electric trolley in Via Vittorio Emanuele, with Giovanni Valentini ('Romano') and Michele D'Urso; Antigone Pesce; and Antonio Guarracino (*last courtesy of Pietro Cerrotta*)

dent of the CCIC, but devotes very little time to it and leaves the running
to the Librarian, Professore Luigi Bladier, an eccentric, autocratic, gruff,
but *au fond* genial pedagogue, who once taught Greek and Latin in the
liceo. The records of the Centro were recently put in order and it is now
possible to do systematic research there. It is much used by foreign
researchers and by those few islanders who are interested in details of
their past.

Finally in this section we must look briefly at those islanders who have
made their mark outside the narrow confines of Capri. The total is very
small, even counting immigrant Italians who have become local citizens;
but then Capri, for all its fame, is a very small community.

The only local writer known abroad is Edwin Cerio, who died in
January 1960 in his eighty-fifth year, but not before marrying a woman 52
years younger than himself, in the hope of begetting a male heir. In 1953
she had a child, but it was a girl. Cerio was a complicated character. Hard,
grasping, intelligent, astute, sarcastic, *estroso* (fanciful, wayward), his
active life spanned 60 years as naval engineer, builder, writer, botanist,
collector of antiquities and businessman; he was also a notable seducer of
women (*chiavatore* in Neapolitan), coveting women as he coveted plots of
land.[7] He was a great lover of Capri and a good *sindaco* from 1920 to 1923,
when he did his best to protect the architecture and countryside of Capri
from the ravages of the developers. It is as a writer that he is best known,
but almost all his writing is flawed by his habit of mixing fact with fiction.
Added to which, whether expounding a light or serious subject, he
persistently adopts a sarcastic approach, allied with a facetiousness which
is often infantile and in the long run tedious – all this when he had the
shining example of his father to guide him, as well as the time, opportunity
and sources at his disposal to write a definitive history of the island in all its
varied aspects. A notable exception is *Capri nel Seicento* (1934), a well-
researched and serious book, which is a mine of information not readily
available elsewhere. Even in a biography of his illustrious father (in which
he makes no mention of his mother) – *La vita e la figura di un uomo* (*c.* 1921)
– the material is badly arranged and the reader wearied by attempts to be
funny; while his *Flora privata di Capri* (1939), where the student would
welcome a straight book on botany, is marred by fantasy, musing and
gossip. In *L'aria di Capri*, a collection of essays on Capri personalities,
fragments of truth are submerged in a sea of fantasy, and throughout is the
puerile *umorismo*. His most substantial work, *L'ora di Capri*, published in
1950 (followed in 1957 by *The Masque of Capri*, a shorter book in English,
published by Nelson, which covered much of the same ground), deals
with the social history of Capri from Tiberius to Munthe, with particular
emphasis on the foreign visitors and residents, and is noticeably reticent
about the Capresi themselves. While the book contains useful material, it

is often impossible to know what to believe. Finally, one may ask, why did Cerio consistently write in such an unsatisfactory manner, when the unembellished truth about Capri is so extraordinary and fascinating?

Of artists whose work is known and appreciated outside the island, one can name a few. Laetitia Cerio, twice married and for many years living a cosmopolitan existence in Buenos Aires, New York and Europe, settled down in Capri in 1971, taking a flat in the Cà del Sole, still haunted, no doubt, by shades of 'Rory Freemantle' and the 'extraordinary women'. A talented draughtsman, she did excellent line drawings to illustrate her father's books. She has exhibited abroad, and her paintings are found in public and private collections. Anacapri claims as its own Rosina Viva (1899–1983), a distinguished 'naïve' painter (although it is also said that she was a *figlia della Madonna* from Naples), who had the good fortune to attract the attention of Benjamin Vautier, a Swiss industrialist, who married her in 1918. Vautier was himself an artist, the son of an artist and grandson of Marc Louis Benjamin Vautier, one of the most distinguished German nineteenth-century painters of genre, and Vautier was no doubt the main impetus to Rosina's development as a painter. Then there is Raffaele Castello (1905–1969), born and bred in the lower part of the island, who had an innate feeling for colour. Later he travelled and studied widely and became one of the most interesting European abstract artists of the inter-war years.

Also known abroad is Capri's leading potter, Massimo Goderecci. Born in 1928 at Castelli, an Abruzzi village, once famous for its majolica and still known for its craftsmen, Goderecci came to Capri in 1946 and after further training and working with other potters in 1960 established his own workshop where he produces pottery, but specialises and excels in enamelled tiles and mosaics. He has built up a commanding position in the island, with an unending series of public and private commissions – tiles for the sacristy of the parish church of Santo Stefano; street notices for the *comune*; tiles for hotels and villas in Capri; and tiles for the houses of foreign visitors who had seen and admired his work. Fully occupied with his many commissions, Goderecci has no need or desire to sell to the general public.

The most famous islander in the arts is, however, a musician, Giuseppe Faiella ('Peppino di Capri'), who comes from a musical family. His grandfather, Giuseppe ('Il Quartino'), had migrated from Naples early in the century, gone into business as a shoemaker and played the *quartino*, an instrument of the clarinet family, in the Capri band. By the 'twenties Giuseppe had become leader of the band, which included his son Bernardo, who played 'cello, saxophone and clarinet, and ran an electrical shop in Via Madre Serafina.[8] Young Giuseppe began to play the piano in 1943 when he was only four and soon became a *bambino prodigio* in the

island, playing American tunes to the US forces on the piano of the Hotel
Morgano Tiberio. When he was a little older he took lessons in classical
piano. When he was fifteen he began to sing, and in 1956 turned
professional, with regular night-club performances. In the next year
Carisch of Milan recorded three of his songs – 'Non è peccato', 'Malattia'
and 'Let me cry' – which were an immediate success and within a few
months were the rage all over Italy. Peppino was fortunate in being able to
display his youthful talent at a favourable moment. Neapolitan song was in
the doldrums. His own style, derived from the then popular 'Rock and
Roll', had its own individuality, and the all-male quintet which he formed
was young, fresh and something new. In 1964 Peppino joined the Beatles
on an Italian tour and, in 1970, after continuous success with his Carisch
records, established his own recording company 'SPLASH' in Naples. By
1971 he had sold 15 million records in Italy alone, and there were also
substantial sales in America and elsewhere abroad. In 1976 he won first
prize at the Festival of San Remo with 'Non lo faccio più'. In 1980 he
created a new group of nine, with himself still as pianist and singer,
supplemented by guitar, bass, two synthesizers, drums, saxophone and
three female singers. Today, in his middle forties, rich, successful,
pursued by autograph-hunters, Peppino and his 'Capri sound' continue
on the crest of the wave.

    From these scattered observations, it will be seen that the Capresi are
now fully emancipated. They have come a long way from the days when all
but a few were poor, led a peasant existence and looked up to the foreigner
as some sort of higher being.

                                    *

From the 'fifties to the middle 'seventies the foreign colony was graced by
individuals who were bewitched by the charms of the island, put down
their roots and set about adding to the annals of pleasure; this was the
golden age of post-war Capri. Prices, although high by the standards of
the mainland, were tolerable compared to the increases which came in the
late 'seventies. Life still had a grace and elegance, which vanished in the
early 'eighties.

    Many of these residents were highly eccentric, and their eccentricity
was often enhanced by residence in Capri. Principe di Sirignano poses the
important question: 'I do not know whether eccentrics are attracted to
Capri or whether the island makes them eccentric';[9] there is much to be
said on both sides of the argument. There was no one, however odd, who
could not be quickly and happily assimilated into a society which had seen
all, was surprised at nothing and knew how to please foreigners, especially
if they were rich; *la vita piacevole* was no longer easy for the eccentric

pauper. Foreigners came as individuals, and individuals they remained. Some had been successes in their own countries, some had been failures. For some, the enjoyment of Capri was enhanced by finding a lover or lovers to his or her taste, if they had not already brought one to share the island's pleasures. And all around was the eternal charm and beauty of the island itself.

First, a word about some of the pre-war residents and visitors who died during the period under review. In 1964 Renata Borgatti, one of the most remarkable of the 'extraordinary women', died in Rome. During the intervening years she had usually been short of money and dependent on the generosity of lovers and friends. Volcanic, warm-hearted, intelligent, and totally honest, Renata attracted much affection throughout her tempestuous life. A fine artist, who had a gift for teaching, she devoted herself to giving music lessons and encouraging young pianists. In the early 'thirties she befriended the Romanian pianist, Clara Haskil, who was to become world-famous; on one occasion Renata deliberately cut her finger just before one of her own recitals, so that Clara could play instead. During and after World War II Renata taught at a school of music in Switzerland, where she remained until the school closed in the mid-'fifties. Then she moved to Rome, lived frugally in a barely-furnished apartment, attracted a circle of devoted pupils, and made enough money by her teaching and occasional recitals to be independent for the first time in her life. She even managed a final visit to Capri, where in the Palazzo Cerio she gave a recital, with all the strength of a man, bewitching her audience but taking no apparent notice of the enthusiastic applause which greeted the performance. Suddenly in February 1964 Renata developed galloping leukaemia. She was well enough to have a birthday-party on 2 March – under the sign of *pisces*, which she had always liked, because fish are difficult to hem in and usually get away. She had expressed a desire to die to the music of Bach's *St Matthew Passion*, and this was played from the early morning of 8 March when her end was near, until she died at midday, surrounded by friends and pupils, among them two Chinese girls, who sat with absolutely impassive faces, while tears streamed down their cheeks. After a Catholic service in Rome – although Renata was an unbeliever – attended by many distinguished Romans and by the American poet Ezra Pound, a friend arranged for her to be buried in the cemetery of Palestrina, an ancient town (the Roman Praeneste) which she had always loved, and the namesake of one of her favourite composers.[10]

Somerset Maugham, frequent visitor to Capri since 1895, spent most of his last years in the Villa Mauresque, Cap Ferrat. In early December 1965 he asked to see Romaine Brooks, who, as 'Olimpia Leigh', had been the most notable of Capri's 'extraordinary of women' and was living nearby in Nice. Fragile, wispy and opinionated, she was the same age as

Maugham, but was to outlive him by five years. Romaine came to the Mauresque with some reluctance, for she knew of Maugham's distressing condition. His stammering was such that she could not understand a word he uttered. Only when he saw her to her car and pointed his finger at her did she grasp what he was saying: 'You need somebody to take care of you', and then he directed his finger at Alan Searle, his secretary. It seemed as though he was bequeathing Alan to her. A few days later Maugham collapsed and was taken to the Anglo-American Hospital in Nice, where he died on 15 December, a few weeks short of his ninety-second birthday. His last words were: 'Why, Alan, where have you been? I've been looking for you for months. I want to shake your hand for all you have done for me.'[11]

1974 saw the end of earthly joys for Hans Spiegel. Released from internment after the collapse of Fascism in 1943, he had returned immediately to Capri, and, deaf and dumb as he was, made the best of his remaining 32 years – wearing his flamboyant red-and-blue clothes, masks, rings and necklaces; dancing and miming his way round the restaurants and *caffè* to entertain the visitors; painting water-colours; and enjoying the company of his friends. As a victim of racial persecution during the war, he received a small pension from the West German Government and was able to rent a room-cum-kitchen in Via Castello. Although he was an incorrigible scrounger – known as 'gratis' because he never paid for anything – he succeeded in making and keeping friends all over the world, who used to send him presents in cash and kind. He died in his eighty-fifth year and to everyone's surprise was found to have left a substantial fortune lodged in a Swiss bank;[12] he joined the many other foreign eccentrics in the *cimitero acattolico*.

Forced to spend the war in Switzerland, where she was free from the risk of internment, Dottoressa Elizabeth Moor hurried back to the island as soon as she could. From then until the middle 'sixties, her 'small square body with the big teeth, the startling blue eyes, the tough electric hair as alive as a bundle of fighting snakes', continued to be seen all over the island where, always miserably poor herself, she resumed her practice amongst the poor. She had a quality of passionate living and a sexual interest in men, which never deserted her – indeed she claimed Edwin Cerio as one of her many lovers.[13] Her final period in the island was marked by a series of daunting blows, which gradually wore her down. First, in 1946, when he was only twenty, her son Andrea died suddenly and in great pain from an internal condition. Next came the demise of three friends and patients, Douglas, Gray and Schack – all of whom died within twelve months in 1951–2. The final shock occurred fifteen years later with the death of her grandson, little Andrea, child of her daughter Giulietta and successor to big Andrea as the apple of her eye, who was electrocuted in front of her eyes in a Zurich shoe-shop. Reduced to a state of chronic melancholy, she found no comfort in religion. 'She never went to Mass. God, she repeated often, had done her too much evil. He was absurd, he was pointless, perhaps he was wicked. It was worse for her than doubting his existence. An empty universe is easier to face than a universe governed by cruelty.'

It was at this juncture in 1967 that Graham Greene, who since 1948 had spent some part of every year in his Anacapri home at 'Il Rosajo' and had a soft spot for the Dottoressa, suggested, by way of therapy, the compilation of her memoirs. In partnership with Kenneth Macpherson, he arranged for her to be interviewed by a Hungarian, who had not previously known her but was briefed about the main questions he should ask. 'Her words were recorded – in German – on tape. The result was then translated literally into English', in order 'to reproduce, if it was possible, the tone of her voice so unmistakably her own'. Macpherson was still working on the task of 'translating the translation', when in 1971 he died of a heart attack. Greene took up where Macpherson left off and finished the book just in time for the Dottoressa 'who had never believed it would be published . . . to hold a proof copy in her hands a few days before she died' in Switzerland on 23 February 1975, in her ninetieth year.[14]

*

A brief reference must be made to mainland Italians, mostly rich Romans and Milanesi, who had second homes in Capri and came there for their holidays. Regarded as 'foreigners' by the Capresi, they also kept to themselves; islanders and foreign residents were rarely asked to their homes.

There were, however, a few noteworthy exceptions. In 1948 Edda Ciano was back with two of her children, staying at the Manfredi Pagano. She regained possession of her villa on Castiglione, often stayed in the island and made friends with Pietro Capuano, who had a jewellery shop in Via Vittorio Emanuele, where in *Vestal Fire* days Lamberti had sold antiques. Eventually Edda got tired of Capuano, who did not fit well into her parties, where English was usually the language spoken, left the island and sold the villa, which was turned into mini-apartments; but she was back in Capri for Capuano's funeral in 1981. Signor Gazzoni, who owned a chemical plant near Bologna, both enjoyed Capri and added to its pleasure. Having a weak heart and afflicted with asthma, he had special dispensation to ride through the Piazza and along the pedestrians-only streets by car, mule or sedan-chair (*portantina*). He gave lavish parties, which because of his condition he could never attend himself. Conte Manfredi bought the Villa Vismara at Punta Tragara and in 1969–70 transformed it into a small, luxurious, hotel; he also acquired the villa next door, as an island home. Manfredi himself, a very rich Roman architect and property-owner, came and went, while his wife Enrica, a plump, warm-hearted blonde, very hospitable and *molto simpatica*, spent much of the year in her villa, ran the hotel through a manager and enjoyed the social round of Capri.

An Italian couple who established very firm roots in Capri were General Carlo Gardini and his wife Milly, whose house in Torina, perched up on the hill-slope below the cliff of Monte Santa Maria, commanded splendid views of the southern part of the island. Carlo, born in 1912, joined the Italian Army, and, after service in Spain in support of General Franco, in Abyssinia and East Africa, and on Rommel's staff in North Africa, became one of Italy's representatives on the staff of NATO. In 1951 he fell in love with Milly Prosdocimo, member of a well-to-do Venetian family and twenty years his junior, and married her. Milly had studied the piano with Cortot and was set to become a concert pianist, until tuberculosis brought an end to her career. After a last job in the Ministry of Defence in Rome, Carlo retired. In 1967 they came to Capri for a holiday, and, like so many others, fell hopelessly in love with the island. Almost immediately they met a *mediatore* who found them a dream house in Torina, which Milly called 'K 488' – Mozart's Piano Concerto No. 23 in A major. Dinner-parties at the Gardini house were always delightful for the guests, who, while they ate and drank on the terrace, could gaze at the dark outline of Castiglione, the twinkling marina and the fishing-boats, each with its light, like a swarm of fireflies, moving over the shimmering sea. Perhaps also they would have a chance to see the launches of the Naples Customs Police vainly chasing the faster boats of the *contrabbandieri* taking American cigarettes and drugs back to Naples after a rendezvous with some ship out at sea.

*

Turning to foreign residents of other nationalities, one need take a few examples only: some artists (in the broad sense of the word); some homosexuals; two American gangsters; two products of 'Old England'; and finally the hostesses and 'party girls' who did so much to engender pleasure. The life and death of Gracie and Boris, who were, of course, a powerful factor in the island, is treated as a subject on its own.

Starting with the authors, we have Roger Peyrefitte, novelist and one-time French diplomat, on a long visit to write the life of Baron Jacques d'Adelswärd-Fersen. He found the Villa Lysis unfurnished and uninhabited, its decoration decaying, its garden deserted and overgrown, the property of Felix Mechoulam, a Turk domiciled in Mexico, who had bought it as a speculation. Peyrefitte applied himself to the task of gathering information about the Frenchman, whose disruption of the foreign colony fifty years earlier is described so felicitously in *Vestal Fire*. To help him over Fersen's years in Capri, several living Capresi were able to provide first-hand information, and among his prime sources was Fersen's sister Germaine, the Marchesa Bugnano, who lived in Naples. *L'exilé de Capri* was published in 1959 – with a foreword by Jean Cocteau, who hoped that the book would 'serve to teach youth that beauty exists only if an inner beauty and hard work strive against and exorcise its arrogance; and that youth is an ephemeral privilege, not the attribute of a separate hardy race setting itself up in opposition to the decaying race of the old'.[15]

L'exilé de Capri is a judicious blend of fact and fancy – with enough of real people and what actually happened to put beside the imaginary encounters and conversations appropriate to the characters. Writing thirty years later than Mackenzie, Peyrefitte could safely be explicit about homosexual matters both male and female. He depicts the Wolcott-Perrys as attended, not by the faithful peasant family of *Vestal Fire*, but by a swarm of pretty girls, who are perpetually being enticed across the water by Principessa Soldatenkov to the Villa Siracusa at Sorrento. Norman Douglas, ready-made for inclusion in a Peyrefitte novel, philosophises to Fersen about hermaphrodites, Uranists and the unwisdom of choosing a Roman rather than a *caprese* boy as his 'secretary'. Apart from a few errors of fact,[16] the book is marred by the author's obsession with homosexuality and an endless parade of homosexuals – distinguished northerners haunting the grottoes, aristocratic *recchioni* in Naples, the goings-on at the Villa Siracusa etc., etc. – who are sometimes only peripheral to the plot. Its value lies in being a reasonably accurate and readable account of a strange character, who was both tragic and comic, vain, theatrical and flamboyant, sensitive and kind, and who left his mark on Capri both as a legend and as the builder of a very uncomfortable house, which no one else has ever wanted to live in and which has already begun to collapse. Some consider that it should be preserved as a cultural monument, but no one knows where the money for its restitution can be found. Unlike any other Caprese or foreigner, Fersen became the central character of *two* important books, one of which (*Vestal Fire*) is the most valuable account of early twentieth-century Capri.

Graham Greene's *An Impossible Woman – The Memories of Dottoressa Moor*, which was published later in 1975, was widely read in Capri, but not well received. The Dottoressa, always a bit fanciful (*un po fantasiosa*) at the best of times, was, when the memories were collected from her, in her eighties, and not a little confused. Add to this the fact that Greene, as he mentions in his Editor's note, had not 'hesitated on occasions to insert memories which did not appear on the tapes because the right question was not asked'. We are, therefore, presented with a book which contains some inaccuracies.[17]

Amongst those who felt that the book might have profited from factual research were two of Greene's island acquaintances and admirers of his novels and stories, Francis and Shirley Steegmuller. Both were experienced writers, he American and she Australian by birth, and they had, like Greene, been visiting Capri for many years – separately and sporadically at first, but after their marriage in 1963, regularly and for long periods. In 1971 they rented a flat in Via Sopramonte, decided not to instal a telephone and communicated with their friends through notes left at a *caffè* on the Piazza. In the flat, hoping, often in vain, to remain undisturbed, they did much of their writing, returning, usually in the late autumn, to their home in New York. While they shared with Greene a deep affection for Capri, the nature of their interest in it was different. Greene deliberately distanced himself from the inner life of the island, never learnt to speak Italian and spent much of his time writing in the serenity of Il Rosajo. The Steegmullers by contrast were interested in every aspect of Capri, conversed with the islanders in their own tongue and kept themselves *au fait* with current affairs. Politically liberal, they were deeply disturbed by the ceaseless triumph of private gain over public interest; by the unimpeded march of unauthorised building and of new building whose authorisation seemed to be at variance with the law.

Despite the unfavourable reception accorded to his book about the Dottoressa, Graham Greene was rightly regarded as one of the greatest living novelists, a master of his native language, and the latest in a line of distinguished English writers who had loved the island and written in and about it. In recognition of his literary standing, a movement was launched in Anacapri to confer on him honorary citizenship of the *comune*, and on 30 September 1978 leading citizens and officials of Anacapri and distinguished guests, among them the Archbishop of Sorrento and Gracie Fields, gathered in the council chamber to see him presented with the document of citizenship, and with a bronze medal bearing his effigy and a commemorative inscription, made by a local potter. In a brief speech of thanks, which was delivered in English and translated into Italian by Laetitia Cerio, the new citizen spoke warmly of two islanders who had been his friends since his arrival at Il Rosajo 30 years earlier; of the 'magic of Monte Solaro', which had influenced all his books during these three decades; and of 'a quiet and happiness in Anacapri, which he had found nowhere else in the world'.[18] The ceremony ended with a concert, at which a guitar arrangement of *The Third Man* theme was played.

Simon Elwes, the English portrait-painter, spent long periods in Capri during the 'fifties and 'sixties. Sixth son of Gervase Elwes, the celebrated tenor and singer of oratorio, in 1926 Simon married the Hon. Gloria (Golly) Rodd, daughter of the 1st Lord Rennell of Rodd, who had been British Ambassador in Rome from 1908 to 1919. The painter was continuously unfaithful to his wife and soon after World War II, he took refuge in Capri, where he relaxed and painted, and enjoyed his freedom. During the war he had suffered a stroke on his right side, which compelled him to paint thereafter with his left arm. He lived contentedly with his *amica* 'Miggie' – Margherita Minnigerone Contessa Willaumez – an American, one-time interior decorator, who had known Capri since her childhood and like Elwes was in love with it. A flamboyant, elegant figure, with big straw hat, red kerchief and a silver-topped black stick, Elwes painted when he felt inclined and enjoyed himself, until in 1967, the year in which he was elected Royal Academician, he returned to his family and a more sedate life in England, where he painted expensive portraits of the rich and fashionable until he died in 1975. Miggie stayed in Capri and started a love affair with a Caprese, which continued until her death in 1972.

In April 1967 David Rawnsley, potter and sculptor, inherited 'Dil-Aram', in the woods of Anacapri below Monte Solaro, from his mother Violet. Before he came to Capri, David had founded the Chelsea Pottery Guild, which still flourishes at 13 Radnor Walk. After two unsuccessful marriages, in 1947 he married Mary Doran, an Irish girl, but this did not go well either, and in 1961, in a deplorable act of abandonment, he returned alone to the family home in Anacapri, leaving her in charge of four young sons with a fifth on the way.

Rawnsley, as well as being a capable potter, could also express himself in drawing, painting and sculpture. While continuing to live at Dil-Aram, he created a small studio at Marina Piccola, where he practised his art and, in particular, did portraits in terracotta and bronze – the moulds taken from his *maquettes* and the subsequent bronze-casting being done by a firm in Naples. He was also a campaigner against the slaughter of small birds in Capri. Much of the senseless killing, which included harmless and inedible song-birds, took place shortly after dawn in the Anacapri woods. Cases of injury to innocent pedestrians in the area were not uncommon, as well as deliberate shooting at islanders who were known to oppose the killing of birds, and the noise was tiresome for those who wanted to sleep. When there were no birds available, the gallant sportsmen shot lizards instead. The authorities did nothing to help the situation and granted licences for shot-guns without any requirement of knowing how to use them or valid reason for possessing them.[19]

As a person Rawnsley aroused mixed feelings. Many of the islanders liked him on account of the interest he took in them and the island. He did

not appeal, however, to some of his fellow-countrymen, who, while acknowledging his qualities as sculptor and potter, found him *antipatico* – insecure, tactless, with an uneven temper, inclined to be hearty, and something of a prig. He died in 1977, but not before marrying for the fourth time and producing yet another son.

Finally, two musicians. Harold Gomberg, one of the world's leading oboists, came with the New York Philharmonic Orchestra to the 1951 Edinburgh Festival. During the Festival he telephoned his wife Margaret in America and said, 'Let's meet in Naples.' They went over to Capri for the day, decided to stay for longer and after many later visits bought a small house near Palazzo Canale, where they still spend much of their time.

Capri always welcomed Jack Emerson and his wife, who usually stayed from April to September at the Manfredi Pagano. A professional singer, he knew several languages, had a good sense of humour and, all were agreed, was *molto simpatico*. Usually dressed in a bath-robe, he talked to everybody and became a great connoisseur of the island. His favourite scenario was Pizzolungo, on the south coast, where he found the acoustics excellent and often went to sing opera, classical songs and Neapolitan ditties. Emerson was one of the few who disliked Gracie Fields, whom he called 'Grasi Filide' (*sifilide* = syphilis).

Capri had lost nothing of its appeal for foreign homosexuals. Maurice Yates, a Capri-addict of many years, who had done interior decorating for Indian princes and designed the film-sets for *The Bridge of San Luis Rey* and *Captain Kidd*, had settled in Anacapri in 1932, and had known both Gwen Galatà and Harold Trower. Uprooted by the war, he returned soon after it and amused himself by identifying some of the characters in Mackenzie's *Vestal Fire* and *Extraordinary Women* and seeing where they lived. He scored a success by finding in Naples an album, which must have belonged to one of the 'extraordinary women', with contemporary snapshots of Mackenzie himself and the main characters in his book. Yates and Kenneth Macpherson toyed with the idea of publishing new editions of both Mackenzie's books, with identifications of the characters and photographs of them and their villas, but nothing came of the project. Yates never found in Capri a house which suited him and moved over to Procida, where he had a lover, but he was often in Capri to see his friends. He found Procida constricting and rather dull, he was occasionally robbed by young men he had taken in for the night, and returned to Capri, where he rented a small flat, which was not large enough to accommodate his numerous possessions, but at least enabled him to enter into the social round, enliven parties with his scandalous gossip, and entertain English friends visiting the island. He died in 1981.

An American, Bob Hornstein, earned himself the reputation of *gran pederasta.* Very rich from business interests in the States, he arrived soon after World War II, lived first in a small house at the south end of Via Tragara, and in 1960 bought the Villa Capricorno at the other end of Tragara, where, secluded behind its walls and spacious gardens, he indulged his fancies. When not in the villa, he was often to be found sun-bathing with his friends on the beach below the Canzone del Mare, where Gracie had given him a private corner. Tolerant as the Capresi usually are of the sexual behaviour of foreigners, particularly when they are rich, and although they liked the money 'Mr Bob' spent in the island during his long stay, there was a feeling that his ruthless seduction of young men, whom he would sometimes reduce to a state of helplessness with drugged wine and of whom one had to be sent for hospital treatment in Naples, exceeded acceptable limits, and for a time he was banned from the island. Hornstein was a very emotional man and when he got worked up would scream at people; he was reputed to have a special room in the Villa Capricorno, where he could cry alone. An English visitor who knew and disliked him described Hornstein as 'a thin, leering monster – very nasty – never affable – a bundle of misery'.

The island was much enjoyed by two American gangsters, Mike Spinelli and 'Lucky' Luciano. Soon after his deportation from the States, Spinelli came to Capri and rented a house. Looking superficially like a retired gentleman, with white hair and a benign expression, it was only his steely eyes that gave away a ruthless character. He gave good parties, and had a German girl-friend, whom everyone found very boring. Luciano, born in Sicily as Salvatore Luciana, had emigrated to the United States as a boy and eventually become a prominent figure in New York criminal life during the Prohibition era of the 'twenties. Tried on several counts in 1936, he was convicted and sentenced to a long term of imprisonment. In 1946 Governor Thomas E. Dewey of New York, who as district attorney had successfully prosecuted Luciano, commuted his sentence and had him deported to Sicily, where this mastermind of the American under-world seems to have been taken for a ride by the *real* mafia.[20] He settled down in Naples, and frequently came over to Capri to enjoy himself and see Spinelli. With Luciano too appearances were misleading. Tall, very elegant, quiet, with gold-rimmed spectacles, he looked like a retired professor and this was the impression created for Gloria Magnus on his first visit to her restaurant at Marina Piccola. His end is said to have been unimpressive. There was a plan to make a film about his life, and in January 1962 the company concerned with the project sent a representative to Naples to discuss it with him. Luciano went to the airport to meet him and there dropped down dead.

'Old England' was represented by two ladies of widely differing character, culture and outlook, who, in choosing Capri, had one thing in common, a desire to escape from their respective husbands – Gloria Magnus, a cockney; and Lady Archibald, wife of Sir Robert Archibald, the distinguished authority on tropical diseases.

We must consider Gloria at some length because she made an important contribution to the annals of pleasure in Capri. Born in 1908, Gloria grew into an attractive young woman and at the age of 19½ married Harold Haverson, a grandson of George Lansbury, feeling very romantic, but without any experience of sex. The marriage was not a success, and, after six years of vainly trying to get her to coincide with his own rapid and vigorous sexual performance, Haverson got bored and went off with another woman. Gloria took dancing lessons and learnt the art of deportment ('contra-body movement') from Victor Silvester, and became an accomplished dancer in the 'ballroom' and 'Spanish' styles. When she was 28 she married Manfred Magnus, a Jew from Portugal. He was good and kind, but his family hated her for being a Gentile, and in an attempt to improve her standing with them Gloria studied Hebrew. Magnus was short and fat, and his member was, to quote Gloria, 'like a pimple on the dome of St Paul's'. Unlike Haverson he was very lazy in matters of sex, which he found difficult because of his shape, and there were no children. With another Jew, Oscar Deutsch, Magnus started a scrap-metal business, which became extremely lucrative, and he emerged from World War II a very rich man. In the post-war years Gloria lived in the lap of luxury and saw much of the world. In 1949 they visited Capri, and here Gloria met Pietro Cerrotta, then a boatman. His mother's family were peasants who cultivated a bit of land near Tiberio, kept a few animals, and had a fishing-boat. His father was a coral fisherman and, being very poor, went to South America several times to earn money and each time he returned added a new bit to the family house near Due Golfi. The Cerrottas had attracted the nickname 'occhi d'argento', because of the silver-grey colour of their eyes. Pietro, who had inherited these eyes, was also a *scorpio* and, according to Gloria, 'very deep'. Pietro and his brother-in-law Antonio Guarracino[21] carried cargo to and from the mainland, caught tunny, and during the tourist season took visitors round the island and on trips to Amalfi and Paestum. It was thus that Gloria encountered Pietro. They were immediately attracted to each other and before long were living together. Magnus did nothing to thwart the affair and in due course they were divorced. In 1953 Gloria and Pietro decided to start a restaurant at Marina Piccola, and for this purpose rented part of the Pensione Weber. The 'Ristorante da Pietro' was an instant success. Although the menu was limited, the cooking was excellent; its situation, with a sunny terrace overlooking the sparkling sea, was ideal; and above all there was Gloria, who came free with every course. Attractive, vivacious and warm-hearted, she was usually dressed in tailored trousers (shorts in hot

Gloria Magnus with a selection
of British sailors, c. 1955

Gracie and Boris, June 1963.
Photo: *Press Association*

weather), a jersey and one of a number of turbans, of which Carmen Miranda would have been proud; sang as she worked; talked a mixture of Cockney and fragments of other languages; and gave orders to the kitchen in inaccurate Italian. Thus *frittura di pesce* (fried fish) became *fregatura mista* (*fregatura* means 'swindle'). The restaurant, which was open throughout the winter, when the Canzone del Mare was closed, soon became a 'must' for all visitors – tourists, celebrities on holiday, and all ranks of the NATO base at Pozzuoli. Noël Coward ate there, and Gloria was the inspiration of 'Mrs Wentworth Brewster' in his 1955 song 'A Bar on the Piccolo [*sic*] Marina'. Rex Harrison ungallantly told her that she would have been the ideal Eliza Doolittle – 'but you're a bit old now'. British warships passed close inshore and blew their hooters, to which Gloria would respond by waving a table-cloth from the terrace. Gloria had many ships' plaques which were proudly displayed.

All this success infuriated the native restaurateurs at Marina Piccola, who took legal action in an attempt to have her removed from the island. All aliens then required work-permits and, as Pietro's *amica*, she lacked the security which marriage would have provided. Pietro and Gloria defended the case, won it, and the restaurant continued to flourish.

One day an old man and his wife came to eat there. As he was leaving, he complimented Gloria on her deportment and asked if she had ever taken dancing lessons. 'Yes', she said, 'I was taught by Victor Silvester and won competitions.' He said nothing, presented his card and departed, before she had time to look at the card and grasp that fifty years on she had again met her illustrious dancing-master.

When the restaurant closed in 1976, Gloria, still a notable character but in a more sober turban, frequented the Hotel Sanfelice, which Pietro and his brother Don Costanzo, the parish priest, had opened in Capri town. She never ceased to make new friends and spent every winter in London. In 1984 illness made a London visit impossible and finally she succumbed on Boxing Day, a few days short of her seventy-seventh birthday.

Lady Archibald, accompanied by her daughter, Anne, left her husband in Rhodesia and came on a holiday to Capri, where Anne fell for Vittorio Gargiulo, who taught gymnastics and painting in the *scuola media*. Anxious to be near him, she got a job as secretary in the NATO Headquarters at Pozzuoli. Her mother, although displeased at the idea of having a 'spaghetti boy' as her son-in-law, did not press the point, and they were married in 1953. In 1955 Anne left her NATO job, went to live in the Gargiulo family home on Via Matermania, while they built themselves a house nearby. In 1957, for something to do, she opened a boutique, 'Oriane' (Vitt*o*rio & *An*ne) in Via Fuorlovado. In 1970, emboldened by its success, she moved the shop to the fashionable Via Camerelle.

Lady Archibald herself was one of the last outposts of Empire. Like

Gwen Galatà many years earlier, she raised the Union Jack on the Queen's Birthday, and sat down to Christmas dinner with turkey, plum-pudding and mince-pies sent out from Harrods; the tea-party was her favourite form of entertainment. She had a good sense of humour, was a keen gardener, stumped about the island in tweeds and sensible shoes, thought all Italians except her son-in-law were beyond the pale, and had only one word of the language – *contadino* – which for her summed up the Capresi one and all. She hated all the gossip for which Capri is famous, because she thought it wrong to talk about people 'behind their backs'. Gloria, who revered Lady Archibald, called her 'my Rock of Gibraltar'.

Party-giving and party-going occupied much of the foreign residents' time. Their festivities and pursuit of pleasure rested on the solid foundation of hosts and hostesses who were rich and, because they enjoyed Capri so much, were prepared to wink at the extent to which they were often 'taken for a ride' by the islanders.

There were four 'party girls' who in their diverse ways added to the gaiety of the island during this period – Norma Clark, Laura Gould, Emily Earl and Blanche Dunn.

Norma Clark, Norwegian by birth, came to Capri after a divorce from Clark, head of Singer sewing-machines. With a settlement from him and with money of her own, she lived first at the Gatto Bianco and then at a villa near Pizzolungo. A woman of tremendous verve and charm, she gave splendid parties. 'Marvellous. Blonde. Very beautiful. A darling,' was the verdict of a resident Englishwoman. Going to bed at 5 a.m. after all-night revels, she would be up at 10 o'clock fresh as a daisy and ready for another party. She entrusted the running of her affairs to a Caprese, who did very well out of her, and finally, having blued most of her money, she returned to Norway.

Drink was the sustaining force for Laura Gould, who got through a bottle of gin every day. Originally a chorus-girl, she married the son of an American oil tycoon. Having divorced him, she married an English actor and lived with him in London for many years. She divorced him too, came to Capri and took a flat in the Palazzo Cerio. Rich, elegant, with short grey hair, civilised, intelligent and liked by everyone, she loved entertaining and, when not giving parties, was a voracious reader. She found a Neapolitan lover and they lived happily together for several years, but he died first and, becoming old and lonely, she soon followed him to the grave.

Emily Earl, a rich American from Virginia, came first in 1947–8, loved the island and later took a home on Via Tragara. Drunk for much of the time, beautiful and beautifully dressed, to be seen at all parties, she was a woman of uncertain moods – cordial one day and rude the next – and thus lacked the popularity of Norma Clark and Laura Gould. She fell in love with her gardener, a rough *contadino*, who readily obliged her for the sake of the handsome pickings. On the first of April 1957 she took an overdose of sleeping pills and died, three days short of her fifty-second birthday. Gloria, who then had a flat on Tragara and was on her way down to the restaurant, encountered the coffin being trundled along on a barrow and with an English friend roused a small party of mourners to go down to the cemetery and give Emily a send-off. Meanwhile Capresi invaded the house to get their hands on what they could – and not much of value remained by the time Emily's daughter arrived to settle her mother's affairs. She was buried in the suicides' corner of the non-Catholic cemetery and over the grave was put a tombstone inscribed: 'To love and be loved and to die in eternal light.'

Blanche Dunn was exceptional as a foreign resident, in that she was black, albeit rather ashamed of the fact and given to powdering and plastering herself, in order to look a bit lighter. Born in Jamaica, she had lived for many years in Harlem, where she had been a successful dancer and great friend of the actress and singer Elizabeth Welch. Blanche came to Capri, loved it (except for its thunderstorms of which she had a permanent phobia), stayed at the Gatto Bianco and then took an apartment on the lower side of Tragara, where she often gave parties. As a rule Blanche's conversation was limited to stories about her profession, and she was also a considerable name-dropper. Those who saw much of her found this tedious, but being black and, therefore, 'different', she was an object of interest to new acquaintances. Warm-hearted, feminine, hospitable, Blanche's ability to live comfortably and cover herself with the jewellery she habitually wore, rested on the solid foundation of being the mistress of one of the Scandinavian ambassadors in Rome, whom she had met first in America and who gave her an allowance and often came to Capri to embrace her. One day the neighbours heard screams coming from her flat and found Blanche with a copy of an American paper recording how the ambassador had been killed by his wife who had then shot herself. Blanche pulled herself up, continued to enjoy Capri and give good parties, until in 1979 after a stroke she died in her sleep. Although Blanche was an unbeliever, a *caprese* married-couple who were fond of her arranged for her burial in the Catholic cemetery with a life-size bronze of her head to stand beside the tomb.

Two notable hostesses of the 'sixties and early 'seventies were Doreen Berrill and Lady Kitchen, who were friends and had many guests in common. Doreen, born in Fiji, had wanted to be a ballet dancer, but because this was not respectable had taught ballet instead. When her husband Adrian retired from the chairmanship of the Central News Agency in South Africa, they returned to the northern hemisphere and divided their time between England and Capri, where they rented a flat.

Doreen became very attached to Capri and soon began to spend most of the year there. For three or four years Adrian did the same, but then, unable to tolerate any longer the avariciousness of the islanders – 'greedy peasants', he called them – decided to live in England, and visited Capri only occasionally. Before he uprooted himself, he threatened to suspend a banner inscribed 'SEMPRE DI PIÙ' across the Piazza. Doreen took the garden in hand, gave a home to some of the island's many stray cats, and became one of the island's leading hostesses. Her parties were always managed by Tonino Esposito, of the Hotel Gatto Bianco, but, except for dinner-parties, these took place in her house and garden. Doreen discovered that servants had not changed much since the early days of the century, when Harold Trower had found them 'not very honest' and Compton Mackenzie had noted the various devices they used to inflate the household books of foreign employers (what the Chinese call 'squeeze').[22]

A hostess who entertained on the same scale as Doreen Berrill was Joan Kitchen, wife since 1946 of Sir Geoffrey Kitchen, Chairman of Pearl Assurance and director of numerous companies. Described by Doreen as 'shrewd Yorkshire', Lady Kitchen had known Capri for many years before the war and had been drawn to it not least by her affection for one of the islanders. The late spring of 1940 found her in Capri, where by chance she met and impressed Count Ciano, who told her that she must leave immediately, to avoid internment. He conducted her personally to North Italy and literally pushed her across the frontier into France, just before Italy entered the war. Both the Kitchens loved Capri and spent much of their time there. At first they took an apartment, but later, disgusted by the relentless increase of rent, moved to the congenial and festive Gatto Bianco, where the Esposito brothers provided an admirable base for her parties, until Sir Geoffrey's death in December 1978 and her own return to England.

Gracie and Lady Kitchen were old friends and, until Boris limited her social activities, she came not only to the grand parties but also to more intimate gatherings in Gemma's *pizzeria*, where Gracie would sometimes sing for the pleasure of the guests, while passers-by in Via Madre Serafina would pause and listen.[23]

Gracie and Monty, who had returned to the island in 1945, were soon compelled to spend periods abroad to earn a living again. A major anxiety for Gracie was Monty's addiction to gambling: 'horses, cards, the wheel, two flies on a wall – he'd put his shirt on anything,' Gracie later told Denis Pitts, 'trouble was – it was usually my bloody shirt'.[24] After she had done shows, concerts and recordings, and Monty had taken a character part in a film which needed an Italian accent, they again based themselves on Capri and, as well as continuing to modernise the *fortino*, decided to create a restaurant and Capri's first swimming-pool – the whole complex to be called 'La Canzone del Mare' (The Song of the Sea). Work on the swimming-pool involved blasting the rocky terraces, to create enough level ground, which temporarily polluted the sea below, and there were cries of outrage that they were ruining the natural beauty of the island. It was at this point that John Flanagan, poor and miserable, paid a flying visit to the island. Whether or not he saw Gracie is not recorded, but he descended on Ettore Patrizi and complained furiously about the Canzone, which had ruined what he had loved. Ettore tried to calm him by telling him what in fact was true, that Monty and not Gracie was the motive force behind the new restaurant and swimming-bath.

In January 1950 Monty died of a heart attack. Never one to give in to private sorrow, Gracie threw herself again into show business, travelled, and, when she was not working, filled the *fortino* with relations and friends. One day somebody broke her automatic record-player and a friend suggested asking Boris Alperovici to repair it. Gracie 'liked his quietness, his steady blue eyes, his unhurried, peaceful conversation', grew more fond of him, and before long they decided to get married. Shortly before the marriage in 1952 Edwin Cerio, who had known Boris for twenty years or more, wrote Gracie a fulsome letter, extolling Boris's virtues, his 'unswerving, true, lovable character . . . profound technical knowledge and constitutional honesty . . . perfectly blended with disinterestedness and reliability'.[25]

Gracie, who knew nothing of Boris's background, had no reason to question Cerio's account. Besides she loved Boris, and when six months later he said that he had found a good housekeeper for them, named Irene Bonus, Gracie enthusiastically took her on. In these days Gracie, who was in her mid-fifties and had all the money, kept the upper hand at the Canzone, where, apart from the restaurant staff, she had a cook, general servant, gardener and caretaker. Content, as never before since the days of John Flanagan, Gracie spent most of her time in the island and became an Italian citizen in 1959. Boris's technical skill was useful in the development of the swimming-pool, and together they raised the Canzone into a *ristorante molto confortevole* (three spoons-and-forks in Baedeker), with swimming and sunbathing, where visitors could spend a pleasant time and have the added excitement of meeting Gracie herself. This was the cause of an early disagreement which was never resolved. Boris, though poor, was a snob and despised Gracie's working-class fans who came to the Canzone, particularly when Gracie insisted on waiving the usual locker-fee of 1,000 *lire* and allowing them to bathe free. But even Gracie objected when they brought picnics as well, and it was made a rule that visitors who wanted to make a day of it must also eat in the restaurant. In character Gracie and Boris were completely different – she, warm, outgoing, generous, unselfconscious and always happy to be 'on stage'; he, cold, calculating, close-fisted and perpetually concerned about his appearance. Gracie called him 'Mr Clean', because he was so often in the bathroom, washing and grooming himself, so that his nails, hands, hair and clothes might always be immaculate; every day he had a man to shave him and do his hair. Nor did it take her long to become uneasy about his relationship with Irene. Boris and Irene had met in the Cerio household, where she had been nanny to Giorgio Cerio's love-child Amabel.

The Canzone was not only something special for Gracie's admirers, but also attracted many visitors who wanted to enjoy good food and a swim amidst the enchanting surroundings of Marina Piccola. The boatman Costanzo Federico, nicknamed 'Pataniello' (small potato), was on hand with his motor-boat to provide a *giro dell' Isola*. In a pleasant *piazzetta* near the Canzone, there was an Emilio Pucci *alta moda* boutique, where visitors could spend their money; and after their swim they could be massaged by Glauco Di Bella. A good-looking young man of Sicilian origin, Glauco had from his youth led a varied life of work and pleasure. After sowing his wild oats, mainly in South Africa, Glauco learned the art of massage at a school in Rome and, having rented a room from Gracie at the Canzone, pursued his new trade; Gracie herself refused to be massaged by Glauco, who as a rule required his patients, of whichever sex, to remove all their clothes. In 1972 he moved up to a room under the swimming-pool at the Quisisana, where he found a better class of client and surrounded his massage-parlour with their photographs and expressions of approval, including one from Roger Peyrefitte: '*Pour Glauco di Bella, dont le nom représente si bien son île de Capri – glauque comme le couleur des yeux de Minèvre, et beau comme le roc immortel de ce lieu . . . et comme lui.* Capri 12. viii. 79.'

The year 1970 found the Canzone del Mare in full swing. Holiday-makers galore, who wanted a glimpse of Gracie, happily paid for what was now a very expensive day of swimming, sun-bathing and eating. There were still Lancastrians in braces who just wanted to dip their toes in Gracie's pool. There were constant demands to photograph her in or out of the pool, and in the goodness of her heart she usually obliged, although sometimes feeling 'like a bloody performing seal', often being kept wet for long periods at a time.[26] Gracie and Boris were to be seen posing confidently beside the pool, but all was not well with their marriage, as Denis Pitts, who at that time was engaged in making a BBC documentary about Gracie, discovered. In a series of interviews with him Gracie poured out her heart about her three unhappy marriages, telling a story which differed notably from what the world believed and what she had already recounted in her autobiography *Sing as we go*. She told Pitts about the misery of her marriage to Archie Pitt; her escape into the love affair with John Flanagan, which led her to Capri; how the charming but scatty Monty Banks had gambled away much of her fortune. Finally she revealed how unhappy she was with Boris, who disliked her singing and despised the very thing that had made her the special woman she was – her public. 'He likes the money they bring in, does Boris, but he doesn't like the working-class English – my sort of people. He's a bit of a snob, is Boris.' Pitts soon realised that Gracie was scared of Boris, who let it be known that he was opposed to the whole idea of a BBC film about her. Finally, on the pretext that Gracie had bronchitis, he ordered her to remain in their Anacapri home until the BBC team had left the island. Pitts promised to keep what she had told him locked away in his files until after her death. 'Wait till I'm dead, luv. Then you can tell the whole bloody world.'[27]

Gracie was now 72 and no longer strong enough to resist the domination of Boris, whom, notwithstanding his treatment of her, which included physical violence, she still loved. More and more he tended not to let Gracie out on her own, accompanied her whenever she went abroad and supervised her social life both in and out of the island. Boris had always been poor and hated spending money, so that under his control the household was maintained less and less for the sake of comfort and hospitality. Nevertheless he was generous to the poor of Anacapri and popular with them.

Not that Boris could or wanted to cut Gracie off from her friends in Capri, some of whom they had in common, and some not. Boris and Laetitia Cerio got on very well and he deputised for her as President of the Centro Caprense; Gracie, however, did not like Laetitia. Gracie saw a lot of Marchese Ettore Patrizi, whom she had known ever since her first visit to the *fortino* in 1927. Gossips talked of an affair between them, but it seems that they were no more than good friends. Anton Dolin, one time ballet-dancer and choreographer, and an inveterate traveller, six years her junior and a lifelong friend, often came to Capri with his friend John Gilpin, who owing to a thrombosis and operation on his legs had been compelled to give up a brilliant career as a dancer. A photograph of 1973 shows a happy group at the Canzone, and in 1975 Dolin and Gilpin spent a whole year in the island.

Gracie, with her warm and generous nature and big heart, was popular with the islanders. Aldo Aprea, who with Edwin Cerio had been a witness at her wedding in 1952, describes her simply as 'a wonderful woman'. By contrast Irene, an abrasive, humourless and German-looking Piedmontese, was not liked; her nickname was ''A Scupilla' (lavatory-brush), in part an illusion to her frizzy hair. Gracie had reservations about what she termed a 'beautiful but wicked island'. While often generous with her money, she hated the endemic avarice of the islanders, disliked being diddled, and, a true Lancastrian, bargained fiercely over the smallest purchases. To a large extent Gracie was thrown back on her own resources and her own memories. She had always been sentimental about people she liked and kept all their letters and photographs. She still cherished her love of John Flanagan, now long dead – a love which he had never returned with any fervour – and, because he was always poor, had sent him money from time to time.

In 1972 a ray of sunshine was brought into her life by an English girl, Hazel Provost, who had been a fan of Gracie since early years. In 1965 Hazel went with a friend to Capri and called on Gracie, made a good impression, and in the summer of 1972 Gracie employed her as a temporary *au pair* at the Canzone. Gracie took a strong liking to this attractive, capable and open-hearted girl, who had an earthy sense of humour and provided much-needed companionship in her difficult and lonely milieu, where English was seldom spoken and English humour rarely available. After the visit Gracie sent Hazel a signed photograph, inscribed 'love to Hazel my glamorous 1972 helper', and from March to November in every year except 1978 Hazel returned to act as general companion; to deal with correspondence both for Gracie and Boris; to go shopping with and for her; to do Gracie's hair; and to make tea, of which Gracie was inordinately fond ('I like me tea. It perks me up') and for the enjoyment of which she had installed innumerable kettles, tea-caddies, sugar-bowls, cups and mugs in the Canzone, where she usually spent the summer, and her Anacapri home, where she retired for the winter.[28] Gracie liked her tea strong, and one of Hazel's unsuccessful brews was greeted with, 'I did say tea, not pee.'

Another valued companion was the dog Sandy, which Gracie and Hazel acquired in 1973 at a fête given in Carney Park – the US Army's sportsground in an extinct volcano near the NATO base in Pozzuoli. Sandy, who was mainly Labrador, with possibly a touch of Great Dane, grew from an incontinent puppy into a large and vociferous guard-dog at the Canzone, and Gracie adored him. Sandy hated Italian men and got his teeth into them whenever he could. Gracie also found comfort in the support of Mario Pollio, her devoted caretaker at the Canzone.

In 1975 Gracie had a bad accident. As she was leaning against the balcony of the Canzone, the balcony collapsed, she fell on the concrete below and broke several ribs. When the news reached Professor Sol Cohen, the London surgeon, who was holidaying in Capri, he visited the hospital and was horrified to find her lying down. By pulling her to her feet, making her walk about and expand her chest, he thinks he may have saved her from pneumonia. Later he sent her some flowers, but these were not well received by Gracie, who had always regarded floral tributes as being associated with funerals. In 1976–7 she had a long and painful attack of shingles, and Hazel stayed on through the winter to nurse her.

Soon after the shingles had cleared up, she fell and broke a wrist. All these were severe trials for a woman nearing 80, who moreover lacked the comfort of a sympathetic husband and well-run home. In 1977 Gracie and Boris leased the restaurant and swimming-pool of the Canzone to the brothers Luigi and Giorgio Iacono,[29] which brought in a substantial rent, relieved them of a major responsibility, and from Gracie's point of view had the added advantage of the good food which was often sent up from the restaurant to her run-down house.

None of these misfortunes however could daunt her spirit, and she welcomed the opportunity to escape temporarily to England in 1978, when in her eighty-first year she crowned her career with a tenth Command Performance, in the presence of Queen Elizabeth The Queen Mother, who was two years her junior, exactly 50 years after her first appearance before royalty in 1928. The performance was in Rochdale, where she had come to open a new theatre named after herself – and here for the last time she sang 'The Biggest Aspidistra in the World' and 'Sally' – both of which she admitted to being tired of. She and Boris wintered in the United States and here on 19 January 1979 they both made their wills, leaving all their property to each other.[30] A final distinction came with her advancement in the New Year's Honours to Dame of the British Empire, and, having returned to England by Concorde, she went to Buckingham Palace to receive the insignia from The Queen Mother.

Back again in Capri Gracie felt tired and disinclined to see anyone. In July she went down with bronchial pneumonia and spent three weeks in the International Hospital in Naples. Amongst her visitors was the Rev. Edward Holland, Anglican chaplain of Christ Church, Naples, who found her, even in a hospital bed, still Gracie the performer and 'on stage'. She talked incessantly *at* him rather than *to* him and even sang a little. Hazel came to look after her during her convalescence at the Canzone and was with her until a week before she died. On what was to be her last day, lonely and exhausted, Gracie struggled up from the Canzone to Capri town to get the post, and then continued on to Anacapri to collect Boris. In the evening she went to bed without eating. On the morning of 27 September she took some coffee but did not get up. Finally she made some utterance which went unheeded, closed her eyes, rolled over and died.

The dead Gracie and her bed were moved to the sitting-room of the Canzone, and there she lay in state, surrounded by little chairs, on which the mourners, having been greeted by the weeping Irene and having kissed Gracie farewell, sat in silent contemplation. On the 28th Holland, having been summoned from Naples, said prayers over the body and agreed to conduct an ecumenical service in the cemetery on the following day. The steamers had chosen this day to go on strike, but he managed to get over by hydrofoil and hurried down to the Canzone. He found Gracie already in her coffin but without the lid on. He said a few prayers, the coffin was sealed, and six of the Canzone staff, dressed in white T-shirts and black trousers, took the coffin on their shoulders. They paused on the terrace and lifted the coffin above their heads to salute the sea-view Gracie had loved, while Sandy, not knowing what was happening, but certain that something was very wrong, barked incessantly. The coffin was put on a hearse, which drove up to Due Golfi, followed by mourners in taxis and buses. At Due Golfi the Canzone staff again shouldered the coffin, which was now decked with 27 deep-red roses from Boris for every year of their marriage. There were wreaths from Rochdale, friends in London and the BBC, and heaps of flowers from the islanders. The funeral procession, led by Boris, Gracie's brother Tommy, Giorgio Iacono and the chaplain, arrived at the cemetery and ascended the steps towards the Cerio mausoleum, where Gracie was to lie until her own tomb had been built. Here the procession was barred by an official of the Catholic cemetery, who directed the mourners back down the steps and into the non-Catholic cemetery at the bottom. The official having been persuaded that the Cerio mausoleum was their goal, the procession, now in considerable disorder and with little room to manoeuvre, advanced again up the steps to the mausoleum, where the coffin was deposited. The party had now been joined by a Roman Catholic priest, Don Giovanni Farella, and there was a discussion as to whether the funeral should be held in the mausoleum or in the chapel of the Catholic cemetery above. The latter having been chosen, the bearers again took up their burden and moved into the Catholic cemetery and along the central path to the cemetery chapel, where the chaplain conducted a short service and pronounced a benediction:

> Thank you, Lord, for the life of Gracie. Thank you for the warmth and joy she brought into the lives of so many. Thank you for her talents and dignity and appreciation of the beautiful things of this world and for all she had given to the world and especially to those who knew her.

As soon as the ceremony was ended, Farella departed and for half an hour the mourners circled round the coffin, commiserated with Boris and Irene, until it was carried back to the mausoleum where, urged by Irene, the chaplain, now alone with Boris and the dead Gracie, said a final prayer for Boris.

In due course Gracie's marble tomb was built beside the steps under the shadow of the Cerio mausoleum, where it could be seen by pilgrims without entering or indeed knowing that the non-Catholic cemetery existed at all; the tomb was even visible over the cemetery wall from a car or bus in the main road – an arrangement which conveniently absolved the Non-Catholic Cemetery Committee from taking any steps to improve its deplorable condition. The headstone was inscribed GRACIE FIELDS IN ALPEROVICI (Gracie Alperovici formerly Fields) 9.1.1898–27.9.1979, and on the tomb itself was placed a free-standing plaque with the words OUR GRACIE and the date of her death. Shortly after the entombment Hazel came out briefly to help, looked after the unhappy Sandy, who continued as guard-dog at the Canzone, and took turns with Boris and Irene to put flowers on the tomb.[31]

Boris died on 3 July 1983. The Canzone del Mare and the house in Anacapri, together with Boris's estate in the United Kingdom and the United States, which he had inherited from Gracie in 1979, went in equal shares to Gracie's brother Tommy, her sister Edith and nephew Anthony Parry. The estate in England was valued at £801,572 net and that in America at a minimum of $1.3 million.[32] Informed opinion put the value of the Canzone property – restaurant, swimming-pool, length of rocky beach, house and stretch of open hillside, which in its undeveloped state Gracie had bought in 1933 for £6,000 – at about 10 milliards of *lire* (around £4,300,000), because even without building on the untouched land, which was unlikely to receive permission, there was considerable scope for developing existing structures. When I visited Capri in May 1984 it was still the property of Gracie's relations, who continued to lease the restaurant and swimming-pool to the Iacono brothers and visit the *fortino*, which was their private property, from time to time; Irene was still housekeeper in Gracie's villa in Anacapri.

By an extraordinary coincidence the *fortino* property at Marina Grande also lost its châtelaine at this very same moment.

After the death from cancer in 1971 of Count Bismarck, Mona had married, as her fifth husband, a young Italian doctor, Umberto De Martino, who also called himself Conte. After his death in a car crash, Mona reverted to the title of Contessa Bismarck until her death in Paris in early July 1983. She left almost the whole of her estate, valued at $30 million, to the Mona Bismarck Foundation in the United States. In Capri there were legacies to her builder Ercole D'Esposito; to her hairdresser, Tonino D'Emilio, now retired and proprietor of the Albergo Canasta; and to Carlo Civitella, but he had died six months earlier. She left the staff of the *fortino* either 50,000 or 25,000 dollars each. Those who got the lesser sum were paid in cash; the 50,000 lot received the annual interest on the capital, which would, however, revert to the Foundation on their death.[33] It was reported that Mona's son by her first marriage intended to contest the will and invoke the Italian law which ordained that no more than a third of any estate could be left to an institution or political party if any offspring of the deceased was alive. Meanwhile the property remained sealed and inaccessible to all.

*

Much of bygone Capri has vanished or been transformed. The Hotel Pagano, whose foundation in 1826 marked the beginning of tourism, became 'Hotel La Palma', under new management, soon after World War II. Although the hotel prospered, it was decided that modern Capri needed a modern hotel, and between 1962 and 1964 the old building was demolished and a smart category I hotel was built in its place; into oblivion went all the festive murals by Jean Benner and other foreign artists of the nineteenth century. On 4 November 1966, its famous palm-tree was blown down in a gale. According to Teodoro Pagano, some of the roots of the palm-tree had been trimmed in such a way that, if it ever did fall, it would not fall on the new hotel. Others said that it had been deliberately weakened, and pulled down in a suitable gale, in order to make way for a new night-club, 'Las Vegas', which was built under the garden where the palm-tree had once stood.

Most of the villas of the *Vestal Fire* period have been divided into apartments. This fate has overtaken the Villa Torricella (Wolcott-Perry), Villa Narcissus (Coleman), Villa Mezzomonte (Palmes), Villa Alba and Cà del Sole ('Rory Freemantle') and Villa Discopoli (various owners and tenants). The Villa Castello, with its substantial garden, in the middle of the town, which is still in one piece, is the home of the Principessa di Sirignano and her colony of aristocratic cats. The Villa Tragara, with shades of Allers and Lady Mackinder, is owned by the Italian shipowner Giuseppe D'Amico, but he seldom visits it. Gorki's Villa Pierina, beside the Via Mulo, has taken on a new lease of life. Bought in 1913 by Enrico Scarciglia, it was restored, redecorated and furnished in opulent style by his son-in-law and daughter, Salvatore and Ornella De Martino, who also collected books by and about Gorki and formed a modest 'Gorki centre' in what was once his studio. Ornella, who owns other properties, is often in residence.

The Palazzo Inglese (Canale), built around 1745 for Sir Nathaniel Thorold; used as a hunting-lodge by the King of Naples; badly battered by French artillery in 1808; finally became an agglomeration of scruffy apartments. Until recently the property of two islanders, who drew rents from the 15 households which occupied it, in 1981 it was bought by a Neapolitan company which wanted to evict all the tenants and convert the *palazzo* into dozens of smart mini-apartments. The tenants who, if evicted, would find it extremely difficult to find anything else, banded together and prepared for battle. A compromise was reached whereby existing tenants retain their possession, but the owners have permission to make new apartments in parts of the *palazzo* which become vacant.

The Villa Fersen, sunless and windswept, houses a caretaker in part of the ground floor. The rest is crumbling, and already the roof and floor of the *salone* have collapsed into the Chinese room. Nobody can decide what to do with it.

Strangest of all was the fate of All Saints Church. It suffered severely during World War II. Taken over as enemy property after Trower's death in February 1941, it had been totally neglected and indeed forgotten, and was still in custody in March 1948, when Edwin Cerio reported to the British Vice-Consul in Naples that the structure was in an advanced state of decay. Originally the site had been acquired and the church built by private subscription, with the stipulation that it should not be sold without reference to the principal subscribers. Lawyers advised the SPG that, as it was impossible to trace the principal subscribers, who were either dead or scattered, a sale would be in order, and it was sold in October 1951 for 900,000 *lire* (£514) to Carlo Talamona,[34] who without delay built the Hotel La Pergola incorporating parts of the church in its structure. One of the walls of the church forms part of the bar, and the arch of the nave can still be seen in one of the double bedrooms. The furniture was scattered. Harmonium, pews and seats went to the Certosa, where the pews are still used for public functions in the monastery church; the garden-gate became the garden-gate of the Talamona house in Via Tuoro, where the brass lectern, missal-holder and paten repose in the drawing-room; and one of the candlesticks sits in the hall of the hotel.

*

The island is administered by two elected communal councils, each of 20 members and each headed by a mayor (*sindaco*), supported by career officials, who sit in Capri town and Anacapri respectively and are fiercely independent of each other. There are more problems in Capri than Anacapri, and this explains why in the *comune* of Capri there are frequent changes of *sindaco* and, when the administration collapses altogether, a *commissario prefettizio*, usually one of the *vice-prefetti*, is appointed by the provincial government. Under normal conditions the *sindaco*, while reserving to himself general control of the most important functions, delegates the detailed work to *assessori*, who are usually his leading *consiglieri*, or, if there is a coalition, include representatives of the parties who make up the government.

From 1957 to 1979, apart from two short gaps in 1962–5 and in 1970, the office of *sindaco* in Capri was held in turn by three local politicians –

Carlo Federico, Costanzo Lembo and Raffaele Di Stefano. Although there was stability in short doses, there was no coherent government over the period as a whole, because politically these three were rivals. Such stability as existed in the affairs of Capri was due in no small way to the permanent officials, who kept the wheels turning.

Carlo Federico, who at the age of 42 became *sindaco* in 1957, was politically on the right but *independente*; he was an admirer of the pragmatic Tommaso De Tommaso, *sindaco* of Anacapri. Federico held the post of Professore di Scienza in the *liceo*, the State-run secondary school for 15- to 18-year-olds, situated in the Certosa, and was married to the hotel-owning Venere, daughter of Antonio Esposito. As a character, Carlo was brisk, lively and quick-witted; as an administrator, strict and unresponsive to outside influences.

In 1960 Federico was followed as *sindaco* for two years by Costanzo Lembo, who had already held office briefly in 1947–48. Lembo was born in 1914, the son of another Costanzo, who was brother of the *parroco*, Don Luigi Lembo. Young Costanzo's mother was Luigia Desiderio, whose uncle Luigi had built the Villa Torricella. Costanzo the father died shortly after his marriage and before the birth of his son. Luigia, although young and attractive, never remarried, not from lack of inclination or opportunity, but because in those days no respectable widow could remarry without incurring the gravest censure, and so poor Luigia had to bring up young Costanzo entirely on her own. The boy followed the traditions of his mother's family and became an architect and builder. In 1960 he married Maria Mellino, once the belle of Marina Piccola. Lembo was nominally Democrazia Cristiana (DC), but his political stance proved difficult to determine – 'tutti colori', said one venerable Caprese, making a circling motion with his hand.

Raffaele Di Stefano, the third of these political rivals, was born in 1920, son of Felice ('Felicione') Di Stefano and Tersilia Federico, and, through his mother, first cousin of Raffaele Vuotto. Around 1870 his great-grandfather Felice had started a butcher's shop at what is now 5–7 Via delle Botteghe, just off the Piazza. The business had continued profitably under his grandfather Costantino and his father Felice, who was said to have kept all his money at home in a large chest. Supported by his good and capable wife Giovanna (Di Franco), Raffaele carried on the butcher's shop, which provided a steady income on top of his inherited capital. He soon accumulated enough wealth to become a money-lender, and one of the richest men in the island, known universally as 'Il macellaio'. Politically DC, he was elected *consigliere* in 1954 and chosen to be *assessore* for public works and trade. He was *vice-sindaco* to Costanzo Lembo from 1960 to 1962, but did not himself become *sindaco* until 1968. Di Stefano was intelligent, quick, shrewd and wary. He did much of his business, whether political or financial, in the butcher's shop, which was popularly known as 'Il Comune'.

In 1970, when Di Stefano was *sindaco*, Capri made one of its rare appearances on a wider stage. As the centenary of Lenin's birth, the year was celebrated by communists worldwide. The Italian Communist Party (PCI), having cast around for a suitable venue, discovered that in 1908 and 1910 Lenin had stayed briefly in Capri for discussions with Gorki and other Russian exiles, and had clearly enjoyed himself there. In February 1969, therefore, a PCI *consigliere* proposed that a monument to Lenin be erected in some public place, and at a meeting, attended by only a minority of the 20 *consiglieri*, there was a narrow vote in favour of the proposition.[35] Giacomo Manzù devised a *stēlē* with a portrait of Lenin in relief, which was erected in the children's playground of the Villa Krupp – the public *parco-giardino* presented to the people of Capri 70 years earlier by the ill-fated 'King of Guns'. Perhaps the communists saw in this spot the chance for Lenin to exorcise the demon of Krupp, in the same way as the statue of Santa Maria del Soccorso had been placed above the ruins of the Villa Iovis, to expiate the sins of Tiberius. Manzù's *stēlē* was unveiled on 21 April 1970 in the presence of the Soviet Ambassador, the Secretary-General of the Associazione Italia-URSS and a delegation of the Soviet Communist Party. The monument was not universally popular, and a year later it was daubed with fascist symbols and slogans by three young men of the political 'right'. It still stands in the children's playground – the only commemorative portrait of a foreigner to be erected by the Capresi in a public place.

In November 1972 Di Stefano came temporarily unstuck when he was arrested on charges of corruption and was briefly imprisoned.[36] His popularity, however, with at least part of the population, remained undimmed, and on his return from prison, to continue as *sindaco*, he was greeted with fireworks. His administration was again embarrassed in February 1974, when the rubbish beside the *bruciatore* collapsed down the cliff, overwhelmed a house and killed the occupants.

In 1975 Di Stefano was succeeded as *sindaco* by Lembo, who at the head of a breakaway group of four Christian Democrats (DC) opposed to Di Stefano, formed a coalition with three Socialists (PSI) and three Communists (PCI). The coalition fell apart in May 1979. Since the opposition also numbered ten, local government temporarily collapsed and Naples was asked to appoint a *commissario prefittizio*, who visited the island on Tuesdays and Thursdays, while the day-to-day work of administration lay with the officials. The *segretario*, Nicola Miele, lived in Naples and spent much of his time there. The main burden, therefore, fell on Mario Ferraro, the *vice-segretario* and his staff; the island owes much to their devotion and hard work.

Raffaele Vuotto; Raffaele Di Stefano; and the 'Scialpopolo' party for the 1981 *festa* of
San Costanzo, led by Tonino Spadaro, son of the group's founder

It was not until July 1980 that the politicians were able to compose their differences and choose a *sindaco* who commanded a majority in the *consiglio comunale*. The new *sindaco* was Dr Costantino Federico, a lawyer aged only 36, politically DC and son of Carlo and Venere. Costantino and his brother Claudio had inaugurated 'Radiotelecapri' – an entirely new venture in the island which hitherto had depended on the mainland for its programmes. The new channel carried the national and local news, sport, musical programmes and films, and was very successful, being watched on the mainland as well as in the island.

Costantino Federico was an unusual *sindaco*. Younger than his predecessors, he was also different in style. Vigorous, straightforward and effective, he was not disposed to be manipulated by other politicians and had a considerable following among the younger voters. In some quarters he was unpopular, because, like his father Carlo, he was strict, tended to throw his weight about in order to get things done and was not disposed to seek agreement by compromise in the usual Italian manner. His enemies and critics dubbed him 'fascist', 'immature', 'dim', but, undeterred and conspicuously *onesto*, he soldiered on.

Federico had to contend with not only the burden of administration but also the hostility of some of his DC colleagues. Di Stefano, who had polled more votes than Federico and was leader of the DC element in the *consiglio*, considered that his exclusion from office had been due to a conspiracy by Federico's supporters and was very vehement on the subject. Few citizens actually wanted Di Stefano again as *sindaco*, and some very uncomplimentary things were said about him. It was felt that he represented the 'old order' and that the young and forward-looking Federico at least ought to be given a chance of proving himself. Also opposed to Federico was a group of four of his *assessori*, who were allied to Di Stefano and known popularly as the 'Banda del Marmo', so-called after the marble slab in his butcher's shop. As a counter to Federico's 'Radiotelecapri', they started a new local radio station, 'Radio Capri Uno', to put out their own propaganda and to blackguard Federico. Not to be outdone, the local Communist Party opened 'Radio Capri Popolare' at Marina Grande to broadcast against the DC as a whole and on any other topics about which they felt strongly.

A new political crisis occurred in November 1981, when Federico was forced into resignation, because eight of the twelve DC *consiglieri*, led by Di Stefano, withdrew their support. The new *sindaco* was Dr Saverio Valente, who had been *vice-sindaco* under Federico. Valente was a nuclear physicist, trained in America, who held a scientific appointment in Rome, where he spent much of his time. Valente and his seven supporters became known as the 'Giunta'; Federico and his three allies, 'Casta 4'. At first Valente governed with the support of all the DC *consiglieri*. Towards the end of 1982, however, 'Casta 4' went into opposition, and, in order to survive, the 'Giunta' had to form a tactical alliance with four Socialists (PSI) and an ex-Communist (PCI) who was now a Republican (PRI).

To bring this involved story of parish-pump politics to a close, we move on to the local elections of June 1985, when the DC, having parted company with Di Stefano, who became leader of the PRI, won only 10 of the 20 seats, thus making settled government more difficult than ever.

In Anacapri the long and largely peaceful reign of Tommaso De Tommaso as *sindaco* came to an end in 1970 after 23 years of office. He was followed successively by a schoolmaster, a surgeon, a retired medical teacher, and in 1978 by Arch. Fausto Arcucci.

Politically DC, Arcucci was an architect by profession and spent much of the week practising in Naples; indeed he was often so little in Anacapri that he became known as 'Il Sindaco del Weekend'. The *consiglio* was mainly DC, with a sprinkling of Independents, Communists (PCI) and Socialists (PSI). Anacapri's problems revolved mainly round water and the use of land. Water distribution was patchy; many farms and peasant homes still operated their own cisterns for collecting rain-water. Unlike the lower part of the island – where almost all the available flat land had already been built upon and only rocks and mountainsides remained – much of Anacapri was potentially suitable for house-building but was also precious as unspoilt countryside. Here there were conflicting interests, as between conservationists and developers. On the one hand were the small farmers who cherished their land; and there were islanders and visitors who loved the peace, the greenness and the wildness of Anacapri; who liked to walk its paths and who thought that road-building had already gone quite far enough with De Tommaso. In the opposite camp were non-residents who wanted villas and apartments for their holidays; residents who either wanted to improve their properties for themselves or, it they had bought them cheap in earlier years, to sell them at a profit to developers; and speculators who wanted to buy and sell land and property and cared nothing about the environment. Interested parties on all sides waited anxiously to see how Arcucci would deal with this sharpening conflict between public and private interest.

*

So far very little has been said about the Roman Catholic Church. This is partly because the priests of Capri have been uncommunicative about their affairs, and I have had to rely mainly on rather fragmentary secular sources; and partly because Don Luigi Lembo, a strong and severe character, priest in Capri since 1914 and *parroco* from 1918, guided his flock firmly and uneventfully until he retired in 1967. He died in the following year.

He was succeeded as *parroco* by Don Salvatore Scavuzzi, who was entirely different. Sicilian by birth, Scavuzzi was keen on the trappings of religion and its *feste* and celebrated every Saint's Day in the calendar; the Capresi, who, like all southern Italians, love *feste* and the outward appearances of worship, thought him *molto bravo* and thronged the parish church. He was not, however, without his critics and was on bad terms with one or two of his priests. He remained in office for only two years, during which he spent much of the Church's funds and even sold some of its furniture to raise money for *feste*.[37]

The new *parroco*, appointed at the end of 1969, was Don Costanzo Cerrotta, elder brother of Gloria Magnus's *amico* Pietro and owner of the Hotel Sanfelice, which he had inherited from his godfather and which, since its conversion from villa into hotel in 1965, had been managed by Pietro. Ordained in 1928, Costanzo had been a naval chaplain from 1936 to 1945. He left the Navy at the end of the war with the rank of captain and became a priest again. A sincere and deeply religious man, tough and practical, and a strong disciplinarian, he set about reforming the parish and imposing his will. All saints of dubious origin were removed from the local calendar. *Feste*, including the traditional Good Friday procession, was abolished. Only San Costanzo was left, but this was no longer high carnival. His curtailment of religious gaiety was widely deplored, but Cerrotta, for whom religion was something inward and deep down, was unmoved by his unpopularity. During the 'seventies he set about modernising the Church of Santo Stefano. The electricity system was renovated; loud-speakers, both internal and external, were installed; and, to the horror of many, electronic chimes replaced the bells of the campanile. Each evening, with startling suddenness, a tune-to-order rang out from the bell-tower – Sibelius one year, Schubert's 'Ständchen' the next. The sacristy was re-tiled; new stained-glass windows were installed; the organ was rebuilt and enlarged; a new altar and lectern were installed; and the vestments repaired. A strong supporter of ecumenism, in 1975 Cerrotta invited the Rev. Edward Holland, to celebrate communion once a month in Santo Stefano for the non-Catholic community of Capri, and he extended a welcome to the many believers and unbelievers who as tourists wandered round his church.[38]

Whereas in the past the *festa* of San Costanzo on 14 May had been one of the great events of the Capri year, enjoyed by Capresi and foreigners alike, it has been stripped to its bare bones, and has little appeal to a *festa*-loving population. There are no longer any celebrations the evening before; no bangs and fireworks; no boys of the Guild of San Luigi Gonzaga trying to look as pure as their patron on his white silk banner; no guilds and fraternities under their assorted banners, except for members of the Congrega di San Fillippo Neri,[39] some in red and white cassocks and others in ordinary clothes with silver medallions around their necks; and greatly reduced numbers of *figlie di Maria*. Nor is there any longer a Capri brass-band, but only one hired for the day from Sorrento. In a largely secular age, it is no longer an event of special interest. For the most part the islanders ignore it, while the visitors display a polite interest in something that is different from the usual Capri day. There is a modest tour of Capri town, which takes place in the earlier part of the morning, so as not to become entangled with the *comitive* of day-trippers. In the old days, San Costanzo's procession through the town had been a separate occasion on the '*ottava*', or eight days after after the 14th, when all the winding streets of medieval Capri north and south of the Piazza, as well as the main thoroughfares of Via Vittorio Emanuele, Via Camerelle and Via Roma had been visited.

The afternoon route begins, as in early days, down the steps of the Via Acquaviva, emerges into Via Marina Grande, then branches right down the new road which reaches the port at its east end. Having arrived at the port, the procession passes the Piazza Fontana, where the Truglio fountain has been a vital source since the timeless past and has never been known to run dry; continues in gathering darkness along the Marina and advances up the first stretch of Via Marina Grande, where from the balconies *ginestra* blossom ('*fiori di San Costanzo*') is thrown. Finally the Saint enters his Church for a night's rest before returning once more to Capri town for another year's repose in the parish church.

May 1984, San Costanzo's month, was the worst for a hundred years – frequent *scirocco* (which used to be popular on account of the quail it brought to Capri but now has no friends) alternating with *libeccio*, a constant variation of sun, cloud and rain. Some felt that this weather was the work of San Costanzo himself, angry because on the night of 6/7 November 1983 thieves had broken into his church on the Marina and into the parish church of Santo Stefano, where the pectoral cross was stolen from his effigy.

The Birth of the Blessed Virgin Mary is still celebrated on 7–8 September with Masses in the Church of Santa Maria del Soccorso and a variety of pagan festivities – and there is the equivalent celebration in Anacapri at Santa Maria a Cetrella. In place of the magical all-night *caprese* occasion of earlier days, when the Caffè Carmela and others were transported *en bloc* to the darkness of the mountainside and the citizens revelled in eating and drinking, singing, dancing and love-making, as a prelude to the celebration of early-morning Mass, there is now a more sedate, more organised and longer *festa*. On the evening of the 7th a small band of the faithful gather on top of Tiberio to celebrate Mass. Meanwhile at the foot of the mountain at the so-called 'Piedigrotta Tiberiana'[40] secular celebrations take place. In 1983, for example, it was an *eccezionale spettacolo musicale* by Francesco Calabrese and his ensemble. For this concert a special stage had been erected in a hollow, where the audience could gather on the rocky hillside with their picnics, to enjoy the tremendous noise of the amplifiers which relayed the concert. The occasion was rounded off by a torchlight procession, before the thousands wended their way home down the Via Tiberio. On the morning of the 8th, Mass was celebrated twice in the chapel. In the afternoon there was a walking-race around Tiberio; in the evening games with prizes – the 'breaking of pots' (*rotture delle pignatte*) by blindfold players, who were rewarded with money, if lucky, and flour or water, if not; a sack-race; a tug-of-war; an eating contest (*gara gastronomica*); and, to bring the *festa* to an end, a *show musicale* by *gruppi folkloristici* from all over the island.

On 5 April 1978, a thunderbolt struck and completely disintegrated the statue of Santa Maria del Soccorso and part of its pedestal, which had been erected in 1901 to expiate the sins of Tiberius. Not a single piece of the statue survived – *un fulmine di buon gusto* (a thunderbolt in good taste), according to one islander, who both disliked the statue and the motive for putting it there. Steps were soon taken to re-establish Santa Maria on the mountain-top. Thanks to the generosity of Guido Odierna, a commercial painter of sea- and landscapes who had a gallery in Via Vittorio Emanuele, a commission was given to the sculptor Alfiero Nena in Rome. He changed the orginal motif from the Virgin with the hands held together in supplication – a copy of the statue of the Madonna at Lourdes – to the Virgin holding the Christ-child; a new concrete pedestal was built; and a lightning-conductor installed to defeat further mischief by Jove's thunderbolts. The problem was how to move the heavy bronze statue to Tiberio and install it. Luckily the US Air Force came to the rescue and, as a gesture of goodwill, provided one of their NATO helicopters to lift the statue up to Tiberio. After being blessed by the Pope in St Peter's Square, the statue was brought to Capri on 6 September 1979, the day before the customary celebration of the Nativity of the Blessed Virgin Mary, and placed on the *campo sportivo* at Palazzo a Mare, where dignitaries of Church and State assembled to await the arrival of the helicopter. Although the day was hot and the ground arid, no one had anticipated the enormous cloud of dust which enveloped the company as the machine landed on the football-ground. When the dust had settled, the statue was slung beneath it, and then all ran for cover as it took off. On arrival at Tiberio the pilot, prevented by a high wind from placing his charge exactly on the pedestal, dumped it on the ground nearby for later instalment and headed off to the mainland. When finally installed, the Madonna was placed, not facing out to sea, like her predecessor, but towards Capri town, and the sailors complained that she was no longer interested in helping them, but only Odierna.

*

It was Edwin Cerio who first sounded the alarm in 1922 with his 'Convegno per la Difesa del Paesaggio'. It was not until 1939, however, that a law for the *'protezione delle bellezze naturali'* was issued. The post-war boom and the developments which attended it provoked expressions of apprehension from those who cared about the environment. Their leader was not a Caprese, but Roberto Pane, a Neapolitan Professor of Architecture, who had a house in Anacapri and for many years had made a detailed study of the architecture of the island. In 1954 he published *Capri*, which was not only a monument of scholarship, with an admirable text, illustrated with copies of early nineteenth-century drawings and with modern photographs revealing known and unknown facts of the island's architecture, but also a *cri de coeur* from one who was greatly disturbed by 'the wide scattering of new houses in areas of greenness' and by the inappropriate styles in which the new houses were built and old ones reconstructed. He recorded the melancholy view that fundamentally it was 'a matter of the usual quarrel between private and public interest, and it is a well-known fact that in Italy the former almost always wins'.[41]

Younger than Pane and an equally vigorous campaigner was Carlo Knight, a free-lance writer and historian, who lived at Naples on the Posillipo. His ancestors, court jewellers in the days of the Bourbons, had stayed on in Naples after the creation of Italy in 1860 and become Italians. Born in 1929, Carlo studied medicine at the University of Naples, served for a time in the Italian Navy, and, with his Dutch wife, subsequently travelled the world as a manager of the Italian food company CIRIO. Having resigned from CIRIO, he devoted himself to writing. Humane and intelligent, fearless in his exposure of inhumanity, corruption and the neglect of national treasures, and in his support of ecology, conservation and culture, he published his courageous articles in the Naples *Mattino* and the national daily *Corriere della Sera*. Knight frequently visited Capri, where his wife's parents have a summer residence.[42]

There was an important test case in the 'sixties. Raffaele and Teresa Vuotto, having established the Hotels La Pineta and Flora, embarked on a third. Raffaele bought a property, consisting of a chalet, a roller-skating pitch and the Cinema Parco Augusto, which adjoined the Villa Krupp public garden. He operated the cinema for a time, then demolished it *'con grande difficoltà'*, (to quote his own words) and obtained permission to build a large hotel on the cliff-top, 100 metres west of the Certosa and cheek by jowl with the public garden. The Hotel Luna, placed in such a position, completely altered the character of this part of the island and was environmentally disastrous. The matter was taken up by the Capri branch of Italia Nostra, a nationwide organisation, which had been constituted with official recognition in 1955, to protect the 'historical, artistic and natural heritage of the nation'. Italia Nostra, although successful in some other parts of Italy, has never been effective in Capri and in this, its first major case, failed to exert any influence. In the introduction to the second edition of his book, issued in 1965 under the title *Capri – Mura e Volte* (walls and vaults) and in 1967 translated into English by Anthony Thorne, Pane wrote bitterly of the building of the Luna in 'a spot so long hallowed by fame, and a source of pleasure to so many, that one would have thought it exempt from the touch of predatory hands'. Undeterred by criticism, Vuotto pressed on with his plans, completed the hotel in the middle 'sixties and in 1970 added a swimming-pool to the hotel only a few feet from the Certosa itself.

The summer of 1967 was marred by a serious fire ('*L'incendio*'), which in the second week of August broke out near Castello Barbarossa and spread southwards along the wooded slopes of Monte Santa Maria and Monte Solaro, until it arrived above the Grotta delle Felci and then leap-frogged to the steep cliffs below Solaro. The Capri firemen were unable to master it and it raged for three days, until finally extinguished by *bersaglieri* and US troops brought over from the mainland, and fire-killing liquid dropped by US planes. It was the first fire of its kind that anybody could remember. It could scarcely have happened in the old days, when all the farmers gathered hay and grasses for feeding the cows and dry branches for cooking. With every family cooking by bottled gas, nobody bothered any more to collect the combustible material which no doubt facilitated the *incendio*.[43]

In 1980 irreversible damage was done to the Scoglio delle Sirene at Marina Piccola, when its rugged surface, on which the Sirens may once have perched, was suddenly concreted by the concessionaires, so that it could accommodate deck-chairs and mattresses. A vigorous but fruitless campaign against what had been done was conducted by George Weber, aged 86 but still active, and in Capri on his annual visit from Florida, who was outraged by the spoiling of a favourite spot a few yards from where he had been born and spent his early years; and Italia Nostra added its plaintive voice. But the damage had been done, and the concrete re-mained. In assessing the conflict between private and public interest in this instance, it must be admitted that the issue was not clear-cut. While the motive for concreting the rock was obviously to attract more visitors to the bathing establishment and nearby restaurant, the bathers themselves no doubt felt that the public interest was being served by being able to relax on a flat surface – and who were the conservationists to deny them this pleasure?

Further along the coast, the concessionaire of the Faraglioni beach and restaurant, again part of the *demanio marittimo*, displayed a similar disregard for conservation by demolishing part of the wall of the old Roman harbour of Tragara, in order to make way for new construction, but timely protests succeeded in limiting the extent of the destruction.

Pane followed up his book with public statements in which he did not hesitate to name the culprits. His efforts received no encouragement from the *comune*, or even from the Centro Caprense, which was at first reluctant to allow him to hold public meetings on its premises. Unable to reverse the political and social conditions endangering Capri, he grew ever more sceptical about the island.

In Anacapri, 1982 was celebrated as 'ecology year', in memory of the birth of Saint Francis of Assisi, 800 years earlier, in 1182. Levente Erdeos, Swedish vice-consul and administrator of San Michele, tried to launch a scheme for extending Munthe's bird sanctuary at Barbarossa to include the whole 'green' zone to the west of Monte Santa Maria and Monte Solaro, but found no interest or support in the *consiglio comunale*. The contribution of Fausto Arcucci's administration to ecology year was to award nearly 400 building licences. About half these licences were uncontroversial, being repairs and minor additions to existing structures. As to the remainder, there was widespread alarm that the beauty and peace of the Anacapri countryside would be seriously impaired. Many of these licences were given to individuals outside the island, and this fact carried with it the suspicion that the administration had been subject to improper influences. Existing property-owners also were apprehensive that new building in the countryside would reduce the amenity value of the land and the actual value of existing properties. Although firm information was difficult to obtain, there were rumours that there was no effective check on illegal building; that complaints by existing property-owners had gone unheeded; and that *camorristi* in Naples were using this opportunity to launder 'dirty money' (*soldi sporchi*), by investing in Anacapri land and property. Later in the year news spread that there was a private scheme, supported by the administration, to make a nine-hole golf-course on the beautiful upland plain of Cetrella, with its freedom to wander and stunning views, convert the existing track up the mountainside into a road and give permits for building beside it. There were vigorous protests throughout the island, the Italian office of the World Wildlife Fund brought pressure to bear in Rome, and the schemes were dropped.[44] The scandal as a whole brought Capri to the attention of British readers, who were warned that 'Capri fears a concrete overcoat'.[45] What was so disheartening was that the issue of so many building permits appeared to have the support of the ruling DC faction. A small number of DC *consiglieri*, however, were openly critical, but unable to influence events.

In a different category, but disturbing for the environmentalists, was a group of co-operative housing projects in Anacapri. Sited on land owned by the *comune*, these new blocks of apartments were built primarily for accommodating working-class families, for whom space in Anacapri had become very tight, as living standards continually improved. Families allotted these apartments, who had to prove at least 10 years' residence in Anacapri, put down capital sums of various sizes, but the money soon ran out and building stopped. The families could raise no more money, and it was reported that some were being bought as 'second homes' by mainland Italians, who could afford to finance continued construction. The main objection of the environmentalists was that the new structures, while possibly appropriate to a town, were hideously out of place in the village and countryside of Anacapri.

There was great rejoicing in Anacapri when in the local election of June 1985 a group of independents, calling themselves 'The Anchor', gained a majority of 11 seats over 9 DC and ousted Fausto Aricucci as *sindaco*, but not before much damage had been done to the countryside. It seems that the Capresi, unconcerned as ever about the fate of Anacapri, do not greatly care, provided that the beautiful plain of Cetrella is spared.

*

Naples continues to exercise a powerful influence on Capri. It provides an administrator whenever local government breaks down. It disgorges hordes of *pendolari*, who are much disliked in the island. Rich Neapolitans buy land and property in Capri as 'second homes' and as a hedge against inflation, which increases the housing problem. The activities of the Camorra, which are so widespread in Naples, and the deeply rooted trade in contraband and drugs, both impinge on the island.

It is difficult for a foreigner to discover the truth about the activities of the Camorra in the island – a sensitive subject about which the Capresi tend to be silent or deliberately misleading. A former English resident, who knew Capri well during the late 'sixties and throughout the 'seventies, was certain that then some profitable enterprises in the island paid protection money to the Camorra and claimed to know the identities of some of the *estorsori* and to have seen them at work. This person cited the instance of a particular *taverna* which at first was unwilling to make the arrangements required by the Camorra but, later, when its business began to dry up, toed the line. One Caprese said that a *camorrista* from Sorrento had threatened a Capri night-club, which had telephoned the police, and the man had been removed bodily; that any criminal who made himself objectionable in this way would find it difficult to escape unseen from the island; that, while there was no protection racket as such operating in the island, there was a certain amount of local corruption over building permits. Another Caprese considered that the leading *caprese* families and the ever-increasing network of rich *commercianti* would not allow *estorsori* to operate, and that, if they tried to do so, their organization and identities would quickly become known. A local businessman said that the only *mafia* he knew – and it was a very gentle one – was a private security firm, which patrolled the streets with guards, who were allowed by the State to carry arms, and in exchange for monthly payments guaranteed to protect business premises against burglary. Yet another Caprese said: 'The *mafia* is not a problem here, yet.' A Neapolitan well-acquainted with the island considered that the only *mafia* in Capri was that of the leading local families who carved up almost everything between themselves and did their best to prevent *forestieri* (which included Neapolitans and all other Italians) from getting a foothold. There was, however, general agreement that *camorristi* invested *soldi sporchi* in Capri and had been helped by the great number of building licences issued in 1982 in Anacapri and by a few islanders who were ready to cooperate with them.

Situated 20 miles out from Naples, Capri is used regularly by the Neapolitan *contrabbandieri*. Much of the contraband is tobacco – which has always been a monopoly of the Italian State – and consists mainly of American cigarettes, but it also includes hard drugs. The contraband usually arrives on sea-going ships, which stand off Capri whenever they have a rendezvous to make with the operators in Naples. The fast, deep-blue motorboats of the *contrabbandieri* cannot proceed directly from their base in Naples without the risk of being intercepted by the launches of the Guardia di Finanza. The smugglers' boats, therefore, leave Naples, well ahead of their rendezvous, and hang around the coves of Capri to await the appointed signal from the carriers out at sea. Having collected their booty, they make full speed to their base, where the goods, once landed, can usually be dispersed in the city without interference by the police. Thousands of Neapolitan families live on contraband and any crack-down by the police would increase the already formidable numbers of unemployed. Sometimes La Finanza tries to intercept at sea, but with slower boats than the smugglers they have a daunting task. If the smugglers' boat is in danger of being apprehended, the contraband is thrown overboard, and all La Finanza can do is to confiscate the boat and, if the smugglers are armed, prosecute them for illegal possession of arms. Whether or not smuggled goods under this system reach Capri is difficult to determine, but there is a suspicion that hard drugs have been finding their way to young people in the island, either direct or from contacts in

Naples, and there are certainly a number of coves, particularly those on the west coast, suitable for clandestine landings. One day, near the Pizzolungo, a foreigner encountered a boy in radio communication with some *contrabbandiere* boats lying inshore near the Faraglioni, waiting to dash out to meet a big ship at sea. There was a decoy boat a little way offshore, and the boy was reporting to the smugglers on the effect which the decoy was having in distracting La Finanza. The machine started to crackle, and the smugglers asked the boy who the stranger was. The foreigner enquired from the boy, who was of Neapolitan origin but at school in Capri, if he minded helping to smuggle consignments which might contain drugs. He said he was solely concerned with getting some pocket-money for his services and did not mind about anything else. A few days later, by chance, the stranger saw the boy with his school-books in the Piazza, looking virtuous and happy.[46]

The smugglers do not always win. In the summer of 1983 a *contrabbandiere* boat, loaded with cigarettes, went aground below the Salto di Tiberio. The Guardia di Finanza kept it under surveillance, but turned a blind eye at night when small boats came to raid 'The Tobacco Shop', as it became known – a real 'whisky galore' situation which would have amused Compton Mackenzie.

*

It is time to bring this saga to a close and end the pilgrimage which began in 1973 in quest for Mackenzie's characters and which broadened and deepened into a much wider study. I must record my deep appreciation of all the kindnesses I have received from the islanders; the fascination of developing many sources of information, in order to unfold a tale which has never before been told; perpetual amazement at the multifarious activities, happiness and vigour of the islanders; the potent spell of lotus-land and the timeless magic which envelops the visitor from the moment he steps ashore. In the words of a venerable islander, *Capri è sempre bella*.

Identities of characters and places described in Compton Mackenzie's 'Vestal Fire' and 'Extraordinary Women'

1. Vestal Fire

Note: Several of these identifications come from source 'M' (see under Miscellaneous sources). Characters not mentioned by the author in his book are indicated by asterisk.

Real name	Pseudonym
Edith Page Andrews	Elsie Neave
William Page Andrews	Joseph Rutger Neave
Alice Tweed Andrews	Mrs Dawson (who is, however, according to 'M' a made-up character)
Vernon Andrews	Nigel Dawson
The Misses Baker	Rachel and Hannah Bilton
Edna Blake	Marian de Feltre
Rev. Francis Burra	Rev. Cyril Acott
The Misses Calvert	The Misses Cooper
Edwin Cerio	Enrico Jones
Giorgio Cerio	Alberto Jones
Nino Cesarini	Carlo di Fiore
Gilbert Clavel (Swiss)	Martel, the Belgian hunchback
Cristina (*amica* of Green)	Fortunata (*amica* of Westall)
Charles Caryl Coleman	Christopher Goldfinch
Dr Pasquale de Gennaro	Dr Squillace
*Marquis de Julien	Marquis de la Tour des Bois
Don Giuseppe de Nardis	Don Pruno
Olga de Tschélischeff	Anastasia Sarbécoff
Doris (niece of Emelie Fraser)	Phyllis Allerton
Norman Douglas	Duncan Maxwell
'Mrs Edwardes' (identity not known)	Adelaide Edwardes – a real person ('M')
Costanzo Federico	Agostino
Baron Jacques (Jack) d'Adelswärd-Fersen	'Count' Robert (Bob) Marsac-Lagerström
Horace Fisher	Francis Cartwright
Emelie Fraser	Mrs Hector Macdonnell
Giovanni (John) Galatà	Peter Ambrogio
Gwendolen Galatà	Maud Ambrogio
Ferdinando Gamboni	Maestro Perella
Rev. Henry Gepp	Rev. William Wills
Mrs Ginsberg	Mrs Kafka
Alexander (Sandie) Grahame	Archibald (Archie) Macadam
Sophie Grahame	Effie Macadam
Alfredo Green	Arturo Westall
Morgan Heiskell	Harry Menteith
Mrs Hinde	Mrs Rosebotham
Thomas Spencer Jerome	John Scudamore
Miss Kennedy	Beatrice Mewburn
Isabel Kennedy (her niece)	Dorothy Daynton
Pietro Lamberti	Cataldo

Real name	Pseudonym
Lady Mackinder	Mrs Onslow
Don Giuseppe Morgano	Don Luigi Zampone
Donna Lucia Morgano	Donna Maria Zampone
Mariano Morgano	Ferdinando Zampone
Rose O'Neill	Sheila Macleod
*Ouloen (a Dane)	Ibsen (a ladylike Norwegian)
Col. Bryan Palmes	Major Natt
Pretore Pestalozza	Numa Fogolare
Mimì Ruggiero	Gigi Gasparri
Henrietta (Yetta) S. Rupp	Nita
San Costanzo	San Mercurio
Sant' Antonio da Padova	San Bonzo
Federico Serena	Don Cesare Rocco
Margarete Sinibaldi	Madame Minieri
Mrs Spottiswood	Mrs Gibbs
Jan Styka	Zygmunt Konczynski
Godfrey Thornton	Anthony Burlingham
Bertha Trower	Carrie Bookham
Harold Trower	Herbert Bookham
Anita Vedder	Angela Pears
Elihu Vedder	Simon Pears
Maestro Vito	Maestro Supino
*Mrs Watts	Mrs Arkwright-Hughes
Annie Webb	Mrs Pape
Kathryn (Kate) Wolcott-Perry	Virginia Pepworth-Norton
Saidee Wolcott-Perry	Maimie Pepworth-Norton
William Wordsworth	Henry Mewburn
*Count & Countess Zukov	Prince & Princess Marlinsky

Pseudonym	Real name
Rev. Cyril Acott	Rev. Francis Burra
Agostino	Costanzo Federico
Phyllis Allerton	Doris (niece of Emelie Fraser)
Maud Ambrogio	Gwendolen Galatà
Peter Ambrogio	Giovanni (John) Galatà
*Mrs Arkwright-Hughes	Mrs Watts
Rachel and Hannah Bilton	The Misses Baker
Carrie Bookham	Bertha Trower
Herbert Bookham	Harold Trower
Anthony Burlingham	Godfrey Thornton
Francis Cartwright	Horace Fisher
Cataldo	Pietro Lamberti
The Misses Cooper	The Misses Calvert
Mrs Dawson	Made-up character ('M')
Nigel Dawson	Vernon Andrews
Dorothy Daynton	Isabel Kennedy
Marian de Feltre	Edna Blake
*Marquis de la Tour des Bois	Marquis de Julien
Carlo di Fiore	Nino Cesarini
Adelaide Edwardes	'Mrs Edwardes' (identity not known, but a real person, according to 'M')
Numa Fogolare	Pretore Pestalozza
Austin W. Follett	An imaginary character ('M')
Fortunata (*amica* of Westall)	Cristina (*amica* of Green)
Gigi Gasparri	Mimì Ruggiero
Mrs Gibbs	Mrs Spottiswood

Pseudonym	Real name
Christopher Goldfinch	Charles Caryl Coleman
*Ibsen (a ladylike Norwegian)	Ouloen (a Dane)
Alberto Jones	Giorgio Cerio
Enrico Jones	Edwin Cerio
Henry Jones	Composite character ('M'); bears no resemblance to Ignazio Cerio
Mrs Kafka	Mrs Ginsburg
Zygmunt Konczynski	Jan Styka
Archibald (Archie) Macadam	Alexander (Sandie) Grahame
Effie Macadam	Sophie Grahame
Mrs Hector Macdonnell	Emelie Fraser
Sheila Macleod	Rose O'Neill
*Prince & Princess Marlinsky	Count & Countess Zukov
'Count' Robert (Bob) Marsac-Lagerström	Baron Jacques (Jack) d'Adelswärd-Fersen
Martel, the Belgian hunchback	Gilbert Clavel (Swiss)
Duncan Maxwell	Norman Douglas
Harry Menteith	Morgan Heiskell
Beatrice Mewburn	Miss Kennedy
Henry Mewburn	William Wordsworth
Madame Minieri	Margarete Sinibaldi
Major Natt	Col. Bryan Palmes
Elsie Neave	Edith Page Andrews
Joseph Rutger Neave	William Page Andrews
Nita	Henrietta (Yetta) S. Rupp
Mrs Onslow	Lady Mackinder
Mrs Pape	Annie Webb
Angela Pears	Anita Vedder
Simon Pears	Elihu Vedder
Maimie Pepworth-Norton	Saidee Wolcott-Perry
Virginia Pepworth-Norton	Kathryn (Kate) Wolcott-Perry
Maestro Perella	Ferdinando Gamboni
Don Pruno	Don Giuseppe de Nardis
Don Cesare Rocco	Federico Serena
Mrs Rosebotham	Mrs Hinde
San Bonzo	Sant' Antonio da Padova
San Mercurio	San Costanzo
Anastasia Sarbécoff	Olga de Tschélischeff
John Scudamore	Thomas Spencer Jerome
Dr Squillace	Dr Pasquale de Gennaro
Maestro Supino	Maestro Vito
Arturo Westall	Alfredo Green
Rev. William Wills	Rev. Henry Gepp
Ferdinando Zampone	Mariano Morgano
Don Luigi Zampone	Don Giuseppe Morgano
Donna Maria Zampone	Donna Lucia Morgano

2. *Extraordinary Women*

Real name	Pseudonym
Renata Borgatti	Cléo Gazay
Romaine Brooks	Olimpia Leigh
Olga de Tschélischeff	Anastasia Sarbécoff
Mimì Franchetti	Rosalba Donsante
Luigi Gargiulo	Carmĭnĕ Bruno
Francesca (Checca) Lloyd	Aurora (Rory) Freemantle (in part)
'Missi', governess of 'Baby' Soldatenkov	Miss Chimbley
Lica Riola	Olga Linati

Real name	Pseudonym
Principessa Hélène Soldatenkov (Gortchakov)	Countess Hermina de Randan
Hélène (Baby) Soldatenkov	Lulu de Randan

Pseudonym	Real name
Carmīnĕ Bruno	Luigi Gargiulo
Principessa Flavia (Bébé) Buonagrazia	Not known
Miss Chimbley	'Missi', governess of 'Baby' Soldatenkov
Countess Hermina de Randan	Principessa Hélène Soldatenkov (Gortchakov)
Lulu de Randan	Hélène (Baby) Soldatenkov
Rosalba Donsante	Mimì Franchetti
Aurora (Rory) Freemantle (in part)	Francesca (Checca) Lloyd
Cléo Gazay	Renata Borgatti
Hjalmar Krog ('Daffodil')	Not known
Olimpia Leigh	Romaine Brooks
Olga Linati	Lica Riola
Zoë Mitchell	Mistress of a Parisian shirtmaker; name unknown
Contessa Giulia Monforte	Not known
Mrs Royle	Not known
Janet Royle	Not known
Anastasia Sarbécoff	Olga de Tschélischeff
Baroness Drenka Vidakovich	Not known
Captain Wheeler	Not known

3. Topography
(both books)

Real name	Pseudonym
Anacapri	Anasirene
Capri	Sirene
Castiglione	Torrione
English Church of All Saints	English Church of St Simon & St Jude
Hotel Quisisana	Hotel Augusto
Monte Solaro	Monte Ventoso
Monte Tuoro	Monte San Giorgio
Morgano's	Zampone's
Tiberio Palace	Hotel Grandioso
Torre Quattro Venti	Villa Aeolia
Via Krupp	Via Krank
Via Tragara	Via Caprera
Villa Alba & Cà del Sole	Villa Leucadia
Villa Castello	Villa Parnassus
Villa Cesina	Villa San Giorgio
Villa Esperia	Villa Botticelli
Villa Lysis (Fersen)	Villa Hylas
Villa Narcissus	Villa Adonis
Villa Siracusa, Sorrento	Villa Castalia, Stabia
Villa Tragara	Villa Minerva
Villa Torricella	Villa Amabile

Pseudonym	Real name
Anasirene	Anacapri
English Church of St Simon & St Jude	English Church of All Saints
Hotel Augusto	Hotel Quisisana
Hotel Grandioso	Tiberio Palace
Monte San Giorgio	Monte Tuoro
Monte Ventoso	Monte Solaro

Pseudonym	Real name
Sirene	Capri
Torrione	Castiglione
Via Caprera	Via Tragara
Via Krank	Via Krupp
Villa Adonis	Villa Narcissus
Villa Aeolia	Torre Quattro Venti
Villa Amabile	Villa Torricella
Villa Botticelli	Villa Esperia
Villa Castalia, Stabia	Villa Siracusa, Sorrento
Villa Hylas	Villa Lysis (Fersen)
Villa Leucadia	Villa Alba & Cà del Sole
Villa Minerva	Villa Tragara
Villa Mortadella	Not known
Villa Parnasso	Villa Castello
Villa San Giorgio	Villa Cesina
Zampone's	Morgano's

APPENDIX B
Administrators of Capri and Anacapri

1. Capri

Date	Name	Position	Profession
1869	Giuseppe Fischetti	Sindaco	Doctor
1869–72	Antonio Bonucci	Sindaco	*Benestante* (well-to-do)
1873–77	Michele Pagano	Sindaco	Hotelier
1878	? Mariano Morgano	Sindaco	Not known
1879–84	Filippo Trama	Sindaco	*Benestante*
1885–95	Manfredi Pagano	Sindaco	Hotelier
1895–99	Federico Serena	Sindaco	Hotelier
1899–1900	Filippo Trama	Sindaco	*Benestante*
1900–09	Federico Serena	Sindaco	Hotelier
1910–11	Nicola Pagano	Sindaco	Hotelier
1911–14	Carlo Ferraro	Sindaco	Pharmacist
1914–20	Carmĭnĕ Vuotto	Sindaco	Hotel manager
1920–23	Edwin Cerio	Sindaco	Engineer & writer
1924–25	Carmĭnĕ Vuotto	Sindaco	Hotel manager
1926	Vincenzo Tecchio	Commissario Prefettizio	Provincial administrator
1926–36	Marchese Marino Dusmet de Smours	Podestà	Business employee
1936–37	Renato De Zerbi	Commissario Prefettizio	Provincial administrator
1937–41	Germano Ripandelli	Podestà	Artillery officer
1941–late 1943	Ammiraglio Stanislao Di Somma	Commissario Prefettizio	Retired admiral
late 1943	Avv. Giuseppe Brindisi	Commissario Prefettizio	Lawyer
1944–46	Avv. Giuseppe Brindisi	Sindaco	Lawyer
1946–47	Dr Giuseppe Ruocco	Sindaco	Doctor
1947–48	Ing. Costanzo Lembo	Sindaco	Engineer
1948–49	Biagino Orrico	Commissario Prefettizio	Provincial administrator
1949	Giuseppe De Martino	Sindaco	Merchant Navy officer
1950–52	Giuseppe Conti	Commissario Prefettizio	Provincial administrator
	Alberti Arcamone	Commissario Prefettizio	Provincial administrator
1952–54	Dr Oreste Prozzillo	Sindaco	Doctor
1954–55	Dr Giuseppe Ruocco	Sindaco	Doctor
1956–57	Dr Oreste Prozzillo	Sindaco	Doctor
1957–60	Prof. Carlo Federico	Sindaco	Schoolmaster
1960–62	Ing. Costanzo Lembo	Sindaco	Engineer
1962–65	Avv. Carmĭnĕ Ruotolo	Sindaco	Lawyer
1965–68	Prof. Carlo Federico	Sindaco	Schoolmaster
1968–69	Raffaele Di Stefano	Sindaco	Butcher

Date	Name	Position	Profession
1970	Giovanni Orefice	Commissario Prefettizio	Provincial administrator
1970–75	Raffaele Di Stefano	Sindaco	Butcher
1975–79	Ing. Costanzo Lembo	Sindaco	Engineer
1979–80	Giovannibattista Mastrosimone	Commissario Prefettizio	Provincial administrator
1980–81	Dr Costantino Federico	Sindaco	Lawyer
1981–85	Dr Saverio Valente	Sindaco	Nuclear physicist
1985–	Michele Salvia	Sindaco	Telephone Service

2. *Anacapri*
Note: No details before 1886 are available

Date	Name	Position	Profession
1886	Francesco De Tommaso	Sindaco	*Benestante*
1895–1900	Diego Massimino	Sindaco	*Benestante*
1901–05	Salvatore Lucca	Sindaco	*Benestante*
	Michele Farace	Sindaco	*Benestante*
	Michele Romano	Sindaco	*Benestante*
1906–10	Michele Romano	Sindaco	*Benestante*
1911–24	Antonino Mazzarella	Sindaco	*Benestante*
1925–26	Salvatore Gargiulo	Sindaco	*Benestante*
1926–47	Anacapri and Capri were one *comune* (see under *Capri*)		
1947–70	Dr Tommaso De Tommaso	Sindaco	General Practitioner
1970–75	Federico Arcucci	Sindaco	Schoolmaster
1975–77	Dr Michele Barile	Sindaco	Surgeon
1977–78	Prof. Alessandro Settimi	Sindaco	Retired medical teacher
1978–85	Arch. Fausto Arcucci	Sindaco	Architect
1985–	Guido Pollio	Sindaco	Bank manager

Sources and Bibliography

1. Individuals
Individuals who have provided information are listed at the beginning of the book under Acknowledgements.

2. Manuscript collections
Archivio Carelli (AC)
   A manuscript archive of matters relating to Capri, compiled from official papers by Ing. Alfonso Carelli (d. 1940) and lodged in the CCIC.
Azienda Autonoma di Cura Soggiorno e Turismo, Isola di Capri (Tourist Office in Capri)
Biblioteca Cuomo, Naples
British Consulate General, Naples
   Records of All Saints Church.
British Museum
   Hudson Lowe papers: 20, 107; 20, 108; 20, 163; 20, 165; 20, 166; 20, 167; 20, 171; 20, 174; 20, 178; 20, 179; 20, 189.
Centro Caprense Ignazio Cerio (CCIC)
   Various files, dossiers, manuscripts and photographs, to which references are made at appropriate points.
International Rose O'Neill Club
   c/o Jean Cantwell, 15 Willow Lane, Branson, MO 65616, USA
Kelsey Museum of Ancient and Medieval History (Kelsey Museum)
   University of Michigan, Ann Arbor, USA
Municipio of Anacapri
Municipio of Capri
National Library of Scotland
Pagano Collection
   Located in Palazzo Cerio.
Society for the Promotion of the Gospel in Foreign Parts (SPG)
   In London.

3. Miscellaneous sources
'M' At the back of a copy of *Vestal Fire*, which has passed through author's hands, there is a manuscript list of the actual names of characters mentioned in the book, which is so detailed and so accurate that Compton Mackenzie himself must have been the source.
VN Visitors' book of the Villa Narcissus in the days of Charles Coleman (1903–28).

4. Published Sources
Sir Harold Acton: *The Bourbons of Naples (1734–1825)* (London, 1956)
—— *The Last Bourbons of Naples (1825–1861)* London, 1961)
Joseph Addison: *Remarks on Several Parts of Italy in the years 1701, 1702 and 1703* (Glasgow, 1755)
Richard Aldington: *Pinorman* (London, 1954)
FM Earl Alexander of Tunis: *The Alexander Memoirs 1940–1945* (London, 1962)
Christian Wilhelm Allers: *Capri* (Munich, 1892)
—— *La Bella Napoli* (Munich, 1893)
Francesco Alvino: *Due Giorni a Capri* (Naples, 1838; reprinted Naples, 1967)
Comune di Anacapri: *Graham Greene, Civis Anacaprensis* (Naples, 1980)
Hans Andersen: *The Improvisator* (1834)
Arvid Andrén: *Capri – From the Stone Age to the Tourist Age* (Göteborg, 1980); includes a useful bibliography, arranged by periods

Apollonius Rhodius: *Argonautica*
Ausonius: *The Twelve Caesars*
Baedeker: *Guide to Southern Italy* (editions of 1867, 1883, 1912 and 1930)
Michele Barbarò and others: *Le Fotografie di Von Gloeden* (Milan, 1980)
Renato Barneschi: *Vita e Morte di Mafalda di Savoia* (Milan, 1982)
Luigi Barzini: *The Italians* (London, 1966)
E. F. Benson: *As we were* (London, 1930)
Blue Guide: *Southern Italy* (1959)
John Boardman: *The Greeks Overseas* (London, 1980)
Jean-Jacques Bouchard: *Un Parisien à Rome et à Naples en 1632*. See extract in *Capri nei Seicento*, trs.
     Edwin Cerio (Naples, 1934)
'Bryher': *The Heart to Artemis* (London, 1963)
Michele Buonuomo *et al.*: *Malaparte–una Proposta* (Rome, 1982)
Antonio Canale: *Storia dell' Isola di Capri* (Naples, 1887)
G. Cantone *et al.*: *Capri – la Città e la Terra* (Edizione Scientifiche Italiane, 1982)
G. C. Capaccio: *Antiquitates et Historiae Napolitanae etc* (Lugd. Batav., 1607)
Bruno Caruso: *Lenin a Capri* (Bari, 1978)
Edwin Cerio: *La Vita e la Figura di un Uomo*; a life of Ignazio Cerio (Rome, *c.* 1921)
―― *Aria di Capri* (Naples, 1926), trs. *That Capri Air* (London, 1929)
―― *Capri nei Seicento* (Naples, 1934a)
―― *Manicomio Tascabile* (Naples, 1934b)
―― *Flora Privata di Capri* (Naples, 1939)
―― *Guida Inutile di Capri* (Rome, 1946)
―― *L'Ora di Capri* (Naples, 1950)
―― *The Masque of Capri* (London, 1957)
Ignazio Cerio: *Flora dell' Isola di Capri* (Naples, 1890)
F. I. Chaliapin: *Pages of My Life* (1927)
―― *Man and Mask* (1932)
Tony Cliff: *Lenin Vol 1, Building The Party* (London, 1975)
P. V. Coronelli: *Isolario*, with map (1696)
Nancy Cunard: *Grand Man – Memories of Norman Douglas* (London, 1954)
Vincenzo Cuomo: *L'Isola di Capri come Stazione Climatica* (Naples, 1894)
Anthony Curtis: *Somerset Maugham* (London, 1977)
Marquis De Sade: *Juliette* (1792), trs. Wainhouse (Grove Press, New York, 1968)
Cesare de Seta: *Capri* (ERI Turin, 1983)
Dictionary of American Biography
Dictionary of National Biography (DNB)
Dio Cassius: *History* (early third century A.D.)
Principe F. C. Di Sirignano: *Memorie di un Uomo Inutile* (Milan, 1981)
Norman Douglas: *Siren Land* (London, 1911); references are to 1929 reprint
―― *Old Calabria* (London, 1915); references are to 1926 reprint
―― *South Wind* (London, 1917; new edition with introduction 1946)
―― *Capri: materials for a description of the Island* (Florence, 1930)
―― *Looking Back* (London, 1933); references are to 1934 reprint
―― *Late Harvest* (London, 1946)
―― *Footnote on Capri* (London, 1952)
Alexandre Dumas, *père*: *Le Spéronare* (Paris, 1855)
Edrisius: eleventh century writer mentioned in Douglas, 1930
A. W. Ellerman: see 'Bryher'
Encyclopaedia Britannica (Ency. Brit.), 15th Edition
Lewis Engelbach: *Naples and the Campagna Felice* (London, 1815)
Edizione Radiotelevisione Italiane (ERI): 34th Session of the Prix Italia in Venice, 1982 (Turin, 1983)
Eustathius: *Commentaries on Homer's Iliad and Odyssey* (12th century)
Giuseppe Feola: *Rapporto sullo Stato Attuale dei Ruderi Augusto-Tiberiani nell' Isola di Capri* (1830). Ed.
     and pub. by Ignazio Cerio (Naples, 1894)
J. A. Fersen: *Et le Feu s'éteignit sur la Mer* . . (Paris, 1909)

—— *Akademos*; monthly review (Paris, 1909)

Gracie Fields: *Sing as we go* (London, 1960)

F. N. Finney: *Letters from across the Sea* (Philadelphia, 1909)

H. A. L. Fisher: *A History of Europe* (London, 1936)

Constantine Fitzgibbon: *Norman Douglas, a Pictorial Record* (London, 1953)

—— *Norman Douglas – Memoirs of an Unwritten Biography*; in *Encounter*, Vol 43, No 3, 1974.

Immanuel Friedländer: *Capri*; trs. De Angelis (Rome, 1938)

Friedrich Furchheim: *Bibliographie der Insel Capri und der Sorrentiner Halbinsel etc* (Leipzig, 1916); contains a list of works on Capri

Fabio Giordano: *History of Naples*
   Author's note: Fabio Giordano, who was born about 1540 and died before 1595, was a lawyer, botanist, poet and archaeologist. He wrote an almost indecipherable but valuable history of Naples, of which only one entire manuscript copy has survived. Norman Douglas did what he could to transcribe it; see Douglas 1930, 49–100; and 1952, 29, 30 and 45.

W. E. Gladstone: *The Gladstone Diaries*, Vol 1 (1832) ed. Foot and Matthew (London, 1968)

Louis Golding: *Sunward* (London, 1924)

A. J. Grant and H. Temperley: *Europe in the Nineteenth Century, 1789–1914* (London, 1927)

Michael Grant: *Cities of Vesuvius* (London, 1971)

Lord Grantley (Richard Norton): *Silver Spoon* (London, 1954)

Manfred Gräter: Programme notes for *Omaggio Musicale all' Italia* (Capri, September 1983)

J. R. Green: see *Saturday Review*

Graham Greene: *An Impossible Woman – the Memories of Dottoressa Moor* (London, 1975)
   Author's note: Mr Greene's account of the Dottoressa's 'memories' should be treated with reserve as a source on Capri. I quote one major example of inaccuracy: *p. 140.* 'Once before the war I (Moor) saw him (Munthe) and the Queen walking with Kaiser Wilhelm from Caprile, where the Queen had her house, down to Materita, to Munthe's tower. Wilhelm was in uniform . . .' In 1904 Elisabeth Moor was a girl of 18 studying in Vienna and certainly not in Capri. Dr Weber, who as a boy witnessed the Kaiser's visit, says he was in civilian clothes. Victoria, then still Crown Princess, was living in the Hotel Molaro (later Hotel San Michele) and not at Caprile.

Ian Greenlees: *Norman Douglas* (London, 1957)

Ferdinand Gregorovius: *The Island of Capri – a Mediterranean Idyll* (1853), trs. Fairbairn (London, 1896)

Grove: *The New Grove Dictionary of Music* (London, 1980)

Ing. Michele Guadagno: *Flora Caprearum Nova* (Forli, 1932)

Peter Gunn: *The Companion Guide to Southern Italy* (London, 1969)

Norbert Hadrawa: *Freundschaftliche Briefe auf der Insel Capri* (Naples, 1793, in Italian; Dresden, 1794, in German)

F. H. von der Hagen: *Briefe in die Heimat* (Breslau, 1818–21); 4 volumes, of which Capri is in Vol III, part 2

Augustus J. C. Hare: *Cities of Southern Italy and Sicily* (London, 1883)

Sean Hignett: *Brett* (London, 1984)

Sir Richard Colt Hoare: *Classical Tour Through Italy and Sicily* (London, 1819)

Mark Holloway: *Norman Douglas* (London, 1976)

Homer: *Odyssey* (trs. Rieu, London, 1945)

Hyginus: *Fabulae* (Ed. Rose, Leiden, 1934)

Henry James: *Italian Hours* (London, 1909)

G. Jean-Aubrey: *Joseph Conrad, Life and Letters*, Vol 2 (London, 1927)

T. S. Jerome: *Classical References to Capri* (Naples, 1906)

—— *Roman Memories in the Landscape seen from Capri* (1914)

—— *Aspects of the Study of Roman History* (posthumous, 1923)

Sir Lees K. Knowles, Bt.: *The British in Capri, 1806–1808* (London, 1918)

August Kopisch: *Endeckung der Blauen Grotte* (1838)

N. K. Krupskaya: *Life of Lenin* (Moscow, 1968)

D. H. Lawrence: *The Letters of D. H. Lawrence*, Volume 3 (1916–21), ed. Boulton and Robertson (Cambridge, 1984)

—— *The Man who Loved Islands*, in Collected Short Stories, Volume 3 (London, 1955)

Lenin: *Collected Works*, Volume 34 (Moscow, 1966)

Norman Lewis: *Naples '44* (London, 1978)

J. Lomax and R. Ormond: *John Singer Sargent*; exhibition catalogue (London, 1979)

Compton Mackenzie: *Vestal Fire* (London, 1927)

Author's note: There are some distortions of chronology and some passages which are contradicted by other sources:

(i) *pp. 132–3*. It is implied that Petrara had been built and was Douglas's home; in fact he never finished or occupied it, but obviously Mackenzie had to put Douglas somewhere.

(ii) *pp. 252–70*. This section makes no mention of the ceremonial flogging in the Matermania cave (perhaps it would have been too daring for a 1927 publication), but there are echoes of it in his account of the dinner-party given by Fersen to his all-male guests and the subsequent revels (pp. 106–18). Mackenzie bases Fersen's banishment on the success of a deputation 'representing the finer elements of Sirenian society' to the 'Prefect of Stabia'. In Mackenzie's account the decree of banishment was served on Fersen in a hotel in Rome.

(iii) *pp. 293–303, 335–7 & 367*. Morgan Heiskell ('Harry Menteith') is represented as having 'lost his beautiful young wife in Florence' and come to Capri with his 'twin baby girls'. In fact his wife Ann was flourishing and living in the Villa Discopoli with their children, Andrew (Bobbie) and Diana (*Oct. 5*, 143, 153–4). When Heiskell was away in France in 1917–18, Mackenzie's frequent visits to the Villa Discopoli gave rise to gossip about a relationship with Ann; perhaps this was why he killed off the wife in *Vestal Fire*.

(iv) *pp. 324–5*. Mackenzie gives May 1914 as the month in which Fersen, Nino and Wolcott-Perrys returned from their world trip. In their respective autobiographies, however, both he and Faith indicate that the party did not return until November or early December, after the outbreak of war.

(v) *pp. 376–83*. The death of Jerome ('Scudamore') is transposed from 1914 to 1919.

Compton Mackenzie: *Extraordinary Women* (London, 1928)

Author's note: Two points are worth making:

(i) *pp. 81–90*. 'Rory Freemantle's' Villa Leucadia is put at the point where the Anacapri road, having reached the top of the cliff, turns sharply left into the village, near the present Hotel Caesar Augustus. This is fictitious. Checca Lloyd, who is part of the character of 'Rory', having bought the Cà del Sole and Villa Alba in Via Castello, turned them into a single property; in the garden of the Villa Alba was an 'amphitheatre' flanked by evergreen trees (*EW*, 85–86 and 319).

(ii) *pp. 283–348*. Rory's party – 'It was intended to be a Sirenian night of nights. And it was' – brings in all the main characters of the book and some others besides. 'Hewetson's' classical dance, wearing 'nothing but a pink silk handkerchief and a paper rose' is based on Van Decker's *pas seul* of summer 1918. The adventures of 'Zoë Mitchell', Mimì Franchetti, 'Captain Wheeler' and 'Carmĭně Bruno' (Baby Soldatenkov's boy-friend Luigi Gargiulo), which nearly ended in Zoë falling over the cliff at Punta Tragara, are related to a party at the Solitaria, where Zoë got very drunk, could not make the journey back to the Quisisana and slept it off at the Mackenzies' house, until she was taken back to the hotel by her severe French maid – 'Madame's behaviour is not at all *comme il faut*' – see Faith Mackenzie, *More than I should*, 18–19.

Compton Mackenzie: *First Athenian Memories* (London, 1931)

—— *My Life and Times, Octave 4, 1907–1914* (London, 1965)

—— *My Life and Times, Octave 5, 1915–1923* (London, 1966)

—— *My Life and Times, Octave 6, 1923–1930* (London, 1967)

Faith Compton Mackenzie: *As much as I dare* (London, 1938)

—— *More than I should* (London, 1940)

—— *Always Afternoon* (London, 1943)

Col. J. C. Mackowen: *Capri* (Naples, 1883)

Denis Mack Smith: *A History of Sicily* (2 vols) (London, 1968)

—— *Mussolini* (London, 1981)

Kenneth Macpherson: *Omnes Eodem Cogimur*; memoir of Norman Douglas (privately printed 1953)

Amedeo Maiuri: *Capri – its History and Monuments* – English edition (Instituto Poligrafico dello Stato, Rome, 1958)

Curzio Malaparte: *La Pelle*, trs. Moore (London, 1952)

William Manchester: *The Arms of Krupp, 1587–1968* (New York, 1968); references are to Bantam edition, 1970

Rosario Mangoni: *Ricerche Storiche sull' Isola di Capri* (Naples, 1834)

—— *Ricerche Topografiche ed Archeologiche sull' Isola di Capri* (Naples, 1834)

Clotilde Marghieri: *Trilogia* (Milan, 1982)
G. Martorelli: *De Regia Theca Calamaria* (Milan, 1840)
Mattino Illustrato: issue of 30.6.79 on Malaparte
Robin Maugham: *Escape from the Shadows* (London, 1972)
Wm. Somerset Maugham: *The Complete Short Stories*, Vol 3 ('Mayhew', 'The Lotus Eaters' and 'Salvatore') (London, 1951)
Bernhard Menne: *Krupp – Deutschlands Kanonenkönige* (Zurich, 1936)
Jeffrey Meyers: *Katherine Mansfield – a Biography* (London, 1978)
Ch. Baron de Montesqieu; *Voyages* (Bordeaux, 1894)
Ted Morgan: *Somerset Maugham* (London, 1980; references are to Triad, 1981)
Axel Munthe: *Letters from a Mourning City* (London, 1887)
—— *The Story of San Michele* (London, 1929)
—— *Memories and Vagaries* (London, 1930)
Gustav Munthe & Gudrun Uexküll: *The Story of Axel Munthe* (trs. Munthe & Sudley, London, 1953)
Malcolm Munthe: *Sweet is War* (London, 1954)
Murray: *Handbook for Travellers in S. Italy and Sicily*; 2nd edn. (1855); 7th edn. (1873); 9th edn. (1892)
National Geographical Magazine: June 1970, on 'Capri'
Nautical Chronicle: Vol XXI (1809), on Anglo–French hostilities in Capri
Alexander Olinda: *Freund Allers* (Stuttgart, 1894)
Josef Oliv: *Axel Munthe's San Michele – a Guide for Visitors* (Malmö, 1975)
Pino Orioli: *Adventures of a Bookseller* (Florence, 1937)
Oxford Classical Dictionary (Oxford, 1949)
Roberto Pane: *Capri – Walls and Vaulted Houses* (trs. Thorne, Naples, 1967)
D. A. Parrino: *Guida pei Forestieri ess. delle Isole d'Ischia, Capri ecc.* (Naples, 1704)
—— *Descrizione della Città di Napoli* (Naples, 1727)
Enzo Petraccone: *L'Isola di Capri* (Bergamo, 1913)
R. M. Rilke: *Selected Letters*, trs. Hull (London, 1946)
Roger Peyrefitte: *L'Exilé de Capri*, trs. Hyams (London, 1969); references are to Panther edition of 1970
Author's note: Three minor criticisms on points of detail:
(i) *p. 56.* Pagano and Serena were the other way round in respect of 'clerical' and 'anti-clerical'.
(ii) *p. 124.* Krupp was habitué of the Grotta di Fra' Felice, beside the Via Krupp and not the Grotta delle Felci, the prehistoric cave-dwelling on the side of Monte Salaro.
(iii) *p. 264.* The *commissioniere* who transported Fersen's body to the mainland was Alberto Lembo. Allers's boy-model was Antonio Lembo, a member of the fishing family of Marina Piccola.
Pliny the Elder: *Naturalis Historia*
Bernardo Quaranta: *Le Antiche Ruine di Capri ecc.* (Naples, 1835)
Ugo Rellini: *La Grotta delle Felci a Capri* (in Monumenti Antichi, 1923)
Elsa Respighi: *Ottorino Respighi* (Milan, 1954)
E. Rhys: *Frederick Lord Leighton – his Life and Work* (London, 1900)
Royal Institute of International Affairs (RIIA): *Chronology of the Second World War* (London, 1947)
Giobbe Ruocco: Collections of Documents, dealing with the history of Capri from the sixteenth to early nineteenth centuries, published in Naples between 1947 and 1958 – twelve volumes in all
Saturday Review: 1873 – articles by J. R. Green on 'Capri', 'Capri and its Roman Remains' and 'The Coral-Fishers of Capri'
Reinhold Schoener: *Capri* (Leipzig, 1892)
Giuseppe Maria Secondo: *Relazione Storica dell' Antichità, Rovine & Residui di Capri, umiliata al Re* (Naples, 1750)
Meryl Secrest: *Between Me and Life* (New York, 1974); biography of Romaine Brooks
Ettore Settanni: *Scrittori Stranieri a Capri* (Capri, 1954)
—— *Miti Uomini e Donne a Capri* (Capri, 1964)
Mary Shelley: *Rambles in Germany and Italy* (1844)
Silius Italicus: *Punica*
Regina Soria: *Dictionary of Nineteenth Century American Artists in Italy* (Associated University Presses Inc., 1982)
William Smith: *Dictionary of Greek and Roman Biography and Mythology* (London, 1854)
—— *Dictionary of Greek and Roman Geography* (London, 1873)

Publius Statius: *Silvae*
Francis Steegmuller: *Silence at Salerno* (New York, 1978)
Cecilia Sternberg: *The Journey* (London, 1977)
Strabo: *Geography* (late first century B.C. to early first A.D.)
S. A. Svensson *et al.*: *The Story of Axel Munthe, Capri and San Michele* (Allhem Publishing House, Malmö, 1959)
Suetonius: see Tranquillus
Cornelius Tacitus: *Annals*
Angelo Tamborra: *Esuli Russi in Italia dal 1905 al 1917* (Bari, 1977)
'Tidief' (Tina de Forcade): *Capri in grigio-verde* (Naples, 1977)
The Times: *History of the Times*, Vol 2 (1881–84)
Gaius Suetonius Tranquillus: *De Vita Caesarum*; references to *Augustus, Tiberius, Vitellius* and *Domitian*
Hans von Tresckow: *Von Fürsten und andern Sterblichen* (Berlin, 1922)
Raleigh Trevelyan: *Rome '44* (London, 1981)
Tribuna di Capri: 'Periodico democratico dell' Isola' – news-sheet and commentary issued at intervals from March 1982 by the Communist Party (PCI) of Capri
Harold E. Trower: *The Book of Capri* (Naples, 1906)
—— *Sunbeam Stories of Capri* (Naples, 1928)
Nikolai Valentinov: *Early Years of Lenin* (University of Michigan Press, 1969)
Gino Verbena: *Anacapri ride* (Naples, 1982)
—— *Schizzetti d'Anacapri* (Naples, 1983)
Vergil: *Aeneid*
Lea Vergine *et al.*: *Capri 1905/1940 Frammenti Postumi* (Milan, 1983)
Wilhelm Waiblinger: *Letters and Songs from Capri* (1828)
Alan Walters: *A Lotus Eater in Capri* (London, 1893)
Margaret Walters: *The Nude Male* (London, 1978)
Carl Weichardt: *Tiberius's Villa and other Roman Buildings on the Isle of Capri*, trs. Brett (Leipzig, 1900)
Claretta Wiedermann: *Capri Vista dai Tedeschi* (*Tesi di Laurea* at Naples University)
Oscar Wilde: *Letters of Oscar Wilde*, ed. Hart-Davis (London, 1962)
L. Patrick Wilkinson: *Kingsmen of a Century* (Cambridge, 1980)
Henry Wreford: Various articles in *Naples and Florence Observer*, 1867–69; and *The Times*, for which he was correspondent.
Jessica Brett Young: *Francis Brett Young – a Biography* (London, 1962)

References and Notes

The following short titles have been used:

1. *Individuals*
    AA   Aldo Aprea
    DB   Doreen Berrill
    CC   The late Carlo della Posta Duca di Civitella
    PC   Pietro Cerrotta
    SC   Prof. Sol Cohen
    AG   Anne Gargiulo
    IG   Ian Greenlees
    GL   The late Gemma Terrasino (Lembo)
    GM   The late Giuseppina Messanelli
    AP   Antigone Pesce
    EP   Marchese Ettore Patrizi
    TP   Teodoro Pagano
    DR   The late David Rawnsley
    MR   Maria (Marietta) Russo
    ES   Enzo Simeoli
    PS   Pino Salvia
    SS   Shirley Steegmuller
    LT   Lidia Talamona
    DU   Baroness Dana Uexküll
    EV   Hon. Mrs Elizabeth Varley
    GWW Dr George W. Weber
    MY   The late Maurice Yates
    AZ   Alessandra Zomack

2. *Manuscript Collections*
    Azienda   Azienda Autonoma di Cura Soggiorno e Turismo, Isola di Capri
    AC   Archivio Carelli in CCIC
    CCIC   Centro Caprense Ignazio Cerio
    Kelsey Museum Kelsey Museum of Ancient and Medieval History,
                  University of Michigan, Ann Arbor, USA
    SPG   Society for the Propagation of the Gospel in Foreign Parts (London)

3. *Miscellaneous sources*
    Source 'M'   List of identifications of characters in *Vestal Fire*
                  (Mackenzie, 1927)
    VN   Visitors' book of the Villa Narcissus in the days
                  of Charles Coleman (1903–28)

4. *Published sources*
    AA   *Always Afternoon* (Mackenzie, F, 1943)
    AMAID   *As much as I dare* (Mackenzie, F, 1938)
    DNB   *Dictionary of National Biography*

Ency. Brit.	*Encyclopaedia Britannica*
EW	*Extraordinary Women* (Mackenzie, C, 1928)
MTIS	*More than I should* (Mackenzie, F, 1940)
Oct. 4	*My Life and Times, Octave 4, 1907–1915* (Mackenzie, C, 1965)
Oct. 5	*My Life and Times, Octave 5, 1915–1923* (Mackenzie, C, 1966)
Oct. 6	*My Life and Times, Octave 6, 1923–1930* (Mackenzie, C, 1967)
RIIA	Royal Institute of International Affairs Chronology of the Second World War (London, 1947)
VF	*Vestal Fire* (Mackenzie, C, 1922)

References and Notes

Introduction
1. *EW*, 223–4. The lady was Gwen Galatà.
2. Walters, 1893, 10–11. The Capresi still refer to the Anacapresi as *ciammurrielli*, a word of uncertain derivation, which today means simply 'stinkers'.

Chapter I: 2,000 Years of Foreign Rule
1. Douglas, 1952, 7.
2. Maiuri, 1958, 9–14; Douglas, 1930, 253–8.
3. The Sirens are discussed by Douglas in *Siren Land* (London, 1911).
4. Homer, *Odyssey* xii, 39–54, 165–200.
5. Strabo, *Geog.*, v. 4. 9.
6. The influence of the Etruscans in Campania is discussed by R. C. Carrington in *Antiquity* vi (1932), 5–23.
7. Suetonius, *Aug.*, 92.
8. In 1892 it was calculated that originally there were about 880 steps from the shore to Anacapri (Petraccone 1913, 47). A good number were destroyed in 1874 by the new road linking Capri and Anacapri. In 1900, according to Trower, only 159 remained. Today the lower reaches of the Scala Fenicia have been replaced by modern steps and stretches of path, to serve the adjacent houses, while the sector on the steep mountain-side, just below the modern road, has disintegrated.
9. Ephebi (ἔφηβοι) were Greek youths who between the age of 18 and that of full citizenship (usually 20) spent a period of, mainly military, training, which included gymnastics. The custom still persisted in Capri because, until acquired by Augustus, the island had belonged to Naples, which retained its Greek customs and language.
10. Suet., *Aug.*, 98.
11. Suet., *Tiberius*, 40.
12. Tacitus, *Annals*, iv, 67.
13. Ingenious scholars have listed known, probable and possible locations of these villas. They certainly included the Villa Iovis (on the summit of Capo at the north-east tip of Capri), which is mentioned by Pliny as 'Arx Tiberii' (Pliny, iii, vi, 82); and by Suetonius as 'Villa Iovis' (Suet. *Tib.*, 65); Damecuta in Anacapri; and the Palazzo a Mare, west of Marina Grande. There were other villas on the northern slope of the Castiglione, on the summit of Monte San Michele and along Tragara.
14. Tac., *Ann.*, iv, 67; vi, 1. Suet., *Tib.*, 42–4, 60, 62, 74.
15. It is not known whether Elephantis was male or female, nor whether the writings were in verse or prose (see Smith, 1854).
16. Suet., *Vitellius*, 3.
17. Greek painter, *floruit* 397 B.C., born in Ephesus and later became Athenian citizen.
18. Tac., *Ann.*, vi, 6 (trs. J. Jackson in Loeb Classical Library, p. 163).
19. Dio Cassius, lii, 43. Of the splendid buildings erected by Augustus and Tiberius only the indestructible foundations of the Villa Iovis and parts of the Damecuta villa and the Palazzo a Mare/Bagni di Tiberio are still visible. Destruction has been continuous. Roman building

materials have never ceased to be incorporated in Capri houses and walls. A succession of wanton excavators have removed marble by the ton: quantities of columns, statues and pavements have been devoured in the island's lime-kilns or exported for this purpose to Naples. Lead-piping, whenever found, vanishes immediately (see Douglas, 1930, 227–9).

20. Pane considers that the present church is not earlier than the twelfth century. Since the tradition of San Costanzo as patron of the island and its protector against Saracen raids was already established in the ninth century, it is likely that an earlier, probably basilican, church preceded the present late Byzantine building (Pane, 1967, 34–7).

21. Eliseo Arcucci is described as *classis praefectus* by the sixteenth-century historian Capaccio. This has been taken to mean Grand Admiral, or Admiral of the Fleet, but his name appears in none of the relevant lists of the time, and I follow Douglas, 1930, 152–3, in regarding him simply as a sea-captain.

22. The funeral monument to Giacomo Arcucci was the work of Michelangelo Naccherino (1550–1622), a Florentine who moved to Naples and became court sculptor there. Originally made for the Certosa, the monument was moved to the Church of Santo Stefano in 1891.

23. The ducat, generally of gold and of varying value, was in use in many European countries. It was first struck by Roger II of Sicily in his capacity as Duke of Apulia and bore the inscription *'Sit tibi, Christe, datus, quem tu regis, iste ducatus'* (Lord, thou rulest this duchy, to thee be it dedicated).

24. Cerio, 1957, 19–20.

25. The full text of Bouchard's narrative is quoted in Cerio, 1950, 32–9; there is an English translation and commentary in Andrén, 1980, 112–19; I am indebted to both for these extracts.

26. A detailed account of Bishop Pellegrino is given in Cerio, 1934a, 70–132; there is a summary in Cerio, 1957, 29–34.

27. For detailed biography of Prudentia, who became Sister Serafina, see Douglas, 1930, 157–212, which is fuller and earlier in date than the résumé in Douglas, 1929, 179–220.

28. Douglas, 1929, 185–6.

29. This is reminiscent of the aftermath of the earthquake of 23 November 1980, when homeless families, who appealed to be admitted to unoccupied church cloisters in Naples, were refused access.

30. The resemblance is set out in comparative tables in Douglas, 1930, 209–12.

31. Douglas, 1929, 205.

32. In 1813 Serafina's coffin was moved from the Convent Church of San Salvatore to the Parish Church of Santo Stefano, where it was laid under the High Altar. In 1820 it was moved to Chapel of the Lesser Crucifix; in 1856, to near the Baptistery; and finally laid to rest in the Chapel of the Crucifix, where an inscription was placed to record these peregrinations.

33. Trower, 1906, 248–9.

34. This account of Thorold is based partly on Cerio, 1957, 39–44; partly on documents kindly put at my disposal by the Rev. Henry Thorold of Marston, Lincolnshire, who has done research into the early history of the Thorold family; and partly on help from Thorold's descendant Vittorio Canale, who lives in Capri. Cerio is inaccurate in saying that Nathaniel made no will. Whatever may have happened to his corpse, Nathaniel has no known tomb or memorial at Harmston or elsewhere in Lincolnshire.

35. Hadrawa wrote 40 letters about Capri to a friend, which were first published in 1793 in Italian and translated into German in 1794 (see Bibliography).

36. The Lembo family emigrated from Lecce (Puglia) to Capri in 1740. The nickname 'Sorechella' still applies to members of the family, e.g. to Attilio Lembo, steward of Hotel La Palma, who gave me this information.

37. The Parthenopean 'martyrs' are commemorated on a tablet which stands at the entrance of the *municipio* of Naples. Arcucci, who was executed on 18 March 1800, is fourth in the list of names. There is also a tablet in his memory on the south-east side of the Piazza of Capri.

38. Manuscript amongst the Lowe papers in the British Museum; quoted in Douglas, 1930, 302.

39. Amongst the property dispersed were the Certosa's documents, which were 'sold for packing purposes, as waste paper, to the shopkeepers of Capri'. Some of these papers were acquired by the antiquarian and historian Giuseppe Feola, who worked in Capri until his death in 1842, when they were again dispersed – altogether the most serious literary loss sustained by Capri since Roman times (Douglas, 1930, 107–8).

40. There are accounts of the Blue Grotto by Alexandre Dumas *père* in *Le Spéronare* (Tome I, 43, edition of 1855, Michel Levy, Paris) and by Hans Christian Andersen in *The Improvisator* (1834). The young German poet Wilhelm Waiblinger stayed for a month in the autumn of 1828 and wrote an ultra-sentimental *Märchen von der Blauen Grotte* (which he never visited) and *Briefe aus Capri*; on his death-bed in Rome in 1830 at the age of 25, ravaged by excesses and disease, he survived just long enough to write his *Lied auf Capri*. Kopisch himself waited until 1838 before publishing *Entdeckung der Blauen Grotte*. A good practical explanation is provided by the Italian archaeologist, Prof. Amedeo Maiuri:

> The lucky concurrence of geological and spelaeological conditions have endowed the grotto with a twofold enchantment. The cave sank during a geological age 15–20 metres below the present sea level and thus blocked every opening through which light might enter directly, except the narrow breach of access, with the result that both the cavity of the grotto and the sea basin that is enclosed in it acquired two different and magical colours, for on one side the sunlight penetrating from below through a veil of sea water springs out and is reflected on to the sides and the vault of the grotto coloured with azure; and on the other side, this light being reflected by the white sandy bottom of the grotto renders the water strangely opalescent so that any object that is bathed in it drips and vibrates with a silvery light. (Maiuri, 1958, 80)

41. Manuscript letter by Edward Lear, dated 4 January 1840, in National Library of Scotland, to which Alan Anderson kindly drew my attention.
42. In a private collection in England (Cerio, 1957, Plate 20).
43. These drawings, which are in the Museum of San Martino in Naples and in the Astarita collection in the Museo Nazionale at Capodimonte, are reproduced at the back of Pane, 1967. Gigante's drawings, and paintings and drawings of other artists were exhibited at the Certosa in 1980–81, under the auspices of the *Soprintendenza per i Beni Artistici e Storici della Campania*; they are illustrated in a good catalogue, *L'Immagine di Capri*.
44. Extracts from *The Gladstone Diaries*, Vol 1 (1832), edited by M. R. D. Foot and H. C. G Matthew, London, 1968.
45. Francesco Alvino, *Due Giorni a Capri*, Naples, 1838 (reprinted Naples, 1967).
46. Shelley, 1844, 262–79.
47. Gregorovius, trs. Fairbairn, 1896, 17–21, 42–68, 78–9 and 86–91.
48. The French monetary system was in force, the lira and franc having the same value; 1.25 francs were the equivalent of one English shilling.
49. The Grotta Verde got its name from the dazzling green colour of the roof and sides as viewed in the middle of the day. See also Douglas, 1930, 151 and 231; Mackowen, 1883, 165–6; Walters, 1893, 186–7.
50. This grotto, whose name occurs variously as Matermania, Mitromania, Matromania, Matremania, and Metromania, is situated amongst rocks which drop steeply down the south-east side of the island. The Romans used masonry, which still survives, to adapt the irregular shape of the cave to that of a rectangular apsed hall. Dripping water which filtered through the rocks above, collected into a small hollow, which was reached by a row of steps. The cave has been linked with the worship both of Mithras and the Magna Mater (Cybele). The facts, theories and arguments are set out in Trower, 1906, 221–8; Douglas, 1930, 243–6; and Maiuri, 1958, 86–7.
51. *Le Camerelle* ('Little chambers'), which are now submerged beneath a street of shops and houses, were a succession of vaulted cells, built in Roman times, probably with the double purpose of supporting a road from Castiglione to Tragara and collecting/storing rainwater. Hadrawa put forward the improbable theory that they were the parlours (*sellaria*) where young people performed sexual acts for the gratification of the Emperor Tiberius.
52. In 1908 a tablet was erected in Clark's honour in the courtyard of the Municipio.
53. A short account of the 4th Baron Grantley and his Caprese wife is given by the 6th Baron in his reminiscences, *Silver Spoon* (London, 1954, 15, 20–1). Edwin Cerio deals very tediously with a nineteenth-century English resident, 'Burton, Lord Bentley', who married 'Luisa', the daughter of 'Mastro Saverio, the baker of Anacapri' (*L'Ora di Capri*, 210–25, and *The Masque of Capri*, 75–89). In yet a third book by Cerio this character becomes 'Marston, Lord Bexley' (*Aria di Capri*, trs. *That Capri Air*, 111–17).
54. Canale, 1887, quoted by Walters, 1893, 148.

55. Mackowen, 1883, 116.
56. Walters, 1893, 152.

Chapter 2: The First Foreign Residents

1. See Wreford's articles of 14 and 21 November 1868 in the *Naples and Florence Observer*, on 'The Small Communes of South Italy', and his account (date unknown) of 'Sardine Fisheries in Capri'.
2. Mackowen's researches were published in *Capri* (Naples, 1883).
3. *The Saturday Review* of 1873 published three articles by Green – 'Capri' (22 March), 'Capri and its Roman remains' (5 April) and 'The Coral-Fishers of Capri' (3 May); the articles were later republished under the title *Stray Studies*.
4. Mackowen, 1883, 116.
5. Wreford, *op. cit.*, 14 November 1868.
6. Mackowen, 1883, 116–17.
7. AC.
8. GWW.
9. Walters, 1893, 144; Mackowen, 1883, 121.
10. Undated despatch by Wreford, filed in CCIC.
11. Green, *op. cit.*
12. Baedeker, 1867, 163; *bajocco* was the smallest copper coin.
13. Wreford, *op. cit.*, 21 November 1868.
14. Dr Ferdinando Bergamo, *Statistica Medica-topografica-igienica di Capri dal Giugno 1876 all'Agosto 1877*, Napoli, Tipografia dei Comuni, 1879; see also Douglas, 1930, 206–7.
15. Wreford, *op. cit.*, 21 November 1868.
16. All the visitors' books have been preserved by Teodoro Pagano, grandson of Michele and present head of the family, and are housed in the Pagano room in the Palazzo Cerio. The caricatures are also reproduced in P. A. Jannini, *Tristan Corbière a Capri*, Rome, 1975.
17. Not to be confused with the better known Villa San Michele, which Munthe built in Anacapri 20 years later.
18. AC.
19. Quisisana prospectus issued about 1880 by Federico Serena.
20. Cerio, 1957, 75.
21. Walters, 1893, 121–3.
22. Grantley, 1954, 15.
23. Cerio, *c.* 1921, 24.
24. In the inscription of 1884 at the entrance to the non-Catholic cemetery, which records its foundation in 1878, Hayward is described as coming from 'Bury St Edmunds, New York'. He was, in fact, English and born near Bury St Edmunds in the County of Suffolk. According to Edwin Cerio, *op. cit.*, 24, his father Ignazio gave or sold for a nominal sum the original land for the cemetery.
25. Mackowen 1883, 124–7.
26. *Op. cit.*, 117.
27. *Op. cit.*, 136–7; Walters, 1893, 20.
28. A visitor of 1853 was Joseph Victor Scheffel, a plump, fair-haired German, who had abandoned the study of law and moved to Italy to become a painter. Staying at Pagano's he decided to be a poet instead and composed *Der Trompeter von Sakkingen*, an 'epic' which was an immediate success in Germany. Although the poem itself was not about Capri, the island, as well as a cat named Hiddigeigei, who acted as adviser to the poet, was mentioned in the preface. This is the origin of the name taken by the *caffè*, which was situated where a travel office (25), a shop (27) and the restaurant 'Casina delle Rose' (29–33) now are in Via Vittorio Emanuele. Later it became famous as the 'Caffè Morgano'.
29. Cerio, 1929, 111–17.
30. Cerio, 1957, 77–8.
31. Lomax and Ormond, 1979, 22–3.
32. Hare, 1883, 191.
33. Until 1915 the main street of Capri town was known as Via Hohenzollern, no doubt to please the

German tourists. When Italy entered the war against Germany in that year, the street was renamed Via Vittorio Emanuele III, as it still is today.

34. GWW, son of Augusto and Raffaella.
35. Cerio, 1957, 72–3; Svensson, 1959, 87, 89; Andrén, 1980, 152–3; dossier in CCIC; Douglas, 1934, 52.
36. Although as a 19-year-old medical student Munthe may have visited Capri, I cannot accept the account he gives in Chapter 1 of *The Story of San Michele* and his foretelling of the building of Villa San Michele.
37. Munthe and Uexküll, 1953, 22–3.
38. Hare, 1883, 185.
39. Baedeker, 1883, 159–64.
40. Douglas, 1930, 28.
41. Giuseppe Catuogno, President of the Società Operaia (1979–82) gave me information about it and allowed me to make copies of photographs of Dr Rispo, its first doctor, and two early members, Nicola Pagano and Mariano Morgano, which hang in its office; TP and GWW also provided details.
42. See Munthe's contemporary account, *Letters from a Mourning City*, and *The Story of San Michele*, chapter 8, for an account of the plague in Naples.
43. Munthe's own testimony to EV, who gave me the information.
44. Svensson, 1959, 242.
45. An early letter by Munthe filed with the Blackwood papers in the National Library of Scotland, to which Alan Anderson kindly drew my attention.
46. GWW.
47. The titles 'Don' and 'Donna' were bestowed on individuals who were above the average, either financially, socially, in age or even criminally. This was one of the usages left in Southern Italy by centuries of Spanish rule. The title gave the right tone of respect and at the same time of intimacy, when addressing someone who was older, richer or more distinguished than yourself. After the turn of the century the usage of 'Don' and 'Donna' was gradually replaced by honorifics like Cavaliere, dispensed by the King at the suggestion of a Deputy or Senator, and by the use of academic titles such as Dottore, Avvocato, Ingegnere, and Architetto (GWW).
48. *VF*, 50–1.
49. The word *esposito* is applied to new-born babies which have been exposed or abandoned. Many foundlings or 'children of the Madonna' as they are called, attracted the surname 'Esposito', which is extremely common in Naples.

Chapter 3: The Gay 'Nineties
1. Douglas, 1934, 454–6.
2. Di Sirignano, 1981, 172–3, writes that Donna Lucia sent Alberino to warn Allers; and that Alberino also procured a boat with four rowers, which collected Allers at Porto di Tragara (Faraglioni) and conveyed him to Amalfi. According to Andrén, 1980, 155, it was a sailing boat, and his destination Calabria.
3. *VF*, 6.
4. In *VF* he is represented as translating Dante's *Divina Commedia*; see also *Oct. 4*, 186–7.
5. Morgan, 1981, 44 and 53. Almost all Maugham's references to Brooks are bitchy – in perpetual resentment perhaps against the man who took his virginity at Heidelberg. The character of 'Hayward', aesthete and failed lawyer, in *Of Human Bondage*, and 'Brown' in *The Summing Up* are based on Brooks. In *A Writer's Notebook* Maugham wrote that Brooks 'has no will, no restraint, no courage against any of the accidents of fortune. If he cannot smoke, he is wretched; if his food or wine is bad, he is upset; a wet day shatters him. If he doesn't feel well, he is silent, cast down and melancholy. The slightest cross, even a difference of opinion, will make him angry and sullen' (see Morgan, 350–2).
6. Wilkinson, 1980, 32; and Michael Sadleir's biography of Benson in *DNB*.
7. Letters of Oscar Wilde, edited Rupert Hart Davis, 1962, 649, 659, 661, 693. Leonard Smithers published *The Ballad of Reading Gaol* and other works by Wilde. An embellished account of the Quisisana incident is given in Peyrefitte, 1970, 15–17.
8. Douglas, 1934, 28–9; Penguin reprint of *South Wind*, 1953; 50; Secrest, 1974, 134.
9. Svensson, 1959, 241–2.

10. Manchester, 1970, 216, 218, 236–7.
11. Article on Fritz Krupp in *Ency. Brit.*, 15th edn.
12. Douglas, 1934, 183–5.
13. GWW.
14. Capri was the birthplace, sometime in the latter part of the third century B.C., of Blaesus, an Italian poet who wrote serio-comic plays (σπουδογέλοια). He is represented only by a single fragment:

    ἑπτὰ μαθαλίδας ἐπίχεον ἁμῖν τῶ γλυκυτάτω
    (Pour out for us seven measures of your sweetest wine).

15. Information from Giovanni Ruggiero, who took over the running of his father's nursery and flower-shop; see also *VF*, 126–8 and *Oct. 4*, 215.
16. AC.
17. The inscription at the head of the Via Krupp reads:

    La munificenza di Federico Alfredo Krupp / auspice il Comune di Capri / consentì / all' ingegnere Emilio Mayer / la realizzazione / di questa ardimentosa e mirabile strada / che facilitò / il godimento di scoscese bellezze dell' isola.
    The generosity of Frederick Alfred Krupp and the support of the Commune of Capri allowed engineer Emilio Mayer to achieve this audacious and wonderful road, which made possible the enjoyment of the precipitous beauties of the island.

18. The usually accepted story of Mackowen's death is that, shortly after landing in New Orleans, he was shot in a bar either in a brawl or during a heated argument about emancipation. His grandson, Mario Maresca, who has a *pensione* at Marina Grande in Mackowen's former house, told me about his death at the hand of a freed slave. Signor Maresca also showed me a copy of Mackowen's will and allowed me to copy photographs of his grandparents.
19. The date of Jerome's birth recorded on his grave in the *cimitero acattolico* is 1854; I am assured by the Kelsey Museum, University of Michigan, who kindly gave me biographical details of him, that 1864 is correct.
20. In Maugham, W. S., 1951, Vol 3, 1278, Jerome is called 'Mayhew'; this short story contains a colourful account of how he came to buy the Villa Castello. A vivid picture of Jerome and Yetta is given in *VF*, *passim*, where they are 'John Scudamore' and 'Nita'.
21. *EW*, 235–6. Vedder died in 1923, not 1916, as in *VF*, 348.
22. GWW, who obtained information from a friend of Jenny's mother.
23. The document of citizenship is in the Pagano collection in the Palazzo Cerio.
24. Peyrefitte, 1970, 102–3.
25. Anonymous source.
26. According to Peyrefitte, 1970, 44, the crossed forks, held by a Bacchic figure, were construed by the Church as an insulting allusion to the Holy Father's crossed keys.
27. Manchester, 1970, 262.
28. Manchester, 1970, 259–60; amongst his sources are the memoirs of Von Tresckow himself.
29. Douglas, 1934, 186–9; see also *VF*, 257–9.
30. Cerio, 1950, 300–1.
31. AC.
32. Manchester, 1970, 263–72.
33. GWW.

Chapter 4: Heyday of the Foreign Colony
1. *VF*, 89 ff. GWW, GM and TP also provided information.
2. Trower, 1906, xxvi.
3. Douglas, 1934, 61.
4. Holloway, 1976, 60–1.
5. Douglas, 1946, 17; 1934, 200.
6. Douglas, 1946, 20–1.
7. Rachel (Nini) Binyon.
8. VN records a visit by Lady Blanche Gordon-Lennox and her daughter, Ivy, on 14 October 1904;

their address was Monte San Michele. The wine press is now owned by Peppino D'Emilio, of Matermania, whose grandmother, Margherita Salvia, worked on the estate.

9. *VF*, 23–5.
10. F. S. Andrus Esquire, Lancaster Herald of Arms, kindly gave me the following description of the Wolcott-Perry 'coat of arms':

'The Shield shows a chevron, possibly ermine, between three chess rooks, and the Crest is a bull's head erased gorged with an heraldic ducal coronet. This is quite distinct from a Duke's coronet of Rank, which has five strawberry leaves.'

11. This account of the Villa Torricella and its owners is based on *VF*, *passim*, and notes made by Edward B. Hitchcock, a cousin of Kate Perry who inherited the Villa Torricella in 1924. I am grateful to the present owner, Raffaele Gargiulo, who provided access to the property, allowed me to take photographs and gave me copies of his own photographs of the big *salone*, furnished much as it had been in the days of the Wolcott-Perrys.
12. *VF*, 16–19.
13. Douglas, 1934, 48–54; *VF*, 19–20, 141–8.
14. *VF*, 59–61; dossier in CCIC.
15. *Oct. 4*, 209–10; *VF*, 44–8.
16. I am grateful to the Household Cavalry Museum for facts about Thornton's brief military service. An account of him is given in *VF*, where he is 'Anthony Burlingham'; Douglas, 1934, 67–9, where he is 'G. H. Townley'; and *Oct. 5*, 157–8, where his forename is wrongly given as 'Charles' and a colourful but inaccurate account, perhaps invented by Thornton himself, provided of his military career.
17. *VF*, 14–15.
18. *VF*, *passim*; *MTIS*, 67–9. According to Gwen Galatà's death-certificate in the *municipio*, she was born Wickham at Aberden, Monthshire (sic); this no doubt is a corruption of Monmouthshire. MY, who knew her in the 'thirties told me that she was a cousin of Lord Tredegar, the Monmouthshire peer.
19. Information about the Caffè Morgano is from GWW, who as a young man frequented it; see also *VF*, 49–51.
20. Italia Rocchi and GWW.
21. *Oct. 4*, 215. Later the Sisters moved to the Villa Helios in Via Croce, where they still are.
22. *VF*, 87–8, 217–19.
23. *VF*, 126–8.
24. The tea-room occupied what is now 17 Via Camerelle (D'Angelo's shoe-shop); the main store was in 19 ('Volubilis' – clothes) and 21 ('Le Camerelle' – mementos).
25. *VF*, 259–61; see also Baedeker, 1912, 184.
26. In *VF*, 146, Gwen Galatà describes old 'Miss Jamieson' in Anacapri – 'Drives up with a different coachman every night. Asks them in and gives them vermouth. Don't know what she does after that, but quite harmless otherwise.' According to Peyrefitte, 1970, 250–1, Hugo Wemyss, the English homosexual, made regular carriage-trips to Anacapri for amorous purposes. On one such visit, in 1922, Wemyss and the coachman were observed by Marchesa Casati and Count Sforza, the Italian Foreign Minister, from the terrace of the Villa San Michele.
27. Barbarò, 1980, *passim*; Walters, M, 1978, 289 and 307.
28. For an account of the Kaiser's visit to Sicily, see Peyrefitte, 1970, 123. GWW says that on his visit to Capri the Kaiser wore civilian clothes and not uniform, as described in Greene, 1975, 140
29. My main sources on Fersen are Peyrefitte's *L'exilé de Capri*; and *VF*, where he is 'Count Marsac'. I have also drawn on Douglas, 1934, 358–66; material in the CCIC; and oral information given by CC, GWW and GM. I paid several visits to the Villa Fersen and photographed the progressive decay of the house and garden.
30. My account of Fersen's first visit to Capri is based on Peyrefitte, 1970, 9–25, according to which it occurred when Fersen was 17, i.e. in 1896. Peyrefitte, however, makes the visit coincide with Oscar Wilde's brief trip of 15–18 October 1897, which gives him a chance to relate the famous Quisisana episode. I do not know whether Fersen's visit was made in 1896 or 1897, or at all. I am giving myself the benefit of the doubt, in order to introduce certain matters relating to Monte Tiberio.
31. The hermit-chapel of S. Maria del Soccorso, originally known as Capella di S. Leonardo, was in

existence in 1632; Bouchard visited it in that year. In May 1832 Gladstone encountered a 'smirking friar' there. Mangoni, 1834, 499, writes of the hermit as custodian of the chapel and the sole inhabitant of the hill. See Douglas, 1930, 68, 164, 226, 272, 296; Pane, 1967, 49, 68 and Plate 36; Maiuri, 1958, 105–6.
32. Maiuri, *op. cit.*
33. *VF*, 101–2.
34. Douglas, 1934, 358.
35. Peyrefitte, 1970, 113–14, says that the workman was *nearly* killed; according to *VF*, 218, and GWW, the workman *was* killed. In *VF* it was the builder who escaped to the mainland and Fersen who was arrested and imprisoned because someone had to be held responsible. The *pretore* was Pestalozza, whom Douglas depicts in *South Wind* as 'Malipizzo'; see also *VF*, 219.
36. Peyrefitte, 1970, 114–18; see also *VF*, 207–8.
37. *VF*, 129–38.
38. *VF*, 151–2.
39. *VF*, 156–64.
40. *VF*, 189–98. The actual name of 'Adelaide Edwardes' is not known, but, according to source 'M', she was a real person.
41. *VF*, 165–7.
42. *VF*, 172–3.
43. *VF*, 173.
44. Peyrefitte, 1970, 111–12.
45. Marchesa Tina De Forcade.
46. *VF*, 50–1.
47. Peyrefitte, 1970, 125–6; Douglas, 1934, 366.
48. Morgan, 1981, 144.
49. The rivalry between Morgano and Serena is amusingly described in *VF*, 50, 175–6.
50. GWW.
51. Hueffer, who later changed his name to Ford, was born in 1873 of a formerly German (naturalised British) father. He wrote history, poems and novels. He was a friend and collaborator of Conrad. His last years were spent in France, where he died in 1939.
52. G. Jean-Aubrey, *Joseph Conrad, Life and Letters*, Vol 2, Chap. X, letter dated 9 May 1905.
53. Most of the subjects on which Douglas accumulated material are covered in his *Capri: materials for a description of the Island* (Florence, 1930), on which I have drawn extensively.
54. Holloway, 1976, 155 and 160–1.
55. According to the *Dictionary of American Biography*, 1936, Coleman's painting of the 1906 eruption is owned by the Brooklyn Museum.

Chapter 5: Maksim Gorki and Compton Mackenzie
1. GWW; and *New Grove*, London, 1980.
2. Peyrefitte, 1970, 115, 144–55.
3. *Extracts from Selected Letters of Rainer Maria Rilke 1902–1926* – introduction p. xii, letters 47, 58, 72, 84, 89, 95 and 117 – translated by R. F. C. Hull. To judge from these letters, the account of Rilke's visit given in Cerio, 1957, 67–9, is inaccurate.
4. Douglas, 1934, 13–19; Cunard, 1954, xiv.
5. The most notable date-palm in the island was that in the garden of the Hotel Pagano.
6. Holloway, 1976, 158–9.
7. *op. cit.*, 169–75.
8. Douglas, 1934, 279–80, 153–4; his visits to Calabria are described in *Old Calabria* (London, 1915).
9. Tamborra, 1977, 136; Krupskaya, 1968, 160.
10. GWW.
11. MR; AZ.
12. *EW*, 14.
13. Munthe & Uexküll, 1953, 70–2.
14. In *VF*, 232 ff, the review is said to have had only one number. This is not so. The CCIC possesses six issues of which the latest is No. 10 of October 1909. The issue of January 1909 contained a photogravure portrait, painted by Sarluis, of a lascivious-looking young man in skin-tight jersey

and trousers, entitled *L'inquiétude*. Mackenzie describes the illustration amusingly and the deep impression it made on Vernon Andrews ('Nigel Dawson')

15. *VF*, 252.
16. The inscribed copy of *Et le feu* ... is in the CCIC; the quotation about Mariano Morgano ('Ferdinando Zampone') is from *VF*, 252–3.
17. For Fersen's novel and review, and the reactions to them in Capri, see Peyrefitte, 1970, 178–94, and *VF*, 232–52.
18. *VF*, 47.
19. Peyrefitte, 1970, 197–204. There is a different account of the Matermania ceremony and Fersen's banishment in Cerio, 1950, 164–70.
20. GWW contributed this account of his father, which, he says, corrects some of the distortions in Cerio, 1950, 268–82 and 1957, 101–5; there is also a short account of Augusto Weber in Andrén, 1980, 157–9.
21. Some of the notebooks, poems and drawings are held by the CCIC.
22. GWW; Soria, 1982.
23. Lenin quotations are from *Early Years of Lenin*, by Nikolai Valentinov, the University of Michigan Press, 1969. In May 1973 I met Maria Stinga (Aprea), who had a gift-shop at 5 Via Croce. Then 77, she had happy memories of her Russian lessons from Lenin; she died in 1979.
24. Lenin, *Collected Works*, vol 34.
25. Amedeo Canfora, son of Gennaro, is proprietor of the present shop at 3 Via Camerelle. Lamberti (*VF* 325, 386 ff) had a shop in Via Vittorio Emanuele where 'Chantecler', the jewellery-shop, now is.
26. Di Sirignano, 1981, 176; GWW; the late General Carlo Gardini.
27. EP.
28. The Petrara property was bought by Ambassador Lago, who built the villa as it now is; later Mussolini appointed him Governor of the Dodecanese, and he lived in Rhodes. For some years past the Villa Lago has been owned by Dr Carlo Poma, of Rome, who in 1981 kindly allowed me to visit the house with his *guardiano*, Salvatore, and to appreciate its unique and rather frightening situation, which Douglas so admired, perched high above Marina Piccola.
29. Douglas, 1934, 15–16, 397.
30. *AMAID*, 188.
31. *Oct. 4*, 182; *AMAID*, 230.
32. *AA*, 21–7. Roberto Ferraro, manager of Hotel La Palma, who is a grandson of Nicola, allowed me to study the visitor's book, which shows that after Nicola's death in 1932 the hotel was continued by his two daughters until about 1938.
33. *AMAID*, 230–1.
34. *VF*, 285–8. Information about Mrs Fraser's swimming is from MR and GM.
35. *VF*, 36–7, 288–91; see also *MTIS*, 51–2.
36. After Capri, Burra became Curate of St Thomas's, Regent Street (1914–16) and then of North Holmwood, Dorking (1916–18). He must have left the priesthood soon afterwards, as there are no further references in Crockford's.
37. *VF*, 88–101, 113, 125–6.
38. *VF*, 291–3, 310–11. Douglas, 1934, 209, mentions *three* Misses Baker, who were Americans and Quakers. On 14 August 1904, VN records a visit by Elizabeth, A. Rebecca and H. Kate Baker, probably the same three sisters, from the USA.
39. *Oct. 4*, 185; Peyrefitte, 1970, 217–8. Peshkov became a senior officer in the Legion; in 1943 was Head of the Gaullist mission to French West Africa; and from 1943 to 1945, as General, was French Ambassador in Chungking.
40. Cicione is an affectionate nickname, which can mean nothing at all. Sometimes it has a sexual connotation and means 'big cock' (*cazzone*). It is not to be confused with *ciccione* (fatty).
41. This account of the *festa* of San Costanzo is based on *Oct. 4*, 185–6; *VF*, 75–86; Walters, 1893, 153 ff; and information from ES, who has made a deep study of the subject. Information about 'Cicione' comes from GWW and Settanni, 1964, 17–21.
42. *Oct. 4*, 189; *VF*, 385.
43. GWW.
44. *VF*, 314 ff.
45. *AMAID*, 232–3.

46. *VF*, 319–24.
47. *Oct. 4*, 217.
48. Maugham, W. S., 1951, Vol 3, 1278.
49. *Cum laude et bonis recordationibus facta atque famam nominis mei prosequantur* (Tacitus, *Annals* IV, 38, trs. Loeb Library).
50. *VF*, 324–5.
51. Secrest, 1974, 173–4, 178–83; *Oct. 5*, 158.
52. Benson, 1930, 338–44.
53. Lieut.-General George Julius Mellis, who died in 1903 and is buried in the *cimitero acattolico*; see Douglas, 1934, 467–9.
54. Kelly was elected Royal Academician in 1930 and, as Sir Gerald Kelly, KCVO, was President of the Royal Academy from 1949 to 1954.

Chapter 6: World War I
 1. Morgan, 1981, 211.
 2. *VF*, 329–30; GWW.
 3. Svensson, 1959, 260; Munthe & Uexküll, 1953, 49–50.
 4. Douglas, 1934, 35. *VF*, 107 ff, 306–7. See also Vergine, 1983, 14, 149–66; Peyrefitte, 1970, 178; and Greene, 1975, 83, 144.
 5. *VF*, 324–8; *Oct. 4*, 232–3; *AMAID*, 250–2. Peyrefitte makes no mention at all of the trip.
 6. The phrase was used by Walter H. Page, American Ambassador in London during the war.
 7. *AMAID*, 237–8.
 8. *AMAID*, 234–5; *Oct. 4*, 240–1.
 9. *VF*, 337.
10. *VF*, 338; *AMAID*, 269.
11. *VF*, 340.
12. *VF*, 347–8.
13. Douglas, 1946, 31–2, 58–64.
14. *AMAID*, 280; Holloway, 1976, 223.
15. Andrews's translation of Goethe's *Faust*, Part I, edited and revised by George M. Priest and Karl E. Weston (William's brother-in-law), was privately printed by the Princeton University Press in 1929; Marchese Ettore Patrizi has a copy.
16. *VF*, 359–63.
17. Notes compiled by Kate's cousin, Edward B. Hitchcock; *VF*, 359, 363.
18. Greenlees, 1957, 22 ff; Holloway, 1976, 239 ff.
19. Fitzgibbon, 1953, 26.
20. *Oct. 5*, 122–5.
21. *Oct. 5*, 129–31.
22. *Oct. 5*, 134.
23. *MTIS*, 11.
24. *Oct. 5*, 136.
25. Vergine, 1983, 13, 75–9.
26. *EW*, 1–35.
27. *EW*, 15–21; *VF*, 80–2.
28. *EW*, 110–31; see also *MTIS*, 15–16, Secrest, 1974, 292–5, and Marghieri, 1982, 330–1, quoted in Vergine, 1983, 65. EV and Etienne Amyot, who knew Renata Borgatti in later life have given me valuable information.
29. In *Oct. 5*, 138, Mackenzie states that 'everyone of the characters in *Extraordinary Women* is an exact portrait, with a single exception; Rory Freemantle is a composite creation of my own.' Contemporary sources are agreed that 'Rory' contains a strong element of Checca Lloyd. Characters whom I have not been able to identify have been introduced by Mackenzie's pseudonyms.
30. *EW*, 92–100, 159–70.
31. *EW*, 57–92, 101–5.
32. *EW*, 124–30, 187–206.
33. *EW*, 120, 324–5, 366–70.
34. *MTIS*, 17–18, 112–16.

35. Aretusa, Titi and Zenaide are characters whose surnames are unknown; they are likely to be persons who feature under other names in *EW*. There are snapshots of them in the contemporary album found in Naples by MY and presented by him to the CCIC. The album also features Principessa Soldatenkov, her daughter 'Baby', Mimì Franchetti, Renata Borgatti, Francesca (Checca) Lloyd, and Compton Mackenzie.
36. *MTIS*, 112.
37. In Capri the victory was celebrated by renaming the street which joins the Piazza to Due Golfi, 'Corso Trento & Trieste'. This street had first been called 'Via Provinciale', because like all metalled roads in Capri, it had been built by the Province. Today it is 'Via Roma'.
38. *MTIS*, 15.
39. Details from the War Memorials of Capri and Anacapri. The Capri memorial by F. Parisi (no further details) is affixed to the clock-tower in the Piazza. It was unveiled in 1921 by Edwin Cerio in the presence of General Armando Diaz, Italian Chief of Staff and victor of Vittorio Veneto. The Anacapri memorial, by Arnaldo Zocchi (1862–1940) and known as 'Il Monumento', is in the Piazza Vittoria.

Chapter 7: The Post-War Pursuit of Pleasure
 1. *EW*, 258.
 2. *Oct. 5*, 145; cf. *EW*, 256–8, where the performance of the *pescecane* at dinner in the Quisisana is described.
 3. GWW; AA.
 4. *VF*, 384–5.
 5. The Italian for gaming-house is *casinò*. Without the accent the word (diminutive of *casa*) means brothel. This subtlety is not apparent in the English 'casino'.
 6. *Oct. 5*, 137–8, 150–1.
 7. See note under Mackenzie's *Extraordinary Women*, in Bibliography, for details of the two villas.
 8. In *EW*, 229–50 and *passim*, Romaine Brooks the painter is portrayed as 'Olimpia Leigh', pianist and composer of antique music.
 9. *MTIS*, 24; *EW*, 229.
10. *EW*, 254–61, 273, 330–49; *Oct. 5*, 158–9.
11. See Bibliography for comments on Mackenzie's brilliant account of this party.
12. Young, 1962, 91–2.
13. *VF*, 385–6.
14. *VF*, 288–91.
15. *Oct. 5*, 158.
16. *VF*, 366–7.
17. When Heiskell returned to Capri after the war he told the Baroness Gudrun Uexküll how miserable and lonely he was (DU).
18. *VF*, 386–90.
19. *Oct. 5*, 158; Respighi, 1954, 133–8.
20. Gräter, 1983.
21. *DNB*, 1951; Young, 1962, 87 ff; *Oct. 5*, 159–60; GWW.
22. *Oct. 5*, 164–71; Lawrence, 1984, 438–77. The friendship between Mackenzie and Lawrence ended abruptly in 1928, when Lawrence published in the *London Mercury* a cruel portrayal of Mackenzie entitled *The Man Who Loved Islands*, which was based on confidences given to Lawrence by Faith Mackenzie.
23. GWW. While working as an engineer for Krupp, Cerio was sent to Buenos Aires in connection with a contract for modernising the Argentine Navy. Here he met and in 1907 married Elena Hosmann, member of a German–Jewish–Argentine family. In 1908 she bore him a daughter Anna Letizia Fiammetta (later known as Laetitia).
24. *MTIS*, 106–7 and *VF*, 64, elaborate on Cerio's appearance: 'He wished to be recognised as an unusual personality, to achieve which he dressed, if the comparison may convey anything, like something between Colline, the bass philosopher in *La Vie de Bohème*, and a Hampshire gamekeeper'.
25. Munthe and Uexküll, 1953, 122.
26. GWW, who is nephew of Vincenzo Desiderio.
27. *MTIS*, 70, 178; Cunard, 1954, 68.

28. Douglas, 1934, 155.
29. *VF*, 392–7; *AMAID*, 252. Kate's cousin, Edward B. Hitchcock, suspected Giovanni Galatà of being involved in the robbery. ES told me that the suspicion still persists.
30. The account of Marchese Casati comes from: *Oct. 5*, 175–6; Munthe and Uexküll, 1953, 122–4; Peyrefitte, 1970, 247–8; AZ, MR and DU, who consider that she was absolutely mad; DU emphasises the evil strain in her character.
31. Munthe and Uexküll, 1953, 146–7; DU. *Kloake* is German for 'sewer'.
32. *MTIS*, 69–70.
33. Information from unpublished autobiography of Rose O'Neill, kindly provided by Jean Cantwell, a leading member of the International Rose O'Neill Club.
34. For information about Dr Ignazio Cerio, see: CCIC; Douglas, 1934, 487 and 490; 1952, 43; Greene, 1975, 119; Knowles, 1918, 28; Maiuri, 1958, 10 and 13; and Trower, 1906, 117, 238–9; and particularly Cerio, *c.* 1921, *La Vita e la Figura di un Uomo*, which is Edwin's biography of his father.
35. *VF*, 410–12.
36. This account of the *Convegno* is based generally on *Oct. 5*, 233–5; *MTIS*, 106–9; *VF*, 411–13; Peyrefitte, 1970, 249–50; and GWW. Details of individual delegates are from: Mack Smith, 1981, 35–6, *Encyclopaedia Italiana* 1934, and Vergine, 1983, 111–18, on Marinetti; Vergine, 1983, 165, or Depero, 75–78, on Tavolato, and 102–110, on Prampolini; *Grove* 1980, on Casella and Malipiero. The CCIC has a transcript of Marinetti's speech and a catalogue of Prampolini's exhibition at Salerno.
37. *VF*, 413–16. A few portable relics of the *caffè* have been preserved by the restaurant Casina delle Rose, which occupies part of what was Morgano's; and by Donna Lucia's grandson, Mario Morgano, in the Hotel La Scalinatella, Via Tragara.
38. *MTIS*, 67–9, 104.
39. *Oct. 5*, 239–40.
40. Cerio, 1957, 99–100.
41. Baroness Budberg, an enigmatic and tricky character, was one of the great loves of H. G. Wells. She was allowed to move freely in and out of Russia, and mixed both with the Bolshevik hierarchy in Moscow and the 'establishment' in London. British intelligence strongly suspected that she was a Soviet agent (letter by Robin Bruce-Lockhart in *Sunday Telegraph*, 7.10.84).
42. Bryher, 1963, 227–38; Holloway, 1976, 314.
43. GWW, who made the arrangements in Naples for Cerio.
44. GWW.
45. The photographs sent to Cerio are in the CCIC; Peyrefitte, 1970, 256–7 describes the visit to Baron Von Gloeden.
46. The account of Fersen's last days is taken mainly from *VF*, 397–406, and Peyrefitte, 1970, 255–65. GWW told me about the treatment of Fersen's corpse. Peyrefitte, 268, describes Nino's return to Rome; GM saw him some years later in his newspaper-kiosk and told me of his death.
47. This inscription is based on one of Kate's treasured possessions – a framed inscription on parchment: 'Happiness is the Only Good; The Time to be Happy is Right Now, The Place to be Happy is Right Here, and the Greatest Happiness consists of Making Others Happy.' Kate's stone in the cemetery reads (ungrammatically) 'consist'.
48. There are references to Sophie Grahame in *MTIS*, 51–2, 68, 71, 154; *VF*, 290, 391, 416–17; Young, 1962, 130; Golding, 1924, 169–73. Louis Golding (1895–1958) spent the spring and summer of 1924 in Anacapri, writing his book *Sunward*.
49. SPG records. The nieces were Mrs Lenon and the late Mrs Sandilands of Lewes, East Sussex.
50. The Villa Ferraro, now Pensione Bel Sito, Via Matermania; GWW.
51. GWW.
52. Young, 1962, 131.
53. *MTIS*, 150–4; quotation from Douglas, 1929, 148.
54. A *commissario prefettizio*, who is usually one of the *vice-prefetti* of Naples, is appointed by the Province to a municipality when the administration breaks down as a result of political squabbles or for any other reason – in this case to fill the gap caused by Mussolini's abolition of local self-government. It is an unfortunate reflection on Capri politics that *commissari* have been all too frequent since 1945.

Chapter 8: Prosperity Under Fascism

1. GWW and TP.
2. Words of the hymn are:

Giovinezza, giovinezza,
Primavera di bellezza.
Il fascismo è la salvezza
Della nostra libertà.
Mussolini's visit to Capri is described in *MTIS*, 183.

3. GWW and TP. Another source told me that Dusmet was sometimes out and about early because he was returning from a night with his *amica*.
4. Peyrefitte, 1970, 267–8; Young, 1962, 162; GWW. Peyrefitte says that Norman Douglas was also due to be expelled in 1927, but was warned by Donna Lucia Morgano and left the island before he could be arrested and deported. Douglas's friend Ian Greenlees, however, told me that Douglas never mentioned the event and thought he would have done, if it had occurred.
5. In Scotland, 'but and ben' are the inner and outer parts of a two-roomed house.
6. *AA*, 98; cf *VF*, 246.
7. *VF*, foreword and dedication; *Oct. 5*, 126–7, 138, 142–3; *Oct. 6*, 93–5, 101, 105–7, 117–18; *MTIS*, 201–3; Appendix A.
8. *Oct. 5*, 138. I cannot provide a complete list of identifications of the characters of *Extraordinary Women*; such as are known are noted in the text and Appendix A.
9. Olga's shop was where Serafina Ferraro, run by Maria Esposito, selling souvenirs, *coralli* etc., now is at 52 Via Vittorio Emanuele.
10. GWW.
11. Secrest, 1974, 292–5.
12. VN.
13. Renata had the drawing copied, and bequeathed the copy to her friend, the Hon. Mrs Elizabeth Varley.
14. *MTIS*, 188.
15. GWW. The Weber family property at Due Golfi consisted of what is now the *pretura* and jail, and a piece of adjacent land.
16. Friedlander, 1938, 149.
17. GWW.
18. *Dictionary of American Biography*, Supplement 3 (1941–45).
19. *AA*, 89–101; Morgan, 1980, 350–2. Somerset Maugham's short story *The Lotus Eater*, is based on Brooks's last years.
20. Douglas, 1934, 99.
21. *MTIS*, 68, 117.
22. *MTIS*, 216–21.
23. *MTIS*, 218–19. 'Tubby Clayton' was the Rev. P. T. B. Clayton, CH, MC (1885–1972), who was a Forces Chaplain in France in World War I. After the war he founded Talbot House (Toc H) – a movement to teach the younger generation racial reconciliation and unselfish service. Between the wars and after World War II, he travelled all over the world on behalf of Toc H.
24. Graham Greene and a Swedish source.
25. Munthe and Uexküll, 1953, 50.
26. *Op. cit.*, 177–8.
27. *Op. cit.*, 100–1.
28. Di Sirignano, 1981, 171–2. The self-portrait of Kluck is owned by Paolo Falco, proprietor of the Ristorante 'La Palette', Via Matermania.
29. Dossier in CCIC; IG; Giovanni Tessitore; Vergine, 1983, 13–14, 35–9, 85–100. Cerio, 1929, 169–79, contains a sketch entitled *The Collection of Macrolepidoptera*, featuring 'Von Lepel', which is a fanciful account of Sohn-Rethel.
30. Fitzgibbon in *Encounter*, 43(3), 1974, 31; Greene, 1975, 157–8; GWW; the late Boris Alperovici; Contessa Maddalena Pozzo di Borgo.
31. Greene, 1975, 17–118; IG. According to IG the Dottoressa was inclined to be fanciful (*fantasiosa*). Without independent evidence, it is not possible to comment on the account of her

life up to 1927. Some passages, however, in Part 3 of Mr Greene's book, which cover the Dottoressa in Capri, do not accord with the facts (see under Bibliography).

32. Conrad Rawnsley. 'Federal Union' was a movement for the abolition of war and the unity and collaboration of the Peoples through World Federation. It attracted some support in the 1930s, and the Rawnsleys played a prominent part in it. Although some individuals may still hold Federalist views, the movement itself no longer survives.

33. *DNB*, 1951–60; Young, 1962, 141 ff.

34. *Ency. Brit.*, 15th edn.

35. Fields, 1960, 198.

36. *Op. cit.*, 45.

37. *Op. cit.*, 66.

38. This account of Gracie's life is based on information from Marchese Ettore Patrizi; Gracie's autobiography *Sing as we go*; Denis Pitts's article in *Sunday People* of 30.9.79; *The Times* of 30.12.74 and 23.11.79; and *Daily Telegraph* of 28.9.79. *Sing as we go* contains some inaccuracies, which probably stem from Gracie's own vagueness about chronology and her deliberate suppression of the truth, principally in respect of her love for John Flanagan, and later her relationship with Boris Alperovici. She did not tell the truth about Flanagan and her three husbands until 1970, when she confided in Pitts, who was preparing a TV documentary about her life, but made him promise not to publish until after her death (*Sunday People*, 30 September, 7 and 14 October, 1979).

39. EP.

40. Maiuri, 1958, 72; Di Sirignano, 1981, 142–4; *Vogue* (New York), 1.4.67; *New York Times*, 20.5.84; *Who Was Who in America*; EP.

41. Cerio, 1957, 124.

42. Fields, 1960, 178–82.

43. Maiuri, 1958, 33–4.

44. Tonino Spadaro, son of Costanzo; AA.

45. GWW on Elefante; MR on Edda Ciano.

46. Buonuomo, 1982; Di Sirignano 1981, 148–51; *Il Mattino Illustrato*, 30 June 1979.

47. All the sea-shore of Capri is the property of the State (*demanio marittimo*) and is administered by the Capitaneria di Porto in Naples, which comes under the Ministero della Marina Mercantile in Rome. The Capitaneria leases concessions to those who want to establish bathing-beaches, cabins, restaurants etc. on the sea-shore.

48. Fitzgibbon, 1974, 31.

49. Giuseppe Savarese ('Scarola'); Di Sirignano, 1981, 174.

50. Maria Lembo (Mellino); see also Di Sirignano, 1981, 173–4.

51. AC; GWW.

52. DU.

53. Maria Strina, daughter of Antonio Esposito; GWW.

54. Paolo Falco.

55. GL; SS.

56. GWW.

57. Mack Smith, 1981, 141–2, 147; IG.

58. TP, via GWW.

59. SPG records.

60. SC.

61. Mack Smith, 1981, 228–37.

Chapter 9: World War II

1. Fields, 1960, 137–9.

2. Tidief, 1977, 18–22. 'Tidief' is the *nom-de-plume* of the Marchesa Tina de Forcade de Biaix, who lives in Via Marina Grande and wrote a book about Capri during the war (see Bibliography).

3. Fields, 1970, 140–5.

4. *Daily Telegraph*, 28 September 1979.

5. *Sunday Telegraph*, 22 January 1984.

6. Mack Smith, 1981, 251–2.

7. IG.

8. Cerio, 1957, 128; Tidief, 1977, 82–3; Vincenzo Russo.
9. *Mattino Illustrato*, 30.6.79; GL.
10. GWW.
11. Caprese source in Palazzo a Mare.
12. *RIIA*, 1947, 38, 83, 86, 98, 127, 157; Tidief, 1977, 58–9; GL.
13. Andrén, 1980, 181; *Ency. Brit.*, 15th edn., on Moravia.
14. Tidief, 1977, 49, 54–5.
15. Mack Smith, 1981, 287–98; *RIIA*, 1947, 195, 205.
16. Tidief, 1977, 69–72; Cerio, 1957, 126.
17. Tidief, 1977, 74–7.
18. Costantino Ferraro; IG; Giovanni Tessitore.
19. Greene, 1975, 157.
20. TP.
21. Greene, 1975, 140.
22. Alexander, 1962, 113–15, 169–71.
23. Lewis, 1978, 25–6, 30–1.
24. Lewis, 1978, 61, 66. A surrealistic account of the banquet is given in Malaparte, 1952, 234–45, where 'General Cork' and the formidable 'Mrs Flat' of Boston are served with the Aquarium's famous 'siren' – a young girl, boiled and served with mayonnaise, on a bed of lettuce-leaves, and garnished by a wreath of pink coral-stems.
25. Lewis, 1978, 46.
26. Mack Smith, 1981, 300–4.
27. GWW.
28. On 9 November 1943 representatives of forty-four Allied and Associated Nations, meeting in Atlantic City, signed an agreement establishing UNRRA. On 25 January 1944, the US House of Representatives voted to appropriate the equivalent of £337,500,000 to UNRRA (*RIIA*, 1947, 221, 235); the Americans were always the largest contributors to its funds and personnel.
29. Information about the Allied occupation of Capri is derived from: Tidief, 1977, 74–99; Di Sirignano, 1981, 154–6; Baronessa Graziella Pennacchio; AA; GL.
30. Lewis, 1978, 101–7; Grant, 1971, 42
31. See Lewis, 1978, 98, 119–20, 134–9, 162, 200, for further details of the black market and the corruption of Allied administration.
32. *Op. cit.*, 110–13.
33. *Ency. Brit.*, 15th edn., on Malaparte.
34. Alexander, 1962, 148–9, 196–9.
35. Mack Smith, 1981, 318–20.

Chapter 10: Post-War Boom
1. Holloway, 1976, 474.
3. GWW.
4. *Vogue* (New York), 1.4.67; Di Sirignano, 1981, 142–4; Sternberg, 1977, 98–109; ES; AA, GM, EP, AG, Tonino D'Emilio; Ercole D'Esposito.
5. Giuseppina, born in 1904, was the eldest daughter of Luigi Messanelli, the *caprese* schoolmaster who gave Italian lessons to Fritz Krupp and Maksim Gorki, and niece of Roberto Serena, the lawyer, and Carlo Serena, Archbishop of Sorrento. Although she inherited a lot of money and property and had no need of extra income, she became a *mediatrice* for fun, because she enjoyed helping people she liked. While many of the islanders regarded Giuseppina as a schemer – and she was certainly a tremendous gossip, which earned her the nickname 'Prezzemolo' (parsley), because she was 'in everything' – many foreigners, including the author, will remember with gratitude her kindness and the depth of her knowledge about Capri past and present. One foreign resident, for whom she had found the ideal house, called her his 'guardian angel'. She died in August 1981.
6. The late Mrs Sandilands, niece of Harold Trower.
7. IG; Holloway, 1976, 429–31.
8. Greenlees, 1957, 8.
9. Holloway, 1976, 469–74.
10. Cunard, 1954, 215.

References and Notes

11. Young, 1962, 308, 314–15.
12. Fitzgibbon, 1974, 30.
13. *ibid.*
14. Holloway, 1976, 483.
15. Young, 1962, 312.
16. Holloway, 1976, 483.
17. Islay Lyons.
18. Buonuomo, 1982; *Il Mattino Illustrato*, 30.6.79; Di Sirignano, 1981, 148–51; *Saturday Review*, 1.3.69; *Ency. Brit.*, 15th edn.; GM.
19. Fitzgibbon, 1953, 9–11; an account of the 'unwritten biography' is in Fitzgibbon, 1974.
20. Carmela's son Arturo Salvia; Peyrefitte, 1970, 271; Settanni, 1964, 23–8.
21. Munthe & Uexküll, 1953, 195–206.
22. Svensson, 1959, 343.
23. DU.
24. Munthe & Uexküll, 1953, v.
25. *Oct. 5*, 127.
26. *Op. cit.*, 128–31.
27. *AMAID*, 242–3; *Oct. 5*, 126–7.
28. Svensson, 1959, 255; the late Duchessa Dusmet; GM.
29. Munthe & Uexküll, 1953; xiv; trs. Peter Collins, of George E. Harrap and Company Ltd.
30. Holloway, 1976, 501; Malaparte (trs. David Moore), 1952, 219.
31. Maiuri, 1958, 125.
32. Pane, 1967, 62, 71.
33. Greene, 1975, 158.
34. Erysipelas is a contagious infection of the skin, accompanied by red swellings, usually of the face and scalp, and a feverish condition; it is also called 'St Anthony's fire'.
35. Maugham, R., 1972, 197–200.
36. For an account of Douglas's death and its attribution to suicide, see Greene, 1975, 194, and Holloway, 1976, 490–2; Ian Greenlees considers that Douglas died of the combined effects of old age and disease.
37. Macpherson, 1953, 28–9.
38. *Omnes eodem cogimur omnium/versatur urna serius ocius/sors exitura et nos in aeternum/exilium impositura cumbae* (We are all driven to the same place; the lot of us all is shaken in the urn, sooner or later to come forth, and embark us in the boat for eternal exile), Horace *Odes*, II, 3, 25–8.

Chapter 11: Reflections on the Last Thirty-five Years
1. Azienda.
2. Azienda.
3. One such was Carlo della Posta, Duca di Civitella, who has been flitting in and out of these pages. Born in Naples in 1904, the son of an Italian duke and an English mother, Carlo took a feudal view of life, which carried with it a determination never to take a paid job. This rule had been broken only twice – once in 1933, when he acted in two films under the family name della Posta, and in 1943/44, when he was recruited briefly to act as interpreter with the British Army. Intelligent, equally at home in Italian and English, well-read, witty, gregarious, possessed of great charm and perfect manners, in short *un vero signore*, Carlo had led an absolutely useless life, apart from being a great asset to his many friends. Now in his early seventies and with only a modest unearned income, he found it more and more difficult to afford the ever-increasing rent of his small apartment in Via Sopramonte. Finally his landlords asked him to go, saying that they needed the flat for their daughter. Carlo was too much of a gentleman to fight the case and even refused an offer by his niece to buy him a home in Capri, saying that it would be too expensive and would absorb capital, which otherwise would produce an income. Instead he retreated to Rome, where one of his great-nephews gave him an apartment. He hated going, but fortunately could stay in Capri whenever he wanted with his old friend Marchese Ettore Patrizi. Not that their relationship was always calm. They often quarrelled and sometimes made such a noise shouting at each other – and as a Neapolitan Carlo considered that he could outshout Ettore, a Tuscan aristocrat – that the neighbours complained. As heart-trouble and Parkinson's disease overtook

him, however, and his memory began to fail, Carlo was more and more confined to Rome. He died in January 1983.

4. Cf. *Il Mattino*, 29.8.82, article by Raffaele La Capria.

5. *Il Mattino*, 8.5.83.

6. Literature of the Società di San Vincenzo de' Paoli; Roberto Alberino.

7. *VF*, 246.

8. Old Giuseppe died in the spring of 1985 in his hundredth year.

9. Di Sirignano, 1981, 175.

10. Information about Renata Borgatti's later life from EV, who was present at Renata's death and arranged her burial in Palestrina; and by Etienne Amyot, pianist and one of the founders of the BBC's Third Programme, to which Renata occasionally contributed.

11. Morgan, 1981; 661-2, and generally 658-64; see also Curtis, 1977, 200-4.

12. AA; Vincenzo Russo, concierge at the Quisisana, from whose family Spiegel rented a room in Via Castello.

13. Greene, 1975, 126, 193-4, 199-202.

14. *Op. cit.*, Editor's Note, 196, 205.

15. Peyrefitte, 1970, 8, trs. Edward Hyams.

16. See under Bibliography.

17. See under Bibliography.

18. *Grahame Greene, Civis Anacaprensis*, Comune di Anacapri, 1980.

19. DR; AA.

20. Barzini, 1966, 270-1.

21. Guarracino stands out in Capri as a rare example of simplicity and selfless courage. Born in 1909, he was blest with a variety of talents. Strong in body and character, he became an experienced gardener and fisherman, he taught peregrine falcons to catch quail, and from his earliest youth he was a brilliant rock-climber; with a German archaeologist he once scaled the Salto di Tiberio in search of the legendary equestrian statue in gold of the Emperor. He often climbed the Faraglioni rocks to catch blue lizards for the tourists and to bring down gulls' eggs for the kitchen, and was among those who took part in the *pulizia della montagna* instituted during the Fascist regime. In World War II he served with distinction as a coxswain in the Italian merchant navy and won the Bronze Medal for rescuing from a sinking ship, at great personal risk, a dog which was the ship's mascot. After the Italian surrender of 1943 he returned to his old occupations of gardening, fishing and climbing. He rescued an American sergeant from the cliff at Unghia Marina and received a personal tribute from Colonel Woodward, and in 1968, a dog which had been thrown from the Belvedere della Migliara. He died in November 1977.

22. *EW*, 349.

23. Information about the mainland Italians and other foreigners was provided in some cases by themselves; and variously by Aldo Aprea, Doreen Berrill, Sol Cohen, Giuseppe Esposito, Gloria Magnus, Ettore Patrizi, Graziella Pennacchio, Alfredo and Antigone Pesce, Pino Salvia, Principe di Sirignano and Lidia Talamona.

24. *Sunday People*, 7.10.79.

25. Fields, 1960, 177.

26. *Sunday People*, 14.10.79; *Radio Times*, 22.1.76.

27. After Gracie's death on 27 September 1979, Pitts published three articles about her in the *Sunday People* of 30 September, 7 and 14 October.

28. Russell Harty in *Observer*, 30.9.79.

29. Giorgio (b. 1937) and Luigi (b. 1940) Iacono are the sons of Mario Iacono, from Ischia, and Assunta Albanese, of the Marina Piccola family. Through their mother they inherited the beach and restaurant concession at Faraglioni. Luigi recently bought the hotel 'La Certosella'. Giorgio, who has a share in both enterprises, also owns the restaurant 'Luna Caprese' at Oxford.

30. Wills filed in the Family Division of the High Court, Somerset House.

31. Most of the information about Gracie's last years comes from Hazel Provost and various newspaper articles. The account of the funeral is based on information from the Rev. Edward Holland; *Sunday Telegraph* and *News of the World*, 30.9.79; *Daily Telegraph*, 1.10.79.

32. Somerset House.

33. Anonymous source who obtained information from a member of the *fortino* staff. Regarding Bismarck's cancer and his marriage to Mona, see Sternberg, 1977, 507-10.

34. SPG. Carlo Talamona died in 1975. His widow Lidia has been a useful source.
35. Municipal records of Capri.
36. *Il Borghese*, No. 49, 3.12.72, 873–4.
37. ES.
38. ES.
39. San Filippo Neri (1515–95) was a jovial and bibulous priest, known as 'Pippo buono', who did missionary work in Rome. His day is 26 May (see *Penguin Dictionary of Saints*, 1965, 284–5). In Capri there is a small oratory dedicated to him under the parish church; and part of the *cimitero cattolico* is reserved as a burial ground for local members of his brotherhood.
40. The term comes from the Festival of Piedigrotta, when the Neapolitans celebrate the Birth of the Blessed Virgin Mary at the Church of Santa Maria di Piedigrotta, preceded by a 'nocturnal procession of carriages from Via Forla, through the Via Roma, to the Madonna di Piedigrotta with many stops and to the accompaniment of music, singing and general uproariousness' (*Baedeker*, 1930).
41. Pane, 1967, 10. cf. Cantone *et al.*, 1982, 319–41.
42. SS.
43. GWW.
44. Information variously from *Tribuna di Capri*, May 1982; Arch. Enrico Lucca; Prof. Gino Verbena; Gelvio Bottiglieri; IG.
45. *The Times*, 15.3.83; *Scotsman*, 26.3.83.
46. Anonymous source.

Index